C000256688

JOHN GORDON DAVIS was born in
Zimbabwe, and educated in South A
Political Science, paying his way throug
a deckhand on British merchant ships a ... ... the Dutch whaling
fleet at the Antarctic. He went on to take an LL.B. degree whilst
serving as a judge's clerk in Rhodesia.

Called to the Bar, he was appointed an assistant public prosecutor
in the Magistrate's Courts during the troubled years leading up
to Rhodesia's Unilateral Declaration of Independence, before
becoming Crown Counsel in the Attorney General's Chambers.
He was later appointed to the same position in Hong Kong.

He quit this post to become a full-time writer when his first book,
"Hold My Hand I'm Dying" became an instant best-seller. Other
bestselling novels followed.

A veteran seaman; he and his Australian born wife, Rosemary,
sailed round most of the world in a succession of yachts. Upon
retirement, they travelled widely and from their home in a lovely
old Spanish farmhouse in Andalucia, Spain, he also ran highly
successful writing courses for both aspiring and published
authors.

John Gordon Davis sadly died in 2014 leaving behind a rich literary
heritage, including several unpublished novels he had worked on
even as he supposedly slowed the pace.

THE WORKS OF JOHN GORDON DAVIS

Hold My Hand I'm Dying (1967)
Cape of Storms (1970)
The Years of the Hungry Tiger (1974)
Taller Than Trees (1975)
Leviathan (1976)
Typhoon (1978)
Fear No Evil (1982)
Seize the Reckless Wind (1984)
　　　　aka Seize the Wind
A Woman Involved (1987)
The Land God Made in Anger (1990)
Talk to Me Tenderly, Tell Me Lies (1992)
Roots of Outrage (1994)
The Year of Dangerous Loving (1997)
Unofficial and Deniable (1999)

Non Fiction
Operation Rhino (1972)

Cape of Storms

John Gordon Davies

HOUSE OF
STRATUS

This edition published in 2015 by House of Stratus, an imprint of Stratus Books Ltd., Lisandra House, Fore Street, Looe, Cornwall, PL13 1AD, U.K.
www.houseofstratus.com

Typeset by House of Stratus.

A catalogue record for this book is available from the British Library and the Library of Congress.

ISBN 07551-5403-7
EAN 978-07551-5403-6

TO JOAN

Cape summer is hot and fair, the Fairest Cape of All; Cape winter is a bitch. In the winter the rain lashes cold and the Southern winds blow the big storms in and the sea is big and rolling and treacherous out there, and they call it the Cape of Storms. There are many great oak trees in the Cape, oaks of England, and vines from the Mediterranean, and the wine and brandy they make is amongst the best in all the world. And fruit, the fruit from the Mediterranean they grow down there in the Fairest Cape, gold and orange and red and green, and in the winter there is snow on the mountains of the Hottentots' Holland. The Cape is as old as when the white men began to sail the seas, and there is a mellowness. There are many old spacious gracious Dutch homesteads and vineyards of the days of slaves, and there are very many Coloured people who are halfbreed descendants of the Hottentots and the Bantu and the Malays. Up the long wild South African coast there are the farms overlooking the rugged Atlantic and the mild Indian oceans, with big fish, and the mighty forests of George and Knysna and Tzitzikama where the great teak and pine trees grow, and on the Drakensberg mountains behind them there is also snow in the wintertime. Inland is the great flat desertous Karoo, the land of sheep and the greatest diamonds in the world. On up the coast there is the River Kei and the Transkei where the Wild Coast goes for hundreds of miles, green hills and valleys of jungle, the land of the Xhosas and Pondos, the people of the Red Blankets and the people of the Blue Blankets, the cattlemen who live in round thatched huts on the hilltops for fear of the tokoloshi evil spirits who live in the valleys; and the fishing is very good there. And on up over the wild Umzimvubu River to the coast of Natal where the land is rich and the sugar cane and pineapples and bananas grow, where live the handsome Zulu people who were the mightiest black warrior nation under King Chaka. And on up north on to the great highveld of the Transvaal where the mighty Johannesburg and the mighty gold mines of the Witwatersrand are, and up through the vast wheat and cattle and citrus country, up to the Limpopo. To the west is the vast flat cattle country of Bechuanaland, where the Botswana people are ruled by their black king under the protection of the Union Jack, and to the south and south-east are the two black British Protectorates of Swaziland and Basutoland, the mountainous lands of horsemen. There is nearly everything in South Africa, gold and diamonds and great farms and fruits and elephants and monkeys and crocodiles and lions and all the buck and fowl, and many climates, from the lands that storm in winter to the lands that storm in summer, and many colours, and many tribes. The Dutch, who are called the Afrikaners, and the English, and the Fingos and Xhosas and Griquas and Pondos and Zulus and Basutos and Swazis, to name only some, who are all called the Bantu, and the Indians and the Malays and even Chinese and the many people in between, those people of the mixed blood who are called the Coloureds, who are yet another race. There are many languages. At the south is the vineyard Cape, which is called the Cape of Good Hope, and old Cape Town with its oaks, which is called the Tavern of the Seas. There are many Coloured people in Cape Town. And there are many fishermen. In the beginning of the long hot summer when the vineyards are getting heavy and the white people turn golden in the sun, the whaling fleets of Europe arrive at the Tavern of the Seas, on their way to the Antarctic. In the summer of that year McQuade prepared to go south with the whalers again.

James van Niekerk McQuade once broke the world record for the hundred metre free-stroke at the South African Inter-University's Swimming Championships, but do not be too impressed with that because it happened like this: when the pistol went and the eight finalists hit the water and the roar went up, McQuade came running out with half a bottle of brandy inside him and big flippers on his feet. He plunged into the Olympic size pool and flailed the water with his flippers and he cleaned up all the universities' champions easily and broke the world record to roars of applause. The next week he received a long telegram from a university in America offering him a scholarship. He telegrammed back to the university that he was very sorry but he had only that morning accepted a scholarship to the University of Moscow. Down at the docks they called him the Professor, but that was only half correct and it happened like this: it took him an inordinate five years to get his Bachelor's degree in Marine Science and another three years to get his Master's in Icthiology because in the summers he went south with the whalers to the Ice, and sometimes he took it into his head to go north to Walvis Bay to work the pilchard boats, where there is very good money indeed. In his eighth year, at the beginning of the final term, he was drinking a bottle of brandy with the Professor of Marine Science when the Professor fell over dead. Now the Department of Marine Science was a small one, a one man band, and icthiologists are few upon the ground. The university could find nobody to take the chair at short notice and so they had to appoint McQuade to hold the fort, which many people thought was a jolly good joke. McQuade had to work so hard that he actually got his Master's, by osmosis he said; and with black ingratitude he declined appointment as lecturer the following year, went back to sea with his degrees, mortgaged the house in Oak Bay and bought a fishing trawler.

At the beginning of the summer he left his boat to his bosun and he went south to the Ice with the whalers again.

Part One

Chapter One

Down at the docks the fourteen corvettes of the All England Whaling Company were tied up against each other around the big black whaling factory ship. There were a couple of hundred Cape Coloured men hanging around the factory decks, and a few white South Africans, trying to get signed on. Every season it was the same. There were some women too and they were mostly Cape Coloureds, belonging to the Coloured men, and some of them were whores. The white whores were in the white bars uptown. The night before a whaling fleet sails is a very big night for the bars and whores of the Tavern of the Seas. It was four o'clock in the afternoon when James van Niekerk McQuade drove his old Ford along the quay and stopped opposite the catcher Number Fourteen. He took his suitcase and haversack out of the back seat, carried them to the narrow gangplank of the Fourteen and took them aboard one at a time. He went back to the car and got out a big cardboard box of books and carried it aboard also. Then he carried a crate of brandy aboard. Then he climbed up to the bridge to look for the Mate. He knew the Captain would not be aboard, the Captain would be uptown in the bars. There was nobody on the bridge so he went below through the officers' accommodation to the Mate's door.

'Oh,' the Mate said, 'it's you again.' He was in his uniform, though it was not necessary in port. He grinned, trying to be friendly, but he was self-conscious. He was plump with thinning red hair and a red moustache and freckles and when he smiled he showed all his gums.

'Reporting, sir.' The Mate liked it when McQuade called him sir. The Mate always started the season trying to be friendly and McQuade felt sorry for him.

'Where were you last season?' the Mate said.

'I was too busy,' McQuade said.

'Oh well,' the Mate said, 'we missed you.' He could think of nothing more to say. McQuade knew the Mate had not missed him but he knew he was trying to be friendly. Soon he would not be friendly any more because of his inferiority complex. He had a hard time.

'Captain Child left a note for you,' the Mate said. He grinned as if he knew what the note would say. He handed McQuade a letter. It read,

'Meet me in the Night and Day you old bastard. Kid.'

The Kid was a very irresponsible young man but his father was the Chairman of the Board and he was the best harpooner and the darling of the fleet. 'Thinks he's on his daddy's yacht,' the Mate said about The Kid.

'Which I unprintably am,' The Kid said, 'and don't you forget it.' The Mate never learned.

'I suppose you want to go ashore now,' the Mate grinned, trying to look like one of the boys.

'Would you like a lift?' McQuade said kindly.

'No,' the Mate shook his plump face. 'No, you go and enjoy yourselves,' he said, the disciplinarian indulging his subordinates and holding the fort. His red mouth was smudged with freckles.

As McQuade walked back down to the deck he thought: The poor bastard would like to come with us but he'd feel inadequate, that's why he's in his uniform. He picked up his gear and went through the hatch down into the alleyway. In front of him was the small Mess and galley. He turned aft to the accommodation. There was the vibration from the engine room below. He felt it again as he did every season, the confinement of work work work and sea sea sea and ice ice ice, four hours on and four hours off, every goddam day for five godawful solid months. It was the same feeling every season.

He put his cases in his cabin, then he walked back up the alleyway and back up on to the deck and on to the quay. The sun was still well up. There was the mighty Table Mountain up behind the warehouses and the slopes were mauve and gold in the late afternoon sun. He started walking along the quay towards the factory ship to see if he could find Big Charlie and Wee Jock and Beulah.

Chapter Two

McQuade and Big Charlie and Wee Jock and Beulah and Buzzy and Lodewijk went ashore in the car. Buzzy's surname was Honey and he could play the piano. Lodewijk was a Coloured off the Fourteen, he was a very respectable Coloured. Big Charlie the bosun had received a letter from his wife saying she was having another baby and he was very happy and he was going to buy them all a drink. Big Charlie and Wee Jock were brothers. Wee Jock was not small at all, they only called him Wee Jock because Charlie was so big. Big Charlie was forty years old with red cheeks and big greying eyebrows and greying hair and a barrel chest and he was always cheerful. Jock was only thirty and he was lean and good-looking and surly, he looked like a cowboy should look, with an oblong face with hollow cheeks. Down at the Ice Jock brewed his own Scotch moonshine. It did not taste at all like Scotch, but it worked. Jock's hobby was painting but he only painted women's portraits and nudes for what was in it for him. 'It's amazing how it works,' Jock said. Jock was the wild one, Big Charlie was the gent, everybody liked Big Charlie and this baby was going to cost him plenty before he got back to Glasgow. Jock was talking about the smashing bit of crumpet who was sailing with the fleet this season, the nurse who worked in the Company's Cape Town shore clinic.

'Who says?' McQuade said. 'I've heard these rumours before about the smashing crumpet that's sailing and all we get is Old Ferguson and Rigor Mortis.' They were driving through the docks still.

'Even Old Ferguson gets beautiful down at the Ice,' Buzzy said.

'It's true an' all,' Beulah said. Beulah was the Old Man's steward and he thought he knew everything.

'Who told you?' McQuade demanded.

'Old Man's missus,' Beulah said loftily. 'Our Ida, The Sunshine of Our 'Ome. This morning. Old Rigor Mortis went down with hippatitus last night.'

'There you are,' Jock said.

'I'll believe it when I see it,' McQuade said. 'All we'll get is Old Ferguson.'

'You are speaking of the woman I love,' Buzzy said, 'after the second month at the Ice. I tell you, I've thought I could screw Old Ferguson.'

They were stopped at the dockyard level crossing letting a goods train shunt by. Beulah was going ashore to look for Pete. 'The faithless swine,' Beulah said, 'I'm good enough for him at sea but as soon as we hit port he sneaks ashore for a bit of hairy pie, what you bastards see in girls I just do not know.'

'That's the trouble with these shipboard romances, Beulah,' McQuade said.

'My mother always told me that,' Beulah said. 'It's only 'cos of him I came back this season, I'm just absolutely sick sick sick of the Antarctic and all that blood and fat, how you boys can *work* in it.'

'We didn't go to grammar school Beulah,' Jock said, 'except maybe the Professor.'

'I wanted to do a Caribbean run this time,' Beulah said, 'there's good tips on them an' all. And it was because of him I had my nose op, two hundred nicker for the plastic surgeon to mash my snout up. National Health don't pay for that jazz unless maybe you're a Jamaican. Beulah you old bitch, he said, you've got the most godawful nose and you talk like an adenoidal bull mastiff.' They laughed again. This was the first time McQuade had seen Beulah with his new nose.

'Now how is it?' Beulah said.

'Now you're beautiful, Beulah,' Jock said.

'Is it a nose you want to be near, a nose you want to kiss? Professor?'

'It's a nose to launch a thousand ships, Beulah,' McQuade said.

They drove through the docks and headed up town and Beulah told them all about his nose op and how positively indecorous it all was. First the surgeon gets stuck in with a mallet and mashes your nose up, then he opens you up and hoiks out the pieces you don't use in a nose one wants to be near, a nose one wants to kiss. You wake up with a king size hangover and for days you can't see on account of your two shiners and you can't eat properly on account of it wriggles your new nose too much. And now he daren't get into a punchup on account of he was carrying two hundred quid's worth around in front of him, and all for that sonofabitch. They promised Beulah they would help him look for his sonofabitch tonight and see nobody punched him on his two hundred quid's worth.

First they went to the Fog Horn, which is quite a good joint. They said goodbye to Lodewijk because he wasn't allowed in and he walked down Adderly Street slowly, looking for a Coloured bar. Big Charlie ordered the first round from the Coloured waiter and they drank to his new baby and Big Charlie beamed. Beulah went around among the dim tables looking for Pete. There was a Coloured band playing rock and roll in front of a dance space. There were plenty of whalermen and most of them were on the way to getting drunk already, young men and old men. Most of the whores were not bad looking except that South African whores go all to hell quickly because they drink too much, they are not very professional about being whores, they enjoy it. It was swinging already in the Fog Horn but they were still quite well behaved. Later there would be the falling and the fighting and the mauling the whores. Beulah came back and said that the sonofabitch was not amongst those present. They had another round of beers and Big Charlie paid again and Jock went off and asked a girl to dance and they watched him. Jock was good.

At eight o'clock they arrived at the Night and Day and they were beginning to get along with the beer and the Cape brandy. Beulah had a quick look round and said, 'He's not in here, I'll go and case the other joints. Toodle-oo my darlings and don't do anything I wouldn't do.'

'That's exactly what we're going to do,' Jock said.

The Night and Day was dark and full. There were red lamps in places and they made the sailors and the whores look devilish. There was a three piece Coloured band at the far end thumping out through amplifiers. Sailors were rocking and rolling. There were wooden partitions along the walls, very dark. McQuade could not see The Kid. The waiters and the barman were Coloureds. There was a long bar counter but there were no bottles of liquor behind it for by law women were not permitted to see liquor being uncorked lest it corrupted their minds. McQuade got the beers and they stood in a row at the bar watching the dancing. A woman with big hips was standing close up against a sailor against his groin and then she laughed shrilly and stepped back and slapped his hand playfully and said shrilly, *'Yiss-like, alreeds steek by sy tent op'* which means 'Jeez-like already he is sticking his tent up.'

A whore with big breasts and fat bare shoulders came to McQuade and put her hands on her hips and jerked them once and fluttered her tongue and said, *'Yirrrr-r-r-r.'*

'I'm sorry,' McQuade said.

'How's about a brandy and Coke man?' the whore said.

'Jakob,' McQuade said to the Coloured barman, 'get the lady a brandy and Coke.'

Jakob walked behind the screen behind the bar so the whore would not see the liquor being poured lest it corrupt her mind.

'Are those real?' Buzzy said.

'Real,' McQuade said. 'Lift 'em up and bats would fly out.'

She stepped back.

'Hoe se jy?'

'He says they are real.'

'Agh of course!' She thrust her hand down her neckline and produced the big breast and squeezed it twice to show its authenticity. She grinned and fluttered her tongue and said *'Lekker!'* and put it away.

The band started thumping again. After a little while Charlie tapped McQuade on the shoulder.

'I've had enough, Jimmy,' Big Charlie said. 'I'm going back to the ship.'

McQuade looked at his watch. 'Okay. Me too.'

He leant over to Jock.

'If The Kid comes tell him I've gone back to the ship, I'll see him in the morning.'

'Don't go!' Jock shouted. 'What about all these broads?'

McQuade shrugged. 'See you in two weeks at the Ice, I'll come aboard the factory first time alongside.'

'Five months mate!' Jock shouted. 'That's how long it's going to fookin be!'

'What about the nurse?' McQuade said.

'She's mine, you sonsabitches haven't a chance. Five months Professor!'

As Big Charlie climbed into the car beside McQuade he sighed and said, 'Aye, Jimmy, I'm gettin' old. These joints are no use to a married man.'

'None, Charlie.' McQuade started the car.

'I keep thinking about the wife,' Big Charlie said. 'You ain't got any idea how bad it feels to sail away.'

'Sure,' McQuade said, 'it must be bad.'

'Ogh, you ain't got any idea, Jimmy, until you been married you just ain't got any idea how bad it feels to sail away.'

'You're lucky to feel that way,' McQuade said. He was driving down the street.

'Ogh Jimmy it's time you got married, you're nearly thirty, don't make the mistake I did and leave it so late. If I'd known what I was missin'.'

'You had a good time didn't you?' McQuade said. 'And now you've got a nice young wife, not an old bag you married fifteen years ago.'

'Ogh,' Big Charlie said, 'I never had a good time, Jimmy. I never gave it a bang like you and Wee Jock and The Kid, I never knew how.'

'You had a good time,' McQuade said.

'Aye, I suppose it wasn't too bad,' Big Charlie said, 'but I'm awful glad it's over.'

'Yes,' McQuade said, 'I'm beginning to feel that way myself.'

He pulled into the yard of a large building. 'Where's this?' Big Charlie said.

'The main police station. My sergeant friend will pick my car up later for me. I'm also meeting my servant here, her young son's sailing with us and I promised to hold his hand.'

They got out and McQuade locked the car. Then they walked back into the street then up the steps into the big Charge Office, up to the counter. There were people waiting on the benches.

'*Ja, Meneer?*' the young constable said. He had a little blond moustache.

'Sergeant van Tonder of the Oak Bay Station said I could park my car here and he would pick it up later.'

'*Ja,* he phoned us about it,' the constable said. 'Your servant girl's also waiting here.'

A very fat Coloured woman with grey hair was walking towards them. A Coloured youth walked behind her. The old woman was beaming. 'Hullo Master James,' she beamed.

'Hullo Sophie,' McQuade said. 'This is Mister MacGregor.'

'You remember Benjamin?' old Sophie beamed around at her son. She was taller than Benjamin and she was not very tall.

'Certainly,' McQuade said. 'You've grown.' Benjamin looked very embarrassed.

'What do you say to Master James, Bennie?' Sophie commanded.

'Good evening Master James,' Benjamin mumbled, very embarrassed. McQuade and Big Charlie beamed at him.

'Stand up straight!' Sophie commanded. 'He's a bit *skaam*, Master James, it's very nice of you to come an' fetch him hey—'

'Not at all—' McQuade said.

'Get your things man Bennie!' Sophie commanded and Benjamin hurried back to the bench to his cases. They followed him and McQuade picked up a suitcase and Big Charlie the bundle. Benjamin picked up the other suitcase and it bent him right over. He was small and skinny. Sophie preceded them out on to the pavement and looked up and down the street for a taxi.

'Agh where's your *coat* man Benjamin!' Sophie cried, 'a fine howdy do when you there by the Ice and no bleddy coat!' Benjamin fled back into the police station.

'*Jere*, no coat! Now Master James,' she commanded, 'jus' you keep an eye on him down there, hey!'

'Don't worry, Sophie.'

'Of course I worry man Master James!' Sophie said peevishly. 'Down there by the Ice an' no coat! An' all those skollie boys leading him astray—'

'He won't go astray Sophie,' McQuade smiled. 'It'll do him good.'

'What good's it done you Master James may I ask hey?' Sophie said. '*Jere*, if your ma an' pa could see you now, it's a wonder they don't haunt you after all the education they gave you.'

Big Charlie was grinning. Benjamin came running out of the Charge Office with his coat.

'That's better!' Sophie said. 'Now jus' you wear it hey, Master James you see he wears his coat – an' you wear your coat too, Master James, we don' want you coming back with pneumonia neither, your pa had pneumonia once and he nearly died. Benjamin jus' you do everything nice what they tell you on the ship—'

'Here comes a taxi,' Big Charlie grinned and he stepped out into the street and flagged it. Benjamin grabbed up his suitcase thankfully and it nearly pulled him over. The taxi pulled up at the kerb.

'Get in man Benjamin – say thank you to Mister McGregor.'

'Thank you man,' Benjamin mumbled. He sorely wished his mother would shut up, he was fifteen now wasn't he, he wasn' a bleddy kid no more was he?

'Here's your *koekies*,' Sophie passed him a packet, 'but don' gobble all at once hey.'

Big Charlie climbed in the front next to the taxi driver. Sophie hurried round to Benjamin's window and put her head in.

'O'right Benjamin, goodbye hey!' McQuade could see her fat brown face was crying. She grabbed Benjamin's small face and gave it a big kiss. 'Goodbye my *lammetjie*—'

'Goodbye—' Benjamin croaked.

She pulled out of the window and straightened up and looked up at McQuade and the tears were running down her fat old cheeks. 'Goodbye Sophie.' McQuade put his arm around her.

'Goodbye Master James,' old Sophie cried, 'and jus' you look after yourself hey!'

'Don't you worry about Benjamin, Sophie,' McQuade said, '*Totsiens, ou ding.*'

'*Totsiens* Master James,' Sophie cried. 'I baked a nice Christmas cake for you. Bennie!' she called through the window, 'remember to give Master James his Christmas cake!'

'*Ja*, Ma,' Benjamin croaked.

'An' don' you eat it before Christmas, Master James,' Sophie wept. 'An' remember to bring back the tin, it's a good tin.'

'Okay Sophie,' McQuade said. 'Goodbye, *ou ding.*'

'Goodbye Master James.'

He walked round the back and climbed into the taxi.

'You'll get a lift back with Sergeant van Tonder, Sophie,' McQuade said through the window.

'*Ja,*' Sophie said. 'An' happy Chris'mas hey, I'll be thinking of youse at Chris'mas ...'

'You too, Sophie,' McQuade said. 'Goodbye—'

The taxi started.

'Goodbye – goodbye,' Sophie waved, '*an' remember to bring back the tin!*'

Chapter Three

McQuade woke up early in his cabin with a clear head. It was still dark. He lay in his bunk, smoking. Every now and again he heard whalermen straggling along the quay. Some of them were singing. When it began to get light he got up and went down to the heads and showered. He felt good and virtuous because he had not got drunk last night. He dressed in his sea gear and then he went to the galley and got some coffee. The whole ship was quiet except for the faint hum from the engine room below. Then he went up on deck into the dawn. There was the factory ship, the Icehammer lying big and quiet in the dawn. There were fumes coming from her funnels aft. There were still lights burning on the bridge. There were two men straggling up the gangway. The catchers all had their canvas shrouds over their harpoon guns up in the bows. There were some lights burning. Two women appeared at the top of the factory gangway and started coming down. He watched them come along the quay. They looked bad, as if they had been drinking and fornicating all night. They were not talking to each other, as if they felt too bad to talk. One was plump and the other was skinny with thin lips and pencil eyebrows. McQuade felt so fit he wished he had taken one or both of them to bed. He would be sorry down at the Ice. Down at the Ice he would remember these two beat-up whores as the last opportunity he had had and he would curse himself for not having gone to them right now and taken them both back to his cabin. He would imagine them both in his cabin, one fat and the other skinny taking it in turns, and they would get ravishingly beautiful down at the Ice. He let them go. The sun was just coming up. The tide was still coming in, it would have turned by the time they sailed. He looked south-west at the fiat sea horizon going on for infinity and he felt the claustrophobia again and the feeling: *five months five bloody months again oh Jesus.*

There were some people about on the quay and the ships now. There were two taxis coming along the quay. McQuade went below to the messroom. The messboy was in the galley. He got another mug of coffee and sat down at a table. It was still quiet aboard the Fourteen although he could hear men moving around. Then he heard The Kid singing loudly on the quay.

'... Watch for the mail
I'll never fail
If you don't get a letter
Then you'll know I'm in jail
O-toot toot toot toot tootsie goodbyee ...'

and the sound of laughing and the sound of The Kid coming aboard.

McQuade got up and went up on deck. He saw Jock and Beulah and Buzzy walking away along the quay towards the Icehammer. The Kid was climbing the companionway up to the bridge. 'Kid!' McQuade called.

The Kid hung on to the companionway and twisted round and then he screwed up his face. '*McQuade!*' he shouted.

'Hullo Kid,' McQuade grinned.

'*McQuade you old sumbitch,*' The Kid shouted. '*Where were you last night?*' His face was bruised and grazed. He clawed up the companionway to the bridge and turned around with his arms outflung beaming. '*Oo-toot-tootsie Hulloa ...*' he bellowed. McQuade climbed up grinning and The Kid flung his arms around him. '*McQuade you old sumbitch—*'

'Good to see you Kid,' McQuade grinned. 'What happened to your face?'

'*Where were you last night,*' The Kid shouted, '*and my lovely face wouldn't look like this!*'

'Let's go to your cabin,' McQuade said.

'This is my fucking ship!' The Kid beat his breast, 'if I wanna be tight on my own bridge nobody can stop me.'

'Come to your cabin, Kid.' McQuade took him by the arm.

'Where were you last season?' The Kid complained following. 'Jesus isn't this an awful ship?'

'Terrible, Kid.'

'It's *my* fucking ship though and no fucking Mate'll tell me what to do, McQuade!'

'Absolutely,' McQuade said. He led him into the cabin and closed the door. 'How are you, Kid?' he grinned.

'See my beautiful face, Jesus you should have been there McQuade.'

'What happened?'

'Can't remember McQuade, got tight you know.'

'No!'

'Got tight McQuade, you should have been there. Looked every goddam where for you ...' He was getting a whisky bottle from his cabinet.

'Have you got a beer?'

'Beers will your eyes bubble! – McQuade isn't it terrible about my beautiful face?'

'It's a tremendous loss. What happened?'

'Can't remember McQuade. Everything happened.'

'Where did you get tight?'

'Everywhere, McQuade. I'm still tight you know.'

'You don't say.'

'Yes McQuade, just a bit. Didn't sleep you know. Except yesterday with the whores. Two whores McQuade, you should have been there, bought these two whores.'

'And after them what happened?' McQuade was drinking the beer.

'Went drinking with the whores, McQuade. Damn nice whores, McQuade, you should have been there, there were two. Ever had two whores McQuade?'

'No. What time was this?'

'Sun was shining McQuade. Remember the sun very well. Remember one whore only had eight toes, popular prejudice is ten. Kept her shoes on all the time. Damn nice girls, they loved it, McQuade.'

'Go on.'

'Think one played rugby for the Springboks but since she's run to fat. But very nice McQuade.'

'Go on.'

'Lost the whores somewhere McQuade. One had false teeth but very nice. Suddenly the whores got lost some place. Soldiered on alone.'

'What time was this?'

'Dark now McQuade. Black you know. Remember looking for them in the murky night.'

'Then what happened?'

'Remember some sumbitch wouldn't serve me drink. That was after the whores. Said I was tight, McQuade.'

'Damn cheek. Then what happened?'

'Looked for you McQuade. Looked every goddam place.'

'Did you go to the Night and Day?'

'Went to the Night and Day, McQuade, you're right! Saw Jock at the Night and Day. Remember now. Remember Beulah came in. Beulah's crying. Dreadful mess, his nose all smashed up, blood everywhere.'

'Beulah's new nose?' McQuade said.

'Remember it now McQuade. Beulah's nose an awful mess. Got beaten up in some cafe. Beulah crying his heart out. Three Japies had beaten him up, remember now.'

'So what happened?'

'Council of War. Remember that. We're goin' to g'on beat up the Japies. Beulah's shedding blood everywhere. Everybody very excited. Barman's trying to talk us out of it. Jock, Beulah and me. Barman's most upset. Have another drink, McQuade.'

'Go on, go on.'

'We gird our loins McQuade, remember clearly now. Great send off, everybody very excited, all the whores shouting. Off we go, with a whoop and a holler. Into the arms of the cops.'

'Cops?'

'Cop, McQuade. One cop right outside the Night and Day. Bastard's waiting for us arms akimbo. Barman must've phoned him. Grabs us by our collars, most undignified, McQuade.' The Kid frowned hard to concentrate.

'Go on, Kid.'

'Cop says "Did you got a licence?" Wants to take us in on a drunk and disorderly. Black maria's parked in the road. Talked him out of it, damn nice cop. Everybody was very nice, McQuade, you should've been there.'

'How d'you talk him out of it?'

'Honeyed tones, McQuade, flowery speeches. Gift of the gab McQuade. You'd've been proud of me. Told him the bastards who beat up Beulah were Russians off the Slava. Said the cafe was a den of communist sympathisers plotting against the fatherland. Good speech McQuade, you should've heard it.'

'And the cop believed you?' McQuade said.

The Kid took a very noisy suck on his whisky.

'Policeman's lot is not a happy one, McQuade. Take our man. Got to choose between notches on his gun and striking a secret blow for the fatherland. Secret blows give you no notches on your gun, McQuade. And this guy needs notches if he's ever gonna make sergeant. So what does he do, McQuade?'

'What does he do?'

'Joins the ranks of the unsung heroes of the fatherland McQuade. Damn nice cop. First class cop. Lets go of our collars and says *okay man achtung Gott in himmel* something like that. Says we can go and punch 'em up provided we make it snappy. Says he'll drive round the block in his black maria and see no one interferes, damn decent cop. Says make it snappy.'

'Christ. So?'

'So off we go with a whoop and a holler McQuade. Second whoop and holler. We all steamed up now. Remember now. Started to run we're so steamed up. When we started to run got so steamed up threw caution to the winds, McQuade. Charged into the cafe like chap coming down like wolf on the fold. Damn fine sight we made, you should've been there.'

'Go on.' McQuade was laughing.

'Charged in there, McQuade, all steamed up. Only then we see how many goddam Japies in the joint, goddam Japies everywhere McQuade. Japies to the left of us, Japies to the right of us, quite frightful McQuade. You know why?'

'Why?'

'Cos that goddam barman at the Night and Day's phoned the sonsabitches and told them we coming that's why McQuade, that sumbitch must've phoned 'em. Cos they waiting for us like those three hundred Spartans at Thermopylae. And there we are, McQuade.'

McQuade was laughing. 'Go on.'

'And the bastards close in on us. And Christ, McQuade, 'twas a serious rout of the Anglo-Saxon peoples. There'll be questions in the House about this.'

McQuade was shaking with laughter.

'We'll have to send a gunboat, McQuade. And you know what?'

'What?'

'Just as some Japie bastard's kicking my head in and I'm screaming for the cops I look through the window and what do I see? I see my unsung hero cop cruising past in his black maria scrupulously keeping his bargain. Deaf to my entreaties McQuade.'

McQuade's eyes were wet with laughing. The Kid was laughing too now.

'Isn't it awful about my face McQuade? How can I woo the beautiful Miss Rhodes with this face?'

'Who's the beautiful Miss Rhodes?' McQuade said.

'McQuade? – You haven't heard about the beautiful Miss Rhodes?' The Kid cried happily. 'Oh McQuade! – Great things are happening in the All England Whaling Fucking Company. We got a bit of class at last, Miss Rhodes's our new nursing sister 'cos old Rigor Mortis's gone sick McQuade!'

'So it's true!' McQuade said.

'Have I ever told a lie McQuade? I'm having her aboard for dinner. And shall I tell you something else? I'm in love with her already McQuade!'

'Is that right?'

'So you keep your grubby cotton-pickin' paws off McQuade before I have you keelhauled. McQuade? – she's a lovely girl.'

'Yes?'

'She's lovely, McQuade. Big big eyes and long strong legs. You keep your cotton-pickin' hands off McQuade, my daddy employed her so I've the moral right.'

'Oh definitely,' McQuade said.

The Kid did a little jig all by himself. He was very drunk and happy and charming with his bruised boyish face and his blue eyes shining with drink and his thick thatch of hair awry. 'D'you think I'd do right to marry her McQuade?'

'Of course,' McQuade said.

'You don't think she just loves me for my money?' The Kid jigged.

'Certainly not,' McQuade said. 'Jock's after her too.'

'That goddam rotten sex-crazed sumbitch better keep his ugly mug right out of this, McQuade,' The Kid said.

'Jock's on the factory with her,' McQuade grinned, 'while you're off at the wars.'

'I got a motorboat haven't I?' The Kid crowed happily. 'Christ McQuade we're going to do an awful lot of hunting near the factory this season. She's going to brighten up that hospital an awful lot, McQuade.'

There was a knock on the door. 'Come in!' The Kid bellowed. A seaman put his head in, McQuade did not know him.

'Twenty minutes to sailing sir,' the seaman said.

'Who says?' The Kid demanded.

'The Mate, sir,' the seaman grinned. He was very young.

'Woods?' The Kid said happily. 'Will you convey a message to the learned Mate for me?'

'Yes sir,' Seaman Woods grinned.

'Thank you Woods,' The Kid said. 'Will you tell him that Captain Child says this ship will fucking sail when Captain Child fucking says so, Woods. Thank you Woods,' The Kid said. 'See you on the Christmas tree.'

'Thank you sir.' Seaman Woods withdrew, grinning.

'Come on, Kid,' McQuade said. He stood up.

'McQuade,' The Kid said. 'I insist we have another drink, I haven't seen you since Pontius was a pupil Pilate.'

'You've got to get ready, Kid,' McQuade said.

'McQuade,' The Kid said peevishly, 'whose daddy is Chairman of this shithouse company?'

'Yours Kid, now get changed.'

'Who's the best goddam gunner in this fleet?' The Kid said plaintively. 'And who's Captain of this godawful ship, me or that granny sumbitch Mate?'

'Nepotism, *get dressed Kid!*'

'Viva la nepotism!' The Kid sang, 'but I got my effing Master's ticket and that wasn't nepotism, McQuade. McQuade, I refuse to be bullied by the Mate, it's so undignified. McQuade? If I get changed will you please please please stop nagging me?'

'Yes.'

'You got to do the first wheel watch, I refuse to endure the Mate alone up there.'

'Okay,' McQuade said.

'You know I got a theory about the Mate, McQuade?' The Kid said.

'Yes.'

'He's my old nanny in disguise. Put on this ship by my demented father to torment me.'

'Yes,' McQuade said, 'I know.'

'Isn't he an awful man, McQuade? Isn't he a prize tit?'

'Awful.'

'He goes sneaking back to my father telling tales, you know that, McQuade?'

'Get ready, Kid!'

'Oh very well, then.' The Kid got up and started getting undressed.

They could hear the loudspeakers calling from the Icehammer. *Now hear this – Now hear this – This ship and her fleet are about to sail.*

'O very well,' The Kid repeated peevishly. 'But I am very happy about the beautiful Miss Rhodes ...'

They were mostly women on the quay, hundreds of women, wives and sweethearts and the whores. They were mostly Coloured women come to see their menfolk sail away, except the whores, the whores were mostly whites who had been with the Englishmen. The loudspeakers were playing *Auf Wiederseh'n*. The rails of the ships were packed with men waving and shouting to their women, and men who did not have women and who were just watching and waiting to sail away, looking at their last women for five months. *Auf Wiederseh'n* sang the loudspeakers, *Auf Wiederseh'n, We'll meet again, Sweetheart*. Many people were singing it. Many of the whalermen were drunk and there was a group of them hanging on to each other in a ring singing it very loud and deep and well. The factory ship had singled up fore and aft and the tugs were hooked up and their lines were taut. The women were all along the quay, clustered round the small black and white catchers too. Some of the catchers had already cast off and they were already turning in the harbour. Then the factory ship cast off and the tugs took the strain and the sea churned at their sterns and the factory ship blew Whoop Whooooop Whoooooop and the tugs answered Whoop Whooop Whooooop and then the catchers took it up, the whooping. Now the loudspeakers were playing It's a Long Way to Tipperary and the crowds and the whalermen were waving and the streamers were breaking and falling into the sea. *'It's a long way To Tippera-ree,'* The Kid sang, *'Ootsie tootsie Good-Byee'*—he waved to the women on the quay from the bridge—*'Watch for the mail, I'll never fail ...'* The Kid had finally decided against changing and he was stall in his sportswear.

The factory ship was well away from the quay now and the tugs were turning her round. The crowds were still waving. The catchers were all out in the harbour too, now, turning round, all the men were on decks of all the ships waving and watching. You could still hear the loudspeakers on the factory.

'*If you don't get a letter, Then you'll know I'm in jail,*' The Kid sang, '*Oot-toot-tootsie – Good-BYEE ...*'

'Come on Kid, let's go,' McQuade said softly from behind the wheel. The Fourteen was still tied up. The Mate was standing there pink with anger. He was staring rigidly at the quay. Fore and aft the deckies were waiting to cast off, laughing and wisecracking to the crowd. When McQuade spoke the Mate burst, it was the last straw.

'Shuttup McQuade!' the Mate shouted.

The Kid turned round slowly with a beautiful smile.

'Permission to proceed – sir!' the Mate shouted at The Kid, pink. McQuade tried to keep a straight face but only because he was sorry for the Mate. Any other Mate would have learned by now to keep his mouth shut and everything would have been fine, but not this Mate. The bridge boy was also trying to keep from smiling.

'Raised voices, Mister Mate?' The Kid said mildly. He could look sober when he wanted to. The Mate's eye-rims were red. He glared at The Kid.

'Permission to proceed, sir?' the Mate controlled himself pinkly. His neck looked swollen. The Kid looked thoughtful as if it was a good question and he picked up his binoculars and studied the scene. He was as steady as a rock. The factory and all the catchers were headed round out there now, hitting the swells already. The factory went whoop whoop whooop and the tugs answered. When the factory blew the Mate closed his eyes. McQuade wanted to put his hand on the man's shoulder and say 'Relax, Mate, what does it matter, you *ask* for trouble.'

'Hmmmmmm,' The Kid said looking through the binoculars. 'Righty-oh-ho, Mister, let's catch up with Miss Rhodes. With a hey-nonny-nonny and a hot cha-cha!'

The Mate snapped around and stamped out on to the wing of the bridge and bawled down at the deckies, red in the face.

'You shouldn't treat him like that, Kid,' McQuade said.

'I've got a theory,' The Kid said, 'that the Mate is my Aunt Agatha in disguise.' He looked drunk again.

Table Mountain was swinging slowly round. The big black and white mother surging churning through the harbour mouth, little black and white catchers ahead of her and astern of her, chopping and pitching and the dark blue sea ahead beyond, the Fourteen way behind. The harbour gates were dead ahead now with the dark blue sea beyond, stretching all the way to the horizon and far far beyond, to where there is only ice. The wind was blowing here now, out away from the shelter of the quay. The others were right through the mouth now, in the open Table Bay, swinging round to port and the south, the big factory and the fleet of tiny catchers scattered about her going up and down and plunging south. McQuade held her steady on the mouth and the telegraph ran up Half Ahead and the Fourteen surged into the mouth pitching in the swells, and the breakwater plunged past. And then they were in the dark blue sea and the bows were pitching higher and lower and The Kid told him to give her port. He swung the wheel and she heeled to the south, plunging in the new sea, the big mother far ahead with the flock of little ships plunging about her and the Fourteen far behind, all headed south for the horizon and the Antarctic.

On the fourth day they reached the Roaring Forties and the dark colding sea swelled high, high above the crow's-nest so now she was down in the shadow of the swells, sun streaking golden blue through the running hills of sea, now she was riding up back into the sunshine. And poised on the ridge of the running peak looking down into heaving shadowed sea valley far below. Then down went the bows, sliding rushing down into the valley and shadows and the sea running way way up there far above the bridge far above the crow's-nest and the crow's-nest swinging way over as she rode up the side of the swell back into the sunshine again. And another valley, and another and another all the way to the heaving horizon and beyond and getting bigger and bigger and deeper and deeper and the sea running harder. The fleet of little catchers was sometimes nowhere to be seen as they plunged and ploughed. And then the sky got very black, and now came the wind, blowing the black clouds across the swinging sky and whistling in the rigging, then it began to tear the tops off the great running swells and the swells ran bigger before the wind and the valleys were deeper and darker. So the fleet plunged into the first night of the Forties churning uphill and shooting down, and clinging wrapped in oilskins in the wildly dipping swaying crow's-nest high above the ship the waves towered high above and the lights on the fleet scattered far and wide about and went on and off and on and off behind the giant swells, now high, now skidding down, now gone. And the wildly spinning compass, and sweating on the wheel. And in the dawn came the rain, and then the storm, and the day was black black black, the wind rose to a gale, then the big galloping swells broke, waves now. They crashed down into the valleys, crashed over the fleet, and the ships shook and shuddered and heeled and fell and then churned up again out of the valley, up up up up churning gritting panting sodden up up up to the top, they poised at the top propellers beating the air with yawning valley below, then *down,* down they slid with bows down skidding skewering tumbling sliding, the waves broke over her, and blind, now, bows and stern and midships under crashing roaring sea, then sucking roaring back, wave way up high above again, bows up in sodden grind again, up up again, and over the top again, then smack down plunging down into the valley again, lunging broadside down. And down below the tiny alleyway rolling wildly and the water rushing up and down and the sailors falling and all the pumps going and the crash of the waves and the deck rushing up steep then plunging sideways falling. And sleeping on the decks of cabins with life jackets on, tossing and pitching and sliding on the cabin deck, and climbing up and weak and crying for sleep and the world still crazy swinging pitching heaving plunging, and crying out: *Oh Christ make the bloody thing stay still just for one minute please please for Chrissake* – and taking over the bucking wheel and feeling the rudder must snap under your hands, and the sea rearing up high in front of you, then the great chasm of sea below you, then the bows smashed from sight before you, and the rain rain rain and the spray beating the glass and then a huge jolt and only white blue sea falling everywhere and the deck heaving over under you. The fleet was invisible now, the horizon all gone, just howling spray and hurtling rearing plunging sea. Nothing in the whole world but the howls and roars and madness of the mighty sea, the madness, and the mighty thuds and jolts and explosions and the sprawlings and the fallings and the whole world swinging and the great sea hurtling and crashing and smashing and flooding and rearing and high high up and sucking way way down. So it was for four days.

And then they were beyond the Forties in the cold calm south sea, and the fleet reassembled and the sun shone and the gentle rolling of the ship was a lullaby, and they slept. And the air was bright and cold and clean and everything stood out clear-cut. On the second day beyond the Forties they saw the first iceberg, a great square dazzling white mountain in bright bright sunshine in dark blue sea under bright blue sky, sheer white cliffs rising up up high above the fleet, her cliffs were streaked with blue and green and her top was soft and flat and snowy, and she was very clean. She was the first, and in the afternoon the faraway horizon became studded with white icebergs scattered across the sea, big icebergs and little icebergs and the fleet ploughed evenly on, snowcaps and heavy gear and gloves now under the sunshine and the ice blue sky, and the steel of the ships was ice cold.

Part Two

Chapter Four

Now in the summer at the Ice the sky is ice blue and the sun shines golden white and the sea is very dark blue, and everything is very sharp and clear and very cold. In the midday the sun blinds off the ice and off the icebergs, very white and clean, towers of shining cold gleaming and you have to screw up your eyes and you burn red and gold and then brown. In the early mornings and the late afternoons the sun shines low and pink and gold over the dark blue sea, and the ice and the sea reflect the light in long low glares and beams and the ships and the icebergs are bathed in a patchwork of many colours, violet and indigo and blue and green and yellow and orange and red, the light moves in a mottled spectrum over the black and white steel ships and on the faces of their men and on the huge clanking bleeding carnage on the big deck and on the pure white cliffs of ice floating so quietly by.

The first week of that summer we sailed way out there far amongst the icebergs looking for whales, four hours on watch and four hours off, on the wheel and in the crow's-nest and on the bows on lookouts, but we saw very few whales. We went alongside the factory three times to bunker in that first week, although we were using very little fuel in view of the scarcity of the whales, because The Kid wanted to visit Miss Victoria Rhodes. We had to await our turn to go alongside to bunker and every time we got alongside it was long after Miss Rhodes' dinner time and she was already asleep or in her nightwear, and so she refused to receive visitors, and The Kid came back aboard the Fourteen very frustrated. He had not even set eyes upon her since we left Cape Town, but the whole factory ship was talking about her, and it was clear that she was growing more beautiful each day, in about a month she would be the most beautiful woman in the whole world, in about five weeks she would be the most beautiful woman that ever lived. I had not seen her myself. A lot of the boys said she gave them the eye, and all day long men on the factory ship were going along to the hospital with aches and pains that baffled medical science. You didn't know what to believe, except that you couldn't believe very much. But it tore at your guts to imagine it, right down here at the Antarctic, where it was womanless womanless womanless, except for Old Ferguson and the Old Man's missus, Our Ida The Sunshine of Our Home, it tore at your guts, this most beautiful woman right here at the Antarctic with belly and buttocks and thighs and breasts and brassieres, all woman and luscious, taking off her panties down her lovely soft legs in her cabin and lying down and opening her legs. Christ it got you right here in the guts if you thought about it. And only two and a half weeks from Cape Town. I did not believe any of it, but sometimes when you're lying in your bunk you do not know what to believe. At the Ice you begin to believe and imagine and hope all kinds of things, you go a little mad at the Ice, very unstable. The Kid did not know what to believe. The Kid was very restless and furtive in that first week at the Ice. He did not talk much, and when you talked to him his eyes went somewhere else and he was just agreeing with you.

'I thought you were going to invite her aboard for dinner?' I said.

'How can I invite her aboard for dinner when I've hardly met her?' The Kid said irritably.

'You're a Captain of the line,' I said, 'and she's a fellow officer. Send her a note.'

I was anxious that Miss Rhodes should come to dinner.

'You would have broken the ice,' I said. 'Then you can call on her again.'

'*Every* goddam time I call on her she's either not in or she's already in bed. Do you think she has some lousy factory hand in bed with her?'

'I should think so,' I said.

'Why?' The Kid demanded. 'Why do you think so?'

'The rumours,' I said cheerfully. I liked to see The Kid worried for a change.

'What rumours?' The Kid demanded.

'Listen,' I said, 'how long do you think you can turn one beautiful woman loose amongst five hundred slavering men before she chooses somebody? You better make it snappy, Kid,' I said.

He looked at me agitatedly.

'Yeah,' he said. 'What rumours?'

'You better make it snappy Kid,' I said, 'and invite Miss Rhodes to dinner.'

The fourth night The Kid would not wait for the Fourteen's turn to bunker: he lowered his own speedboat and went to the factory by himself. It was a good glass fibre speedboat that he had bought and installed himself and it had a fifty horse-power Johnson outboard. He did not tell me to come with him, as he had all the other seasons. The other seasons The Kid and I had used the speedboat to be able to get to the factory when he wanted, for Christmas and to go and have a pint of beer in the Pig or to see a movie they were showing. The whole crew watched him drive off into the sunset into the icebergs, and we all knew why he was going. When our turn came to go alongside the factory to bunker there was his boat tied up on the leeward. It was late and I went to bed. I was almost asleep when we pulled away from alongside the factory. The Kid had not yet come aboard when we left. When I woke up we were waiting drifting about a mile from the factory. I heard the noise of the outboard coming alongside, then The Kid calling for a deckie to help him heave the boat aboard on the davits. Then I heard him clatter down into the accommodation alleyway and he beat once on the door and flung it open beaming.

'James I made it!'

'Do you mind?' I said, 'I may have been asleep.'

'I said I made it James-baby!'

'Close the door before I catch my death. Made what?'

He closed the door and slumped down on the foot of my bunk.

'James,' The Kid said, 'I want you to know this girl is really something. Really something.'

'Yes?'

'James,' The Kid said happily, 'she is beautiful. I really think I'll marry her.'

'Oh good,' I said. 'Told her yet?'

'Seriously. She is something. Those big brown eyes, James. Those teeth. That long black hair, James—'

'What happened?' I said.

'James, she has the most gorgeous eyes and hair. You guys certainly breed them in South Africa.'

'What happened for Chrissake?'

'She let me into her cabin James.'

'Big deal,' I said. '*Quiet!* There's guys trying to sleep next door. And then?'

'Well ...' The Kid said. 'It was a very pleasant evening.'

'What happened?'

'Well – we had coffee.'

'Coffee?'

'Yeah.'

'Yeah?'

'Very nice too. I didn't want to invite her down to the Pig, the boys would have gone mad.'

'So you had coffee. Then what?'

'We talked,' The Kid said.

'You talked?'

'Certainly we talked.'

'Okay you talked, then what?'

The Kid looked at me and then he burst into smiles. 'We had a very pleasant evening.'

I lay back and closed my eyes. 'Okay,' I said.

The Kid felt ashamed, which was very unusual for him. 'Okay. We only talked,' he grinned.

'What did you talk about?' I said with my eyes still closed.

The Kid sighed happily.

'Just things. Told her what a big deal I am, etcetera. She's a lovely girl.'

'And that's all?'

'That's all. Well,' The Kid said, 'I did make a kind of pass at her.'

'Oh?'

'I kissed her.'

'Good,' I said.

'What do you mean "Good" in that tone of voice?' The Kid said.

'Nothing. I've never seen the girl.'

'How can you be jealous about her then?'

'I'm not jealous, for Chrissake.'

'Okay, Jimmy-baby,' The Kid said.

'So it's in the bag?'

The Kid looked at me. 'I haven't said anything dirty about her,' he said defensively.

'I don't care if you do. I don't know the woman from Adam.'

'Okay James,' The Kid said. 'You'd know her from Adam all right.'

'How does she like the whaling?' I said.

'She's not exactly crazy about it. And she was seasick.'

'Shame.'

'She and Old Ferguson get on famously apparently.'

'Good.'

'I saw Old Fergie, she sends you her regards.'

'Thanks.'

'Okay,' The Kid said, 'I'll leave you, seeing you're in such a beautiful mood.'

'I'm not in a bad mood,' I said.

'Not half, I don't know what I've done.'

'When's Miss Rhodes coming aboard for dinner?' I said.

'Aha!' The Kid said. 'So now we know! Next week, but you'll be scrubbing the bilges that night you bastard.'

'Okay,' I said.

'All right, you can come to dinner too.'

'Don't strain yourself,' I said.

'Just leave us alone after the liqueurs.'

I didn't say anything.

'Actually,' The Kid said, 'I'd like you to come to help keep the conversation going. She's a bit shy.'

'Sounds like a great evening.'

'I'm going in the boat to see her again tomorrow night,' The Kid said. 'You can come for the ride if you like, but only for the ride.'

'Okay,' I said. 'Maybe.'

'And now I must go to sleep,' The Kid said, 'to be beautiful for Miss Rhodes tomorrow. And seeing you're in such a beautiful mood.'

'How about going to sleep so you can shoot some beautiful whales tomorrow,' I said. 'That's what most of us are here for.'

'James-baby,' The Kid said, 'when it comes to shooting whales I'm your only man.'

Chapter Five

The whole eastern sky was red ahead, deep rich and then fanning up and out to overhead, pink. There was a big iceberg way ahead, sheer and flat on top, like Table Mountain, and it had one high solitary peak of ice. At the edges the new red light shone through the iceberg and glinted off it and it glowed vermilion on the edges, and the peak glowed translucent red and at the tip it seemed on fire. There were no swells, only a very little choppiness and the tips of the chops were catching the light also and the sea was dancing red and silver black. On the horizon there were more icebergs and they were black in the centres and on fire on the edges too. We were far away from the factory and Miss Rhodes. In the radio room the machine was going bleep bleep bleep and ping ping ping, quietly.

The Kid said, 'I think I got the clap, Jimmy,' staring ahead.

'What about this iceberg?' I said.

'What about it?' The Kid said.

I stood easy at the wheel and leant on it.

'We're going to hit it,' I said.

'Don't hit it,' he decided.

The Kid nodded thoughtfully.

'Very well. Port or starboard? Port is left, starboard is right.'

He sighed.

'Decisions, decisions, decisions. *You* decide, you're the helmsman.'

'Okay,' I said. 'Left.'

I began to turn the wheel to port.

'Why did you choose left?' he said after a while.

'I guess it's because I'm just naturally sinister.'

That's how it is with the whaling, after a while you get to talking a lot of crap. I took her south of the iceberg. The cliff face of the berg was glass blue with deep veins of white reaching far above us. There was a little bay and a small ice beach and you could see the white icebed of the beach sloping down under the clear blue water. As we came round the cliff face it caught the sunrise and the blue face flashed blinding red and mauve, and the ice beach turned gleaming red.

'That'll make you very popular with Miss Rhodes,' I said. 'The clap.'

'Yeah,' The Kid said.

'Why don't you take it along to her to fix?' I said cheerfully.

'Give her a preview of Charlie?' The Kid said. 'The delights in store when he's back in fighting form?'

'Or put her off for life. Make a kind of test case out of it,' I said.

'Yeah,' The Kid said. 'No,' he said, 'I'll take him along to Old Ferguson. I don't want to jeopardise my beautiful romance with Miss Rhodes. Old Ferguson's used to it. She's seen him at the beginning of every season for the last nine years, she's on first name terms with him. "Hul-*lo there*, Charlie!" she says. "Welcome back! Had a good year?"'

'Yeah?' I was grinning.

'Sure,' The Kid said miserably.

He sighed, frowning into the sunrise. 'Where're the goddam whales?'

'You should have broken out before this,' I said. 'It's nearly three weeks.'

'Yeah.'

'Can't be gonorrhea,' I said cheerfully. 'Must be syphilis.'

'Yeah,' The Kid said miserably. 'And me just starting my beautiful romance with Miss Rhodes.'

'You leave Miss Rhodes alone,' I said. 'You with your syphilis. Three to four weeks for the cure,' I said cheerfully. 'It's a shame.'

'I've never had syphilis before,' The Kid mused. 'Only gonorrhea.'

'Gonorrhea's nothing,' I said.

'A cold in the nose.'

'Almost a social asset,' I said. We churned on into the sunrise.

'The worst I've ever copped before is gonorrhea,' The Kid complained. 'Maybe it's only gonorrhea,' he said hopefully. 'Maybe I've overlooked the symptoms.'

'No,' I said firmly. 'Like you're pissing razor blades.'

'Yeah. Or fishhooks.'

'Or fishhooks,' I said reasonably.

'I think I'll go and have another check.'

He walked behind into the chartroom and clattered down the companionway. The sun was just sitting on the horizon now, and the bridge was turning gold and everything was very clean. It felt good on the bridge, all gold this morning. Perhaps it was knowing there was a Miss Victoria Rhodes at the Ice this year, but it was a beautiful morning. The Kid came back up the companionway.

'Still there,' he reported sadly. 'It's the fishhooks all right.'

'That's it then,' I said, 'that's the Works.'

That is how we were talking about Miss Rhodes that mid-December dawn, after a while with the whaling you get to talking a lot of crap, when the cry comes from Mike up there in the crow's-nest, *'There she blows! Port – there she blows ...'*

'Oh very well then,' The Kid said. He looked up to see where Mike was pointing and then raised his binoculars. He leant out and pressed the Panic Button and the muted bell started burring below.

'Yeah, there she blows,' The Kid said languidly. 'Half to port.'

'Half to port,' I said.

'Where's that goddam Mate?' The Kid snapped. He strode to the telegraph and rang up Full Ahead, with a snap. It rang faraway down in the engine room and there came the big throb and then the surge. Boots were running along the deck. Lodewijk and the English boy whose name I could never remember were running up fo'r'ard to the gun. The bows were coming round hard. The Mate came clattering up the companionway, pink and balding, red hair ruffled.

'Where—?' he puffed.

'Where our bows are heading, Mister,' The Kid said languidly in his best Oxford drawl. 'Steady as she goes, James,' The Kid said, very Oxford for the Mate's benefit.

I looked at the compass and gave her some starboard. 'Steady as she goes,' I said. 'She's steady,' I said.

'Give her a little port.'

'Give her a little port.'

'Steady.'

'Steady,' I said. I let the wheel go and then gave her a little starboard. 'Steady she is,' I said.

'What kind?' the Mate said. He was trying to make his presence felt.

'It's a sperm,' The Kid drawled. 'Did you see her blow, James?'

'No,' I said.

'It's a sperm,' The Kid said conversationally to infuriate the Mate. 'He'll blow his top again in a minute,' The Kid said. He gave a long slow charming smile at the sea. '... The whale, I mean.'

I felt sorry for the Mate. We were picking up speed hard now, the bows were beginning to smash up and down and the mauve-gold sea was beginning to spray over and in the air it was white gold. The Kid stamped his heel.

'Faster you bitch, *faster.*'

I was watching the compass to keep her steady. The sun shone gold and orange into the bridge and I had to screw up my right eye. We were going almost flat out now. 'Faster,' The Kid stamped his heel again, '*faster* you bitch ...'

'There she blows ...' the Mate said fussily, disapproving of The Kid stamping his heel like that.

And there she blew five hundred yards ahead in the orange sunlight, a hump of black swirling up out of the orange blue sea, then the big swelling strength heaving itself up out of the sea, bigger and bigger, a great mound of black back, then the mighty tail sucking up out of the sea, great flukes running water in the sunlight and then thrashing down back into the sea so it splashed far. Then the great throaty idle gush of spray up through the hole on the top of his head, high and forwards, then the great wet back humping itself and the great flukes thrashing again and down he went again in a big sucking swirl and churning and eddying of the frothing golden blue sea, and he was gone.

'Okay, starboard a little,' The Kid said.

'Starboard a little.'

He had not yet seen us. The Kid was taking off his duffle coat, watching the sea as he pulled on his skins. 'Starboard, starboard.' I was watching the sea where I thought he would blow again. The catcher was going fiat out now, bows smacking up and down, up and down, the spray flying over the gun in the golden sunshine.

'Right – steady now then steady as she goes ...'

'Steady up, steady as she goes,' I said.

'Faster you bitch – okay ...' The Kid said.

He strode on to the bridge wing, the wind flapping his hair and walked down the causeway to the bows, his hands on both rails, and the bows were going up and down. He jumped down on to the gun platform and took the curved handle with both hands and he crouched down behind it and swung it experimentally. Then he waved his hand forward like a cavalry officer, which meant Steady as she goes. Then he stamped his boot three times which meant *Faster you bitch,* and spray broke over him and he stamped his boot again *Faster faster faster* you bitch ...

She was going flat out now, up and down and spray smacking over and the sun was over the horizon now, golden bright. The Kid crouched on the gun platform, the water running off him and the sea was empty ahead, just bright early morning sunshine horizontal over the sea, but he waved his hand forward again, dead ahead into the empty sea, and he stamped his boot, *Faster.* The Mate was looking through binoculars. Twenty seconds, thirty, forty, fifty, still the sea was empty, the whole horizon empty, sixty seventy eighty, still he waved us forward.

'I think he's wrong ...' the Mate said.

Ninety seconds one hundred, two minutes.

'He's wrong,' the Mate said, he swept his glasses round, 'The Kid's all wrong.'

'No he isn't—' I said.

Ahead, no more than five degrees to starboard, he came up again, the big swirl and then the big hump again, and then the great lazy thrash of the flukes again. He still had his back to us, he still had not seen us or heard us. The Kid's right hand was up now pointing, hand up to shoulder then forward twice, I swung the wheel over to starboard and she came over, running like a terrier now. Still the whale had not seen us, he swirled on the surface and then he blew his giant breath again silver in the sunlight. Then he sensed us, or he felt the throb of our screws, he raised his giant head so he was almost all above the water and he curled and thrashed his tail once and he turned broadside on to bring his left eye on to us, and he looked at us churning down on him. He stared at us for an instant, the water running off him, then he arched his huge old back and he lifted his giant tail and humped himself once and he ducked his huge perpendicular head under and his huge flukes came up out of the water, and he kicked once, and he dived. He disappeared in a swirl and one thrash of his tail and the water whirlpooled and foamed where he had been.

'Poor old bastard,' I said.

Port port port The Kid was signalling. I spun the wheel, she keeled and came round throbbing hard. The Kid was stamping his boot hunched over the gun and the spray was flying over him. *Faster* The Kid stamped.

The old whale sounded deep with a cry of fear that only I could hear. He whipped his great horizontal flukes and down he dived, great square head bursting down down down into the dark icy sea and his long jaw clamped shut, blind as to what lay before him for his eyes can only look sideways, and swirlings streamed behind him and whirled up to the surface telling us where he was going. The Kid stamped and waved and pointed and the spray broke over him and the ship keeled and followed. Then the old whale levelled out and he whipped his tail up and down, he swam furiously along for three hundred yards with the fear knocking in his great body, blindly under the water, and as he fled he emitted high-pitched grunts of warning and fear which only other whales and I could hear.

Thus he fled panic-stricken, in a straight line, and The Kid could follow him. The Kid stood hunched over the gun shouting into the wind and the spray breaking over him, he waved and waved us forward and stamped his boot. Thus we ran across the Antarctic, the old whale fleeing underneath and the ship pursuing on the top, and then the old beast wanted air again. He lifted his great square head upwards and he galloped his mighty old tail, galloped up up up out of the darkness up to the silver surface, he was tired but not yet finished, by no means finished yet but very afraid. Up he charged to the surface and we could see his great blackness coming up, he broke through black and huge and snorting and blowing into the bright sunshine with a great sucking surge and upheaval, he blew and sucked in air and he skewered round and looked panting and snorting and heart beating for us, and there we were bearing straight down on him, the sea curling up sharp over our bows so it flew over the deck, galloping down on him. The Kid was whooping and stamping his boot and beating the bows like a horse, only one hundred and fifty yards away now. The whale stared at us, blowing and panting and his great tail swirling on the surface. Then he turned his great scarred perpendicular forehead to us, scars of clashes and crashes and battles long ago, with the giant squid with great carnivorous beaks gouging and snapping and long tentacles clawing him as they wrestled to the death in dark deep icy ocean battles of long ago, and with other young bulls in better warmer days in warmer seas, great angry young bulls fighting over a lady, huge rushes and charges and giant jagged jaws gaping and snapping and eyes rolling red and hateful and the sea boiling and thrashing, swiping each other with their tails and charging, the mighty jarring crash of heads and bone and muscle, giant jaws with the giant teeth crashing and locking together, mighty threshing tail crunched in giant jaws, the long bloody herculean wrestle to the death, over the young cow, long ago, in better days, in warmer seas. And for the moment that this forehead glinted in the sun at us the old whale could not see us, and in that moment of blindness the old whale panicked and he skewered and sort of wagged his great head as if he was trying to shake it clear, he looked all confused in his fright, and it was pitiful to see. We churned down on him and The Kid was crouched over the gun and sighting it on him and I held the sharp bows dead on his great forehead and whispered, *'Dive, man, dive ...'*

One hundred yards dead ahead the old whale shook his big head at us and his great tail threshed the sea and the spray flew over the bows and The Kid crouched lower over the big harpoon. One hundred yards, ninety, eighty – *Dive old whale dive,* I willed – seventy yards, the big harpoon poised now – *Don't charge old whale, dive, man, dive* – I held the sharp steel bows straight on him, sixty yards – 'He's going to charge!' the Mate said, 'The Kid'll get us all stove in ...' – *Don't charge old whale, you can't win because we're made of steel, dive boy dive* – Fifty yards and The Kid had his eye right down to the long steel harpoon sighting along it – 'Fire,' the Mate urged, 'Fire!'

Fifty yards and the old whale slewed around with a mighty thrash of his tail, and there was his huge flank exposed to us, and he took a big snort breath and he lifted his tail for the sounding, and there was the thud and jolt and the puff of smoke. The long steel shaft with the big grenaded barbed head flew out over the sea and the long white nylon rope was whistling out behind it, it whistled through the air and he lifted his tail and he pushed his big square head down and the harpoon flew at him. It flew down dead at him, and in the second it took the huge tail kicked and the big black head went under, and the harpoon smacked into the sea, and it was gone. And the big tail flashed black silver wet in the sunlight and the sea closed over it.

'Fuck!' the Mate cursed. Lodewijk and the English boy were bent double under the pitching spray picking up another harpoon, cursing.

The Kid turned and leant with one hand on the gun, a grin all over his wet face and he wagged his finger at us and shouted, 'Now-now! I know you're thinking horrid things about me up there.'

The Mate glowered down at him. I grinned at The Kid. He gave me a wide wet grin.

'Thinks he's on his daddy's yacht,' the Mate glowered pinkly.

'Which he is.'

'Shuttup McQuade!'

'Just a teeny weeny bit of old port, Jimmy-baby,' The Kid called up sweetly, grinning.

'Christ!' the Mate said.

The old whale ran, less deep this time and more tired and frightened, you could see his turbulence as he whipped his great back galloping under the sea, and we tore after him, our spray curving viciously. It was easier to follow him now, the man in the crow's-nest could see him quite easily under the sea.

The old whale was tired now. He was running as hard as he could but he was not going so fast now. He could hear us and feel us hot after him, our propellers and our engine roar, he ran flat out and straight for three-quarters of a mile under the sea hearing and feeling us hard after him, and making his noises of fear that only I could hear. *Run, whale,* I willed him, *run old whale.* For three-quarters of a mile he ran and we were two hundred yards behind him, his turbulence a long swirling trail behind him, the spray curving up in the sunshine and The Kid whooping and stamping his boot again. Then the whale needed to blow and breathe again, and he was going slower now and we were catching up with him. Still he ran and we were a hundred and fifty yards behind and then he just had to come up to blow, and he started coming up and Mike up there in the crow's-nest hollered, *'Here she comes!'* and his arm was outstretched. Then up on the bridge I saw him coming up dead ahead, great black shape galloping up from the sea's blackness up to the morning, bigger and bigger in a flash he came in his great turbulence and then he broke the surface in a roar.

In a great gush and surge he broke, great black and shining silver and gold humpback he broke through in a curve, one hundred yards ahead so you could see the lines on his hide silver and gold and black in the sunlight, huge tired galloping mighty exhausted strength with a gush so mighty and magnificent and frightened and tired and pitiful to see, and he blew, the great beast terrified on the run from man, he blew with a gush and roar and terror that broke your heart to hear it, a mighty snorting blow, half whimper, and I hated the whaling as I hated it every season. You could see the rainbow in his blow up into the morning, and then you smelt it, the great oily, giant breath-scream up into the morning. And it got you right here, and you felt you had no business down here with the great beasts, no right. So the old whale blew, ninety yards dead ahead, and it was only a matter of time. His great tail came up and he plunged back down under but he did not have enough air, he was very tired and he ploughed straight back up again in his tired roaring gallop and he blew again, a smaller roaring gasp, then he sounded. He sounded off to starboard and The Kid was whooping and stamping *starboard* and I brought the wheel over.

But the old whale could not run very fast nor very far now before he had to come up for air again. He broke surface and blew and plunged again, bucking and whipping his huge tail, but not going very fast. We could easily see which way he was headed when he began to sound. And he came up and blew desperately again, but we were only seventy yards from him now and he did not know which way to go for the best, and he lunged down with only half a breath and he staggered as he fled, and The Kid swung after him whooping and shouting and beating the deck with his boot. He came up to the surface again and we were only fifty yards behind with the bows swinging round on him and he blew and roared and he plunged under again and he ran again but he was staggering as he swam.

He came up forty yards ahead in a great surging exhausted blast, he turned wildly to look for the ship and he saw it and he gave a bellow which only I could hear, and he turned to plunge away and his great weary back arched and the gun exploded and the harpoon flew. It flew as a missile and it came screaming down on to the huge wet black heaving flank, screamed into the huge flesh and it exploded and meat and hide and guts flew up and out and into the sea. And a cry went up.

The shock, the shatter, the silent screams of pain. The old whale kicked and thrashed and reeled and staggered and thrashed and his blood pumped clouds into the thrashing sea and the great foam and splashes frothed and flew red as he thrashed and kicked in his first great shock and fight and agony, and then he ran. He ran with the big steel harpoon buried into his guts and the long white nylon rope strung tight from it and his blood was a big fat smoke cloud behind him.

He sounded and ran dragging the long tight white line stretched hard from his guts and The Kid signalled Half Ahead to break his run and the throb of the engines slowed down, but still the whale dragged out the line from the great electric winch, and we gave him line. He ran and ran dragging on the line and the winch and the ship, he twisted and shook and kicked and bucked deep under the sea to shake out the harpoon and its tight long white line from his guts, but he could not and we only dragged him tighter and he ran again. But he ran slower now dragging on the long tight line and then he just had to come back to the air to breath and he broke surface. He broke in a plunging thrash and he blew, fifty feet of black shining beast bleeding thrashing blood, and he heaved up his great tail and thrashed and swept and twisted trying to shake out the harpoon and he twisted his head and shook and opened his giant jaws and snapped the air and he tried to twist around and snap at the harpoon and the line and he blew and snorted and beat his tail on top of the sea and the sea and his froth splashed crimson far about him. We stood still on the clean cold sunshine sea sixty yards from his great suffering and pulled with the big electric winch on the long strong white rope that was pink now.

For one hour the old whale fought. He plunged and snapped and twisted and he sounded and ran ran ran kicking and twisting and fighting and then he had to come back to the sunlight again to blow, he blew and kicked and twisted and snapped and then he sounded and ran again, and all the time his blood pumping out into the sea. For one hour we followed him slowly in the sunshine, the long red line strung tight, the big electric winch winding him in and giving him a little line, engines stopping and starting and stopping again as he dragged us, then the winch reeling him in again, waiting and watching him dying in the ice cold blue sea under the bright morning sun, and reeling him foot by foot, and then giving him a little, on the big winch.

The blue sea was deep mauve with his blood now. One hour, and then the big last desperate instinct of escape came and he plunged again and he tried to run but he could not run any more, and he came back in a big thrash, and he went into his flurry. He came out of the sea and he was shuddering, shuddering and shaking and trembling all over his mighty fifty feet, and the sea shook red about him, he heaved himself high on to the water and there was the great hole in his flank and the harpoon sticking deep, and the white rope soaked red there, and the sea shone red satiny on his big black flesh in the sunshine, he shuddered and shook and he keeled. He keeled on top of the red sea and he beat his tail flat on top of the water and his fins flapped against his side making great wet clapping sounds, and then they stuck out rigid away from his side, stuck out there for a long moment trembling. He reeled again and his long lower jaw stretched out rigid and quivering and his big scimitar teeth white and red, and his long jaw snapped and snapped and then it stuck out open and it shook. And then he slewed around on top of the water and he faced the ship, as if he was going to charge it, one last valiant reckless charge. Then he keeled over, he rolled over and over trembling and shaking and splashing as he rolled, and his fins shook and beat his side and his tail flapped and his jaw trembled and snapped and the red and pink foam flew high. And then he came right side up and he blew. It shot up high into the air as if at last released, blood, a long high plume, deep thick dark rich red blood shining scarlet in the sunlight, then spattering down into the red sea. And he gave a dying bellow which only I could hear and he trembled all over and then he keeled over. His belly came up into the sunshine, satiny red, and he was still.

Chapter Six

That night The Kid was going to the factory in his boat to visit Miss Rhodes, and to have his clap looked at by Old Ferguson, and he asked me to come with him, for the ride. The Fourteen would have to await its turn to go alongside to refuel.

'Do I get to visit Miss Rhodes too?' I said.

'No,' The Kid said. 'You can come to see Old Ferguson if you want.'

'I'm crazy about Old Ferguson,' I said.

'You'll see Miss Rhodes at the dinner party,' The Kid said. 'And I want you to know I am having very grave misgivings indeed about having invited you.'

'You can stick your goddam dinner party,' I said, 'right up your backside, cutlery, dinner-service and all. It's Miss Rhodes I'm coming to see.'

We were drinking my Cape brandy in The Kid's cabin. The Kid had shot four whales and everybody was very pleased with him, except the Mate. The Kid was very pleased with himself. The sun was going down and the Mate was on the bridge heading us back towards the factory. The Kid had showered to make himself smell nice for Miss Rhodes and now he was at the mirror making himself beautiful for Miss Rhodes. 'Do you think I should put a little brilliantine on my beard?' The Kid said.

'Definitely,' I said.

'"Bless your beautiful hide,"' The Kid sang. He decided against the brilliantine. 'Am I or am I not a dead ringer for Gregory Peck?'

'All women want to bear your children without anaesthetic,' I said. 'It's just a pity about your syphilis,' I said.

When The Kid was dressed we were only a few miles from the factory ship. The sun was going down over the icebergs, so the icebergs glowed red and black, and the sun caught the ice and glanced off at angles up into the sky, long red beams, and orange and yellow. There was an iceberg to far starboard which sparkled, a great ruby sitting on the horizon. The blue sea turned to dark purple and as the sun went down the beams of light moved, higher and higher and they would stay there a long time and then when they were gone there would be the red red glow behind the icebergs, fanning out high and pink into the sky. We went down on to the deck and walked down aft to the boat. I heard the telegraph ring down in the engine room and the screws and the noise and vibrations stopped and we coasted and suddenly it was very quiet and beautiful, very private, and also very cold. The Kid was grinning. I was happy also. It was the first time that season that I had used the boat, it was exciting to be going aboard the factory and seeing the strange faces, you get very sick of the sight of each other on a small corvette. We spoke of going aboard the factory as going ashore because after the crazily pitching corvette the factory seemed as steady as a rock. We each took a cleat on the davits and swung the boat outboard and lowered her down on to the sea. The corvette was almost stopped, now. I made the painter fast and held the boat steady, and The Kid climbed into the boat and hooked up the fuel lead and pumped the juice through to the big outboard motor. Then he said, 'Okay,' and I untied the painter and shoved us away out into the Antarctic and sat down behind the wheel. The Kid pulled the engine cord and the Johnson coughed but it did not start. On the corvette the Mate rang up Half Ahead and the screws churned up the sea suddenly and she moved away.

'The bastard,' The Kid said, 'he knows he mustn't move till we're started. He does it on purpose.'

He pulled the cord again and the engine spluttered. Now we were rocking in the wake of the corvette.

'That bastard,' The Kid said, 'he'd love to see us have to row ashore.' I was grinning.

He pulled the cord again, and she coughed and started. 'Hoo-bloody-ray,' The Kid said irritably. He clambered up for'ard and sat down beside me. I opened the throttle and the engine roared and the nose came up. 'Take her past the Fourteen,' The Kid said.

I opened wider and we raced over the water, the sea smacking under the nose, smackerty smackerty smackerty and the boat shuddering and the spray flying. It was very cold, and very free-feeling. We swept past the bridge and The Kid held up his fingers and gave the Mate the V sign. I wished he wouldn't do that. Then I slowed her down and we headed gently for the factory, watching out for ice in the moonlight.

It was a good speedboat. Glass fibre, twelve foot, it had navigation lights but no windshield. It was good to be driving her again. Two seasons back The Kid had taken it into his head to go hunting seals from this boat, he wanted six sealskins to take home for sealskin coats for three of his women. He had ordered me to go with him, and I had refused, so he took two deckies with him, and then I had gone also to try to see to it that there was no massacre. We came to an ice jagged beach sparkling in the sunshine, with two herds of females clustered around two massive roaring bull beachmasters, and the pups were snuffling and flopping around. I warned the bastards that if they took more than six I would bloody murder them, or try to, and I stood on the edge of the ice while The Kid and the deckies walked up to the herds with their fire axes, and the beachmasters roared and the females cowered and snuffled and flopped and simpered about the bastards while they stood amongst them, choosing. Then The Kid lifted his axe and cracked the first female's head open, and then the deckies started, and oh Christ the flapping and the flopping and the roaring and the cowering and the crying and the simpering and the blood, and the pups flopped and snuffled over their bloodied mothers and got in the way and by Christ I couldn't stand it and I charged the bastards with a piece of rope. I swiped The Kid across the face with the hank of rope so he had a great black welt for a long time afterwards and then I hit him on the jaw with my fist and I knocked him flat and thereby rendered him hors de combat. The deckies didn't know what to do, though they knew they should do something seeing that assaulting an officer is a serious offence under anybody's Maritime Law. We compromised by pulling out The Kid's half-jack of whisky and sharing it while he came round and when he came round I advised the bastard that hunting seals during the mating season was an offence and if he didn't mend his ways I would report him to Oslo, or The Hague, or the United Nations, or Somebody.

We could not yet see the factory, it was behind the icebergs ahead in the gloaming. We did not talk, we were watching out for icefloe. Then we came round a berg and we could see her twinkling in the distance. Then my knee touched something and I put my hand down and it felt like a coil of nylon rope. 'What's this?' I said. 'Down here.'

The Kid grinned at me, his hair was flying.

'Nylon line.'

'Yes and for what purpose?'

He grinned at me harder in the wind. 'Nothing.'

'What's it for, for Chrissake?'

'What do you think?'

'Christ, if it's what I think it's for.'

'Yes?' The Kid grinned.

'You're out of your tiny mind,' I said.

The Kid laughed, delighted with himself.

'You're out of your tiny mind,' I said. 'You're crazier than we all think you are.'

The Kid laughed.

'What's the matter James-baby?'

'Listen,' I said, 'those days are over thank God.'

'Don't worry James-baby,' he laughed, 'you needn't come with me if you don't want to.'

'You're dead right I'm not coming with you. I might be mad but I'm not stupid. Where're the harpoons?'

'Down there. Exact replicas of the old fashioned ones.'

'Jesus,' I said. 'You're clean round the bend, Harpic. I suppose you've been practising in your Chelsea back yard?'

'Certainly,' The Kid laughed. 'A secret ambition of mine. And in the old days they didn't have fifty-horse Johnsons to get them out of the way.'

'It's not you I'm worried about,' I said. 'It's the boat, it's useful.'

The Kid laughed, delighted with himself. 'I don't believe it,' I said.

One hundred yards away from the factory you could smell her in the icy night, rich wet stench of fatty blood and the oily stink of the boiling vats, like very oily gravy, and in the floodlights you could see the huge jawbones and the yards of hide swinging through the air from the derricks. I took the speedboat wide around the stern. There were about ten whales in tow behind the slipway, cables round their great tails, floating with their huge bellies up, bloated with air, in a row like sardines and the penises of the males lolled slack in the sea, six feet long and tapering, slopping and bumping about. We went wide around the whales and there were the factory's windows open, the big steel windows in the side to let cold air in. I edged her up to them and The Kid tied us up, I cut the engine and we clambered up over the oily edge of the window and dropped down on to the hot humming stinking vibrating factory deck.

The boiling pots towered high and grey, stewing up the meat dropped into them from the open cutting deck above, and there were pipes and dials and ladders and platforms running everywhere, and the air was grey and misty with fat fumes. It was very hot, and the crew working down here amongst the vats were grey and greasy also, everything glistened with fat oil, and the air vibrated and hummed with the din of the machinery, and everywhere was the thick grey oily steamy stink of fat fumes that clung like steam. We climbed over a big pipe and into the narrow slippery avenue between the huge vats and made our way aft, up the greasy steel companionway, into the aft crew accommodation. There were rows of bloody thigh boots lining the alleyway outside the cabin doors and the alleyway was trampled black and slippery with blood, and a deckboy was scrubbing it with a pail of steaming water and caustic soda. He would scrub it clean and within a couple of hours it would be trampled black and slippery again and he would scrub it clean all over again. That was all the poor little bastard did aboard the ship for five solid months, scrub the blood and fat off acres of alleyways and lavatories and bulkheads. We came to the hatch leading out on to the deck and we stopped. 'How do I look?' The Kid said.

'Old Fergie doesn't care how you look,' I said, 'that's one thing you can say for her.'

'Do I look beautiful for Miss Rhodes?'

'Beautiful,' I said. 'It's just a shame about your clap.'

'Jealousy will get you nowhere,' The Kid said.

'Where's Miss Rhodes' cabin,' I said, 'so I can rescue her when I want to go home to the Fourteen.'

'I'm not telling you,' he said. 'You can go back with the Fourteen when she comes alongside, if you get bored.'

'Okay, you miserable bastard.'

'Okay, you miserable bastard. Do I look beautiful?'

'Smashing,' I said. 'Absolutely.'

I stepped out on to the aft winch deck above the cutting deck.

The stinking carnage. Sixty yards of deck vibrating with the rattle of the winches under congealing blood and lumpy fat. Reeking gore like great lumps of red phlegm, and the music blared over the loudspeakers and the roar of the winches and the shouts of men, it was a quagmire of blood, the deck, vibrating and running and oozing. Two red raw whales bleeding, ninety foot long, being hacked and chopped and torn apart and snaking with the rattle of the winches and the factory below. Bloody men in thighboots with long steel hooks and long flensing knives were wading up to their shins in blood and fat. And everywhere the sharp stench of thick rich blood, and the rattle of the winches and splashing thuds and the shouts under the glaring yellow floodlights in the icy Antarctic night. There was a metallic clang beneath my feet and below in the slipway the big tail plyers dropped over the next whale's tail and the big winch amidships rattled and roared and hissed steam and it took the strain and heaved, and up the cold steel slipway the next whale was dragged, mighty tail first, deep through the blood. She was a female, ninety feet, her long vagina with the two small breasts on either side, and her belly big. And there in her side was the great jagged raw red hole with the harpoon buried deep in it, a bad shot far from her spine, a long fight, a long slow animal death, fighting all the way. And the calf in her belly. And even as she came up over the slipway on to the cold blooded deck, the flenzers braced their legs and sank their long knives into her tail and as the great dead beast was dragged past them the flenzing knives sliced her hide open from tail to jaw. Then the other flenzers ran up her high back in their high spiked boots with their sharp flenzing knives buried into her like ploughs, skinning her. They slit her great hide into long skeins and then they hooked flaps of hide on to the winch cables and the winches gushed steam and tightened and the hide was ripped off her in great skeins with a great tearing noise. And underneath she lay naked, and white and bleeding, ninety feet of red raw flesh. Then they started chopping off her great spreadeagled fins and hacking away down at the root of her great jaw at the muscles and sinews as thick as your thigh, then they hooked a winch cable on to her jaw, and they hooked another winch cable into her upper mouth, and then both winches rattled and strained and her jaw was torn back with a big tearing crunch and then a crack, then it lay there askew and broken and a flenzer chopped the last big sinews and muscles away. Then the flenzers moved in on her belly and back. The two rows of men could not see each other over her, they lifted their long handled knives up high above their heads with both hands and then swiped down. The huge flesh swiped open, and out it spewed on to the deck and on to the men with splashes and splatters and gurgles, the blood, thick rich blood, and the veins it spewed out were as thick as your arm. And the flenzers buried their long knives deep into her belly and then plodded down the sides of her and ran her great guts open and out it avalanched with a great splash, her blood and guts, and out it slipped with a big bloody splash into the long high red pile of its mother's guts, the foetus, the baby whale, twelve foot long and perfectly formed. It was shiny and brown and black and its fins were folded flat against its sleek flanks and its mouth was wedged tightly shut, and its eyes were closed, and it had the grooves and folds and spots, exactly like its mother, and you could see it was a bull foetus. And then the potmen moved in with their long steel hooks and they sank the hooks into the great lumps of flesh and they dragged it off across the deck through the deep blood to the open smoking pot holes. Then they brought the winches in again and they hooked the big cables on to her great eighty foot backbone which was red and clinging with her flesh and they tore her skeleton apart, then the derricks hoisted the huge ribs and chunks of spine up into the air so the flenzers could better get at them, they swiped with their long knives and slashed the meat off the huge dangling bones, and then the bones were dropped back to the deck with a thud and a splash that went far, and then they were dragged over to the great humming screaming bonesaws and sawn up. And all the time the deep rich stink of blood and the glare of the yellow floodlights on the blood and the bones and the bloody steel and the swinging flesh in the icy still Antarctic night, and the roar of the winches and the shouts of men and the music over the loudspeakers.

I went forward and stepped out of the blood into the galley alleyway and put my head through the galley door. 'Hello Elsie,' I said.

He was chopping up radishes, holding a row of radishes under his finger tips and chopping the knife down very close, chop chop chop chop. His big round face lit up but the knife still went chop chop. 'James darling!'

'Mind your fingers, Elsie.'

'I've plenty of 'em. Come and give us a big kiss.'

'Can't step into your nice clean galley with my bloody boots Elsie, or I would,' I said. 'A lovely girl like you.'

Elsie came and shook hands through the hatch, beaming. His hairiness was very black.

'Want some of the Captain's dinner?'

'Aha ...' I said.

'Mutton, chicken and veggies.'

'Mutton, please, Elsie. Thanks.'

'Okay, darling,' Elsie said. 'You nip up to the Mess and I'll bring it up to you.'

I walked up the bloody alleyway to the labourers' Mess. The dayshift had finished their evening meal and the messboys were nearly finished their scrubdown, but where the table legs were fixed to the deck there was old blood and fat encrusted. I sat down in the far corner, leaving footprints of blood. Elsie came tripping in with a plate piled high. 'Here you are, luv. Nice Captain's din-din for a growing lad.'

'Thank you, Elsie. My salaams to the Captain.'

Elsie sat down opposite to watch me eat. His big blue jowls puckered with pleasure each time I took a mouthful, his big hairy knuckles clasped in front of him. He lit a cigarette and puffed at it and then he blew the smoke in a stream up the deckhead.

'So how's things?' I said. 'How's old Beulah?'

Elsie clicked his tongue.

'Poor dear! Her nose has healed up quite nicely but it's still all squiff and wonky, poor girl. Two hundred nicker.'

'And how's his heart?'

'Oh,' Elsie said, 'you know Beulah, a regular gadabout. Oh, I think she does still miss Peter very very much, poor girl, but she keeps her smile on and she'll get over it.'

Seems Beulah's sonofabitch Peter had knocked off a Coloured whore that last night in Cape Town and the cops had caught them and knocked them off and Peter had missed the boat, on account of he was doing a stretch in prison. Anyway, that's the story we heard. 'What d'you think he got for that, Jimmy? Whatcha callit, the law?'

'The Immorality Act,' I said.

'Immorality Act.'

'Three to six months,' I said. 'Because he's a foreigner. If he was a South African he'd get more.'

'Cor-er,' Elsie said. 'Hard isn't it? Just for knocking it off with a Coloured. Even if it is a girl.'

I smiled. 'What we see in girls you do not know?'

'Quite,' Elsie said. 'Not that I have any sympathy for the sonofabitch, exposing Beulah to the risk of the clap an' all. Oo, he made me so cross'—Elsie clicked his tongue—'I was drinking with Peter that last night, you know, and I saw him pick up that girl. We were sitting in the Carlton bar and there was this Coloured girl sauntering up and down the pavement outside, big fat thing she was, fiat nose and frizzy hair, absolutely *nothing* to look at.' Elsie tossed his prize fighter's head. 'And I could see Peter giving this lot the eye, like, and I says to him: "Yer not going to go with *her* are you?" and he said Yes he thinks he is, an' I said: "What about *me*, surely I'm better than that big fat brown thing, 'ave *me*", I says. But oh no, 'e doesn't want me 'cos he knows he could go with me any time, he *actually prefers* that big fat thing to me! I was so hurt. Honestly,' Elsie said, '*men!*'

'Bastards, Elsie,' I said. It was very good mutton.

'But don't you tell Beulah that I propositioned Peter!' Elsie warned.

'Promise, Elsie.'

'I mean, all's fair in love and war and I wouldn't like to hurt Beulah any more, poor girl.'

'Quite,' I said. Elsie puffed his cigarette.

'You hear there's a thief aboard. All kinds of things missing, we've never had that before. You got to lock your cabin nowadays.'

'Really?'

'Mmm. God help him if they catch him, the boys'll murder him.'

'Yes.'

The two messboys were standing with their brooms at the far end of the Mess room, arguing. Elsie turned on the bench and shouted at them, 'Come on then, finish this deck and get on with them sandwiches!'

One, the bigger one, was European and he looked angrily at Elsie, the smaller one was Coloured and he looked cross with the big one. Elsie turned back to me.

'You Japies! That big one, he's also South African. No end of trouble he is, I'm going to kick him in the arse one of these days.'

'What's wrong with him?' I said.

'Everything's wrong with him. We started him as a messboy but he was impossible, wouldn't wait on the Coloureds, said he's not a bloody kaffir.'

I listened while I ate.

'Says when he signed on he didn't know he'd have to serve on Coloureds. So I made him scrub shithouses instead. Now he only comes in here to scrub but he's still impossible. He doesn't like working with the Coloured boy even.' I looked down the mess at him. He was lean and wiry with curly hair. Elsie said, 'Maybe you could give him a talking to, James. He may listen to you, you're a Professor an' all.'

'I was a lecturer,' I said. 'For a short time.'

'You can speak to him like a Dutch uncle,' Elsie said. 'In his own language an' all. There's another white South African messboy this season, a university student, he says he knows your name. Cameron, d'you know him?'

'No,' I said. 'How does he get on with the whaling life?'

'He's fine,' Elsie said. 'Works like a black. But now some of the Coloureds are giving him a hard time, on account of this one being such a Dutchman.' Elsie jerked his head, 'The Coloureds give this one a hard time of course. Especially that one, Jakkals.'

'Jakkals? Hmm.'

'He's a bad bastard is that Jakkals,' Elsie said.

'What's this one's name?' I said.

'Geradus van Wijk,' Elsie said. He pronounced it Jeradus van Wike, instead of Geradus fun Vake.

'How's the Coloured messboy Benjamin?' I said.

'Oh Benjie's *sweet!*' Elsie said, 'he's a little *darling!*'

I was pleased for Benjamin. 'He's my housekeeper's son,' I said, quite proudly.

'Oh *is* he?' Elsie coo-ed. 'He tries *so* hard. Everybody makes a great fuss of him, he's only a baby. He works in the foremen's Mess, all by himself – he's doing *very* well.'

'*Good.* His mother said I must see he wears his coat, or else.'

'Don't you try to mother him,' Elsie warned with his podgy finger, 'he'll take strong exception to that!'

'Will he?'

'Oh, quite the little man is our Benjamin,' Elsie said emphatically, 'puffs around with his chest stuck out being very tough about it all and taking life all very seriously. Don't you try to mother him about his coat or anything.'

'Okay,' I smiled.

'How's that Kid this season?'

'He's fine. He's got hotpants for the new nurse,' I said.

'Oh *Vicky*,' Elsie cried, '*everybody's* got hotpants for Vicky.'

'Yes?' I was not surprised.

'*Everybody*,' Elsie said, 'it's very tough on us girls, but she's very sweet.'

'Tell me about Vicky, Elsie,' I said. I smiled at his joke about the girls.

'Oh *Vicky!*' Elsie said. 'She's *sweet*. A bit shy at first but such a nice girl when you get to know her. And very ooh-la-la,' Elsie twinkled.

'Yes?'

'Very pretty, James,' Elsie said. 'If you like that sort of thing. Why did the good Lord make me big and fat an' ugly?'

'You aren't ugly, Elsie, you're beautiful really.'

'There you go, teasing again,' Elsie said. Elsie was one hell of a good soul.

'What else?' I said. 'Who in particular is after her?'

'*All* the boys,' Elsie said. 'You know what men are, *Animals!* Sounds to me like you've got hotpants for her yourself.'

'I've never clapped eyes on the woman,' I said.

'It makes things pretty tough on us girls,' Elsie twinkled. 'Even Beulah. It was okay with Old Ferguson, but with Vicky?'

'It's tough, Elsie,' I said.

'Of course,' Elsie said brightening, 'it *could* work to our advantage, like, I mean with all the boys with hotpants an' all.'

'Quite,' I said. 'Look at the bright side. Is she particularly friendly with anybody?'

'Jock's chasing her, and a radio officer,' Elsie said. 'They all were at first, the field's thinned out a bit now, like.'

'And?'

'And what?' Elsie said unhelpfully. 'You mean is she sleeping with anybody?'

'Okay,' I said. Elsie tossed his head.

'Of course,' he said, 'there's all kinds of rumours about 'er having it off with everybody. That she's always giving the boys the eye an' all. I don't know, good luck to her, as long as she doesn't take 'em *all*, I says. But I don't think she's as fast as they make out, she seems the quiet sort. Perhaps a dark horse like.'

I didn't say anything. It broke your heart to imagine it.

'They *say*,' Elsie said, 'or rather some boys say she got a bit of the tarbrush in her. But I can't see it myself, she looks white to me.'

'Oh yes?' I was shocked. I had heard some rumours but not this one. Elsie was watching me, to see my reaction.

'Don't look at me like that,' I said. 'What else? Does she ever go down to the Pig for a beer?' I was very disappointed. But then I thought, it's only a rumour.

'No, dear,' Elsie said. 'You're awfully interested in Miss Victoria Rhodes, aren't you darling?'

'Why not?'

'Sure,' Elsie shrugged, 'why not, if you like that sort of thing.'

'Where does she eat?' I said.

'He even wants to know where she eats,' Elsie appealed. 'On the bridge with the Captain darling. She has one meal a day on the bridge with the officers and the others at the hospital. Same as Old Fergie. Anything else?'

'I guess that'll do. And she's pretty?'

'Very.'

'Okay Elsie,' I said.

'Am I dismissed, darling? Are you going to run up to the hospital to see her for yourself?'

'The Kid's with her,' I said.

'That Kid,' Elsie said.

We talked about something else while we had a cigarette. Then I went to the Pig. You could hear the Pig from quite a way off. We called it The Pig and Whistle, or Pig for short. It was just a big room on the starboard side with benches and tables and some portholes and a big hatch for the bar, which only sold English bitter. The Sports Committee had managed to wring a couple of dartboards and a piano and a microphone and half a dozen pairs of boxing gloves and a ping pong table out of the Company over the years, but that's all. The American whaling fleets had first rate gyms on their Factories and a proper cinema with a stage for the Dramatic Society, and so also, according to our information, did Onassis' fleet and even the Russian fleet, the Slava. But not the All England Whaling Company, mate. The Slava even had female deck labourers, which made us very restless to contemplate whenever we saw the Slava in the distance. The Kid always made a bee-line for the Slava whenever we saw her on the horizon, 'Just to smell 'em,' he said, and we went close alongside and gave them a big hullo and stared up at the women deck labourers and they laughed and shouted and waved to us. They looked awful in their oilskins and plastic caps to keep the blood out of their hair, and their faces all bloody and without make-up and burned by the sun and wind, but they all looked very good to us. Once one fluttered her tongue at me. We could only cruise alongside for a short while waving and blowing kisses to the girls while the Comrade Captain glared down at us from his bridge, but it brightened the day up a bit.

The Pig was full. Mickey had brought out his homemade double bass and Buzzy was on the piano and Elvis was on the microphone singing Poor Boy and throwing his pelvis around. Elvis was not his real name, they called him Elvis because he fancied himself as Elvis Presley and he was always working on it. Sometimes the boys squealed like Elvis Presley's fans do, just to rib him, but Elvis was so thick he thought they were squealing because they were really sent. The Pig was full of smoke and beer-swigging and noise. There were sweaty engine-room firemen and factory hands jostling with pimply messboys and fresh faced deck hands and bloodstained deck labourers, and the queers billing and cooing, wigs, dresses, falsies, high heels and all. I worked my way up to the hatch and got a pint on the book. I looked around for a seat but there was standing room only.

A voice behind me said, 'Hullo Van, hey man,' and there was Jakkals standing, fat flat face surly and surly eyes and cropped hair.

'Hullo Jakkals,' I said and he waited to see if I offered to shake hands. I extended my hand and he took it with a grunt.

'Long time no see, Van,' he said without smiling.

'Are you still fishing out of Table Bay?' I said in Afrikaans.

'Mostly,' Jakkals said in English. 'And you, still Oak Bay?'

'*Ja.*'

'It's a *fokkin* bad season, *ou,*' Jakkals said.

'All the females are pregnant,' I said.

'It's getting *fokkin* worse each *fokkin* year,' Jakkals said.

'It's a shame about the females,' I said. I had known Jakkals ever since I started fishing. He was a skolly from way back, but he had never given me a hard time. It was a bit embarrassing now, we had nothing to say to each other. Lodewijk waved to me from across the Pig. 'See you Jakkals,' I said.

I worked my way across the Pig to Lodewijk. He was sitting with Beulah and Mother, the old queer of sixty. Somebody shoved Elvis away from the microphone and began singing Apple-Blossom Time. 'Professor darling!' Beulah shouted. His nose wasn't a nose one wants to be near, any more, a nose one wants to kiss.

'Evening ladies,' I said.

'How do I look, Professor darling?' He patted his long golden wig, his stick-on fingernails were long and purple.

'Ravishing, Beulah,' I shouted. 'Even shaved the hairs off your chest, that's what I like, attention to detail.'

'Sit down, mate,' Lodewijk squeezed up for me and I squeezed down. Lodewijk and I had sailed together for a long time but we always had difficulty talking to each other.

Beulah leant over to shout at me, 'Where's The Kid, Professor?'

'Up with the new nursing sister,' I said.

Beulah made big blue eyes and nodded his head and his lipstick mouth went oh-oh. 'Getting his end away is he?'

I shrugged. 'I doubt it.'

'Not from what *I* hear,' Beulah leant over again. 'Regular little hussy if you ask me!'

'I can see your padded bra, Beulah,' I said, 'when you lean over like that.'

'Okay, touche, darling!' He sat back and smiled at me. Then he leant over again, 'I haven't told you the great news.'

'What news?'

'I'm going to have the treatment, I've finally decided!'

'What treatment?'

'This hormone treatment they've been experimenting with for years. To turn us queers into women! Real women, imagine! Won't that be lovely?'

'That'll be lovely, Beulah,' I said.

'Of course, it'll involve the knife in the end result – that's a pun, darling – but after my nose op I can stand anything.'

'Certainly,' I said.

'Will you go with me when I'm a real woman, Professor darling?'

'Try The Kid, he'll try anything.'

'Oh *Professor!*' Beulah cried.

I went up to the hatch to get some beers. There was a short Jew with thin hair and a thoughtful squint at the hatch.

'Izzy?' I said. 'Aren't you Izzy?'

'Right,' Izzy squinted.

'So you're with us again?'

'Right,' Izzy squinted at me.

'Will you have a beer?' I said.

'I've got the angel-feathers,' Izzy said.

'Angel-feathers?'

'Gimme a Coke,' Izzy squinted.

'Mac, give this man a Coke,' I said. 'What are angel-feathers?'

'Sometimes I hear angel-feathers,' Izzy said. Mac handed over the Coca-Cola.

Izzy pulled out a half-jack of brandy and poured it into the Coke. 'Just to kill the germs.' Then he squinted thoughtfully at me, waiting.

'Where've you been these years?' I grinned.

'Israel,' Izzy said. 'We held those goddam Arabs like whatsisname held the bridge.'

'Horatio.'

'Got the VC for that, the Yiddish model. Ever been into battle on a bicycle?'

'On a bicycle?'

'Prior to that I was working in Jerusalem. Ever seen a thirty inch midget striptease?'

I was grinning.

'Nor had the Yanks and it went over big. Made a fortune and retired to Galilee. Started a home brewery. Have you,' said this Izzy, 'ever fallen in love with a home brewery?'

'Fallen in love?'

'I mean Love, man, Love, the stuff that makes the world go round,' Izzy said irritably. 'Queerest goddam thing. Bought this empty ten gallon Eau de Cologne bottle from a chemist, cost me a quid. Chucked in the hops and yeast and malt. You supposed to brew it in a dark place and my villa's a bit sunny so I drape a black petticoat over the bottle. Soon the gas is bubbling through the test tube. Goes blip blip blip and then it goes bloep blip bloep-bloep. Kind of gets on a man's nerves sitting there for a week waiting for it to brew. Like waiting for your wife to have a baby. Keep peeping under the petticoat to see how it's getting on. I tell you she became like another personality in that house. Got pretty fond of that Eau de Cologne bottle.'

I was laughing.

'Syphoned it off, bottled it, proud as punch I was. Kind of wanted to sit on 'em and hatch 'em out, ever tried to sit on sixty pints all at once?'

'No, and I never saw a forty inch midget striptease—'

'Thirty inch. That's how I got to hear the angel-feathers. Gave up the brewery and went and fought the Arabs. I nursed infants with a Molotov cocktail in my free hand, I taught school by day and I started a bicycle business.'

'Is that where this thirty inch midget rode a bicycle into battle?' I said.

'Shall I ever forget that sight? My Coke's finished.'

'Mac,' I said.

'That's why I'm back at the Ice again. To get some dough. To start a new bicycle factory. You know what our country needs?' Izzy said. 'Bicycles. That's what we need to beat the Commies – Happiness. Why shouldn't every man afford a bicycle in this day and age of sputniks and sliced bread and instant mashed potatoes? Why?' Izzy said. 'I'm going to make a bicycle so cheap every man can afford one. A man's happy when he's got a bicycle. Weren't you happy with your bicycle?'

'Very,' I grinned.

'And in a corner of my factory I'll start making something else,' Izzy said. 'I'll make lots of things in my factory.' Izzy squinted. He had not smiled once. He hadn't changed. Five years older, over sixty now.

'How come you left Israel, Izzy?' I said.

'Became a Christian,' Izzy said. 'Heard the angel-feathers and became a Christian. You know what those schmoes did don't you?'

'What?'

'They *crucified* Him!' Izzy said. 'No!'

'Yes *sir*. That's what they did.'

He squinted at me. I had to work on it to keep a straight face. Izzy squinted at me, waiting. It didn't seem as if he was going to say anything else.

'Izzy,' I said. 'About these bicycles. Flog 'em to the Army. Soldiers can ride them into battle.'

'Could be,' Izzy said quietly.

But it did not start him off again. He looked at me. Then he said, 'You know. I sometimes wonder if I'll ever make the grade.'

And he left his brandy and Coca-Cola and walked out of the Pig.

'Izzy!' I called him back but he did not look round.

At ten o'clock I left the Pig and I walked down through the hot factory deck and climbed up back into the aft accommodation and up to the hospital deck. At the hospital alleyway there was a big red sign that said,

Take Your Boots Off. No Oilskins Allowed. Silence. – Captain.

I took my seaboots off and put them against the bulkhead. They were bloody. I smoothed my hair with my palm and looked at my fingernails. Then I walked up the alleyway. It was very clean and it smelt nice, of antiseptic. The surgery door opened behind me.

'What do you want, young man? Come here!'

You got the impression that Old Fergie even called the Captain Young Man in that tone of voice. I turned and walked back. She stood in the door with her big hands on her big hips. Her uniform was starched crisp and white. Old Fergie clearly had magistrate blood in her.

'Long time no see Fergie,' I said.

'Matron to you! How are you?'

'Fine thanks, and you?'

'What you doing here then?' Old Ferguson said.

'Came up to say hullo to you, Fergie, long time no see.'

'Matron! What were you doing pussyfooting up the alleyway, it's private up there, you know that. Come to say hullo to Old Fergie, my eye!' Old Ferguson said.

'Sure I did, Fergie.'

'My eye! Come inside, don't fool around in the alleyway!'

I went into the surgery. There was only Old Ferguson inside. She was big and fat and as strong as a horse and her hair was greyer than last time I saw her and her face a bit more leathery but her eye was just as steely. It was said she was quite a looker, way back, and you could still see it a bit.

'Sit down,' Fergie said. She sat down herself and crossed her big legs. 'How're your bowels?'

'My bowels are fine thanks,' I said emphatically. Old Fergie's treatment for everything always began with a strong dose of salts.

'Are you taking your vitamin D tablets?'

'I get enough sun, Fergie,' I said. 'Four on, four off.'

'Take 'em anyway,' Fergie glared. 'And your vitamin C? You don't get enough greens down here you know.'

'I take the vitamin C,' I said.

'When you remember!' Fergie glared. 'Want a cup of tea?'

'No thanks, Fergie, I'm full up with beer.'

'You would be. You and that Kid. Isn't it time you settled down, young man, instead of this fooling round on the ships year in year out? It's a crying shame wasting all that education!'

'I've got my own fishing trawler,' I said. 'I'm in business.'

'Business,' Fergie glared. 'Fishing! With your education!'

'I'm a marine biologist, Fergie,' I said patiently, 'I'm working with the sea.'

'Skippering a fishing trawler, young man, is hardly the practice of marine biology.'

'It's my own trawler, Fergie,' I said patiently.

'What you doing fooling around down here at the Ice every year for, then?'

'My bosun runs my boat during the whaling season, Fergie, it's not idle. I make more money this way,' I said patiently.

'No conscientious businessman would leave his business in the hands of a Coloured bosun five months every year young man and you know it. You come on this expedition every year because you've grown into a bum!'

'Balls, Fergie,' I said.

'I beg your pardon, young man?' Old Ferguson said.

'Balls,' I said.

'That,' Fergie glared, 'is what I thought you said. It is *not* balls!'

'Okay, Fergie,' I grinned. Fergie was exasperated.

'And you with a Master of Science,' she said. '*Master's,* they don't *give* those degrees away you know, it takes brains.'

'They don't give those fishing trawlers away either Fergie,' I said. 'I come whaling to help pay it off.'

'I bet you squander your pay-off in riotous living,' Old Fergie glared.

'I squander most of my pay-off on my bank manager,' I said. 'One day I'll be like Onassis.'

'You shouldn't be paying for damn-fool fishing trawlers! You should be paying for a nice house or something! It's all right for a worthless playboy like The Kid, he hasn't got any brains and he's got all his father's money …'

I had something like this every season from Old Ferguson.

'He was sent down from Cambridge,' Old Fergie glared. That was enough for Old Ferguson. 'You were a university lecturer—'

'That was an accident, Fergie, the Professor dropped dead,' I said.

Fergie looked at me. 'Haven't you met any nice girls, James?' she appealed. 'Can't you find a nice wholesome girl and settle down to a sensible life?'

'My life's pretty sensible, Fergie.'

'Haven't you ever met a girl you want to marry?' Fergie implored. 'You're thirty years old! A nice girl who loves you and all? – there's plenty of nice girls James!'

'Maybe that's the trouble,' I murmured.

'Haven't you?' Fergie pleaded. 'Haven't you ever been in love, James? I mean, love, James,' she said irritably, 'not your hotpants for one of your damn sluts.'

'Once, Fergie,' I said, 'I think.'

'And what happened?' Fergie glared.

'She married somebody else.'

'While you were away fooling around on some damn ship!' Fergie glared.

'Okay,' I said.

'Down here at the Ice,' Fergie glared accusingly.

'Yes,' I said.

'See!' Fergie said. 'See what happens!'

I didn't say anything. She glared at me, then she softened.

'Poor boy. Poor James. Did you love her very much?'

'I guess so,' I said.

Fergie stared at me with her head on one side.

'And since she ran off and married this other man, James?'

'I'm fine,' I said, 'I've had a bloody good time.'

'Not really,' Old Fergie said.

'I've had a bloody good time,' I said.

'But you haven't ...' Fergie stared at me with her head on the side, then she closed her eyes and bit her old lip and then she sat up straight.

'You see! You see what comes of your damn fooling about on ships!'

She stood up and turned away and lumbered over to the porthole. I could see she was shaking.

'Fergie?' I said.

'What?' She didn't turn round. I got up and walked over to her.

'Fergie? What's the matter?'

She turned her back more on me and put her big knuckles to her eyes. 'Fergie?' I put my hand on her shoulder. 'Don't cry, old girl.'

'I was in love once!' Old Fergie shook with her broad back to me with her knuckles to her eyes. 'With somebody just like you! He was also going to be like Onassis—'

'Fergie—'

'Why do you think I'm here?' Fergie sobbed. 'Why do you think I'm big and fat and old and ugly? D'you think I couldn't control my weight if I tried – I'm a big woman but d'you think I couldn't be a reasonable size if I'd tried?'

'Sure you could, Fergie,' I said.

'Don't touch me,' Old Ferguson said.

I took my hand off her shoulder.

Fergie gave a big sniff and squeezed her knuckles into her eyes. She lumbered off to the corner and blew her nose on a Kleenex and rubbed her eyes. Then she turned around.

'Forget I said that. Forget I told you any of that!'

'Of course.'

'Forget I said anything. I didn't say anything!'

'I promise, Fergie.'

'On your word of honour?'

'Of course, Fergie,' I said.

'All right,' Fergie said. She came back and sat down.

'You've got a word of honour, you're a decent boy, really. Forget I said everything,' Fergie said. 'Sit down.'

'Fergie, I've got to go,' I said.

'You've got to go and see Miss Rhodes,' Fergie glared again, and I felt more comfortable. 'Sneaking up the alleyway in your socks.'

'It says on the notice no boots.'

'Coming to see me, my eye!'

'I would have come another time,' I said.

'When there was something wrong with you. They all come to Old Fergie when there's something wrong with them. I'm not so old, either.'

'You're not, Fergie,' I said.

'All right, go and see Sister Rhodes. She's a very nice girl.'

She glared at me.

'You've no idea the number of malingerers who come along to the surgery when *she's* on watch,' Old Ferguson said. 'I tell her to give them all a dose of salts and make them drink it right here in front of her, that'll fix 'em.'

'And does she?'

'I don't know,' Old Fergie sighed. 'I guess not, you know what young girls are like, I suppose she's flattered.'

She glared up at me again.

'But she's a very nice girl! And remember, it's only because you've got your Master's that I'm letting you up my alleyway. She's a very good girl. Don't you go breaking her heart. Not,' Old Fergie said, 'that I think for one moment she's interested in you.'

'Actually,' I said, 'I've never set eyes on her.'

Old Ferguson's mouth opened.

'Then *what* on *earth* makes you think you can go calling on her at this time of night?'

'I'm going to rescue her,' I said. 'The Kid's with her and it's time we went back to our ship.'

Old Fergie's face went furious.

'The *Kid's* with her!' She stood up. 'My God! If you knew what I know about that young thug!'

'I know,' I said. 'He's got the clap.'

'He's got more than the clap!'

'I know.'

'Get up there young man and rout him out! My God! That Kid. Go on, get him out! I don't want that thug messing about with Sister Rhodes! Go on!'

'Okay, Fergie. Good night.'

'Go on!' She was making shooing motions. I smiled and turned away. 'And James?'

I turned back.

'Be nice to her, James. She's much too nice a girl for that scallywag.'

'Okay, Fergie.'

She stood in the door and watched me walk up her alleyway. I walked past the sick bay, up to the top of the alleyway, then round the corner. Everything was white and shiny and there was only a slight vibration from the engine room way below. There was a door marked Stores Staff Only and another marked Bathroom and then three cabins. I stopped at the door labelled *Sister V Rhodes* and knocked. A second later the door opened and there she stood, Miss Rhodes.

'*Ja, goeie avend,*' she said.

'*Goeie avend, Mejevrou,*' I said.

The Kid said irritably from the background, 'Hullo, James.'

'I'm sorry,' Miss Rhodes said, she looked back at The Kid and then back to me, 'I wasn't thinking, it was automatic.'

The light was behind her. She was in her white uniform with her shoes off. She had long thick deep brown straight hair hanging in a plait and scraped back from her head so her ears seemed to stand out a litde too much. She had big dark eyes and high cheeks and a wide mouth and I thought she was beautiful. The Kid was reclining in her only chair under the porthole, looking peeved with me. It was a small cabin. 'Are you looking for Captain Child?' Miss Rhodes said.

'Yes,' I said.

'Well,' She held out her palm indicating, 'there he is.' It was clear she didn't intend inviting me in unless she had to. She spoke coolly, politely, like a very efficient secretary. The Kid sat up.

'This is James McQuade,' he said. 'The Professor, the chap I've mentioned to you.'

'Oh,' Miss Rhodes said, and she smiled politely and her teeth were perfect. 'How d'you do.'

I didn't feel very welcome.

'I've just come to find out, to advise the – Captain,' I said, 'that we better be going back to our ship.'

'Come in for a moment if you wish.' She had an Afrikaans accent, stronger than mine, but very mellifluous.

'Thank you,' I said. She stepped aside and I stepped in. 'These are nice little cabins,' I said.

The Kid looked very displeased and I ignored the bastard.

'The tea is cold now I'm afraid,' Miss Rhodes said, 'but I can make some more if you like.'

'No thank you,' I said. Her face was in the light now, and her lashes were very thick and long. 'We mustn't keep you up,' I said.

She didn't deny that we were keeping her up. 'Won't you sit down?'

'Just for a moment,' I said. I sat on the edge of her bunk and Miss Rhodes sat on the end. Her calves were good and strong and her ankles were slim. 'How do you like the whaling?' I said.

'I hate it,' Miss Rhodes said, 'but I think the Antarctic is beautiful.'

'I suppose everybody asks you that, how d'you like it?'

'Yes,' she said. 'You're an old hand, I suppose.'

'What made you come?' I said.

'I work in the Company's Shore Clinic in Cape Town and the chance came up so I thought why not.'

'I suppose everybody's asked you that too. Where in Cape Town do you live, Miss Rhodes?' I called her Miss Rhodes intentionally to give her the chance to invite me to call her something else.

'In Oranjezicht,' she said, looking straight at me. 'I come originally from Woodstock, Mr McQuade. You know Woodstock, of course.'

'Yes,' I said.

'But not very well,' Miss Rhodes said.

'Oh, well enough,' I said.

'Well enough for what?'

'I know Woodstock,' I said firmly.

'What's this about Woodstock?' The Kid said irritably. 'Wherever the hell that is.'

'Nothing's wrong with Woodstock,' I said.

'Woodstock,' Miss Rhodes said to The Kid, 'is not a very classy area. Where do you live, Mr McQuade?'

'I live over the Nek in Oak Bay,' I said. 'That's not a very classy area either.'

'Parts of Oak Bay are very nice,' Miss Rhodes said.

'Parts,' I said. 'Do we have to carry on like this?'

'All right,' Miss Rhodes said.

'What the hell's all this about?' The Kid demanded irritably.

'Nothing,' I said. 'Nothing,' Miss Rhodes said. There was a silence.

'What do you do off season, Mr McQuade?' Miss Rhodes said politely. 'Are you really a Professor?'

'No,' I said, 'I'm a professional fisherman.'

'How lovely,' she said very politely. 'Why do they call you Professor, are you very clever?

'That's a long story,' I said. 'Did you get sick?'

'I was very seasick the moment we left Cape Town. Then as soon as I got better we reached the Roaring Forties and I was sick all over again.'

'And you're all right now?'

'I'm perfect now. It's just the smell if I go on deck, you'd think I was used to blood, but I'm not really.'

'You get used to the smell,' I said. 'It's only at certain times, but I suppose you know all that by now.'

'There's no smell here, of course,' she said. 'And on the poop deck and on the for'ard deck of course it's odourless.'

'Odourless,' The Kid said, injured.

'I love the Southern lights,' Miss Rhodes said, 'and the icebergs. And the snow, I'd never seen snow before, not to touch.'

'The ice is superb,' I said.

The Kid was sulking.

'Isn't it lovely, Captain Child?' Miss Rhodes said politely.

'Oh yes,' The Kid said. 'Superb.'

'Well,' I said to The Kid, 'hadn't we better be going? They're waiting for us out there.'

'Oh very well, then,' The Kid said.

'Thank you, Miss Rhodes.' I stood up. 'I believe we'll be seeing you at dinner on the Fourteen, next week.'

'Yes,' Miss Rhodes said. 'If it can really be arranged. Then you can tell me why they call you Professor.'

We said goodbye to Miss Rhodes, and The Kid and I walked in silence down the hospital alleyway, then out. The ordinary crew accommodation seemed very drab and bloody after the nice clean hospital and the nice clean Miss Rhodes. When we were on the next deck down The Kid said, behind me, 'You bastard.'

'I wanted to meet the beautiful Miss Rhodes,' I said.

'Well? What d'you think, you sonofabitch?'

'She's beautiful,' I said.

'I'm not so sure she altogether likes you,' The Kid said.

'She's got some Coloured blood in her,' I said. 'That's why.'

'*What*?' The Kid said. '*Rubbish!*' He was still walking behind me.

'She has,' I said. 'Though very little, probably one grandparent. Probably Malay.'

'Oh rubbish!' The Kid said, astounded. He caught up with me to argue properly but the alleyway was too narrow. 'How can you tell?'

'We're used to spotting these things in South Africa. You can tell around the eyes, and other things.'

'Her eyes are beautiful!' he protested. 'Certainly.'

'But her skin is pure white!'

'Not entirely. A shade sallow.'

'It's beautiful skin! That was probably the light. She's no more sallow than most Spanish, for Chrissake. It could be suntan.'

'No,' I said.

'Good God!' The Kid said, 'fancy you noticing. Would she be regarded as white in South Africa, for Chrissake?'

'Probably,' I said. 'She's a borderline case.'

'For Chrissake!' The Kid said. We were walking down the alleyway towards the factory deck companionway. 'In South Africa, could you take her into a hotel or a restaurant?' he appealed.

'Probably,' I said. 'In most places she wouldn't be challenged. It would depend on the season.'

'The *season*, for Chrissake?'

'Whether it's winter or summer. In summer you could say it was suntan.'

'Well for Chrissake!' The Kid said. 'Well Jesus Christ! And you go along with this?'

'I don't say I go along with anything,' I said. 'I'm just telling you the score.'

Chapter Seven

The next week Miss Rhodes came to dinner. Everybody was very excited, except the Mate, who regarded it as an affront that he had not been invited to the dinner party also, which was correct and intended. The day before The Kid ordered all the bulkheads and deckheads soojied, out of schedule, which nobody seemed to mind except the Mate and I, because it was done for the fabled Miss Rhodes. Soojying deckheads is most unpleasant because the caustic soda drips into your face and runs down your arm into your armpit and eventually down to your underpants. In fairness it must be noted that The Kid took me off the job as soon as he noticed the Mate had put me on to it, and told me to get back on the wheel. He had all inner decks scrubbed, the main alleyways and Mess room repainted. All this was very unusual for The Kid, who in truth and in fact could not care less what his goddam ship looked like, as long as the damn thing went. In the afternoon he ordered everybody to put on clean gear tonight. Then he announced that all hands would attend in the galley Mess room from eight o'clock to nine for a cocktail party to meet Miss Rhodes. This confirmed that he was a goddam hero, except in the Mate who considered it preposterous. On top of it, he had shot three whales that day. You had a job getting into the showers for jubilant bodies scrubbing themselves clean for Miss Rhodes.

The factory had been cruising east, away from the sun and it was sunset at seven. The Kid stopped engines a mile from the factory, and all kinds of willing hands swung his boat out. The Kid had consulted me about how long the boat ride should be. Miss Rhodes must not get cold, nor seasick, but on the other hand there must be sufficient time. Sufficient time for what? I asked. We settled on one mile. The Kid took Pete with him. I was also looking forward very much to having Miss Rhodes aboard. The Kid set off, very dashing, to "For he's a jolly good fellow" ringing out into the Antarctic sunset. The Kid was very popular.

Miss Rhodes looked wonderful. Her long hair was loose and blowing behind her in the Antarctic sunset and she wore a white woollen scarf tight over the top of her head and ears, and her big eyes were sparkling from the cold wind and the excitement of the motorboat ride. All the boys were gathered on the deck to watch her arrive, and she gave them a big smile up from the boat. They all fell in love with Miss Rhodes when she gave them that smile.

Miss Rhodes was a great success. The cocktail party was a great success. Her cheeks were flushed pink from the icy ride and then flushed warm with the brandy and her big eyes were sparkling, she was very much enjoying herself. She was very gay and friendly. She was introduced to every man and she gave each a big smile that looked personal for absolutely them. She made a great fuss of the fat squint bad-tempered chef and he was so excited he blushed and cast desperately around for something to give her and he could think of nothing except an apple and he said 'Would the lady like an apple?' And when Miss Rhodes said 'No thank you very much, your snacks are delicious,' he looked crestfallen and said 'You can take it back to your cabin and eat it for your breakfast.' Then Miss Rhodes said, 'Oh, thank you very much!' and the fat bad-tempered chef scuttled away into his galley and polished up a big red apple and came back and presented it to Miss Rhodes very shyly, and everybody cheered and he fled back to his galley until his blush had gone away. She made a fuss of the Mate who went very pink and puffed up and pulled nervously on his moustache and showed all his gums when he grinned. I said to The Kid, 'I didn't know the Mate showed his gums like that, I've never seen him smile before,' and The Kid said, 'Oh yes, I saw him smile in the summer of fifty-one when I broke my tooth on a walnut.' Everybody asked her why she had come whaling and how did she like it and did she get seasick and how did she find the smell and she answered each time brightly as if she had never been asked it before, and each person listened very intently and nervously and could then think of nothing more to talk about and moved away smiling and blushing nervously to stare at her and talk about her, how smashing she was, *Cor, not 'alf a darlin'* and imagine the skipper getting his end away with 'er like. Everybody wondering if he did and everybody hoped he didn't because they were all in love with her. I did not speak to her myself except to ask how she was because I couldn't think of much else to ask her myself in the noisy Mess room with us all crowded together. Lodewijk the Cape Coloured came up to me and said quietly, 'She's not a European, hey, Jimmy, she's got some Coloured blood okay.'

'Do you think so?' I said. 'I hadn't noticed.'

'I think so man, jussa bit.'

I pretended to study her across the mess room.

'I don't think so,' I said. 'Anyway, so what?'

'You know so what. You better leave her alone, Jimmy.'

I said, 'I haven't been near the woman. Who says I better leave her alone?'

'I says, Jimmy, hey? The other Coloured *ous* won't like it. An' if you can't touch her ashore you got no right to touch her here, I hear 'em say that, I'm jus' telling you, hey?' Lodewijk said.

'You heard who say that, for Chrissake?'

'Jakkak an' 'em. Not jus' you, any white Sout' African. An' there's not many of yous about, I'm just telling you,' Lodewijk said.

'Jakkals,' I said.

'I'm jus' telling you,' Lodewijk said defensively.

'Anyway, I think she's white,' I said.

'It's up to you man,' Lodewijk said, 'I'm jus' telling you.'

When the singing started The Kid and Miss Rhodes adjourned to The Kid's little suite for dinner and I followed a minute later. Everybody was very sorry to see Miss Rhodes leave the party. When I arrived in The Kid's suite they were already seated at the table because, with the table laid in the centre, there wasn't much other place to sit. The messboy had already uncorked the wine and they were drinking it instead of other stuff, because Miss Rhodes preferred wine.

'If I'd known we were going to have such good company,' The Kid said, 'I'd have bought better wine in Cape Town.'

'This Tasheimer is very nice wine,' Miss Rhodes said. 'I drink it a lot at home. Don't you like it, Mr McQuade?'

It was clear that the conversation wasn't going so well.

'Yes,' I said. 'And it's only five shillings a bottle.'

'That's another thing I like about it,' Miss Rhodes said.

'On the fishing boats,' I said, 'the crew drink a lot of Vaaljapie, and so I do too, that's only five shillings a gallon and you get half a crown back when you return the demijohn.'

'How's your Braille, Mr McQuade?' Miss Rhodes said.

'My Braille?'

'Your Braille,' Miss Rhodes smiled. 'Vaaljapie turns you blind in the end.'

'Is that right?' The Kid said.

'Oh yes,' Miss Rhodes said and we all laughed and then we finished laughing and looked about the table for something else to talk about.

'When I was a student,' I said, 'Vaaljapie was about all we drank, of course.'

'Oh yes?'

'A gallon of Vaaljapie among three or four friends goes like this,' I said, not being very original, 'The first pint, normal chat about whatever. The second pint, animated chat about whatever. The third pint animated and loquacious and gesticulatory harangues about anything. The fourth pint, loud argument. The fifth pint, loud and long arguments and threats both overt and muttered aside. The sixth pint'—they were laughing now and I was encouraged—'fights. The seventh is taken up with loud pacification and first aid. The eighth pint, loud brotherly songs and avowals of lifelong friendship.'

Miss Rhodes and The Kid and I were laughing. 'It sounds good stuff,' The Kid said.

'Oh, it is,' Miss Rhodes said, 'as long as you keep up with your Braille as you go along.'

She turned to me, 'Is that why you were a perennial student, Mr McQuade?'

The Kid raised his eyebrows.

'Why do you accuse me of being a perennial student?' I said.

'Oh, I've heard,' Miss Rhodes smiled. 'I also know why they call you the Professor.'

I was very gratified. 'Oh, do you?'

'Oh, I do.'

'Have you also heard,' The Kid said, 'how he got the name "Peaceful?"'

'Peaceful?' Miss Rhodes said.

'"Peaceful McQuade,"' The Kid said. 'Because he was once hauled before the Magistrate and Bound Over to Keep the Peace.'

'That was long ago,' I said. 'I'm rather respectable now.'

The laughing died down and Miss Rhodes said, 'Tell me how you live your rather respectable life, Mr McQuade. Do you have a servant or somebody to look after you?'

'Or somebody,' The Kid said.

'Yes,' I said. 'An old woman who looked after my parents and who nursed me as a child. She's been part of the McQuade family since God knows when. She's about a hundred, I think, and twice the size of Miss Ferguson,' I said.

'My old nanny's like that,' The Kid said. 'Old battleaxe. Also about a hundred now. Gives me what-for every time I come home from the Ice. Habit. But then,' The Kid added brightly, 'she also always slips me half a crown wrapped in toilet paper to go buy myself some sweeties. The old girl is under the impression I'm still at Eton and just home for the hols.'

We all laughed.

'What does your old servant do while you are at sea, Mr McQuade?' Miss Rhodes asked.

'She stays at home, in my house,' I said, 'and looks after it. Looks after my chickens and my ducks and the vegetable garden and so forth.'

'She doesn't go to her own home?'

'My home is her home,' I said. 'She's been there for forty-five years. She remembers my father's schoolgirl friends and so forth. She remembers the day my father first brought my mother home to meet the family,' I said.

'She lives in the house?' Miss Rhodes asked.

'She's got a room in the back yard,' I said. 'As a matter of fact there are two servants' bedrooms, she uses one as a sitting room, to entertain all her old cronies. And to put up her relatives for the night when they come to town for a few days.'

'Isn't that illegal?' Miss Rhodes said. 'Having non-Europeans who are not employed by you staying on your white premises?'

I got the feeling I was being persecuted by Miss Rhodes.

'I guess it is,' I said, 'but old Sergeant van Tonder in charge of our police station is a good old stick, he turns a blind eye to that sort of thing.'

'Within reason?' Miss Rhodes said, 'of course?'

'Of course,' I said, 'within reason.'

I looked deliberately at The Kid and said to him, 'In the Cape we are much more liberal about this colour question than they are in other parts of South Africa. The Cape is the oldest part of South Africa, and the Coloured people are much more accepted by the whites than elsewhere.'

'Accepted?' Miss Rhodes raised her lovely eyebrows.

'Sure,' I said, 'I mean they are accorded much more human consideration and dignity.'

'That's great,' Miss Rhodes said. 'Captain Child, don't you think that's really great of us Cape whites?'

I was relieved to hear her declare herself, even if she was spoiling for a fight. 'Have some more wine, Miss Rhodes,' I said pointedly. I topped up the glasses. I was getting a bit tired of Miss Rhodes. You get very tired of this subject as a South African, you never hear anything new. The Kid didn't take my hint.

'What I can't understand,' The Kid said, 'is how you know who's mulatto and who's not, with the borderline cases I mean. I mean who decides and says—'

'The Government,' Miss Rhodes began, 'is classifying all the people into colours and issuing certificates—'

'There's a new Act of Parliament,' I said, to shut Miss Rhodes up, 'in terms of which all people have to register themselves with the Population Registration office. Like getting a passport. The Population Registry records who you are etcetera, looks at you and issues you with an identity card saying who you are, and what race – white, Asian, African, Oriental, Mixed etcetera. In due course your ID card arrives by registered post. If you disagree with the racial classification the local Registration Officer has given you, you can appeal to a special Race Classification Board. If you don't like the Board's decision, you can appeal to the Supreme Court and let them decide.'

'And that's you for life,' Miss Rhodes said.

The Kid looked fascinated.

'And has the whole population now been classified?'

'No,' I said, 'it'll take years. I've been done,' I said.

'And does your card bear the magic word *White*?' Miss Rhodes said sweetly.

'Yes,' I said, 'as a matter of fact it does.'

I smiled at Miss Rhodes innocently and then reached for the wine bottle. I was waiting for The Kid to open his big tactless English mouth and put his foot in it.

'I haven't got mine yet,' said Miss Rhodes. She gave a laugh that was meant to be playful. 'Do you think I'm safe, Master James?'

'Oh, I think so, Miss Victoria,' I laughed gaily. 'But then you can never be sure – my Registration Officer was squint.'

We all laughed very heartily at that one.

After that it was quite a pleasant evening, although Miss Rhodes refused to get around to Christian names.

Part Three

Chapter Eight

The next week it was December and The Kid went to the factory every night in his speedboat to visit Old Ferguson to get his disease treated and to visit Miss Rhodes. McQuade went aboard the factory most of the nights that the Fourteen went alongside to bunker, but he only went to say hullo to Beulah and Jock and Charlie and see how Benjamin was getting on, and to have a pint in the Pig, he did not visit Miss Rhodes. He did not go with The Kid in his speedboat because The Kid did not invite him, because he wanted to be alone with Miss Rhodes. The Kid did not report back to McQuade about his progress with Miss Rhodes, and McQuade did not ask. But that week at least McQuade knew that The Kid was not making love with Miss Rhodes, because he was sure that even The Kid would refrain from trying, and he was also sure that Old Ferguson had warned Miss Rhodes in words of one syllable about The Kid's unhappy condition.

There were very few whales that December, it was a bad season, and the sea was grey and rough and the wind blew grey and cutting and the skies were grey and there was much loose ice to worry about, and on deck and in the crow's-nest it was fiercely cold. The catchers went very far out into the ice on the horizons to look for whales but they saw very few and because of the big loose ice it was very hard to chase them, there were long and dangerous and freezing lashing and fruitless chases through the loose ice and icebergs and the grey cutting wind, and everything going up and down and swinging and rolling and the icy spray flying. It was a bad season and it seemed worse to McQuade because Miss Rhodes was there on the factory going about her duties looking lovely, and he could not go to visit her. It was work four, sleep four, the narrow bunk in the narrow cabin going up and down and up and down and rolling, never ceasing, awake and asleep going up and down and rolling, narrow alleyways up and down, tiny Mess room up and down and food falling and spilling, deckheads above you going up and down and bulkheads closed about you swinging, always swinging, and cold, work eat sleep work day in day out and months and months ahead – and out there only the sea and the ice and the cold cold cold, icy sea and ice and ice and ice four hours on four hours off, and Miss Rhodes way out there inaccessible, lovely Victoria Rhodes, with her loins and her belly and her wide soft mouth. And the date never seemed to change, the date is the worst part. And the goddam god-rotting mother-fornicating shitbastard ship never effing shitsake STANDING STILL – Oh God make this bastard ship STAND STILL FOR JUST A GODDAM MOMENT – But no, the bastard never stands still for Chrissake, up and down and Christknows side to side, four hours on and four hours off and night and day and Christ Christ CHRIST I hate the WHALING!

A man goes a little mad down here at the Ice.

Chapter Nine

Benjamin Marais shared a messboys' cabin with Geradus van Wijk and Mark Cameron, facts which pleased nobody. Geradus van Wijk was displeased because he found it outrageous that he should live with Benjamin Marais and Benjamin was most displeased because Geradus van Wijk had told him the moment he moved in to get out to where he bladdy belonged or else. Mark Cameron was displeased because he did not want to share with either a Coloured boy or an Afrikaaner but he stood up for Benjamin on principle, which made Geradus call Cameron a fokkin *kaffirboetie* and Cameron called Geradus a bloody Dutchman. Benjamin felt very bad and nervous in his cabin.

Benjamin Marais wanted very much to become a man. As long as he could remember he had been the smallest and the youngest, it seemed every single person was bigger and older and more important than him. All his life he had been very unimportant indeed. Whaling, however, would end all that. On the whalers he would be regarded as a man, hey man, because only men got to go on the whalers. An' when he got back, hey man, the peoples would bladdy well see he was a man, hey man, because of course only a *man* goes whaling, man. Of course yes, man. He would bladdy show 'em at home, hey man, he would talk about the ships and the sea hey man and say clever things that people like to hear, hey man. An' the girls would look at him an' like him hey man because he was a *man*, now, man. Not a bladdy kid no more, man. Benjamin was very irritated to find that he was the youngest and smallest aboard the whalers and everybody made a fuss of him.

'I'm a *man* not a bladdy mascot, hey man!'

Benjamin scowled and stomped his way around his duties as messboy with a tough frown and his jaw stuck out and his chest stuck out, but it did no good: the whalermen thought this was very cute and made a fuss of him, which made him very mad indeed and he scowled and stomped harder and the men thought this was cuter. The only person who called him a man was Elsie, when Benjamin came running into the galley with a big frown demanding more food for his Mess room in a deep voice, which is difficult with your chin stuck out, and Elsie called him his 'little man' and beamed at him and pretended to feel his biceps. Which was more of a backhanded compliment than Benjamin realised because Elsie entertained no ulterior motives towards Benjamin, it being a rule of Elsie's that he didn't make passes at kids. Once Beulah found Benjamin all by himself weeping because the men made a fuss of him, and Beulah added insult to injury by cuddling him and saying 'There-there little Benjie, tell your Auntie Beulah all about it.'

Benjamin had never had a girlfriend in his life but he knew something about girls especially by the feeling between his legs. Benjamin heard the men talking about women and the things you do to women and the things women let you do to them, and he lay in his bunk afterwards and thought about what he had heard the men say and the feeling between his legs was very pronounced. He was very shocked when he thought about his father having done those things to his mother, but the feeling between his legs stayed there all the same. Sometimes he got the feeling when he was waiting on the men in the Mess room, even when they were not talking about it, and he was very embarrassed and scowling because his pants stuck out, and he had to try to keep his back to the men and press his hard thing against the edge of the sink to make it go down, but usually it wouldn't go down, the pressing only made it get harder and stick out more. One day one of the foremen saw Benjamin's pants sticking out and he shouted and pointed and everybody laughed very loud and applauded him and Benjamin thought he would die of shame and dearly wished he would. His thing went down immediately and he fled down to the lavatories and locked himself in and wept and refused to come out until everybody had gone away. Finally Elsie came down to the lavatory and coaxed him into unlocking the door. Elsie told him not to worry or listen to the jokes, it was only because he was growing up that that happened. Benjamin felt a bit better, and then Elsie went and spoilt it all by patting him on the head and telling him to stop crying and be a big boy. The next meal some of the foremen teased Benjamin again about his thing and Elsie got to hear of it and he came lumbering into Benjamin's mess and announced that if anybody said one more word to upset his little man, Elsie would personally punch him up the froat, and other things.

Benjamin, for all his scowls and jutting chin, without discrimination hero-worshipped most men on board, but the men he currently hero-worshipped most were James McQuade, who came to see him occasionally, and Mark Cameron. He lay on his bunk and scowled open-mouthed and all ears whenever Mark Cameron opened his mouth. *Got,* man, he wished he were like *ou* Mark and Master James an' be clever in the *kop* an' say clever things without having to think hard first, hey man. Not like that *ou* Geradus, that bladdy *ou* Dutchman never said nothing 'cept frown. Benjamin had never heard Mark or Master James say anything about women but Benjamin bet they had plenty of girlfriends, he could imagine them saying their clever things to lots of girlfriends and the girlfriends all listening with big blue eyes, being in love with them, and kissing them, Benjamin was a little in love with Master James and Mark himself. Benjamin lay in his bunk practising over and over in his *kop* the clever nice-sounding things he had heard Master James and Mark and his other heroes say, and he heard and saw himself saying clever sounding cutting things to that bladdy *ou* Dutchman Geradus.

'Hey you! Stop talking to yourself you bladdy little Hottentot!' Geradus van Wijk said. Benjamin's eyes burned in the darkness in helpless rage.

'Shuttup your bladdy *ou* self,' he retorted, 'you bladdy *ou domkop* bladdy Dutchman,' but he only said it inside his *kop* and he could not think of any of the many other clever things he was going to say to Geradus van Wijk. He remembered them the next day and he even thought up some new ones, and some of them were very clever indeed.

Since he had heard the men talking about their women, and particularly when he got the feeling between his legs, Benjamin Marais had tried to attach affection to one or other of the skinny brown fuzzy-haired girls of his acquaintance back home in Malmesbury, because it was clearly appropriate for a whalerman to have a girl. He tried very hard, and thought a long time, but he failed. No female had ever shown any interest in him, except his mother and possibly one Violet Pressure who had once smiled at him at Sunday school. Violet, however, had no front teeth at the time and anyway that was five years ago now and Violet had since gone to Capetown to work where she had children by Februarie Blom and others. The fact that Violet had liked him, who was unquestionably a woman, had impressed him as evidence of his own adulthood, and when asked if he had a girl back home he nonchalantly replied that he had had one but she had just run off and got married, a charitable detail he made with a swagger-scowl representing the man biting the bullet. Learning one night of the Foreign Legion, he subsequently added that he had come away to sea to forget it all. In the solitude of his bunk Benjamin worked hard on Violet Pressure, but he could not get over the two missing front teeth. Then one day Benjamin visited the hospital clinic to get some opening medicine and he fell in love at first sight with Sister Victoria Rhodes.

Oh, how much he loved her! Benjamin fell so hard in love with Miss Rhodes when he saw her close-up that he was too shy to bring himself to confess that he needed opening medicine and he complained of a headache instead and he left the surgery clutching a handful of aspirin in his small hot hand and a song in his heart. He swallowed the aspirin fervently in the amount and at the intervals prescribed by the goddess Miss Rhodes; if Miss Rhodes had prescribed the swallowing of two six-inch nails every four hours it would have been all right with Benjamin. The next day his constipation was worse and he went back to Miss Rhodes and got another handful of aspirin. The third day Benjamin's constipation was so bad that he really did have a headache, but Miss Rhodes refused to give him any more aspirin and told him that if he still had a headache next morning he must see the doctor. The fourth day Benjamin tottered in to see the doctor, with very uncomfortable constipation indeed, and Miss Rhodes was on duty and she took him personally before the doctor and she explained the history of headaches and about the aspirin. The doctor asked him if his bowels were working all right and Benjamin was so embarrassed in front of Miss Rhodes, for whom his constipation had not abated his ardour at all, that he hotly denied anything like that and announced that the headache was now localised in his ears. Benjamin emerged from the surgery with two codeine and very syringed eardrums. On the fifth day the true nature of Benjamin's condition manifested itself to the doctor despite Benjamin's loud disavowals and the doctor prescribed an enema. Benjamin did not realise what an enema was until Miss Rhodes took him into another room, and he saw the equipment and she told him to take down his trousers and lie down. Benjamin was so horrified he scrambled into the corner of the surgery and he stood throbbing with mortification with his face into the corner and absolutely refusing to take his pants down. Miss Rhodes patted him and tried to put her lovely priceless arm about him and coaxed him and cajoled him but Benjamin trembling red and shaking absolutely refused to entertain the idea. It was only when Miss Rhodes finally threatened to call the doctor who would call the Captain that Benjamin in redoubled horror submitted to taking down his pants, after several false starts, and exposed his baggy underwear and his skinny brown legs trembling to his goddess. Then in inarticulate shame he absolutely refused to take down his baggy underpants. Miss Rhodes put her lovely arms around him again and pleaded with her lovely eyes and smile up into his mortified face, and Benjamin was in such mortification he would gladly have laid down his life for Miss Rhodes, but take down his underpants he would not. Finally Miss Rhodes used the Captain threat again and Benjamin tore down his underpants on condition Miss Rhodes looked the other way and he jumped on to the table and faced the wall and buried his shaking face into his shaking hands, and his skinny buttocks were shaking.

And oh the vaseline and Miss Rhodes' crooning cool hands and the hard rude tube. Benjamin dearly wished the sea would just gobble him up in one big gobble for ever and ever. For the week after that Benjamin absolutely refused to talk to anybody and he would rather have suffered a million deaths than go back to Miss Rhodes, and Benjamin very seriously considered jumping into the sea, and in the privacy of his bunk he cried tears of shame.

Benjamin loved Miss Rhodes so very much that he did not go back to see her again, because of his shame, and he only saw her in the distance, and it was because he loved Miss Rhodes so much that he determined to catch the thief.

Chapter Ten

In December the whaling was bad. All the catchers between them only shot enough whales to keep half a shift working half a watch. By the time a whale was brought into the factory the shift had already knocked off from working the last one, and the decks had already been hosed down and the men had changed out of their oilskins already, and Big Charlie and his boys pulled the whale up the slipway and they left it lying on deck for the next shift to work when it came on in the morning. On the factory the boys sat around their Mess rooms and in their cabins and in the Pig, talking and playing cards and arguing and getting very disenchanted with the whaling, and with each other, and sometimes there were fights. Mostly everybody liked the fights. Nobody tried to stop them, unless it was unfair. It is best to let them fight it out and knock each other about a bit, then afterwards it is all right. If you stop them they are bitter with each other for a long time and then they have another fight, so you might as well let them fight it out in the first place and afterwards everybody is satisfied, especially the spectators. They were usually good fights at this stage of the season, after only a month and a half at sea, and usually nobody got badly hurt, only beaten up. The bad ones would come later, after three months at sea. Mostly the fights were between two English or two Coloureds, the English were afraid of fighting with a Coloured, because the Coloureds may gang up on the Englishman, and the Coloureds did not have a very high reputation for fighting clean; if you beat a Coloured in a fight, the theory was, he was likely to creep up on you in your sleep with a broken bottle and ram it in your face, or something like that. This theory was not particularly true, although it had happened in the history of the All England Whaling Company, but it was legend amongst the Englishmen, and the Coloureds knew it and took advantage of it. The English also believed that if you beat up a Coloured he would lie in wait for you in Cape Town when the fleet got back and set a gang of his shore friends on to you. All a Coloured needed to say to an English was, 'I'll fuck you up in the Cape' and usually the Englishman shut up. The Cape Coloureds had a very bad reputation. This December there were so few whales and so much sitting around that the Bridge only permitted the Pig to be open during normal English Sunday licensing hours, from twelve to two and from six to ten in every twelve hours, lest the whalermen drink and fight too much. This December was the beginning of the bad times.

The Bridge showed movies to the crew every second night, to keep them out of the Pig. The movies had names like Berlin Beauties and London Lovelies and Parisian Pussies, much naked woman-flesh, followed by a bad Western. All that woman-flesh flaunting and leering and rubbing itself on the screen in the jammed smoky Big Mess was not very good for the men, but it made them happy for half an hour. Sometimes Miss Rhodes went to the movies with the other officers but she only arrived after the woman-flesh films, and the men all whistled and clapped and stamped their feet when she arrived, she was very popular. They only made the noises to joke her, but many did not feel very funny about it, and after the shows there was a lot of thinking about what they would like to do with Miss Rhodes.

The night Benjamin heard it said that Jock was screwing Miss Rhodes was a very bad night for Benjamin. He spun his back on the foreman and buried his arms in the soapy sink and screwed up his face to keep back the tears of rage at the lie and the heartbreak that it was true. He went red and trembling with his face screwed up and he clenched a spoon in his hands under the suds in the sink and he tried to buckle it and he couldn't, so he banged the dishes in the sink very loud instead. Then when the last foreman left the Mess his red puffed face suddenly burst into tears and he turned from the sink and faced the door with his small fists bunched with soap suds and the tears running down his red screwed-up face. Then he charged out of the Foreman's Mess.

He clattered down the alleyway with his face screwed red and furious and his fists bunched in soap suds, he skidded round the corner and ran down the alleyways and then he skidded to a stop at the door of the Sailors' Mess and he stood heaving in the doorway with his fists bunched up. There was Jock sitting with some other sailors and they looked up surprised at the soapy figure and then Benjamin gave a high gargle scream and he charged at Jock. He charged at him with his chin thrown back and his fists beating in front of him so the soap suds flew and Jock stood up startled and retreated a step and Benjamin beat the air with his chin still thrown right back and a big soap sud flew into Jock's eye. Jock retreated rubbing his eye and Benjamin was beating up at him with his small fists, crying, he beat Jock's chest as Jock cursed and rubbed his eye. Then Jock put his hand on to Benjamin's forehead and he held Benjamin at arm's length while Benjamin beat the air with his soapy fists, and Jock rubbed his eye cursing. Jock held Benjamin at arm's length like that until he had rubbed the soap out of his eye and all the time Benjamin was beating the air. Then Jock stopped cursing and blinked at Benjamin flailing the air and said, 'What's the matter laddie, mon, what's all this?'

Benjamin beat the air.

'What's the matter, laddie?'

Benjamin was crying and he changed his beating to left and right hooks under Jock's arm. The sailors were laughing.

'Stop laughing!' Jock shouted at them. 'What's the matter laddie?'

Benjamin was getting tired now. He was leaning his head heavily on Jock's hand and swinging his hooks slower and the tears running down his face.

'Stop laughing,' Jock roared at the sailors. 'Come on now laddie, come on.'

Benjamin was grunting and sobbing now as he swung very slowly. Then Benjamin was too tired to swing any more. He dropped his hands to his sides and he just leant there against Jock's outstretched hands and the tears just ran down his face. Jock said 'Come laddie,' and tried to take him in his arms and Benjamin gave a howl and he turned and fled out of the Mess room with his knuckles to his eyes. He fled up the alleyway and down the companionway into the heads and locked himself in a lavatory.

He stayed in the lavatory a long time crying and shaking in rage and shame. 'They think I'm just a bleddy little fool!' he shook.

Chapter Eleven

On the twentieth of December McQuade went to the factory in the motorboat with The Kid for the first time in two weeks. The Kid was in an ebullient mood. McQuade was in a good mood too. He realised that he had missed The Kid. The Kid was somebody he took for granted, he was there with his bullshit every season and he got very sick and tired of The Kid sometimes. This season he missed The Kid because The Kid was running to and from the Fourteen and the factory like a dog when a bitch is on heat.

'Ramona ...' McQuade sang, '*I don't believe you wash at all ...*'

They sang Ramona to the words they had made up seasons before. 'Old James,' The Kid grinned at him. He passed the whisky bottle.

'Old James, you're a good bastard, you know that?'

'You shouldn't drink so much with the clap,' McQuade said.

'You shouldn't drink so much, period,' The Kid said.

The Kid was driving at only half throttle, they could see the factory lights twinkling in the sunset way ahead. It was good to be going to the factory, and only five days before Christmas.

'I'm a good drunk, James,' The Kid said. 'You're a good drunk, James. Jock is a good drunk. Izzy Isaacson's a bad drunk. Sings hymns.'

'I'm not a drunk,' McQuade said.

'You just love it,' The Kid said. 'I'd go crazy on that ship if it wasn't for you to get drunk with and shoot the bull and tell me what a bastard I am. Vicky also says I'm a bastard.'

'Miss Rhodes is a bright girl. Perspicacious.'

'But she likes me, James, she likes me. She told me that herself also. She thinks I'm bloody marvellous. She hasn't told me that much yet, but she's thinking it. She also thinks I am a real gentleman because I haven't tried to screw her yet. She hasn't told me but I know.'

'Miss Rhodes knows you've got the clap,' McQuade said. 'Old Fergie will have told her.'

'Old Fergie doesn't like me, you know that James? Thinks I'm a bastard.'

'You're kidding.'

'I rely on you to put in a good word for me with Old Fergie, James. Old Fergie likes you, James, though Christ knows why. Miss Rhodes doesn't like you James.'

'She doesn't?'

'Vicky thinks you're a fascist white South African bastard, James. She told me so herself. And as you say she's very perspicacious.'

'She said that?'

'Certainly she said that, you fascist white South African bastard.'

'Why the hell should she say that – boy, has she got a chip on her shoulder!'

'She says she can sense it, James, you typical goddam South African fascist you.'

'Boy, has she got a chip on her shoulder!'

'She can tell that you think she's got Coloured blood in her, James.'

'She told you that?'

'She told me that a lot of the Coloureds seem to think she's one of them.'

'She said that?'

'Certainly.'

'And how does she like that?'

'She laughed when she said it. She didn't seem to mind what anybody thinks, James.'

'Well,' McQuade said. 'Anyway I've changed my learned opinion, I don't think she's got any colour.'

'How big of you James, I must run and tell her.'

'Go to hell,' McQuade said. 'You're half tight.'

'Old James,' he was in a very good mood, 'tonight I have my fifth last jab from Old Fergie for my clap, you know that?'

'Congratulations.'

'I'll be a nice wholesome boy like you on Christmas Eve, James, won't that be nice? It's going to be my Christmas present to Vicky.'

'You're tight,' McQuade said.

'Won't that be a nice present for Vicky, James? That, plus some seal skins for a coat.'

'You lay off the seals,' McQuade said. 'And you shouldn't talk about a respectable woman like that.'

'Jesus, you *are* a good bastard, James. You're quite right, James. You know something, James?'

'What? It better be good.'

'Certainly it's good. I think I'm in love with her, James.'

'You're tight,' McQuade said.

'No. I've been doing a lot of thinking, James—'

'You've got to have brains to think with.'

'Even when I'm sober I've been thinking, James—'

'You're never sober—'

'I remember distinctly being sober day before yesterday, James—'

'Okay, tell me what you've been thinking.'

'Pass me that bottle. I've been thinking, James. And I think I love her.'

'You said that, now tell me why.'

'She's so bloody *good*, James – that's a difficult characteristic for a sonofabitch like you to comprehend, but it's goodness, James. And she's bright and she makes you laugh and she laughs. She's *good*, James.'

'All the qualities you've hitherto abhorred in women?'

'Maybe I'm getting old, James. They say it gets you like that. You run around like a dog on a tennis court screwing your arse off with anything with a fanny and not giving a damn, and then one day— Kerpow!—you meet this girl. She'll make a first class wife, James.'

'*Wife?*'

'She'll make a bloody fine wife, James.'

'You mean you're thinking of *marrying* her?'

'Well, I mean the season only just begun, and, of course, I haven't slept with her yet. I haven't said anything to her yet. But I really have been thinking.'

'Jesus,' McQuade said.

The Kid laughed. 'I'm happy, James, see what I mean?'

There was one whale in tow behind the factory slipway and one on deck, but they were leaving them for the day shift to do in the morning. They were both female Blue and The Kid had shot one of them that afternoon. She lay on the deck, ninety feet long, looking like a crashed jet aeroplane without wings. Her stripe grooves ran the length of her belly from her jaws to her tail and she had black spots the size of halfcrowns on her belly. Her big jaws were a little open and you could see into her huge mouth, big enough to drive a car into, way down to her gullet.

McQuade and Big Charlie walked slowly up and down the length of the long cutting deck, their arms behind their backs. The snow was trampled hard pink from the blood-soaked planks beneath. There were a number of men walking up and down the deck in the early evening in twos and threes, talking. The sun was gone, but the big red orange glow was bright in the west behind the black icebergs with the glowing pink edges, and the sea was mauve.

'Do you feel like a drink Jimmy?' Big Charlie said.

'Presently. Elsie's just fed me.'

'Poor old Elsie,' Big Charlie said. 'I don't think many guys go with Old Elsie.'

'Yeah,' McQuade said. 'Still, a whaling fleet is about the best place for him. The competition would be too fierce for him in the ordinary merchant navy.'

'Yeah,' Big Charlie said. 'Some of those British lines are so goddam queer they sail out of the harbour stern first. You're coming to the Christmas party aren't you, Jimmy?' Big Charlie said.

'Sure. I've paid Elsie my quid.'

'She puts on a marvellous spread for a quid, does Elsie. Miss Rhodes is coming, of course.'

It was good to think of Miss Rhodes coming.

'We couldn't have a Christmas party without Miss Rhodes,' McQuade said. 'I would mutiny.'

'Wee Jock's painting her portrait for her Christmas present,' Big Charlie said.

'Oh?' McQuade was madly jealous. 'Painting her portrait is he? Seeing a lot of Miss Rhodes is he?' McQuade said.

'You know Wee Jock,' Big Charlie said. McQuade detested the bastard.

'She'll be the cause of a lot of trouble,' Big Charlie said, 'will Miss Rhodes.'

'How's she causing trouble?' McQuade demanded.

'Ogh,' Big Charlie said, 'she's not doing anything, except she's a pretty young missie. You can't have a lassie like that on a whaler.'

'Oh so!'

'Would you like a drink Jimmy?'

'Let's do another turn on deck, it's nice for me to be able to walk.'

'I miss the wife, Jimmy,' Big Charlie said, 'you ain't got any idea.'

'Sure,' McQuade said.

'Especially at Christmas time,' Big Charlie said, 'you ain't got any idea.'

'Professor darling!' Beulah called. Beulah was on the top of a ladder sticking up Christmas decoradons. He had the paper bells and chains and streamers festooned round his neck and strips of cellophane stuck in a line across his lower lip. At the other corner of the Pig were Kitty and Elsie and Mother, also festooned with decorations. 'Careful you don't fall, Beulah.'

'Jimmy!' Jock shouted. He waved his arm. 'C'me here.' Jock was a little tight. He had a half-jack of his moonshine in front of him. The Pig was full but the musicians were not out yet, although Elvis was sitting wistfully near the microphone waiting to sing Poor Boy, waiting for the SPEBSQA boys to finish. The SPEBSQA boys were standing around in fours, woodshedding. SPEBSQA stood for The Society for the Preservation and Encouragement of Barber Shop Quartets in the Antarctic, or so they said. On SPEBSQA nights the quartets harmonised the old songs like 'I Wanta Girl, Just Like the Girl' and 'Swanee' and 'Basin Street' and 'Birth of the Blues.'

Tonight the quartets were woodshedding 'Good King Wenceslas' and 'Hark the Herald Angels Sing' and 'Jingle Bells.' Each quartet was woodshedding a different song at the same time, but they were doing it moderately and they did not sound in each other's way. They were very serious and enjoying it and swigging beer between songs. When they finished one song they would take a swig and listen for a moment to the quartet next to them, then suddenly one would take a breath and start a song and the others in his quartet would come in at different keys. You would see them cock their ears at each other's mouths now and again to get the next man's key and tune themselves up or down. It was very clever and nice to listen to, McQuade liked watching them. It was festive in the Pig, getting ready for Christmas, getting up the steam. McQuade made his way through the SPEBSQA quartets over to Jock's corner.

'Where you bin?' Jock demanded.

'I haven't been aboard for ten days, it hasn't been convenient.'

'Here,' Jock said, he poured two inches of moonshine into a glass, 'indulge in some of this. Hasn't been convenient, hey?'

'Jesus ...' McQuade said. The homemade liquor burned his throat and belly. 'Warms you up though. Could learn to live with this stuff.'

'Why's it been inconvenient? Because The Kid hasn't invited you in his dandy speedboat? Because he's trying to screw Vic?'

'You know he's after Victoria Rhodes,' McQuade said, 'why ask me?'

'Indulge in some more of this,' Jock said. He threw another shot into McQuade's glass. 'That bastard better watch out, captain or no Captain.'

'Now listen,' McQuade said. 'The Kid, you and me have been mates for Christ knows how long. All's fair in love and war. Now cut out this crap and dry your eyes.'

'He mustn't pull his rank on me,' Jock said. 'He mustn't pull his rank that's all.'

'How's he pulling his rank on you, for God's sake?' McQuade said irritably.

'The playboy Captain bit. The speedboat bit. The we're both officers together, come up to the bridge and have a drink Miss Rhodes bit. It makes me tired.'

'For Chrissake,' McQuade said. 'You've got her here aboard all day, what you bitching about?'

'That bastard's barking up the wrong tree,' Jock said belligerently.

'Then that's fine. So you've got her in the bag.' McQuade looked at Jock closely.

Jock took a big slug of his moonshine. He smiled to himself, then took a puff on his cigarette.

'You've got her, haven't you?' McQuade said.

'I ain't saying nothin' James-baby,' Jock smiled. 'A gentleman never does.'

McQuade disliked Jock just then. Jock leaned over and punched McQuade lightly on his shoulder. 'Indulge in some more of this.'

'That stuff's firewater.'

'And another thing,' Jock said, 'I want you to tell your Coloured friends to lay off me.'

'*My* Coloured friends?'

'You know their language,' Jock said, 'they know you. They're giving me a hard time, Professor. Telling me to stop fucking around with Miss Rhodes, or else.'

'Oh? Why?'

'They say she's one of them, Coloured like, and I've got no right because I'm white.'

'Which Coloureds?'

'That brown bastard Jakkals, but he said he was telling me on behalf of them all like. I told him to fuck orf—'

'When was this?'

'Last week.'

'What happened?'

'He come up to me in the Sailors' Mess, like, I was alone, and he tells me he's warning me to lay orf or else. I told him to mind his own fucking business and fuck orf.'

'What did he say to that?'

'He just gave me that look of his and told me he had warned me and I better watch out or else. Then he fucked orf.'

'Jakkals?' McQuade said.

'He's your pal,' Jock said. 'Tell him to mind his own fucking business.'

'You told him, didn't you?'

'The Coloureds like you, Professor, you speak their language and all. Just tell 'em to mind their own fucking business.'

'Jakkals,' McQuade said. 'He's a bad bastard.'

'You're fuckin' right he's a bad bastard. You know me, Professor,' Jock said, 'I'm not afraid of a fair fucking fight, but these Coloureds? And that Jakkals bastard?'

McQuade didn't say anything.

'Jesus,' Jock said, 'I don't fancy that Jakkals bastard.' McQuade took a sip of his firewater and then he grinned at Jock. Jock looked at McQuade and then grinned.

'Jesus, no *sir*! I do *not* fancy that Jakkals bastard.'

McQuade laughed.

'No thank you!' Jock laughed. 'You can have your pal Jakkals. You can have *all* your Coloured pals, Professor!'

McQuade threw back his head and laughed and Jock also laughed.

'Your pal Jakkals,' Jock laughed, 'would not stop at sneaking up on yours truly in his innocent sleep and cutting off his defenceless little balls!'

McQuade laughed out loud. Suddenly it was all terribly funny, they were both laughing loudly.

'You misunderstand Jakkals,' McQuade laughed. 'Really he's a very nice boy.'

'That's what Mrs Capone said about her little Al,' Jock laughed. 'No thank *you*.'

Beulah came over. He was in a pair of tight orange slacks and a blue sweater, but no falsies and hairdo tonight.

'What's the joke boys?'

'Jock's about to get his balls cut off,' McQuade said. 'What a shocking waste ...'

'That's how I feel,' Jock said. 'That's *exactly* how I feel.'

'Who *is* the horrid man?'

'It's a joke,' McQuade said.

'It's not a very funny joke,' Jock said. 'Indulge in some of this.'

Beulah reached out and took a sip. 'How you drink the stuff!'

'Gives you hair on your chest, Beulah.'

'I don't want *any* more hairs on my chest. Have you come to help us with the decorations, Professor darling?'

'No,' McQuade said, 'I've come to have a beer.'

'Miss Rhodes is coming along to help in a minute, darling, she's on the Christmas Committee.'

'I've come to help you with the Christmas decorations, Beulah,' McQuade said.

'So it's not me you love after all!'

'I'm really crazy about you, Beulah.'

Jock said to Beulah, 'Now how come I didn't know Vicky is coming to the Pig for the decorations?'

'You don't own her do you?' McQuade said. 'Beulah says she's on the Committee. Are *you* on the Christmas Committee?'

'No,' Jock said, 'I don' wanna be on the effing Committee.'

'How do I get on this here Committee,' McQuade said to Beulah. 'I'm a keen committee man, me. I love committees, they make me drunk with power.'

'You're hired,' Beulah said. 'I'm the Madam chair.'

'Okay,' McQuade said, 'I baggies working on Miss Rhodes' ladder.'

Jock scowled at him. 'I'm holding Miss Rhodes' ladder, I'm not having a randy sonofabitch like you lookin' up her lovely legs.'

'You can't hold Miss Rhodes' ladder,' McQuade said, 'because you're not on the goddam Committee.'

'Then I'm joining this here Committee,' Jock said.

'Indulge in some of this,' McQuade said. He was learning to live with the moonshine. 'You can't join our Committee, we're very particular who we have on our Committee.'

'I was on a Committee once,' Jock said.

'That must have been some Committee.'

'It was,' Jock said. 'It was a very swinging Committee called Spike's Committee. A small but stouthearted body of men.'

'And what was this Committee concerned with?'

'Spike's Committee was concerned exclusively with the well-being of Spike's Committee, was Spike's Committee.' Laughter. 'Spike's Committee, see, thought up ways and means of making the Committee members rich and happy,' Jock said. 'This guy Spike was no peanut, a sort of maritime Al Capone.'

'Sounds gorgeous,' Beulah said.

'Once,' Jock said, 'once we came to Zanzibar, see, where there's the Sultan of Zanzibar, see. This Sultan is king, and he's got his big castle with his harem inside and his eunuchs guarding the gates with big cutlasses an' all, and nobody ever gets to visit inside the Sultan's castle because he's the big noise, see, nobody can see his harem or it's off with his head and all that jazz. Well this is a passenger ship I'm workin', an' we anchor out in the bay, an' all the Arab bumboats come out and flog the passengers dirty pictures and so forth. Well, before we reach Zanzibar, Spike's Committee picks the lock of the printer's shop where all the menus are printed and we print five hundred invitation cards to a Ball at the Palace, including a Conducted Tour Through His Majesty's Harem, price of invitation two nicker. An' we give these invites to the Arab bumboats to flog to the passengers on a commission basis. An' by Christ, we cleaned up four hundred quid!'

McQuade and Beulah were laughing loudly.

'Well,' Jock said. 'At nine o'clock two hundred odd passengers all pitched up at the Palace gates in their dinner jackets, and the eunuchs start waving their cutlasses and there's hell to pay. An' the passengers come back all indignant and the police come aboard looking for the culprits an' all.'

'And The Committee?' McQuade did not believe the story but he was still laughing.

'The Committee's all sitting in their bunks writing letters 'ome to Mum, aren't they?'

They were all laughing.

'Not for them the fleshpots of Zanzibar,' Jock laughed. 'Four hundred nicker. I wonder how many Arabs had their heads chopped orf?'

He pronounced it Ay-rab. Izzy came and sat down. Izzy had just woken up. Izzy did not sleep in his own cabin very much. He slept wherever he finished talking, when there was nobody left to talk to and sing hymns to. He sat down absently, his piggy eyes red. He had a cup of coffee.

'Hullo, Izzy,' McQuade said. 'Ever been into battle on a bicycle?'

'Oh Christ,' Jock said.

'Don't blaspheme,' Izzy said. He meant it. He felt in his hip pocket and brought out a half-jack of brandy. He poured a big shot into the coffee. 'Just to kill the germs,' he said to them.

'Izzy,' McQuade said. 'You shouldn't drink first thing in the morning.'

'Me?' Izzy said, injured.

'That's the handy thing about working nightshift,' Beulah said. 'It need never *really* be morning.'

'Me?' Izzy said. He was serious. 'Me – I can take it or leave it.'

'It's just that you *prefer* it ...' Jock said tiredly.

'It's just that I prefer it,' Izzy said to McQuade, ignoring Jock. 'You blokes,' Izzy said to McQuade, 'you prefer your early morning coffee straight. Me, I don't really like coffee that much, I just prefer a shot of brandy in it. But I can take it or leave it.'

'And after breakfast?' Jock said.

'And after breakfast,' Izzy said to McQuade, ignoring Jock, 'you blokes like your coffee. Me, I don't like coffee much—'

'I just prefer a shot of brandy,' Jock said.

'I just prefer a shot of brandy,' Izzy said, ignoring Jock.

'Then comes teatime,' Jock said.

'Then comes teatime,' Izzie said to McQuade, ignoring Jock, 'and you blokes like your tea. Me, I can't stand tea, turns your guts to leather—'

'I just prefer to have a shot of brandy,' Jock said.

'I just prefer to have a shot of brandy,' Izzy said to McQuade. McQuade was laughing, he was feeling very good from Jock's moonshine. Jock had his chin propped in his palm leaning over the table and his face pent watching Izzy's mouth.

'But you can take it or leave it,' Jock prompted.

'But I can take it or leave it,' Izzy said to McQuade.

'An' the same at afternoon tea,' Jock said, 'tea turns your guts to leather—'

'Tea turns your guts to leather,' Izzy explained to McQuade.

'But I can take it or leave it,' Jock and Izzy chorused.

'Certainly.' Izzy ignored Jock.

'And *then* comes knock-orf time,' Jock prompted, staring at Izzy with his chin in his palm. McQuade was laughing.

'Well, *then* comes knock-orf time,' Izzy agreed without acknowledging Jock, 'and everybody goes into the Pig for a drink, don't they? Now, *that* drink,' Izzy confessed reasonably to McQuade, 'I really do enjoy.'

Jock stared sloshed at Izzy and wagged his finger sideways.

'That drink you can't take or leave?'

'That drink,' Izzy said to McQuade, 'I must agree I *enjoy* that drink.'

McQuade and Beulah were both laughing at Izzy and Jock. Izzy and Jock had straight faces, and Izzy was staring earnestly at McQuade and Jock was staring at Izzy.

Jock took a breath, 'And then comes bedtime when all the blokes have cocoa?' he said. His voice went up encouragingly on the 'cocoa.'

'Then comes bedtime,' Izzy said to McQuade with simple finality, 'and all you blokes have your cocoa—'

'I just don't *like* cocoa,' Jock said, 'it gives you fatty heart, angina pectoris—'

'Cocoa gives you angina pectoris,' Izzy explained to McQuade. 'I prefer to have my shot of brandy, but as I say—'

'*I can take it or leave it,*' Jock and Izzy chorused.

Izzy frowned very reasonably at McQuade and flicked his eyes peevishly at Jock once. McQuade was laughing and Jock was still staring at Izzy, waiting for him.

'But how do you feel Izzy?' McQuade laughed.

'I—' Izzy said.

'He feels just fine,' Jock said. 'It's just that when he *leaves* it, he wants to go Eeeeeeeeeeeeeeek!'

Jock's face screwed up and all his fingers thrust up rigid.

McQuade and Beulah had their heads thrown back laughing. Izzy looked at them all and then got up and walked away.

'You upset him, Jock.'

'Christ! How many times have I heard that story?'

'Here comes Victoria,' Beulah said. 'And The Kid ...'

They were standing at the door looking around.

'*Coo-ee!*' Beulah waved his hand up and down. The Pig had quietened down a moment as everybody looked at Miss Rhodes.

McQuade thought she was ravishing. She *was* ravishing. She wore a pair of faded blue jeans that fitted tight and her long legs were full and perfect inside. She wore a bulky grey sweater and there was a good strong bulge for her breasts, and her hair was pulled back into a pony tail and her ears stuck out a little and her cheeks were red from the cold and she smiled her gay wide creamy smile. They came threading towards McQuade's table and the good strong bulge under the sweater vibrated a little with each step, and by Christ she got McQuade right there, right there in the guts.

'Hullo you chaps – good evening, Mr McQuade, haven't seen you for a long time.'

'Hullo Jock,' The Kid said.

'How's your speedboat?' Jock said.

'Sit down, boys and girls,' Beulah said.

'How's your speedboat?' Jock demanded.

'My speedboat's fine.'

'Did you know Captain Child's got a speedboat?' Jock said. 'Beulah, did you know?'

'Of course, I know,' Beulah said.

'It's a lovely speedboat,' Jock said, 'frightfully swish. Just the job, donchaknow. Victoria did you know about Captain Child's swish just-the-job speedboat?

'Of course, Jock,' Miss Rhodes said nervously. Her gaiety was gone.

'It's just the ticket, donchaknow,' Jock said in an Oxford accent. 'Frightfully useful for a chap down here—'

'Okay, knock it off, Jock,' The Kid said.

'Of course,' Jock said to McQuade, 'you used to ride in Captain Child's speedboat a lot, but I believe of late it hasn't been convenient.'

Victoria Rhodes was blushing.

'Okay, Jock,' McQuade said, 'indulge in some of this ...'

He shoved the moonshine across the table.

'What's all this in aid of?' The Kid demanded.

'Do you remember Professor,' Jock said, 'the year I worked on the Fourteen and you and I and Captain Child went hunting seals?'

'I remember,' McQuade said guardedly. He was not sure whether Jock was changing the subject.

'We went hunting seals in Captain Child's speedboat, see,' Jock said to Beulah, 'because Captain Child rather wanted a couple of dozen sealskins to make up into fur coats to give to his London lady friends.'

Victoria Rhodes laughed politely. The Kid was scowling at Jock. Beulah was enjoying the situation.

'Oh yes?' Beulah said.

'Oh yes,' Jock said. 'Captain Child, you see, is a very dashing sort of chap, donchaknow. Gives away sealskin coats. Hunts the seals himself. Dashes about the Antarctic in his dandy little speedboat, just the ticket. Very dangerous, too, hunting seals, seals are such ferocious animals.'

'Okay Jock,' McQuade began.

The Kid was very annoyed because his Christmas present to Miss Rhodes was spoilt, but he was trying to laugh it off.

'More dangerous than you think,' Jock said to Miss Rhodes and then to Beulah, 'very dangerous it was, because Professor James McQuade knocked Captain Child out cold.'

They all laughed except The Kid, and Miss Rhodes clapped her hands together once. 'Did he!'

'He did rather,' The Kid smirked.

'Oh yes he rather did,' Jock said to Miss Rhodes. 'Frightfully bad show it was, donchaknow. The Professor got kinda sore, see, with Captain Child butchering those poor defenceless little seals so he could lavish fur coats on his London birds so the Professor went up to Captain Child and smote him one. *Kerpow!*'

They were all laughing now, even The Kid. It seemed Jock had worked out the nastiness. McQuade was pleased with the story about himself. Miss Rhodes clapped her hands again once.

'Jolly good show, Mr McQuade – poor seals!' she said to The Kid and The Kid grinned guiltily.

'So, Victoria,' Jock said, delighted with himself, 'if you happen to get any sealskin coats for Christmas, you'll know all about them, *poor* little seals ...'

McQuade laughed out loud. The Kid was looking livid at Jock.

Jock looked at Miss Rhodes with big enquiring eyes and wagged his finger sideways in front of her, 'You wouldn't want to join the Chelsea Ladies Sealcoat Club, would you Victoria?'

'Certainly not!' Miss Rhodes laughed, and then she shot The Kid a big suspicious look and The Kid blushed and McQuade and Beulah and Jock were laughing.

McQuade decided to step into Jock's applecart.

'How's the painting going, Jock?' he said. 'Painted any good portraits lately?' Beulah guffawed high pitched.

'The painting's going fine, thanks,' Jock said suspiciously.

'Painted any good portraits recently, then?' McQuade asked blandly.

'Well ...' Jock said sheepishly, 'I try to paint, you know-landscapes, that's what I—'

'Icebergs?' Beulah said. 'He's good at close-ups of icebergs.'

'And portraits.' The Kid nodded at Miss Rhodes. 'He's very good at portraits.'

'Is he?' Miss Rhodes said, expecting the mickey was being taken. Jock waved his hand denying it, but you could see he was laughing underneath, waiting.

'Oh yes he is,' The Kid said earnestly, 'he's a very popular portrait painter. He's kept busy painting the whole season, there's hardly a floosie in Glasgow and ports south who hasn't had her portrait painted by Jock some whaling season or another ...'

'Really!' Miss Rhodes pretended to be shocked. McQuade was laughing, Jock was looking cheesed off.

'Really!' The Kid said. 'Dashing sort of chap, dashes off portraits. Keeps the home fires burning, donchaknow. So,' The Kid laughed pretending he was making a joke, 'if you get a portrait Vicky, you'll know you've joined a very select gallery—'

'Okay, Kid,' Jock said, very peeved.

When they stopped laughing Beulah said, 'Well, about these decorations, boys and girls? Kid can you help me in yonder corner?'

The Kid looked disappointed.

'And Victoria and the Professor can work in the other corner …'

McQuade shot Beulah a grateful look and Beulah gave him a wink. The Kid looked cheesed off with Beulah. They stood up and Jock still sat.

'Wot about the workers?' Jock said.

McQuade leaned over Jock's ear and said,

'The working class
Can kiss me arse
I'm working with
Miss Rhodes at last.'

Beulah turned to Jock, 'You! You can sit there and blow up balloons with all your hot air!'

McQuade could not have cared less about Christmas decorations but he worked with Miss Rhodes as if he just loved Christmas decorations. McQuade was very happy. Miss Rhodes was very friendly and McQuade, with a few of Jock's moonshiners inside him, was very witty and Miss Rhodes laughed at his jokes and they didn't seem to be getting an awful lot of decorating done. The Pig was warming up now, the SPEBSQA woodshedders had stopped and the band had started up, and the men were singing with the band. Once when McQuade and Victoria were bending over a pile of paper decorations and McQuade said something funny and she burst out laughing and their faces were close together, and McQuade knew from her eyes he could have kissed her then, he could have put his arms around her while they were laughing into each other's faces and their laughter would have disappeared and she would have let him kiss her but of course he could not, but he was very happy. And Victoria climbing up the ladder to stick decorations on to the deckhead, and looking up the line of her legs and the bulge of her breasts and he could see the end of her panties underneath the tight jeans and he felt Oh Christ and it got him right there in the loins. Then McQuade cut his finger with a razor-blade cutting string.

'You must go along to the surgery and get that dressed,' Miss Rhodes said.

'It's nothing,' McQuade said, he squeezed it with his handkerchief.

'You must, come with me then and I'll dress it,' Miss Rhodes said.

'Okay,' McQuade said cheerfully.

They crossed the long frozen cutting deck and she took him to her cabin to dress it because there was a queue of men waiting to see Old Ferguson. She disinfected it thoroughly, because infection sets in very easily on the whalers on account of all the blood and fat, and then she dressed it. When she straightened up from dressing his finger he put his arms around her and kissed her. She yielded momentarily and then she broke free and slapped him. She slapped him hard and swift and there was a bright flash in his head. Then he blinked himself clear and she was standing back from him with her hands on her hips.

'I'm sorry,' McQuade said.

She didn't say anything.

'I wouldn't have done it if I'd realised you felt so strongly about it,' he said.

'How did you expect me to feel, Mr McQuade?'

'Nothing,' McQuade said.

'Did you expect me to collapse in your arms? I know what you think I am, Mr McQuade.'

Oh so! McQuade thought.

'I don't think anything, Miss Rhodes. Let's just forget it.' He looked at her standing angrily in front of him and then he grinned his most charming grin. 'I'm sorry.'

She also broke into a grin.

'All right,' she said. 'Let's go back now.'

Chapter Twelve

There was a long queue outside the pantry hatch when McQuade and Miss Rhodes walked back, the nightshifters queuing for their bi-weekly free ration of rum. They whistled at Miss Rhodes and called 'Hullo sweetheart,' and 'Come here sweetheart,' and 'Be careful of that man, Victoria.' She grinned, blushed, and somebody cried 'Oh-ooh, that's how it is,' and then the cry was taken up 'Oh-oooooh,' and they laughed and Miss Rhodes laughed and blushed harder and McQuade grinned, she was very popular with them. As they reached the corner a Coloured man stepped out of line and grabbed his genitals and shoved his groin forward and shook his genitals and his hips at Miss Rhodes' back and stuck out his tongue and said, 'Jere! – Kom hierso vrou-mens!' and many laughed uproariously. McQuade guessed what they were doing behind them. When they got back to the Pig the decorations were all up and the band was in full swing and there was singing and smoke and crush and beer-swigging with the gentle roll of the factory. The Kid and Jock and Beulah were standing crushed round the bar hatch. Jock shot an accusing look at McQuade and The Kid immediately asked Miss Rhodes to dance. Before he got involved in explanations, McQuade said 'I'll be back' and turned and walked out of the Pig.

He walked down the alleyway then down the companionway to below. He stopped at Benjamin's cabin and tapped quietly on the door, listened and then opened the door.

The cabin was in darkness, the electric light from the alleyway shone in. He opened the door wide and peered at the bunks. They were all empty except one, the bunk's curtains were drawn,

Benjamin's bunk. He felt for his matches and struck one and advanced. He saw the watch lying on the table. He looked at Benjamin's bunk and then he saw the sheet over the feet trembling. McQuade parted the curtains.

'*Aaaaaarh!*' Benjamin screamed. '*Aaaaaarh – aaaaaarh!*' He had his face screwed up tight and his hands over his face, jerking as he screamed '*Aaaaaarh!*'

McQuade swept the curtain back. '*Benjamin! Benjamin!*'

'*Aaaaaaaarh!*' Benjamin screamed with his face screwed up and his hands over his face, '*Aaaaaaarh.*'

'Benjamin!' McQuade said. '*Stil!* Benjamin, *wat makeer, jong?*'

'*Aaaaaaaaaarh!*' Benjamin screamed jerking.

'Benjamin! *Dis ek,* Master James, *dis ek, moenie bang wees nie—*'

'Huh?' Benjamin screamed, and he opened his eyes and peered through his fingers and his eyes were flickering terrified in the match light, '*Huuuuuuh—*'

'*Dis ek,* Benjamin,' McQuade said.

'Huh?' Benjamin stopped jerking and parted his fingers wider and stared terrified at McQuade. Then he took his hands away from his face, still trembling. 'Hullo, Master James ...' he quavered.

'*Wat makeer jong?*' McQuade blew out the match. 'Climb out Benjamin, and tell me everything, come.'

McQuade closed the door and switched on the light and suddenly the cabin was very white and bright and safe. Benjamin blinked sheepishly in the light. He was still trembling. He climbed down and sat in his underwear hunched up on the bench with his hands clasped between his shaking knees and looked at McQuade with big shy eyes and as soon as McQuade looked at him Benjamin looked away.

'Now tell me, Benjamin,' McQuade said in Afrikaans, 'what's all this about? What's your watch doing lying on the table like that tied to your foot with string?'

Benjamin wriggled on the bench with his hands between his knees.

'It's nothing Master James,' he said in English.

'And don't call me Master James,' McQuade said in Afrikaans, 'we're all whalermen, right?'

'Okay, Master James,' Benjamin said, blushing and glowing underneath his shaking.

'Remember that your Ma is like my Ma,' McQuade said encouragingly, 'so we're all men together, right?'

Benjamin nodded vigorously and glowed and he rolled his eyes adoringly once up at McQuade and then he looked away in extreme shyness.

'And your Ma said I've got to keep an eye on you or else,' McQuade said. 'But I know you're big enough to look after yourself so I've just come to say hullo ...'

Benjamin wriggled on the bench once happily.

'And what do I see? I see your watch tied to your foot with string. Now what's all this Benjamin?'

'It's nothing, man, Master James,' Benjamin said in English and waggled himself once, mortified.

'Tell me Benjamin!' McQuade said firmly in English.

Benjamin waggled on the bench with his hands clasped between his skinny brown knees.

'It's a trap for the thief,' Benjamin confessed in whispered Afrikaans.

McQuade stared at the little embarrassed brown profile and then he leaned back.

'Oh so! A trap for the thief!' Benjamin glanced up at him once and then shot his eyes back to his knees and waited. McQuade took a breath.

'Well, Benjamin,' he said in Afrikaans, 'that's a very good idea. A very good idea indeed ...'

Benjamin flushed with furious happy incredulity.

'... but from what I hear the thief has stopped stealing. And don't you think that you're rather risking losing your watch, I mean encouraging just anybody to take it? It may not be the real thief,' McQuade pointed out.

Benjamin had not thought of that one. *Got,* but it was difficult, hey, to catch a *skellum,* hey man! He waggled on the bench defiantly, nonplussed.

McQuade decided to pass over the question as to what exactly he was going to do when he trapped the thief.

'I think,' McQuade said, nodding very reasonably into the middle distance for Benjamin's benefit, and Benjamin had his big brown eyes glued on McQuade's profile, hanging on his words, 'that maybe the thief has stopped stealing, and even Scotland Yard couldn't trap him.'

Benjamin shook his head with big eyes.

'And I think,' McQuade said, 'that you're running the risk of losing your watch for nothing.'

Benjamin looked up at him with big eyes aghast.

'*Got!*' Benjamin whispered aghast.

'So I suggest,' McQuade said, man to man, 'that you put your watch back on your arm – *I* would.'

Benjamin scrambled to obey. McQuade looked at him as if nothing had happened. Benjamin sat back clutching his wristwatch, and waited.

'And how goes it, *Boet?*' McQuade said. *Boet* is a slang Afrikaans endearment, meaning brother. 'How goes it with your cabinmates?'

Benjamin waggled on the bench looking at his hands between his knees.

'They're okay, Master James,' Benjamin said in English. 'Except one, he's a bleddy Dutchman.'

'Are they all Europeans?'

'*Ja,*' Benjamin said, 'I'm the only Coloured *ou.*'

'And what's the Afrikaaner doing?' McQuade demanded.

'Agh,' Benjamin waggled again, 'he doesn' do nothing really, he jus' don' like me in the same cabin as him, man. He always frowns, man, an' tells me to shut up, hey.'

'He doesn't bully you?' McQuade demanded.

'Well,' Benjamin said, 'he tried to make me do the dirty jobs, man, cleaning the cabin and making his bunk, but *ou* Mark stopped him.'

'Who's Mark?' McQuade said.

'Master Mark,' Benjamin said.

'You don't have to call anybody Master, Benjamin!' McQuade said.

Benjamin waggled with embarrassment.

'*Ou* Mark,' Benjamin said, 'he's nice, hey.'

'Is he South African or English?'

'He's Sout' African, man,' Benjamin said, 'but he's English, hey. But he talks Afrikaans of course. He goes to the university hey, jus' like you did, Master James.'

'What else does the Afrikaaner do?' McQuade demanded.

'Agh,' Benjamin waggled. 'Nothing. He jus' frowns and tells me to shut up, and calls me a bladdy Hottentot and to shut up. An' he tells me I stink. I'm not a bleddy Hottentot,' Benjamin waggled hotly, 'I'm half European an' half Coloured—'

'Of course you're not Hottentot, *Boet*,' McQuade said.

'I'm *not* a bleddy Bushman!' Benjamin said.

'Of course you're not, *Boet*,' McQuade said. 'Remember I know most of your brothers and sisters and they're fine people!'

Benjamin shot his eyes up at once at McQuade adoringly.

'I'm the same as Miss Rhodes, aren't I?' Benjamin said, 'an' she's not a bleddy Hottentot, *she's* Malay same like me.'

McQuade sat back.

'Sure,' he said.

Benjamin was blushing furiously, horrified and happy at what he had said. McQuade looked sideways at Benjamin. Benjamin was staring rigidly at his hands, blushing.

'What makes you think Miss Rhodes is Malay, *Boet*?'

Benjamin's heart bounded with happiness.

'All the Coloured *ous* say so,' he declared, blushing with furious happiness. He sat rigid, glaring joyfully at his hands between his knees.

McQuade looked at Benjamin. Then he smiled.

'Do you like Miss Rhodes, Benjamin?'

Benjamin went into a spasm of joyous mortification.

'She's okay,' he blushed furiously.

You poor little bastard, McQuade thought. He slapped him once on the back and stood up.

'Okay, *Boet*,' Benjamin shuffled to his feet uncertainly and stood there in his baggy underpants and vest, looking at McQuade's chest. He was disappointed that they weren't going to talk any more about Miss Rhodes.

'Well just you take care of yourself. *Verstaan?*'

'*Verstaan*, Master James,' Benjamin blushed.

'And stop worrying about this thief, and if you get into any trouble just you get word to me. *Verstaan?*'

'*Ja, verstaan* Master James,' Benjamin said to McQuade's chest.

'Okay, *Boet*. And you work hard and don't you worry about that old Dutchman and don't you be tempted to give him any cheek, okay?'

'Okay,' Benjamin blushed.

'And when we get back, if you want a job with me on the fishing boats it's okay,' McQuade said. '*Verstaan?*'

McQuade punched him lightly on the shoulder. Benjamin took a step back blushing furiously with pleasure under the blow. 'And just you look after Miss Rhodes!' McQuade joked him and Benjamin thought he would die with delight. He swivelled around on his heels and screwed up his hands behind his back. McQuade walked out the door, switching off the light.

Benjamin stood in the darkness gaping at the door and then he swivelled and he wanted to shout with joy. He wiped his hands over his face four times for joy then he did a little dance and then he scrambled up into his bunk and screwed himself up into a ball and pulled the sheet up over his head. Then he pulled the sheet back down and he lay there screwed up in a ball in the dark staring at the bulkhead and he said over and over again to himself in the dark, *Okay, Boet. Just you look after Miss Rhodes, hey? Okay, Boet.*

'*Boet!* man!'

McQuade took one turn on deck for fresh air before going back to the Pig. The deck was floodlit now and they had decided to call out the nightshift to work the two whales, and men were gathering in their oilskins and thighboots but they had not yet started. The Twelve was alongside bunkering, her crow's-nest just above the deck of the factory and McQuade could see the Fourteen a hundred yards off, waiting her turn, twinkling on the black sea. He walked back to the for'ard hatch and up the alleyway to the Pig. He could hear the singing from way off. As he got to the door he met The Kid and Miss Rhodes coming out.

'Are you off?' McQuade asked, disappointedly.

'Yes,' The Kid said. 'See you, James.'

'Good night, Mr McQuade,' Miss Rhodes smiled politely.

'Good night,' McQuade said.

Chapter Thirteen

When the calf was born he was twenty-two feet long and his mother laboured at the surface of the sunny South Pacific, as a woman labours, and two other female whales attended her, as our women tend each other at such times. After many contractions he was born tail first down into the sea, without a breath in his mammal's body and his mother and her attendants dived down and came up underneath him and nudged him up to the surface, and so he blew for the first time and took his first breath of air, and the females came up blowing and wallowing about him, and he knew how to swim already, and after a little while and a few experimental blows and wallows they swam off to join the rest of the pod, the females around him and he on the inside. And when she first fed him she rolled on her side and he knew exactly where to go; and he could not get his wide jaws around her teats, which are no bigger than a woman's breast, and he just opened his mouth wide and she squirted a jet of milk into his mouth very accurately, and without him swallowing any sea water, which of course would have made him very sick. For six months they stayed in the sunny South Pacific, following the shrimp shoals, and she fed him milk.

The calf was six months old now and he had almost stopped his suckling, and the hairy baleen plates in his mouth were strong and hard enough for him to eat the krill shrimps. He was nearly fifty feet long, that six-month whale, half as big as his mother already, so nutritious was the milk which she had squirted into his mouth, but he was still a calf and he still swam beside her all the day and he slept beside her in the night. She looked after him, calling to him where the krill were and giving him milk when he didn't get enough krill, and calling him away from any danger, and playing with him in the late afternoons when the sun was going down and all whales feel frolicsome. They dived and twisted under the water and nudged each other and chased each other and then shot up to the surface and jumped, jumped almost clear out of the sea in the sunset with the sun glinting red and gold and sleek down the big arched streamlined backs, and the water streaming blue and gold off them, and diving again and calling to each other, for whales are happy trusting animals. And so the calf whale waxed strong and he took less milk and he ate more and more krill, and when he was six months old there came the sweet natural call that only whales can hear that it was now spring in the white cold south seas thousands of miles away and that soon it would be summer and much of the sea would be unlocked where the krill would be fat, and then he went with his mother and her mate, south to the Antarctic.

James McQuade was the first human being to see him, on Christmas Eve. Two miles away to starboard, under an ice blue sky and a bright white sun on a dark blue sea, James McQuade saw him blow a white plume of spray, then another blow appeared beside it, bigger, and then three more at once and McQuade filled his lungs with icy air and he pointed and he hollered *'There she blows!'* and he kept pointing to the place where he had seen them.

The muted alarm bell was ringing below and the sailors were running up on deck to their stations. The Kid came up on to his bridge yawning and he took the binoculars from the Mate, because he had forgotten his own in his cabin. The Mate was very annoyed. McQuade was still pointing, dead ahead now, and the catcher was churning full speed. The blows did not reappear and The Kid gave an order and the catcher swung a few points to starboard and kept running. McQuade kept pointing to the place where he had last seen the blows. Then the blows came again almost dead ahead to where The Kid had headed the bows and McQuade shouted again and pointed anew. For ten minutes they ran thus, shouting and pointing and changing direction a little, and the four blows were coming every minute, for the whales were feeding, and they were not running much. Then the blows did not come for some time, and The Kid slowed the ship down to half ahead, for they were now only a quarter of a mile from the place where they had seen the last blow, then he cut engines altogether and the ship coasted. He came down the causeway from the bridge to the gun platform. McQuade waited, and everybody on deck waited. Then came the surge of black hide dead ahead and then another and then the blows and McQuade pointed and the telegraph rang on the bridge and McQuade shouted down to The Kid below, '*There's a female and calf.*' The Kid nodded without looking up. There was another blow, the bull, and he rolled over on his side as he went up and over so one great flipper came out of the water and there was his huge long striped silver belly flashing long in the sun and his cavernous mouth was open hugely happily gulping in seawater, and then McQuade saw it in the sea ahead, the tinge of dirty pink cloud under the surface, the krill. From the crow's-nest he could see the big dark shapes flit and disappear and reappear close under the surface, the bull and the cow and the calf skirting shallow through the cloud of krill.

'They're feeding,' he called down to The Kid. The Kid nodded and signalled with his right hand and the Mate rang up full ahead. The engines throbbed hard and the ship surged, one hundred yards, two hundred, towards the pink cloud of krill, and then he signalled and the engines cut again, and it was suddenly dead quiet and the hunter glided on under its own momentum silently, treacherously, towards the krill patch, and all on deck waited. Then The Kid signalled a spurt of half ahead and the telegraph rang and the ship surged forward again and then he cut the engines again and they glided again, silently, treacherously. The Kid shuffled himself in front of the big harpoon gun and crouched a little, his hand was on the butt. He swung the gun back and forth, once, and then crouched lower.

McQuade leaned over the rim of the nest and called down to him, 'You're only allowed to shoot the bull!'

The Kid said without looking up, 'Okay, Jimmy-boy, okay, okay.'

They glided on, losing momentum now, and they were a hundred yards from the beginning of the krill patch, and The Kid called up to him but without looking up, 'Why the hell do you come whaling anyway, you goddam ichthiologist?'

'Because I'm soft in the head.'

The Kid muttered, 'We're all goddam soft in the goddam head.'

The Mate shouted from the bridge, 'Shuttup McQuade and watch the bloody sea,' and The Kid shouted without turning around, 'Shuttup, Mister, you're frightening the goddam whales with your goddam shouting!'

The deckhands grinned. The Mate clamped his lips together and he looked as if he had finally had a gutsfull of this goddam outfit and was going to report the goddam Kid to his goddam Old Man. Goddam him! His eyes looked as if he were imagining The Kid disowned by his Old Man, then being disembowelled by his Old Man. Some men are born frustrated deck officers, some achieve frustration, others have frustration thrust upon them. With the Mate it was the last. With The Kid it was perversely the reverse. If ever a man deserved to be low man on the Company totem pole it was The Kid. The horrible perverse fact of the matter was that The Kid came across more whales, missed more whales, and hit more whales than any other gunner in the fleet. And nobody knew it better than his Old Man, the Board, the Shareholders, and the Mate, who declared there was no justice in this world, no God, and most of all no sense. No nothing. And here was The Kid and that bastard McQuade who set himself up as some kind of Solomon on this ship, bearing down on a pod of blues which according to all the laws of nature should have the wind up and be fleeing across the ocean and The Kid and that bastard McQuade are conducting a bullshit conversation between the crow's-nest and the gun that should even put the krill to flight. But what were the whales doing? The Mate glared at them through his binoculars as if the beasts were in league with The Kid and that bastard McQuade to get harpooned.

The bull and the cow and the calf had been following the shoal of krill for an hour and they were half full and the sun was shining and they were fat and they intended following the shoal of krill until they were completely full. When they were full they would rest a little, and then play together a little, snorting and diving and jumping and blowing, and then they would go to sleep together, right there in the open ocean whenever they felt it was time to go to sleep. They would go to sleep resting at the surface of the sea with their blow holes above the sea, close together, not for warmth but for contact, and the calf in the middle, his side touching his mother's side. Now they were feeding and they were feeling very friendly towards everything. The cow saw the catcher bearing silently down on them, and she was not afraid, for she had never been hunted before, the only ships she had ever seen in the Pacific Ocean had never tried to harm her. Some of the ships she had seen in the Pacific she had swum towards out of curiosity, and she had swum beside them and underneath them and cut across and back of them, and she had seen human beings on deck and they were as harmlessly curious towards her as she had been towards them. She would have swum towards the ship to greet it now had she not been feeding. The bull had been hunted before but he did not see the hunter until it was one hundred yards away, because he was very intent on gulping in the krill in great tons of salt water and then squirting the water back into the sea out of the sides of his huge mouth so the krill were caught in the hairy baleen plates. But the bull was not unduly alarmed by the ship because it was coming silently and smoothly and slowly, and he was very intent upon the krill that were abounding, and when you are intent upon filling your belly you are less disposed towards suspicion of your fellow creatures than at other times. The bull blew and he rolled an eye at the catcher, and he opened his cavernous mouth and he kicked his tail and shoved himself through under the water like a bulldozer with his huge mouth open sucking more tons of water and thousands of krill shrimps. The cow saw the ship gliding so close towards them and she was thrilled with a moment of anxiety, she twisted around under the water and placed herself between the ship and her calf. Then the calf saw it, the keel gliding towards them under the sea, and he had a bellyfull of krill and he was feeling very happy and friendly and full of curiosity and he turned and dived under his mother and he came up and blew and he gambolled towards the ship.

'*It's the calf!*' McQuade shouted. '*You can't shoot the calf!*'

The Kid waved his hand at McQuade petulantly.

Now the big cow turned and she chased after the calf, and they were both ploughing towards the ship. They were seventy yards away. The Kid made a signal and the telegraph rang up Slow Ahead and the engines throbbed. And then the bull signalled alarm. Then The Kid signalled Full Ahead.

The cow overtook the calf in a big plunging blow shrieking danger to him and she cut across the front of him and headed him off. They turned and blew and plunged off back towards the bull, the calf galloped beside the cow, and the catcher was churning after them, seventy yards behind. The bull blew and snorted and shouted for them and he started off, but slowly, waiting for them to catch up with him. The cow ran under the sea, bucking her great back and beating her great tail and the calf was galloping beside her, but the cow was not running as fast as she could, on account of the calf. The bull was stopped now, watching them, and still making his *run run run* noises and waiting for them to catch up with him, and he could feel and hear the urgent throb of the engines, and he turned around and around under the water waiting for them. Then the calf had to come up for a blow because he had not taken a proper breath before running, and so the cow came up too and she also blew and the catcher was only sixty yards behind them. The cow and the calf were still fifty yards from the bull where he was milling around waiting for them. And the bull roared at them under the water and he churned around furiously and then he humped his huge back and he beat his giant tail and he sounded.

The bull charged back under the seas, back towards the cow and the calf and he passed them and then he bent his huge head upwards and he roared up to the sunlight again and he broke surface huge and snorting and blowing angrily fifty yards in front of the hounding catcher. Only once did he blow, to show himself, and then he sounded again. He made off shallow under the surface, away from where the calf and the cow were running. McQuade could see him from the crow's-nest, the blur of his great pounding tail and his great flat head bounding forward, and he felt sick in his guts, and he struck out his arm and shouted, '*There, there he goes!*'

Already the ship was heeling to starboard, for the Mate and the helmsman had also seen him. And The Kid threw both his arms in the air and he turned around screaming and punching his arm pointing, '*There – there – follow the cow you goddam idiots!*'

The helmsman faltered. The Mate's red-rimmed eyes were wide open, then McQuade and the Mate hollered in unison, '*But you can't shoot the cow!*' and McQuade added at the top of his lungs, '*It's illegal,*' and the Mate screwed up his face and screamed, '*Shuttup McQuade,*' and then screamed at The Kid, '*It's illegal to shoot the goddam cow!*'

The helmsman swung the wheel back and the ship headed the other way, after the cow and the calf. The Kid's hands were on his hips now and his back was to the gun, and to the whales, to everything except the Mate and McQuade, and he looked up at them and he hollered, '*Thanks for your advice, gentlemen! And thank you Mister Helmsman for getting the goddam message!*'

He glared at them again and then he screwed up his face again and he screamed, 'We're following the goddam cow because I'm Captain and I'm gunner and I'm godalmighty on this goddam ship and I say we're following the goddam cow because I'll be goddammed if I'm going to chase my guts out after that goddam bull who has set his heart on deluding me and we'll be running around here all goddam day like a dog on a goddam tennis court and he'll *still* get away because he's no peanut this bull!'

The Kid stopped and glared at the Mate on the bridge and then up at McQuade in the nest, and then he took another breath and then he screwed up his face again and he started screaming again, '*And if we keep chasing his cow he'll come back to his cow and he'll be a sitting duck because that cow is a peanut it sticks out a goddam mile like the rest of you are!*'

The Mate was looking pinkly down at The Kid with impotent fury. McQuade looked down at him unabashed, mollified.

'Okay, then,' McQuade said.

The Kid dropped his fists from his hips and he dropped his voice and said only loudly, 'Thank you, gentlemen, *all* the same—'

'Oh very well then,' McQuade said.

The Kid turned round back to the gun and then he turned up to McQuade and shook his finger up at him, 'And any more goddam crap from you McQuade and I'll have you keelhauled!'

'Keelhauling's also illegal these days,' McQuade said.

The cow and the calf were a hundred and fifty yards ahead running in a straight line shallow under the sea, side by side. They blew once each, short snort blows, one big one and one small one, then plunged on again. The catcher pounded after them smacking through the water, the spray flying up over the gun platform soaking The Kid so he cursed. The bull galloped on away at a tangent, shallow under the surface bucking his great back and tail and trying to listen for the throb of the engine, he ran for a quarter of a mile and then he came up to blow and he swirled as he blew and he looked back for his enemy and then he blew again. For there he saw the ship a long way from him and it was not chasing him, it was chasing his cow and the calf. And he gave a high angry blow and he took a huge breath and he humped his great back and he charged at an angle back across the sea towards his cow and the calf and at an angle to the ship, to get himself between it and them.

'*Here he comes,*' McQuade shouted and he pointed, as was his duty. The Kid grinned without looking around, then he held his fingers at his ear and gave the Mate the V sign, and then pretended to scratch his ear with the V.

The cow and the calf came up and blew again, a hundred yards ahead, short quick panic blows and sounded again, running as fast as the calf could run. The bull was cutting across towards them, huge angry galloping thrashes of his mighty tail, he was only two hundred yards from them now and he could hear them but he could not yet see them. He made his angry urgent run run run noises under the water as he galloped but the cow had not yet heard them. In the crow's-nest McQuade was pointing with both arms outstretched in a V, pointing to the two places he had last seen the big fish, and The Kid was hunched over the bows cursing at the spray and stamping his foot, and shouting *faster faster,* only ninety yards behind the cow and the calf now. The bull galloped across towards them making his run run run noises, only a hundred and fifty yards from her now. And then she heard him, and her female heart gave a leap and she turned towards his noises, and the galloping calf also turned. Up in the crow's-nest McQuade was snouting and pointing, and the ship was turning also. The calf and the cow had lost twenty yards in the turning and the ship was only seventy yards behind them now. And the cow and the bull converged and they plunged on, side by side, with the calf between them. Then the bull sounded deep and they followed him.

On the gun platform The Kid gave the Mate the V sign again, then he signalled for the engines to be cut down to half, then down to quarter. It was suddenly quiet, the engines suddenly just a background purr and the ship stopped pitching and the spray was no longer flying, and everybody was waiting and watching. For minutes it was so, only the sun and sssssh of the ship. Then McQuade saw the dark shadows galloping up under the sea and he pointed and shouted.

'*There she blows!*' And the ship was heeling hard over and the telegraph was ringing and the engines were surging and roaring again.

The whales blew again and sounded again, together, the calf between the bull and the cow. They plunged off to starboard and McQuade pointed and the catcher heeled over to starboard. They ran under the ocean, great tails beating, plummeting down into the darkness as fast as they could with the calf, and getting tired now, the calf going slower now, but down down down, then they levelled out and galloped deep, then the bull swerved to the right and so the cow and the calf swerved also, the calf was beating his tail and bucking twice as hard as the cow and the bull. The calf was getting tired now and he needed to breathe but he galloped on because the bull and the cow were galloping, sticking with it because of the fear. Then he lifted his head and kicked and galloped upwards to the faraway silver surface, up up up blind for air, and the bull and the cow came up too because of the calf.

They broke the surface together and blew, and McQuade's shout rang out in the cold sunlight and the ship was heeling over and pounding down only fifty yards away now. They sounded and then ran again, in another direction deep under the sea, but the ship was heeling over after them. And the galloping and the sounding and the zig-zagging and the calf flagging and galloping on between them but flagging more now and having to go slower. And the cow and the bull were galloping slower and making their urgent noises to him, and he was trying and his spine and his tail were growing trembly now and his heart was pounding. And rushing up to the sunshine for air and blowing and sucking in air so it whistled down his blow hole, and not wanting to sound again just lie trembling on the surface and rest and blow and get his strength back, and there was the ship cutting down on them and the water cutting up high over her sharp bows, and the cry of man in the cold clear air. Desperately plunging again and running running running, then back up to the sunshine for air; and every time the ship cutting down on them closer and the spray cutting up from the sharp bows. For one hour running, diving, plummeting, swerving, galloping, gasping up for air, blowing and snorting and having to blow again and again and then heaving the great tails to drive them on, and down again, and round again, round and round slower slower and exhausted and trembling now, staggering now, and crying up out of the sea for air. And always the catcher, the clang of the telegraph and the engines surging again.

Shoot, McQuade prayed. For Godsake shoot and get it over with ...

The three whales came up and blew, close together. They were staggering now, and they were forty yards ahead, and the calf was in the middle and the bull was closest. The three black backs surged up blowing out of the sea, and the bows were swinging round on them and the spray was flying, the three black backs in a row together, and The Kid fired at the bull. There was a jolt and a bang and a puff of smoke, and the harpoon flew, swift and vicious trailing its long white tail behind. It flew high and then it began to drop, and the bull's back was going over and down, the back of the bull was almost gone now, and the harpoon was coming down. As it fell the big back of the bull went over and down, and the harpoon fell into the back of the calf. It screamed down deep into the back of the calf and then it exploded and the barbs flashed out and the white line went tight.

'*You fucking murderer,*' McQuade screamed.

'I didn't do it on purpose!' The Kid shouted.

'*You bloody murderer,*' McQuade screamed.

The calf reeled and staggered and screamed and thrashed and bucked and then he ran, screaming the scream that only McQuade could hear. He bucked and thrashed and ran, the harpoon sticking right out of his bucking back and the blood was a long red trail behind him and his guts were blown to bits inside. Down he galloped blindly under the sea screaming his pain and his terror, running running running as hard as he could and the harpoon pulling tearing screwing at his guts as he ran and the blood pumping out. Down down down he bucked and twisted deep down into the sea, screaming his pain and his terror, running running running as hard as he could and the harpoon pulling tearing screwing at his guts as he ran and the blood pumping out. Down down down he bucked and twisted deep down into the sea, then he was screaming for air and then he was turning and galloping and shaking and twisting back up to the sun, and the line pulled in tight on him, the big barbs tearing at his innards. And breaking the surface and blowing and thrashing his tail and blowing again and twisting and beating his fins trying to shake the big barbs out of his back and his guts, and his blood frothed red in the sea. The cow came plunging up beside her calf and she blew and snorted in horror and terror and fury and she shouted at him to dive, but he would not dive because he was trying to shake out the harpoon, twisting and thrashing the water red. Then he dived down kicking and fighting and twisting and the cow dived beside him, and she was crying at him and urging him to run run run, and consoling him. And then the bull came back and he swam beside them, also, shouting to the calf, and to his mate, to run run run and so they swam, the calf pulling on the line and crying out and bucking and twisting and fighting and the harpoon was wrenching at his guts, and his blood pumping out. But only for two hundred yards could he run and fight and he had to come up for air, he came up blowing and kicking and thrashing, but weaker now because of the blood that was muddying the water and the agony in his guts and he was shocked and in great fear, and the catcher heaved in on the line and dragged him still kicking a little closer. The cow came up beside him and called to him dive again. And he did dive again, he dived again and again, kicking and twisting but weaker and weaker now, and his blood pumping out fast and the pain in his guts getting worse and worse, the catcher was pulling him in a little more each time, and all the time the cow was swimming beside him and crying out to him. And so it was for half an hour, the great thrashing and fighting under the sea and then the running and the fear and then the thrashing and the fighting again at the harpoon in his guts and the long strong line, and then the having to come up for air and the thrashing on the surface and the great clouds of blood and the foam was red, and then the sounding and the running again. And all the time the cow stayed with him and blew in his blood when he blew.

And then he came up for the last time. He was kicking very slowly now and his blood spread crimson in the sea about him and he twisted about and clawed the air with his fins, and he only clapped the water with his big tail. The cow came up beside him red in her calf's blood and she blew and then the cow did something that McQuade had never seen before. She came up beside her calf, red in his blood in the sunshine, and she rolled on to her side beside him and she lifted her great fin high out of the air and she brought it down over her calf, and she tried to take the calf under her fin and pull him down under the sea with her. And again and again she lifted up her fin and tried to take him under it, thrashing beside him in the sunshine in his blood, and all the calf could do was flop his tail and blow and twist, and McQuade stood in the crow's-nest and whispered, '*Die! Die, for Godsake die! God, help that calf to die,*' and the tears were standing in his eyes.

But he took a long time dying, and all the time the cow lay beside him lifting her great fin in the air, and the winches on the catcher were pulling him slowly in. And then he gave one last big flap of his tail and one last big shudder and he blew for the last time, a jet of ruby blood gushing up out of his blow hole high and red and sick into the air and it cascaded down on to the sea and on to the cow like big red raindrops, and then he went into his flurry. He rolled over and over and over in the crimson sea flapping his fins and flapping his tail and twisting the long white line around him. And then he was still, only twitching in the crimson sea. And the cow milled and blew about him and still she rolled over on her side lifting up her great fin and trying to take the dead calf under her fin, swimming and milling red in his blood. And the winch pulled the calf slowly in and she came in with it. The Kid was at the gun and he was following the cow with the gun.

'Oh not the cow, not the cow as well for pity's sake!' McQuade screamed.

The Kid looked up at McQuade and said, 'I'm sorry, Jimmy. But she's not a cow with calf any more.'

And he took careful aim and as her fin came up over her calf's red-black body there was the big bang and there was the jolt and the flying harpoon. And the thud and the kick and the line screaming out, and the cries of the cow that only McQuade could hear. And the bull ran with her until the end.

Chapter Fourteen

Christmas Eve.

McQuade refused to speak to the Captain except in monosyllables. It was the only way to upset the Captain.

'Are you angry with me?'

'Yes, you sonofabitch.'

'I didn't mean to shoot the calf.'

No answer.

'McQuade?'

No answer.

'McQuade! Open up the door!'

'My cabin.'

'And I'm the Captain!' The Kid shouted.

'Ha!'

'Open up.'

'No.'

'Are you denying your Captain admission to your cabin?'

'Yes.'

'Why?'

No answer.

'Are you pulling your wire in there?'

McQuade stood at his mirror with a big shot of brandy in one hand and a pair of scissors in the other, trimming his beard.

'Yes.'

'You're not.'

No answer. McQuade trimming his beard.

'Are you punishing me?'

McQuade snorted softly to himself.

'I heard you snorting softly to yourself in there.'

No answer.

'*McQuade?*'

No answer.

'It's Christmas Eve.'

'Yes.'

'Peace on earth and goodwill unto all men.'

'Humpf.'

'And all that jazz.'

No response.

'All right – go and get stuffed!'

The Kid shoved himself away from the cabin door and stomped away. He turned around and stomped back.

'It's a fucking good thing for an insubordinate sonofabitch like you that you're a fucking good helmsman!' he shouted.

McQuade snipped at his beard and took a mouthful of brandy. The Kid stomped away again. He stomped back.

'And even if you are a fucking good helmsman which is debatable, it's a fucking good thing for you that I don't give a fuck about the All.England Fucking Whaling Company Limited!' he shouted. He scowled at the door then he stomped away again.

Half an hour later McQuade walked up the companionway towards the Captain's cabin and went in. The Kid was reclining in his armchair, drinking whisky.

'Ah,' The Kid said, 'The Seldom-Seen-Man!'

McQuade looked at him.

'Look,' The Kid said, sitting up straight and looking as if he had had a gutsful of this, 'I've had a gutsful of this, it was an error of judgement.'

'*It was an error of judgement because you were half drunk!*' McQuade hissed. 'You were half drunk you rotten lousy disaffiliated spoilt sonofabitch, I don't care if you slobber around tight all season and park this godawful ship on an iceberg but I do care when you drunkenly, criminally destroy the life of a six-month old Blue, you sonofabitch—'

'Don't you talk about my mother like that,' The Kid murmured, trying to assuage McQuade. 'It'll embarrass my father.'

'And then shooting the cow, you sonofabitch, why couldn't you leave the bloody cow, why didn't you go after the bull? Because it was too much trouble?'

'It wasn't an offence to shoot the cow,' The Kid said, 'after she'd lost the calf.'

'*It was an offence against Nature, you sonofabitch!*' McQuade shouted. 'Do you know how many blue whales marine scientists estimate there are left in the whole world? Fifteen thousand, that's all, in the whole rotten stinking world, and fifteen years ago there were *hundreds* of thousands of blues! And you had to shoot the cow and she was probably even pregnant again, you sonofabitch. And you committed that crime against nature *because you were drunk,* you sonofabitch!'

'All whaling is a crime against nature then,' The Kid said. 'Why the hell do you come?'

'This is the last time! This is the last time, so help me God!' He sighed and relaxed his shoulders.

'You'll come again,' The Kid said, 'because you're a bum. Like me.'

McQuade sat down.

'No,' he said, 'not like you, thank God.'

The Kid pushed the cork firmly into the whisky bottle and tossed it to McQuade. He caught it lethargically.

'Am I forgiven?'

'Only God can forgive you for that. You sonofabitch.'

'There is no God,' The Kid said tentatively relieved. 'You told me that yourself.'

'For Chrissake,' McQuade stretched for a glass. 'Oh well,' he said, 'the whales are dead whether I drink your rotten stinking whisky or not.'

'Sure,' The Kid said contritely. He added quickly, 'And I'm very sorry. Ashamed,' he said.

McQuade decided to let it go. He took a long suck of whisky and he breathed into the glass so it made a weary sound.

'Christmas,' The Kid said tentatively, 'cheers!'

'Okay. Cheers.'

'Jesus, you're a pain in the arse,' The Kid said.

McQuade took a sip of his whisky. The Kid glared at him.

'Why do lavatory chains sometimes refuse to pull?' The Kid demanded.

'I beg your pardon?' McQuade said.

'I said,' The Kid said, 'why is it that sometimes lavatory chains don't pull properly?'

McQuade stared at him.

'I mean,' The Kid continued earnestly, 'the principle upon which lavatory flushing systems work is very simple indeed. The tank fills up. When you pull the chain you are pulling on a lever which pulls out a plug and the water runs out the plughole into the lavatory and flushes it. It's an exceedingly simple and intelligible system. Now,' The Kid says, 'my question to you is: why does this simple plug-chain-pulling system so frequently refuse to work the first time you pull the chain?'

McQuade stared at him.

'I've no idea,' he said.

'You get the point?' The Kid said. 'Sometimes you have to pull it two or three times. Sometimes half a dozen times. And then at last, as if with monumental reluctance, the damn thing decides to flush. Now, why?'

McQuade shook his head.

'I mean,' The Kid said, 'either that goddam chain is connected to the goddam plug or it is not. Right?'

'Right,' McQuade said.

'Right. And logic says it is so connected and, ergo, must be continuously so connected. Right? So my question is—'

'I've no idea,' McQuade said. 'I'm not a plumber. I'm a marine biologist. Related but subtly distinct professions.'

'Good,' The Kid said. 'Very good!'

'What is?'

'I've got you talking! Dale Carnegie, see? I drew you out with my polite small talk about lavatory chains. Bound to provoke a marine biologist into thought.'

'You didn't provoke much,' McQuade said.

'I have my last penicillin jab tonight,' The Kid said brightly. 'From that vivisectionist. For my VD.'

'I hope she hurts you like hell,' McQuade said.

'Thank God it's the last,' The Kid said. 'Even though there is no God. I hate people sticking things into me.'

McQuade snorted. The Kid soldiered on.

'But what I really hate,' he said, 'is that goddam torch of hers.'

'Torch?' McQuade said, interested despite himself.

'Yes,' The Kid said, encouraged. 'Dreadful instrument. A torch, see, with a sort of tapered nozzle, the nozzle bit's as thick as a knitting needle. Light shines down the nozzle, see. And she takes the dreadful nozzle instrument,' The Kid said slowly, 'and she rams it up my chopper six inches, and shines her goddam light up into my intestines.'

'Jesus,' McQuade said, despite himself.

'Exactly,' The Kid said.

'What for?'

'To see if there is any obstruction to my urinary system. I have assured the old hitch in words of one syllable that I experience absolutely *no* obstruction in my goddam urinary system, I urinate beautifully. And I have a strong suspicion that syphilis does not *cause* obstructions in urinary systems anyway. But she rams it up all the same.'

McQuade snorted to suppress a laugh. The Kid laughed to jolly him along.

Chapter Fifteen

Christmas Eve.

The mirror in the heads was five feet above the deck and Benjamin had to stand on tiptoe to comb his hair, which is very tiring and very trying with hair like Benjamin's. Usually he used the cabin mirror, but Geradus van Wijk was there tonight and Geradus made Benjamin very nervous and very embarrassed. That bleddy *ou* Dutchman hey man. Tonight Benjamin was very excited already. When he finished combing his hair he had to jump up and down to get a full view of his face. This was not very satisfactory after a while because he needed to make sure of a lot of things. After jumping up and down a while he went off to look for a box to stand on. After a long time he found a box and he carried it back to the heads. There were men inside the heads now who would joke him about the box and the mirror so he hid round a corner in the alleyway with the box, peering round the corner watching for them to go away. When they came out they saw him peering round the corner with his box and they joked him. When they went away he carried his box into the heads tiptoeing carefully so as not to get blood on his shiny shoes and set the box up under the mirror and he very carefully climbed up on top of it. It was not a very strong box and it wobbled a lot and he had a hard time balancing on it, so he went off to find another box to place beside it. He found another box and carried it back and there were more men inside the heads again so he had to wait round the corner again. When they left he carried his box into the heads and placed it beside the other below the mirror and climbed up on top of them, one foot on each box. He stood poised and shaking on top of the two boxes and straightened up and now he was too high for the mirror. He could only see his chin. He carefully crouched down a bit until he could see his hair and examined himself carefully, his clean brown face, his clean brown ears, his elaborately combed brown hair, his clean blue shirt and his clean blue jeans with the swashbuckling belt with a dagger and a snake with red glass eyes. He rolled his eyes from side to side, and his face from side to side to get all the angles and to check them, but mostly to get them. He wished he had some beard under the soft smooth of his shaved face, but no matter how hard he shaved no beard ever came through. It was the same with his chest, he was thinking of giving up shaving his chest, it didn't do any bleddy good, man. He twisted his head as far round as he could to see what he really looked like in profile and he lost his balance. He crouched horrified wavering on the boxes with his backside stuck out waving his hands trying to catch his balance and then he fell. He fell back with a bang in the blood and got his shirt and his jeans all bloody and he bumped his head. He sat in the blood rubbing his head and got his hair all mussed up and bloody. He sat there rubbing his sore head and then some men came into the heads and saw him sitting in the blood rubbing his head with his face screwed up and they saw the boxes and they laughed and joked him. Benjamin ran out of the heads. He ran to his cabin alleyway and stopped outside his cabin and wrung his hands and cussed and lamented the condition of the back of his nice clean shirt and his nice clean jeans that he had steamed and washed and ironed especially for Miss Rhodes. What the bleddy hell was he bleddy going to do now hey man? A bleddy fine how-do-you-do now hey man! Benjamin stood in the alleyway screwing his hands, he dared not go back into his cabin and change his nice clean bloody clothes in front of Geradus van Wijk because Geradus would shout at him for making a bladdy nuisance running in and out here the whole time changing his stinking *ou* clothes. Worse, Geradus would jeer at him because his nice clothes were all messed up. Benjamin did not know what to do. Then he ducked his head down and put on his most ferocious scowl and quick as a rabbit he ran crouching into the cabin and threw open his locker and grabbed Miss Rhodes' Christmas present and turned and ran as quick as a rabbit out the cabin again before the startled Geradus could challenge him.

Benjamin Marais ran down the alleyway clutching Miss Rhodes's present to his bosom as if Geradus were chasing him, he skidded round the corner and slipped in the blood, picked himself up and scrambled on. When he was two alleyways away he stopped scurrying and he just walked as fast as he could with his head down over the present and scowling up from under his eyebrows. He clattered sideways down the hot oily steel companionway down to the factory deck and scurried along down the hot oily avenues of the huge grey fat boilers. He was scowling up from under his eyebrows to deter any of the boiler crew from stopping him and joking him. When he got near the end some Christmassy crewmen saw him and shouted at him, to stop and joke him. Benjamin scrambled up the companionway at the aft end of the factory as if demons were chasing him. He ran aft down the alleyway and skidded round the corner and nearly slipped in the blood again. At the foot of the companionway leading up to the hospital deck he stopped. He was panting. He ran his fingers through his hair so it all stood up spiky and bloody, thrust out his chest and lowered his head, re-clutched his present and started up the companionway scowling up from under his eyebrows but his legs were trembling. He got to the top and there was that smell of everything clean and white and disinfected and Benjamin nearly got the funks. He stopped, hunched and scowling and shaking. Mercifully there were no men outside the surgery to joke him. Then Benjamin screwed up his courage and lowered his head and scurried on tiptoe up the alleyway.

Then Old Ferguson's big voice boomed out behind him, 'And where d'you think you're going young man!'

Benjamin jumped.

'What are you doing in those shoes!' Old Ferguson boomed. 'Don't you know you must take off your shoes on the hospital deck?'

Benjamin stood cowed, looking down the alleyway at her.

'Well, can't you speak?'

Benjamin nodded.

'Can't you read the notice?' Old Ferguson said peevishly.

Benjamin dropped his head and waggled.

Old Ferguson mellowed. 'Aren't you little Benjamin Marais?'

Benjamin nodded miserably.

'Come here lad, what're you doing up here?'

Benjamin looked wildly up the alleyway for escape.

'Come here lad!'

Benjamin came tiptoeing.

'Take your shoes off!'

Benjamin sat down with a thump and scrambled to take his shoes off. Then he stood in front of Old Ferguson in the surgery doorway scowling nervously at her bosom.

'What about a nice cuppa tea, laddie?'

Benjamin shook his head miserably.

'A nice biscuit?'

Benjamin again shook his head miserably at Old Ferguson's bosom.

'What've you got there, laddie?'

Benjamin clutched his parcel tighter and glowered.

'Nothing man!' he croaked.

'Is it a Christmas present for somebody, laddie?'

Benjamin shook his head fiercely. Old Ferguson looked at him then she smiled a wisp of a smile and she could feel tears burn.

'All right Benjamin,' Old Ferguson smiled. 'You can go up to Sister Rhodes to give her the present, just remember your boots next time.'

Benjamin blushed, mortified, and clutched his parcel and rolled his eyes and waggled once and fled. He fled mortified up the alleyway and out. 'Benjamin! Benjamin!' Old Ferguson called him back but he kept running to the companionway and down. He ran down the bloody alleyway and into the aft heads. He threw himself into a lavatory and locked the door. He stood panting a while listening, then he turned and he sat down on the lavatory seat lid and looked at the parcel miserably. They thought he was a bleddy little fool, hey man. Now Benjamin was ashamed of his present. Miss Rhodes thinks I'm a bleddy little fool hey man also hey! Now everybody will know I wanted to give a present to Miss Rhodes an' they'll all joke me hey man. He was very ashamed of his present now. She would think it was a bleddy silly *ou* present. He sat hunched up on the lavatory seat scowling miserably into his lap at his parcel for Miss Rhodes, turning it over miserably in his hands. Maybe it was jus' a nothing hey man, a bleddy silly *ou* kid's present. He looked at the parcel hatefully, very ashamed of it and scowling hard at it. Benjamin felt very foolish, and then he turned the parcel over a few more times regretfully. He began to unwrap it miserably. He looked at it sadly lying there unwrapped in his lap. Well, he liked it all the same. It wasn't such a bad *ou* present, man. It was a big piece of baleen from a blue whale's mouth that he had sandpapered and polished up. In the top right corner he had drawn a picture of a whale and in the left top corner a picture of an iceberg and in the bottom left corner a picture of a ship and in the right a picture of a nurse who was Miss Rhodes. It was not a very good likeness of Miss Rhodes because her face was round and her eyes were round, but anyway you could see it was a nurse. And in the space between the four pictures he had written ...

to sister V Rhodes
Compliments of the season
Happy Xmas
from B Marais (Mr)

... and he had painted the hair on the baleen edge red, white and blue. He liked it. Benjamin had given it a great deal of thought and he had started many times and messed up many pieces of good baleen. And he had had to do it all in the lavatory which was the only place nobody could see him and joke him. He looked at the present sadly. It was an okay *ou* present reely hey man. He particularly liked the Mr bit and the picture of Miss Rhodes right close to his name and the Mr. He cocked his head on the side and examined the present from all angles. He liked to think of Miss Rhodes admiring it. When she got home she would hang it on the wall in her lounge and people would say '*Got* what is that?' And Miss

Rhodes would explain it proudly and say, 'Mr B Marais who is a whalerman gave it to me last Christmas hey, when we were whaling together he is a very nice man and I am going to marry him one day,' and other nice things like that, like, 'My husband Mr B Marais gave me that when we were whaling you know, now he is the famous gunner much better than Captain Child even,' and things like, 'That is a souvenir of our first whaling season, I can't go whaling with Captain B Marais these days any more because now I got all these babies, we have a baby every year you know.' Benjamin throbbed with pure pure love when he thought of Miss Rhodes and the present hanging on the wall and all their babies and he blushed with pure pure joy.

Benjamin sat on the lavatory seat glowing and then he thought of Old Sister Ferguson upstairs knowing about his present and then he was very ashamed again. He sat there a long time on the lavatory seat scowling and hating the present and blushing and feeling very ashamed and then he felt he would die of shame and foolishness. He scowled at his present like that a long time and the tears were running down his cheeks now but he was not yet crying, he was just feeling very foolish and ashamed about his hateful present. He sat crying at it a long time and then he jumped up off his lavatory seat and he bundled his present back up in the paper and he ran out of the lavatory. He ran up the alleyway aft to the poop deck and he flung open the door and he ran out on to the ice cold steel deck into the night and the snow. He ran to the freezing rail and he lifted the parcel up and he looked at it once with the tears running down his face and then he flung his present to Miss Rhodes out into the sea.

'*Voetsak,* you bleddy stupid *ou* fool,' he sobbed.

Then he turned and ran back to the lavatory. He stayed locked in the lavatory a long time. Then he crept out and crept into the Pig and sat down in a corner scowling, and his heart was breaking.

The factory was swinging. There were coloured paper decorations swaying everywhere from the deckheads, in the blood-trampled alleyways and Mess rooms and in the Pig, and red Santa Clauses pasted on doors and reindeer and holly with red berries and silver-speckled Virgins and children in stables with cows and asses and Wise Men with crooks, and, yea, even mistletoe, so you had to be careful of Beulah.

The Pig was jumping. Spike was on his homemade double bass with his buck teeth grinning and his long hair jerking and Buzzy was on the piano and Elvis was throwing his pelvis and his guitar and his head around singing Let's Rock Around The Clock Tonight. Somebody was rocking with Beulah and Izzy had changed his pants and was grinning under his old hook Jew nose as he was dancing with Mother, the bitter old bitch. Mother was too old and awful to even dress up any more but he was doing his best and looking very peeved with Izzy because Izzy couldn't rock and roll, he was just gyrating and grinning under his old hook Jew nose. McQuade was standing at the bar hatch with Charlie and Lodewijk and Smokey and singing Silent Night. Charlie and Smokey were singing it in English and McQuade and Lodewijk were singing it in Afrikaans, Stille Nag, it harmonised very well. Next door some SPEBSQA boys started singing Birth of the Blues and then they all sang The Lavender Cowboy With Only Three Hairs On His Chest. They were all crushed close in the Pig. And in the background the double bass and Elvis and the jabbering and the guffawing and the jostling and the beer-swigging and the bottles of hard tack and the smoke and the ship rolling and the decorations swaying, and the blood running off men's boots. The Kid and Victoria were at the officers' cocktail party up on the bridge, they were coming down to the Pig later. Benjamin sat squeezed up on the bench at the doorway staring at all the jolly whalermen with big eyes, forgetting to scowl. Then the hooter blew midnight up top and it was Christmas Day at the Antarctic and on the cutting deck the labourers cheered and they plodded and sucked their way red and sticky and bloody out of the mud of blood and fat through the mountains of bleeding flesh and dangling fins and tails and jawbones and hanging flesh dripping red and yellow under the bright yellow floodlights. There was a gentle fall of white light snow filtering down out of the icy night into the yellow floodlights and on to the bleeding meat. They jostled down the alleyway into the big scrubbed Big Mess with the blood running off them, and there were the long tables decked in white cloths with oranges and crackers and nuts and raisins under the swaying decorations. They trampled their blood over the Mess deck and slid their bloody oilskins on to the benches and leaned their bloody arms on to the tables and stretched out their bloody hands and grabbed the wine jugs and the beer jugs and the nuts and the raisins and the crackers. And they were noisy and singing and stamping and thumping and swigging beer and wine waiting for their dinner, and blood smeared and fingerprinted everywhere, and now the throwing of bread and the laughing and the contests of beer-swigging and then the, 'Elsie! Elsie! We want Elsie!'

And then fat Elsie came in in his big bellied apron and his chequered chef's pants and his chef's white hat high and coy on his head, beaming all over his big fat coy sweating blue-shaven jowls, and the row of messboys came behind him carrying the big tin baths piled high with whole brown roast chickens, and a roar and whistles and shouts and stamps and clapping went up from the whalermen, Good girl, Elsie! and Attaboy Elsie! and We love Elsie! and big fat strong bad-tempered bluebearded sweating Elsie who had been cussing everybody all season went all coy and cocked his big fat double-chinned blue-jowelled head and beamed flushing all round and flicked his hand coyly Get Away with you boys! and fled sweating and blushing and giggling, very happy. It was the same every season. And the bloody oil-skinned arms and blood encrusted fingers grabbed out at Elsie's roast chickens, a chicken a man, and tore the hot brown flesh apart with their bloody fingers so the steam and delicious stink of them rose above the sharp fresh stink of blood, and they shoved the brown hot meat and bones into their bloody hairy faces.

Outside in the yellow floodlights the snow fell white on to the great red meat bleeding unattended, the winches still, the derricks poised, fins and jawbones swinging with the ship through the falling snow, dripping, and the black silent sea, blackness and sometimes the looming out of the blackness a white wall of ice, sliding past. And the swinging and thumping of the Pig and the Big Mess.

The Pig was jumping. Elsie bellied into the Pig sweating and glowered around through the smoke and the thumping and the singing and the jostling. He nodded abruptly here and there without smiling and stood with his fists on his hips, looking, and then he saw him, Geradus van Wijk, standing in a corner by himself drinking. Elsie bellied through to him and stood in front of him sweating with his fists on his hips.

'Well! Didn't ye get the message then?'

'What message?' Geradus sulked, guiltily.

'The order that you were needed to help out in the Big Mess tonight!' Elsie was quivering now.

Geradus shuffled guiltily again but he looked Elsie in the eye. Elsie's hairy nostrils were dilated.

'What you think I am to serve on bladdy Coloureds—'

'Get in there!' Elsie jerked his big fat head, fists on his hips. Some of the noise had stopped so men could listen. Benjamin was craning his neck eagerly.

'How can I serve in there?' Geradus said. 'There's Coloureds in the Big Mess.'

'Jimmy!' Elsie shouted. He turned round. 'Jimmy? Come 'ere an' talk to your countryman!'

McQuade came over carrying his beer. It was quiet at their end of the Pig now.

'Talk to your countryman! His last chance. He won't help out in the Big Mess tonight.'

McQuade looked at him.

'*Waarom nie?*' he said.

'*Got!*' Geradus burst into Afrikaans. 'Half of them is Coloureds in the Big Mess, what they think I am, a kaffir or something?'

'What's he say, Jimmy?' Elsie snapped dangerously. He was looking at Geradus, not at McQuade. McQuade looked at Geradus a long moment then he said, 'Okay Elsie. Give him the works, it's the only way.'

'*Christ!*'

Elsie's big hairy hand gave Geradus a backhander across the face. He staggered sideways, men jolted and beer sloshed. Suddenly it was dead quiet in the Pig. He hit against a table and the men drew back. He leant on the table, stunned, then he looked up incredulously at Elsie standing over him, big belly and big chest heaving.

McQuade said to him quietly, 'Now go to the Big Mess.'

'You fucking *kaffirhoetie*,' Geradus whispered, and he charged big Elsie.

Elsie let him come and then he sidestepped and hit him with his ham fist on his ear. He fell and in one big fat bound Elsie was after him and grabbed him by the collar and yanked him up. Geradus was choking. Elsie let him go and then he hit him in the guts so he doubled over with a *wooof.* Then Elsie grabbed him by the back of the collar again and by the back of his pants and he ran him out of the Pig like that. The men scattered and fat Elsie ran him, pushing his head forward and lifting him forward by the back of his pants so he just had to lurch-run ahead of Elsie as fast as Elsie was pushing him, out the Pig and down the bloody alleyway towards the Big Mess. Benjamin was jumping up and down for joy.

Elsie got Geradus to the door of the Big Mess, and inside the Big Mess the big clamour of the shouting and the singing and the drinking and the gorging stopped and the gory faces turned, and Elsie held him there for a moment, bruised and winded and wild-eyed and shocked. Then Elsie gathered himself all panting and big bellied and sweating and hairy and he heaved Geradus van Wijk into the Big Mess so he pitched forward at a run and then he sprawled.

'*And you'll stay there the whole season!*' Elsie shrieked, '*and you'll scrub shithouses as well!*'

When The Kid and Miss Rhodes came down from their Bridge Christmas cocktail party, the Pig was jumping again. When Benjamin saw Miss Rhodes his Christmas was complete. Geradus, and now Miss Rhodes. He screwed and hunched himself up on the bench by the door and he clasped his hands between his knees and waggled, no scowls. Then came the whistles and the shouts and the *Hullo Vicky,* and *Yahoo darling's* and the *Watch it Vicky's* and the thumps and the whistles and the throaty growls. Miss Rhodes smiled and blushed and every man loved her. McQuade thought he loved her.

He stared at her and it felt as if his stomach turned over overjoyed to see her and it felt as if he loved her. She was blushing at the commotion and her wide brown eyes were sparkling and her wide red mouth sparkling and she wore a black heavy sweater and a wide flared tweed skirt and black wool winter stockings and high heeled shoes. She wore high heels! It was the first time McQuade or anybody had seen her in high heels. She was stunning. McQuade felt he was in love with her, and so was every man. The Kid was grinning beside her, very pleased with himself.

'Go home, Kid!' somebody shouted.

McQuade came through the crowd, smiling his most charming gmile. He felt in love and full of booze and on top form.

'Good evening, Victoria, Happy Christmas!'

'Good evening, Mr McQuade! Happy Christmas to you.'

Men were submissively making room at the bar hatch. Jock came up.

'Keep away from the mistletoe,' McQuade warned her, 'or you'll be trampled to death.'

'Happy Christmas Vicky!' Jock said possessively. 'Been up to the Bridge party? You can take off your oxygen mask!'

'Hullo James, hullo Jock.' The Kid grinned.

Jock held his arm up straight suddenly and waved his hand and a chorus broke out from his pals at the other end of the Pig, 'Go-Home-Kid!'

Everybody laughed and Jock pretended to look surprised. 'Why, fancy that!'

'Drinks,' The Kid said – he was looking embarrassed.

'Been to any good oxygen mask parties lately, then?' Jock said to The Kid – he turned to Victoria, 'I say Vicky,' he said in his mock Oxford accent, 'you do look smashing! Just the job for an oxygen mask party.'

'Vic darling!' Beulah cried – he grabbed Miss Rhodes and kissed her cheek. 'You look absolutely gorgeous! Your hair! How *do* you get the oo in your shampoo?' Everybody laughed. McQuade was relieved that Beulah had come. 'You *do* make us all look so dowdy!' Beulah explained without malice, 'Oh I *wish* I was a girl ...' He took

Victoria's elbow and said in a loud whisper, 'I'm not like the other queers you know, my dear, they're just homos; me, I actually *wish* I was a girl.'

Victoria laughed, a little shocked, everybody laughed.

'If you were a girl you'd have to have an oxygen mask Beulah!' Jock shouted dangerously.

'If I were a girl I'd have all your money, Jock!' Beulah said.

The jabbering and the singing had taken up again in the Pig.

'Tell us about the calf you shot today, Kid,' Jock shouted. He turned to Victoria, 'Captain Child shot the cutest little calf today, you know.'

'Old Jock,' The Kid grinned. McQuade was grinning too.

'Got to be a very good gunner to hit such a cute little calf,' Jock said, 'such a small target, you know.'

'She knows about the calf, Jock,' The Kid said wearily, 'she gave me hell.'

'The Professor also gave him hell,' Jock said to Victoria.

'Good for you, Mr McQuade,' Victoria said.

'James always gives me hell,' The Kid said. 'James is in league with the Mate to make my life a hell.'

'Okay,' Beulah said. 'What about this food?'

'Yes, what about this food?' Miss Rhodes said brightly, 'I'm starved.'

'No caviar at this oxygen mask party, then?' Jock said.

'Come on then,' Beulah said. 'Vicky darling, would you like to join me in the Ladies Room?'

'I took the precaution of using Our Ida's before I came down,' Miss Rhodes laughed.

'Oh very swish …'

Benjamin had left his corner of the bench and he had been peeping round men's backs at Miss Rhodes. As he turned to flee McQuade saw him.

'Benjamin!' McQuade said and he thrust out his hand. 'Happy Christmas, *Boet.*'

Benjamin froze. He stared at Miss Rhodes' bosom and he could not speak. McQuade gripped his shoulder and shook it. Beulah whispered to Miss Rhodes, 'He's standing under the misdetoe – *go* on.'

'Happy Christmas, Benjamin!' Miss Rhodes laughed and she thrust out her arms and gave the horrified Benjamin a big kiss on the cheek and the men roared *Ooooooh!* and everybody laughed. And the horrified Benjamin smelt the sweet bliss of Miss Rhodes and felt her lovely soft face against his and he was so happy he thought he would die of horror, and the roar and the whistles of the men in his ears, and he broke away from them all and he fled. And the roars and the shouts and the laughter in his horrified ears were incomprehensible bliss.

Benjamin raced all the way down to his cabin, skidding and thumping and clattering so horribly happy he did not know what to do except run. And he flung himself into his dark cabin and slammed the door shut and he stood panting and dizzy with happiness and then he began to jump up and down for joy and he rumpled up his hair and then he began to throw punches in the dark ka! ka! ka! as he did heroic stuff for Miss Rhodes, great uppercuts and hooks, and then he jumped on to his bunk and screwed himself up in a ball in the dark.

And Benjamin knew that he just had to catch the thief for Miss Rhodes.

Now Elsie's little Christmas parties, one pound a head, were no small affairs, although they were very select. They had happened every Christmas since McQuade had joined the fleet, when McQuade was only a deck potman and The Kid was only a Mate. Only about twenty people got invited to throw in a pound to Elsie's little Christmas parties, what Elsie called the Ladies and Gents of the Outfit, and if a newcomer was invited that newcomer had thereby arrived. Like Miss Rhodes had arrived. This year there were sixteen guests including Old Ferguson. Elsie and Beulah had adjacent cabins at the end of a short alleyway and they had collapsed their bunks and spread a trestle table. And loaded on the table was fare such as the Captain never saw, whole turkey and whole suckling-pig, the whole works down to crayfish cocktails and eggnog and champagne, more booze than you could shake a stick at. Nobody knew how Elsie did it. It started at midnight and went on until breakfast. It always started very formally.

'Ladies and gendemen,' The Kid said, as senior officer present, 'I ask you to rise and drink a toast to Our Sovereign Lady, The Queen.'

'The Queen,' everybody said.

It was always a very good party indeed. McQuade thought it was the best party he had ever attended, he was very happy on account of Miss Rhodes, she made him happy and strong and vibrant. The guests milled between the two cabins and overflowed out into the alleyway eating and drinking and singing and talking and laughing above the music of Elsie's gramophone, and McQuade took Miss Rhodes away from The Kid and Jock and danced with her in the alleyway.

And he felt her soft and sweet-smelling in his arms and it seemed the happiest thing in the whole world and he whispered to her, 'Victoria, I love you.'

And she said softly, 'That's very unstable of you, James.'

Chapter Sixteen

It was dawning by the time McQuade and The Kid were smacking in and out of glinting red and white icebergs, looking for their ship. With Izzy singing hymns in the stern of the speedboat and Beulah standing with his long blond wig flying holding his gorgeous cocktail hat on his head and singing Aye Aye Cathusalem, The Harlot of Jerusalem. Nobody was sure how Izzy and Beulah got in on the act.

The Kid was driving and McQuade was swigging whisky and singing Good King Wenceslas. Then The Kid was chasing whales, screaming after them at top throttle and swooping down on the startled blowing beasts seven times the size of the boat and then veering aside at top throttle so their spray flew high across the whales' blows and the huge startled tails rising high above them, and McQuade was shouting *For Chrissake you crazy bastard* and The Kid shouting with glee into the icy wind *See how easy it is!* Beulah was making snowballs and throwing them at the whales and Izzy was sitting in the stern hanging on for grim death and saying he wanted to go home. Then they were parked against an iceberg and sitting in a row on the ice having a littie rest and then McQuade discovered the whisky bottle was empty, then they were boarding catcher Number Nine to ask the way to the Number Fourteen and to bum a bottle of whisky off the Captain to sustain them till they got to wherever the hell that sonofabitch of a Mate had hidden the Fourteen in an effort to kill them all, the rotten lousy stinking ballaching pain in the ass of a sonofabitch. The Captain of the Nine reluctantly giving them all a drink and telling Izzy to for Chrissake stop singing hymns on his bridge, Christmas carols okay but no more hymns for Chrissake, and telling Beulah to please stop flirting with the goddam helmsman it was a disgrace at Christmas time for Chrissake and would McQuade and The Kid please sing a little softer and did they know there was a general emergency call out to all ships to look for them on account of they had been seen leaving the factory and the Old Man was demanding that Beulah bring his breakfast and the Mate of the Fourteen was complaining bitterly that he had been on watch for twelve solid hours and where was the Captain? The Kid was saying the Mate could go and get stuffed and Beulah was saying the Old Man and his breakfast could both go and get stuffed and McQuade saying that the whole damn All England Whaling Effing Company could go and get stuffed and Izzy saying that everybody could go and get stuffed he wanted to go home. And McQuade jollying the Captain into giving them all another drink and The Kid staggering into the radio room and sending a long rude message to his Mate telling him amongst other things that McQuade said he could go and get stuffed and sending eleven long and expensive cables to eleven London birds telling them all that certain rude things were going to happen to them on his return and forbidding the radio operator on pain of keelhauling to tell the Old Man of the factory where they were. And The Kid bullying the Captain into lending them the bottle of whisky to sustain them on the long hazardous arduous and perilous search for the Fourteen and the four of them clambering down into the speedboat and The Kid ordering McQuade to drive because he was too drunk to sing and Beulah blowing kisses to everybody and Izzy putting the One Hundredth and twenty-first psalm to song, which is a difficult psalm to sing no matter what beat you try. And everybody waving and cheering and McQuade roaring the boat off in the direction the radio officer had told him the Fourteen lay, the bows smack-smacking and the spray fly-flying and Beulah's wig blowing and The Kid sucking and passing the whisky bottle and them all singing The West Virginee Skies, except Izzy. And McQuade took the boat in a wide whisky sweep round an iceberg and *suddenly there were whales all over the goddam place blowing the living shit out of them.* Whales to the left of them whales to the right of them whales in front of them blowing and thundering, and sperm whales at that with their great perpendicular battering-ram foreheads and their huge ten foot jaws with great crescent teeth and their huge fluked tails that they liked to flatten whale boats with and their huge high stinking blows filling the air and drowning the sun and making stinking rainbows raining down on them and the giant tails high in the air. And everybody shouting at once except Izzy who blinked at the spectacle of heaving spouting whale flesh all about him open-mouthed with deep interest and said 'Gosh, whales, gee ...' Beulah was screaming and trying to grab the wheel and McQuade was shouting '*Leggo you stupid bitch!*' and trying to swing out of the pod and then mountains of back rearing up in front. And spinning the wheel back and all falling over and the stench of whale blow beating McQuade's face and a giant tail rearing up high in front. And spinning the wheel back and Beulah screaming and grabbing at the wheel again and McQuade swiping Beulah backwards on to his bum gargling and clutching his solar plexus, and The Kid shouting and McQuade swinging the wheel around in a tight arc trying to get the hell out of it, and Izzy holding tight in the whales flashing about him and saying '*Gosh, whales, gee ...*' To left the long ragged peninsula of ice cutting them off and to right the big wing of ice floe chopping and dead ahead six big sperm whales blowing and McQuade screaming *Chrissake why aren't they scattering*, and spinning the wheel tight round. And suddenly there was The Kid standing brandishing a harpoon and shouting *Yahoo!* and McQuade screamed *You crazy bastard!* And The Kid hurled the harpoon.

'Jesus Christ!' McQuade screamed.

The rest was very confused. McQuade sobered up very fast but it was all terribly confused. The Kid was jumping up and down and shouting *I got him! I got him by Christ!* The nylon rope was whistling out and McQuade was clutching the wheel screaming curses at The Kid and looking wildly for any sharp instrument to hack the line. Nothing, no axe, no knife, cursing the axe, knife, The Kid, the whale, Beulah, the sea the ice the sky the heavens Jesus Christ. Screaming after the tight white line, half dragged by the beast with the ten foot jaws half driven by the Johnson, the spray flying into his contorted face and the horizon swinging and the bows going smack smack smack and The Kid jumping up and down and Beulah sobbing blood. White ice loomed crazily and he spun the wheel and there was more ice and he was spinning the wheel back, the boat swinging and keeling and more ice and icebergs. And suddenly the line was going slack and The Kid was whooping as he wound on the hand winch and suddenly the beast was surfacing in a great eruption of scarred battering-ram head flashing in the sun. McQuade swung the boat wildly round the huge beast's tail coming up higher and higher into the air high above McQuade's terrified head. And swinging the boat jerking and jolting and McQuade screaming *Give him line you sonofabitch*. The winch handle was screaming and Beulah was holding his bloodied nose stupidly, the winch handle had broken Beulah's nose all over again, and then they were tearing off over the ocean again in and out of ice, and the horizon was swinging crazily and the bows going smack smack and the spray flying. And then the line was streaking up up up in the water and the huge angry mass of muscle was coming up up up to the surface right before McQuade's terrified eyes.

'*Give out the line!*' he screamed. And there was the great seething rush of water heaving apart and the furious beast came through and blew and reared his great angry head right up on top of the churning water, and he pivoted on his great belly, his huge yellow white jaws agape, and McQuade screamed and swung the boat round him.

And the great sperm swished his great tail in the sunlight and he pivoted following the boat round and round, and he blew short angry snorts of rage. With the harpoon buried in the back of his head and the blood running red down his big black back and his huge head jerking so he could see them with his small fierce eye on the churning frothing water-line. And the great fluked tail suddenly bent upwards and the great fifty foot spine humped itself and he gave one big angry blow and the tail crashed down and he charged. McQuade's second last terrified image of him was the huge scarred perpendicular head gushing steam galloping down on them as he spun the wheel frantically trying to get the hell out of his way. Then the sickened screaming crashing flying jolt as he crashed the living shit out of them. Flying backwards and sideways and upside down through the air in all directions, icebergs and horizons sideways and upside down all over the place and screaming horrifying snorting gnashing fifty foot beast with ten foot jaws and eight foot flukes gnashing water and teeth sideways and upside down all over the place. And the stunning explosive shock of deep bitter ice water knocking them stupid and shocked and gasping and numb like a kick in the guts all over the place. The kick in the guts of the roaring ice water, stars, fighting and kicking to get right way up and back to God's air, kicked breathless by the icy sea and beating frantically.

McQuade broke surface beating wildly snorting salt ice water and a choked sickened scream of terror in his throat: he saw the great flukes high and mighty in the sky above him and whistling down with a crack like thunder and then the great head high flashing huge and wet and scarred and terrible and bloody in the sunshine, giant yellow and pink and white jaws snapping heavenwards into stinking wrinkled upper sockets; the last thing McQuade's terrified eyes took in as his boots dragged him under was Beulah's wig flashing sodden gold in the sunlight across those white crescent teeth.

McQuade was dragged under by his boots with half a gasp of air and ice sea water in his nostrils and a gargle of terror in his throat, he bunched himself under the sea and yanked and wrestled off one boot and let it drop, he kicked and clawed back to the surface for air and gasped and sank again and clawed at the other boot, and then he was thrashing wildly on the surface again. The beast was gone and there was no boat.

'*Beulah!*' he shouted wildly. '*Beulah!*'

'Here I am Jimmy ducky darling honey bunch,' the gay falsetto calling him from all around, 'Here I am Jimmy you old sonofabitch,' the long elegant cigarette holder pointer and the bloody nose wrinkled at him.

'Beulah!' McQuade bellowed and he thrashed spinning round and round in the water looking for him, 'Where's Beulah!'

But there was no Beulah, only Izzy and The Kid clinging to a piece of ice flow and Izzy weeping and saying he wanted to go home and The Kid was shouting at him 'Here comes the ship,' and the Fourteen was cutting down on them round the bergs. And there was Beulah clawing up on the ice.

The last thing McQuade remembered before he passed out was drinking the hot whisky and calling The Kid a sonofabitch. Then he dreamed the Mate was shaking him and calling him a sonofabitch and saying that he was demoted to deck labourer on the factory and he woke up and the Mate *was* shaking him and calling him a sonofabitch and telling him he had been demoted to deck labourer on the factory.

'Go'n get stuffed,' McQuade said and he went back to sleep.

Part Four

Chapter Seventeen

I slept the whole of Christmas day in the hospital and in the evening when I woke up I felt bad but I didn't know whether it was just all hangover or the shock of the ice as well. Old Ferguson was on duty and she came in and gave me hell for gadding about with The Kid in that damn speedboat, I deserved everything I had coming to me.

'What've I got coming to me?' I wanted a beer very badly, a hair of the dog.

'Fined a day's wages and demoted to deck labourer!' Old Fergie snapped.

'Can I have a beer, Fergie?'

'Certainly not! This is a hospital you know!'

'It's medicinal, Fergie.'

'And don't call me Fergie, Matron to you! Booze is your trouble, young man! If you hadn't been full to the eyeballs you wouldn't have fallen in the sea. Here's your dinner.'

'If I hadn't been full I would have frozen to death, Fergie. And I didn't harpoon the bloody whale, that bastard Kid did.'

'You and that Kid!' Old Fergie glared at me and then she had to look away to stop herself smiling. She got to the door and shook her big finger at me. 'You and that Kid! I tell you, it's the best thing that ever happened that you two are separated!'

She stomped out before I could press again for a beer.

I ate the dinner, then lay there feeling hungover. I was the only person in the hospital. Must have been a good Christmas, most Christmasses some Coloured got himself stabbed by another Coloured in a nice Christmas brawl or somebody fell down somewhere or something. It was still broad daylight outside the porthole but I reckoned it must be evening. I wondered what had happened to The Kid and Izzy and Beulah. I felt very bad and I wanted a beer badly, a cold one. I wondered when Victoria would come on duty. How long would I be in hospital? If they wanted to keep me here the rest of the season it was okay by me. Then I felt very sleepy again and I don't know how long I lay there half asleep, and then Victoria was standing over me.

'Hullo, Vicky,' I said.

'Good evening, Mr McQuade,' she smiled. She looked very beautiful in the dim daylight looking down at me.

'Why the hell can't you call me James?'

'I never mix business with pleasure, Mr McQuade,' she smiled.

What the hell does that mean, I thought.

'Isn't it a pleasure nursing me?' I said.

'That remains to be seen, Mr McQuade – how do you feel?'

'Like death. Call me James.'

'Are you hungry?'

'James.'

All right, Mr McQuade: *James*. Are you hungry?'

'I sorely need a beer.'

She smiled.

'That's against the rules.'

'Miss Rhodes,' I said, 'if you have one iota of the Florence Nightingale in you you will bring this dying man a beer – two beers.'

She grinned at me.

'All right. I suppose a beer won't hurt you. But promise you won't tell Fergie?'

'Miss Rhodes,' I said, 'I cross my heart.'

She walked out of the ward. I watched her walk. She was lovely to watch move, her long legs and straight back. I lay there thinking about Vicky Rhodes; I was very happy I was in hospital. She came back in one minute with one small bottle of beer and a glass, the bottle was frosted cold.

'This is very unprofessional of me,' she said, 'but I know you're all right – Fergie and I keep our beers in the surgery fridge.'

For The Kid and Jock, I thought.

'Thanks Victoria, I'll replace them,' I said.

'Nonsense,' she said.

I sat up and she puffed up the pillow behind me.

'Where did I get the pyjamas from?' I asked. 'I don't own pyjamas.'

'Hospital issue,' she said. '*Sip* that, don't gulp it.'

It went down like a mountain brook.

'God that's good!' I felt much stronger already.

'Sip it,' Victoria said. She sat down by the bed. I could feel the balm of the beer strengthening my shoulders and hands.

'What happened to The Kid and Izzy and Beulah?'

'They're all right. They were sent back to their own bunks, you're the only privileged patient.'

'How come?'

'They haven't allotted you a bunk yet and Old Fergie said she'd have you. She likes you.'

'Well!'

'You also had one pupil bigger than the other, could be concussion.'

'Aha! How long's that good for?'

'Back to work tomorrow, Mr McQuade.'

'Oh Christ.'

I was feeling much better and my mouth felt clean as if the beer had corroded the muck out of it. She smiled at me as I drank it and I wanted her very much. I put the beer down deliberately and then I stretched out and put my hand on hers. She left her hand where it was but she did not turn it over to hold mine, she just did nothing when I squeezed her hand. She was looking at the deck steadily.

'Vicky,' I said and she turned her head and looked at me and I smiled at her and then she smiled back. I felt at a disadvantage sitting up in bed. I tried to pull her to me and she pulled her hand free.

'No,' she said. She stood up. 'I must go,' she said calmly. 'I've got work to do. Go to sleep.'

'How the hell can I sleep?' I said.

But she turned and smiled briskly and walked out of the ward.

I lay there a long time, thinking, I tried to laugh it off, not to think about it, but I could not laugh it off. I felt uncomfortable that she had rejected me, even that little. I had not thought of whether she had Coloured blood for a long time, but now I wondered again because I was angry. But I wanted her, oh I wanted her all right, I remembered telling her last night I loved her and I felt angry and foolish and I knew I didn't love her, but wanted her. I wanted her so much it felt as if I loved her. After a long time I went to sleep. I woke up once with somebody holding my eyelids open and a bright light very close to my eyes and when I focused I saw it was Miss Rhodes holding a small torch in her teeth and shining it into my eyes to check the relative sizes of my pupils, which is a hell of a way to be wakened by the woman you've been trying to make love to unsuccessfully. She said, 'You're all right, Mr McQuade,' and I tried to take her hand and detain her but she laughed softly and squeezed my hand once briskly and she walked out of the ward. I lay there thinking about the brisk woman sound of her clean white uniform, and after a while I went back to sleep.

Chapter Eighteen

Next morning Old Ferguson got me up and dressed as if I were a malingerer, as if it had been my idea that I spend Christmas day in her hospital. Miss Rhodes was off duty, the night was like a dream. Old Ferguson took me before the doctor who gave me the once over and declared me fit. He was German.

'And may I a suggestion make?' he said.

'Yes?'

'No schnapps today. Beer a little if you want but no schnapps.'

'Who's got schnapps on this ship?' I asked, interested.

'You know what the doctor means, young man!' Old Fergie snapped.

Then I had to go up to the bridge to report to the Mate of the factory. The Mate was not looking very clever either, he also had had a good Christmas. I had thought I was going to have a tough time, and I could not have cared less. I was glad I was on the factory. Quite apart from Miss Rhodes. That goddam Fourteen going up and down and The Kid had begun to get on my nerves. It was about time that Kid grew up. That was my attitude. The Mate tried to look fierce and he just looked tired and told me that The Kid and I had had it coming to us, don't think our goings on had not been noted, not just this season but seasons past, and he told me to go and sleep it off and look alive tonight in the nightshift. It seemed everybody was telling me to go to sleep. I said yes sir no sir three bags full sir, like you do to Mates, and that seemed to settle him. I think he then went off to sleep it off. I was feeling good, brilliant sunshine out of a bright blue sky on to a dark blue sea and the icebergs were sparkling white all about and the ships' rigging and superstructures sparkled white and the air was clean and I had been asleep a long time and I had no hangover. And the factory was big and spacious and steady as a rock and there wasn't a catcher in sight. It all felt very good, even apart from Miss Rhodes. When I thought about her I felt happier, as if something delicious was going to happen in the cold beautiful bright Antarctic summer sun. I clattered down from the bridge to the office of the Chief Steward, to find out which cabin I was in. The Chief Steward looked like the Mate and he was drinking a beer by himself, sitting in a lump in his office. He offered me a beer as if he were offering me aspirin, he presumed I was feeling worse than he. I had a beer with him cheerfully and he winced every time I spoke. He told me that he and the Mate had really tied one on yesterday, oh boy. He shook his head when he said Oh boy, very softly. The beer was making me feel very good, I felt strong and good and happy. When he didn't offer me another I went down to my cabin. My suitcase and books were already there. I didn't mind who I shared a cabin with as long as there was one other European and as long as he was neither Izzy Isaacson nor a queer. I would have preferred to have all Europeans in my cabin but that was too much to hope for. Coloureds are all right, except you usually have nothing in common and they often smell because they don't shower every day. But then a lot of those Limey bastards were the same about bathing. But Coloureds sweat more. I put my gear in the empty locker and then I went along to Elsie's cabin. Elsie was lying in his frilly nightie in bed, reading.

'Hullo Professor,' Elsie said dredly.

'Hullo Elsie. Heard the good news about me being demoted?'

'Yeah, luv,' Elsie said. Elsie's hairiness was very black against the green nylon nightie. 'How're Beulah and Izzy?'

'Beulah's nose is in plaster again, poor girl. Izzy's okay.'

'Poor Beulah's having bad luck with that nose.'

'The Kid,' said Elsie tiredly. 'Isn't he a sonofabitch?'

'They've taken his command away, you know,' Elsie said.

'Yes, but he's still gunner, so he's still the big-shot on the ship.'

'Still the big-shot in the fleet,' Elsie said, 'that Kid.'

'A good gunner gets away with murder,' I said.

'Want a beer?' Elsie said.

'I'm on my way to get some breakfast,' I said. 'Okay.'

The beers were along the outboard bulkhead, keeping cold against the steel.

'That was a helluva good party, Elsie,' I said.

'You're welcome, darling. I saw you whisper sweet nothings in Vicky's ear. She fancies you.'

'I'm not so sure.' It made me happy to hear him say it.

'Oh, Elsie can tell. You better watch out for Jock, he gets nasty.'

'That bastard better behave himself. All's fair in love and war.'

'Now James,' Elsie said. 'You see what a woman does? You three were always such friends, now see what a woman does?'

I took a swallow of beer. It was good and cold and I was happy.

'Jock's all right.'

'Sure he is, but he's a peasant, just you behave yourself,' Elsie said. 'Why you bastards must get all hot and bothered over a girl I just do not know, when there's all us nice boys available. Aren't I beautiful enough or something?'

We had a good laugh. When I finished the beer I left Elsie to sleep and I went to the galley and I eventually persuaded the dayshift third cook to fry me some eggs. Why are cooks always such bad-tempered bastards? Even Elsie. Out of his galley he was a nice homosexual, show him his chef's cap and he became a perspiring culinary Captain Bligh. The nightshift had finished their supper and the messboys were scrubbing down. I ate the eggs and bacon in the Big Mess and some of the dayshifters lounged around. Everybody had heard about The Kid harpooning the whale and everybody thought it was a grand joke. The rumour was that we had gone looking for whales and that I had chased the whale and then The Kid harpooned it. Anyway it was a good story. Then I went back down to my cabin and to the heads and brushed my teeth very carefully and combed my hair. Then I went aft through the factory deck and then up to the hospital deck and down the alleyway to Miss Rhodes' cabin. I knocked and she opened the door.

'Good morning.'

'Good evening,' she said. 'This is my evening now.'

'Of course, mine too. Shall we go for a walk, it's such a lovely day.'

She considered, surprised. 'Yes, *let's* go for a walk!'

'We can walk up and down the lifeboat deck.'

'I'll have to change out of my uniform then, I haven't got my passion killers on ...'

'Passion killers?'

'My thick woollen bloomers,' she laughed, 'you should see them, put any man off for life!'

'Want to bet?'

She laughed again.

'Would you mind waiting outside while I change?'

I walked up and down the alleyway in my socks while I waited. She's a strange one, I thought, sometimes she talks like an easy lay. Maybe it's just that she's natural. I was very happy as I waited, I had thought she would be cool after last night. The door opened and she came out smiling in her jeans and heavy sweater and her snowboots, she had a woollen cap on her head which she could tie under her chin to keep her ears warm.

'You look lovely,' I said.

'Thank you, Mr McQuade.'

I wished that she would drop the Mr McQuade. 'Have you got your passion killers on under all that?'

'No, with this lot I can afford my scanty-panties!' she grinned. I didn't know what to think.

We walked down the alleyways in silence. Both of us were suddenly self-conscious. I put my boots on and then we went out the for'ard hatch on to the lifeboat deck. As I opened the door the noise of the cutting deck below flooded in, and the cold, and a breeze blew her hair. She smiled at me as I held the door open for her. Some flenzers down below on the skin deck saw us and a wolf call went up and then all the men took up the call. She blushed.

'You must get rather tired of that,' I said.

She smiled. 'I'm getting used to it. Sometimes I like it.' Then she grinned. 'It's nice to be appreciated – even if it's only lust!'

We turned the corner and the cutting deck was out of sight.

'You don't mind being lusted after?'

'Few women do, Mr McQuade, as long as they can choose their ultimate company themselves.'

I thought that was good: ultimate company.

'It is a novel experience,' she grinned, 'being the local masturbatory image for several hundred men!'

I wondered if I had heard right.

'I exaggerate, of course,' she laughed.

We were walking down the deck under the lifeboats.

'Isn't it a lovely day,' she said. Her cheeks were pink from the cold and she looked so good and fresh. She smiled at me.

'Yes, it is.'

'Look at that!' There was a big iceberg with a long flat top and it had a big hole right through it, so you could see the sea sparkling behind it.

'It's like The Hole in the Wall,' I said. 'That's a place on the Wild Coast, about a thousand miles from Cape Town, the Transkei Coast. It's all native reserve, it's the most beautiful part of Africa I've ever seen. Europeans aren't allowed to live there. It's absolutely wild and unspoilt.'

We came to the after rail and leant against it, looking at the iceberg.

'And at one spot there's a big rock island that shape, with a hole through it. It's called Hole in the Wall. The country,' I said, 'is green rolling hills and valleys and sub-tropical jungle, it's lovely. The Wild Coast is about six hundred miles long.'

'It sounds lovely.'

'My father had a mud and thatch cottage at one place, we used to go there for holidays. Whites can only build ron-davel-type cottages costing less than two hundred pounds and they can only spend short holidays there because it's a native reservation. And the fishing! And the natives are nice people. They are Red Blankets and Blue Blankets, depending on what part of the coast you go to. They wear the blankets instead of clothing. You don't see any of that in the Cape. They're very primitive, but they're very pleasant friendly people.'

'I'd love to see it. I've hardly been out of Cape Town all my life. My father was on the Railways there. He was only a guard,' she said.

'Oh yes.' I wanted her to talk about herself. But when somebody says their father was only a guard on the Railways you hesitate to ask more.

'Oh look!' she cried delighted, pointing, 'a *seal!*'

A big piece of ice was floating by and there was a big seal on it. He had his nose stuck in a hole in the ice, looking for something and then he lifted his head to look at us and he sniffed the air.

'Oh isn't he *lovely!*' She suddenly turned to me. 'Tell me something about yourself.' We stayed on the lifeboat deck a long time, leaning over the rails and talking, and walking up and down a bit. There were half a dozen whales in tow behind the factory, bloated striped bellies up. It was nice on the lifeboat deck, nobody came up there. I was very happy to be with Victoria Rhodes on the lifeboat deck, and she seemed happy too, and it was very nice talking about myself. I did not try to touch her.

After a long time she said, 'Come and have some coffee. Then I'm afraid I must go to bed, it's way past my bedtime,' she said.

We went back to her cabin. There was a small queue of men outside the surgery and they stared at us. They didn't dare make a noise in Old Ferguson's alleyway. It was nice and cosy in Victoria's cabin.

'I don't think those boys would bet much on my virginity,' she said.

'I don't suppose so.' I really didn't know which way to bet myself.

It was a very good little cabin. She had put her own cover on the bed and a few ornaments around. Under her mirror was her hairbrush and hairclips and face-cream and stuff. It smelt good. She had a nylon dressing gown hanging behind the door, and a thick towelling dressing gown also. There was a door leading off.

'What's through there?'

'My shower and lav. Look inside if you want.'

It was a tiny shower booth with a lavatory beside it. There was a plastic shower cap hanging on the door.

'Brought your own pink toilet paper, I see.'

'Nothing but the best,' she laughed. 'Actually I got it from the Chief Steward.'

'The officers get pink toilet paper? Why the hell don't we get pink toilet paper?' I grumbled. 'It's enough to turn you Commie.'

She thought that was very funny.

I sat on the chair and drank the coffee, she sat on the edge of her bunk. I spent a lot of time screwing up the courage. It's awkward when you're both sitting down separately. It must needs be a very deliberate movement. Then I put down my cup and I got up and went and sat down beside her on the bunk. She sat rigid, and stared in front of her.

'Vicky,' I said and I put my arm around her. She sat rigid. I could feel myself trembling, it was nerves and the thrill of feeling her. She did not yield.

'Victoria?' I said and I put my hand to her chin and tried to turn her face to me.

'No,' she said.

I put my hand behind her neck and tried to bring her to me to kiss her. Then suddenly there was a jerk and a crack and that blinding flash again. Jesus, all right Miss Victoria Bloody Rhodes, that's your lot, mate!

'Jesus!' I said. 'You're a great one for that aren't you!'

She was standing up. She looked angry and she had her hands on her hips.

'And I'm getting bloody tired of you thinking you can walk in here and tumble me into a bunk, Mr McQuade! I know what you think of me!'

'What do I think of you for Chrissake?'

'You think I'm a Coloured and therefore an easy tumble and you think you're going to *use* me, you think you're quite safe because when we get back to South Africa you won't be able to have anything to do with me!'

'I don't think you're Coloured, for Chrissake!'

'Yes, you do, Captain Child told me!'

The *bastard,* I thought.

'And anyway I could see what you thought the moment we first met, I've lived in South Africa a long time!'

'Did Captain Child also tell you that I withdrew my opinion and that anyway it doesn't matter to me what bloody colour you are technically?'

'Oh it doesn't matter to you! Oh doesn't it just! I've met your kind, Mr McQuade, South Africa has plenty of liberals to whom colour doesn't matter! It matters all right, it doesn't matter in their flowery speeches but it matters all right when it comes down to brass tacks. It matters in restaurants and cinemas and taking a girl out in public, they'd rather die than stick their white necks out in public—'

'Well if it's any damn consolation to you I *don't* think you're Coloured!'

'Well, if it's any damn consolation to you, I'm *not!*'

'Good!' I said. 'What are you so hot and bothered about then?' She stopped looking so angry.

'At least I don't think I am. I didn't really worry until this damn Registration of People thing came in, then the witch hunts started. Since then everybody's looked at me sideways. There's a pretty girl, they think, but *hasn't* she got a touch of the tarbrush?'

'Don't be silly.'

'Oh yes they do! I've seen it. Oh, it's all right in summer!' she laughed brittly, 'when everybody's tanned, but in winter? Oh dear dear! She *is* a bit swarthy, my dear, better not take a chance. Bus conductors and cinema cashiers look at you sideways and then decide to give you the benefit of the doubt. Oh, it's *charming* in winter!'

'Victoria,' I said and she stepped back.

'And shall I tell you something, Mr McQuade?'

'Yes.'

'It's a terrible sin, but you know deep down in here,' she tapped her breast, 'I think I do have a teeny weeny bit of Malay in me, isn't that terrible?'

'That's not terrible.'

'Oh it's so terribly *terribly* terrible. It's so non-*u*, Mr McQuade, and it's got such inconvenient consequences, like maybe the bus conductor will tell you to go sit upstairs and maybe the cinema cashier will say sorry Europeans Only and maybe one day the Housing people will come and say sorry, but you've got to go and live in District Six, we've just decided—'

'Nobody's going to say that to you, Victoria.'

'We hope not, Mr McQuade, oh we *do* hope not. How frightfully non-u to have it official.'

'You said you didn't think you were,' I said.

'Just a sneaky doubt, Mr McQuade. With all those nice liberals being so frightfully nice and liberal, don't you know, and all those nice bus conductors making their agonisingly important little decisions every day, it must be hell being a bus conductor with all those decisions all day long, they really *should* be paid more.'

She looked at me.

'And my suntan does survive the winter rather too well to be … sociable?'

'Vicky?' I said.

'What?'

'You're beautiful. You've got beautiful skin.'

'I'm a wow in summer,' she said. 'But in winter?'

I smiled at her.

'Look,' I said. 'You haven't got any Coloured blood in you, I can see that. You've got a lovely complexion.'

'Have I? Say that again.'

'You're beautiful,' I said. She smiled at me.

'You're a nice man, Mr McQuade. I'm sorry I slapped you.'

'That's all right,' I lied.

'No it isn't, you can kiss me now if you still want to.' I looked at her. She was very beautiful. 'Do you still want to?'

'Yes,' I said. I stood up in front of her. I was trembling again. I had wanted her so much, thought about her so much I was nervous and trembling. I kissed her and she kept her eyes open at first and then she shivered and closed her eyes and yielded a littie. I was shaking as I kissed her. I could feel my mouth and breath trembling. She felt blissful, soft and woman and beautiful and it felt so urgent. She was not trembling and she did not have her arms around me, and then I put my arms right round her and then she put her arms right around me and yielded and kissed me hard. I tried to put my tongue in her mouth, then she broke the kiss but still clung to me.

'Oh darling,' she said, 'you won't love me and leave me will you?'

Christ! I thought. But I was still shaking from wanting her.

'I won't love you and leave you Vicky,' and I wanted her so much I meant it.

'You won't abandon me when we get back to South Africa? You won't be ashamed of me?'

'Oh Vicky,' I said.

'You do love me, don't you, you did say the other night you loved me?'

Christ, I thought, this means trouble, McQuade; but I wanted her so much I didn't care.

'Yes, I do love you,' I said.

'Oh darling,' she said, she held me tight, she felt marvellous against me. 'I've liked you too, that's why I was such a bitch to you, because I thought you'd love me and leave me. Never mind darling, I won't be a bitch any more, I'll be good to you.'

I was very happy, and shaking, I didn't care what bloody colour she was I wanted this beautiful woman so much. Her breasts felt so marvellous against me. 'Vicky,' I said and I put my hand on her beautiful breasts and she kissed me again and she let me keep my hand there a moment, and it was absolute bliss, then she pushed it gently away.

'Not tonight darling, please, I'll be good to you darling, don't you worry, but not tonight.'

She stroked my face.

'Poor boy, I can feel you, how badly you want me but not tonight darling, not the very first night.'

'It's not the first night,' I said.

'No, but it is really. I know it's awful to send you away like this but please understand. I will soon, darling, soon soon, if you still want me.'

I didn't care what kind of trouble I was getting myself into.

'Poor boy,' she smiled. 'You're a good boy, James. There, please go now, there's a good boy. And you will come back and see me tomorrow?'

'Of course,' I said.

'That's good. You *are* good to me. You see? Good night darling, sleep tight. And keep warm on that deck.'

'All right. Good night, Vicky.'

'Good night,' she kissed me briefly and smiled and patted my face. 'Sleep tight, you are good to me.'

It seemed to me I was out of her cabin before I knew it. Maybe, I thought, maybe I *am* a good boy. Christ! I was happy as I walked back for'ard through the factory to my cabin. I wanted to laugh and shout, I felt I was in love with a crazy beautiful girl. She was crazy, no doubt about it, and I was in love with her.

Chapter Nineteen

When I woke it did not seem such a good idea. When I first woke up, at my lowest ebb, I thought: Oh Christ, you're in trouble again, McQuade. I thought: she's a little crazy, McQuade but she's genuine and you're in trouble, you can't love and leave a girl like that, you won't be able to get rid of her very easily when you get home, she's the clinging type. I like the clinging type, but you know what kind of trouble you get into. And what's more, I think she's dead right, I think she is a bit Malay, and you know what that means. That's really trouble. She had the good sense to give you a chance to get out of it, so take it, don't go back to her, that's the only sensible and honourable thing to do. Go and masturbate and it will all seem different afterwards, you'll get it in perspective. But I lay in my bunk smoking a cigarette and I woke up properly and I knew that I was looking forward very much to seeing Victoria Rhodes tonight and I knew I would go to her and I thought: what the hell, you're lucky. You're a lucky bastard.

I finished my cigarette and I got up, although it was early. The cabin was dark, for it was inboard, and my cabin mates were still asleep. I did not fancy meeting them for the first time first thing in the morning. Christ, I thought, I hate shipboard life, living squashed up with a bunch of sweating, snoring, farting bastards, it's time I quit. It was better on the catcher, she rolled and pitched but at least she was airy and I had a cabin to myself. It was very warm in the cabin, I had been sleeping naked under a sheet. I put on my shoes and a pair of shorts and got my toothbrush and towel. Outside in the alleyway there was the blood. Not much, but sticky. It also stank, the steamy gravy smell from the factory deck billowing up the alleyway. There must be plenty of whales in tow. Why couldn't I have been demoted when there were no whales? The bulkheads of the heads were vibrating hard, and the deck was very sticky with blood. I washed and brushed my teeth and I thought: another four months of this. While I was brushing my teeth a potman came in. He was a Coloured I did not know, but he seemed to know I was a South African.

'*Avend,*' he said.

He stood at the urinal and the blood shone in streams down his oilskin trousers and ran off his spiked boots on to the deck.

'*Goeie avend,*' I said. I had forgotten it was evening. '*Veel walvis bo?*' Many whales above?

'Plenty.' He grinned. If there's one thing a whalerman doesn't mind it's whales. 'We're working like kaffirs,' he said.

It wasn't that he had a sense of humour. Coloureds don't have much time for natives, Kaffirs.

'How many?'

'They shot twenty-four today, and the sun has not gone under yet so perhaps they will get more.'

He was grinning.

'Hell,' I said.

'Money,' he said. His hands were red and wet with blood and he had blood on his face. 'Cheerio, hey,' he said and he strode out of the heads.

I walked back to the cabin. The hot stale air and the smell of bodies got me. The alleyway smelt much better now I had got used to it. I held the door open to get some fresh alleyway air in while I took off my shoes at the door. There was only a small patch of blood inside the cabin, at the door. A bunklight went on and a man leant up on his elbow and looked at me.

'Close the fucking door,' he said, 'you're letting all the stink in.'

'Jesus,' I said. I left the door ajar on the hook and walked to my bunk.

'I said close the fucking door!'

I could not see him clearly but I could tell from his accent he was Coloured.

'Quiet man,' I said in Afrikaans, 'you will wake the others. We must have air.'

'*Got!*' he grumbled and he lay back in his bunk. I could tell he was looking at me.

'Who are you?' he asked in Afrikaans.

'McQuade,' I said. I was getting dressed.

'Are you Rooinek or Afrikaans?'

'Rooinek,' I said. Rooinek means Redneck, or English. I don't mind being called Rooinek but I'm a bit off being called English.

'Oh,' he said. It seemed that that made the door ajar a bit better. I continued getting dressed.

'Who're you?' I asked.

'Januarie. You can call me Jannie.'

'Okay Jannie. I'm James.' I thought it was too early in the relationship for jokes like 'You can call me Baas James'. Maybe he didn't have a sense of humour. I finished dressing. 'Why is it so stuffy in here?' I whispered.

Januarie sat up. He was wearing a singlet and his underpants. I could see now he was very Coloured, with the short curly hair and thick lips, but his nose was more European than native. He pointed to the air vent above the door.

'Fokkin' thing doesn't fokkin' work hey man.'

The grill was broken and a lifebelt was stuffed in the hole. Some air squirted into the cabin round the sides of the lifejacket and I felt it with my hand, it was very hot air. The edges of the lifejacket were charred black from the hot air. That could start a fire. 'Why didn't you get the carpenter to fix it?'

'Hey, man?' Januarie said.

'The carpenter,' I said. 'Okay, I'll tell him.'

I pulled on my oilskins and then pulled on my gumboots. I would have to get some boots with spikes from the slopchest.

I walked up the alleyway and then up the companionway on to the messdeck. Down the alleyway the sunshine and the clamour and clatter of the cutting deck shone in, you could see the mountains of meat and the sea and the men wading in the slough of blood. I stuck my head in the galley hatch and asked for a cup of coffee. I did not know the day galley crew. They looked busy and sweaty and bad-tempered, the way galley staff always do. A galleyboy gave me a mug of coffee from the urn as if he was sick of people sponging on him. I stepped out into the galley alleyway into the blood on to the cutting deck and plodded round behind the winches and up the companionway on to the fo'c'sle. It was clean and cold and quiet and empty on the fo'c'sle, and there were only a few tracks in the snow. The sun was beginning to settle to port and it was beautiful, pink and gold and mauve, some icebergs far away catching the late sun and I felt good and young and strong and rested and my guts winced in excitement when I thought of Victoria Rhodes.

I went right up to the peak with my mug of coffee and I looked over down at our sharp bows far below cutting through the freezing clean dark blue sea going God knows where, and I knew why I was a sailor. And I thought of Victoria Rhodes getting up out of her bunk now, soft and sweet-smelling and woman, promising to be my lover.

Then I walked back across the fo'c'sle down to the carnage of the cutting deck, through the blood and into the clean scrubbed Big Mess. I tramped blood up to my place. I was the first man in the Big Mess, and that felt good too.

After breakfast I went below to the slopchest and bought a pair of spiked seaboots on account. You've got to be quick to find a ship's slopchest open. I also bought a new denim shirt to wear to Miss Rhodes' cabin tonight because I was wearing my last clean shirt until I did my laundry. Laundry would be hell on this ship, with all the blood, and I decided I would hire Benjamin to do mine. Coloureds are good at laundry, they have the patience. I went back to my cabin and pulled on my new spiked seaboots. I realised I had forgotten to buy a padlock for my locker. We never used padlocks on the catchers, theft was an unthinkable offence, but it would be different on the factory, with all the Coloureds. Men were coming down from breakfast into the changing room to get into their oilskins and boots. The oilskins hung from pegs, red and sticky with yesterday's blood congealed and the bulkheads were smeared and there were pools of blood where the oilskins had dripped. I climbed the companionway back to the messdeck. The dayshift had not knocked off yet. I went past the Big Mess and looked in the small Sailors' Mess. This, I felt was where I belonged. Charlie and Jock and two others were finishing their breakfast. I sat down next to Charlie.

'Ogh,' Big Charlie said, 'the new boy!'

'Wish I was your new boy and not going out there to the abattoirs,' I said.

Jock looked at me sourly from the next table.

'I hear you were steppin' out with our Vicky last night, wee James?'

'Yes,' I said.

'That's a marvellous story about The Kid and the whale,' Big Charlie said quickly, to change the subject.

'Yes,' I said, 'but a little goes a long way.'

'Peggy!' Big Charlie said to the messboy, 'bring Mr McQuade some coffee.'

'No thanks,' I said, 'it's almost time for my debut.'

'Keen boy, hey?' Jock said from the next table.

'Well, James,' Big Charlie said, 'now that you're aboard we expect to see plenty of you, come and eat in here whenever you like, same grub but better company!'

Jock looked as if he was about to say something to all that, and Big Charlie said quickly, 'Cigarette, James?'

The hooter went up top, signifying seven pm, time for the dayshift to quit.

'Too late,' I said. 'Dammit! I forgot to get a cigarette holder for the deck.'

'You can get one tonight,' Big Charlie said, 'I'll come out now too.'

'See you, Jock,' I said.

'You sonofabitch,' Jock said.

When we got outside the Mess room the dayshift were toiling out of the blood into the alleyway.

'James,' Big Charlie said and he held my arm, 'don't mind Wee Jock, he's a good lad really.'

'Sure he is,' I said, 'I know Jock, I've sailed with him long enough.'

'No, he wouldn't be like that ashore where there's plenty of lasses, he'd say all's fair in love and war, but here where there's only one lassie you know what it's like.'

'Sure, Charlie,' I said.

'I'll talk to him,' Big Charlie said.

'Don't bother with that,' I said. 'Jock and I understand each other, if he keeps it up I'll talk to him, don't worry.'

'Just don't fight over a lassie,' Big Charlie said.

'Okay, Charlie,' I said.

'Okay, James,' Big Charlie said. 'Good luck.'

The dayshift were filing past, smeared and dripping blood, blood shining red on their black oilskins, faces wet and bloody and cold and smeared, jostling out of the blood straight up to the Big Mess to eat. The night shift were filing down the alleyway in the opposite direction. I plodded out into the blood, pulling on my gloves, then I lowered the ear flaps on my snowcap. I looked around for a foreman to tell me where I was detailed. The rows of big open potholes in the deck leading down into the factory below were steaming and fuming in billows, hard. There were two eighty-foot blues on deck, in different stages of decimation. I saw a foreman and plodded over to him. He told me to get a pothook from the Blacksmith's shop, which is what I had feared. Goddam potman! A dragger of meat from the flenzer to the pots. A hewer of wood and drawer of water.

I plodded aft through the blood to the Blacksmith's shop. It was also the Carpenter's shop. There was a pile of bent and buckled harpoons for him to straighten. The harpoons were solid steel, three feet long and about two inches in diameter, with the big barbed head which held the grenade. Yet the whales were so tough that many of the harpoons got bent when they hit. The Chippy, the carpenter, was also in there, at his bench, and I told him about the air vent in the cabin. I had half a cigarette with the Chippy and the Smithy and then I took my pothook on deck. The foreman put me on a gang on the for'ard port section.

The flenzers swiped with their long broomstick knives at the eighty foot skinned beast, swiped so the blood flew. They hacked out blocks of meat the size of an armchair and they crashed with a splash to the deck. The blood gushed out of the big veins, red and splashing. Buzzy was flenzing on the starboard side of my whale.

'Hullo, Professor,' he shouted. He swiped hard at the hump of flesh high above him and he hit a vein and a thick jet of blood cascaded on to him and he jumped back.

'Hullo, Buzzy, you happy in your job?'

Jakkals was one of my flenzers, on the port side. The rest were Englishmen. Jakkals was a bad bastard. He had a bad reputation and it was considered surprising that the English, who are afraid of skollies, gave Jakkals a flenzing knife, but he was a good flenzer. Even the Coloureds were afraid of Jakkals. Nobody quarrelled with Jakkals. He was nearly six feet, which is unusual in a Cape Coloured. I walked up beside Jakkals and I sank my pothook into a block of meat.

'*Got!*' he said, 'you working here now?'

'*Ja*,' I said. 'Nice job.'

'*Got!*' he said, 'long time no see, man.'

'*Ja*,' I said. 'How're you?'

I dragged the block of meat through the blood to the nearest pothole. The pothole was flush with the deck and it was four feet across, and a man could easily fall down it. I heaved the hunk of meat into the pothole and it fell with a swoosh and a thump down the funnel into the boiling vats in the factory deck below. I plodded back to Jakkals and sank my hook into the next lump of meat.

'Careful you don' fall down the pot, Van hey man,' Jakkals said.

'And you be careful with that knife,' I said.

'Just don't get behind me when I swing it,' Jakkals said. He lifted both arms above his head so the knife hung down behind his back. Then he swiped it forward with a vicious whistle over his head into the beast.

'Just keep reminding me,' I said.

Aft of us, on the skin deck, the flenzers were running the hide of the next blue open. The flenzers on my whale were down to her ribs and innards now and they ran open her huge belly and there was a big slippery crashing sound and her guts and intestines thudded out in a great wet red pile, the intestines were as thick as a man's leg and the coils piled up high and then slid out in all directions, and then on top of them, out crashed her calf. It slipped over the heap of intestines and slid a little way in the blood. The calf was a female. She was twenty feet long and she was perfect. Her hide shone black and yellow and slimy red and her fins were pressed tight against her sides and her mouth was clamped shut and her eyes were closed. She had the grooves down her belly, just like the mother. The umbilical cord snapped as she skidded out. She was much too big for two men to heave over the side and the foreman came up with a flenzing knife and hacked through her, down through her backbone. It took him some time to hack her into four manageable sections. Then he called me and my mate over and we dragged the sections over to the rail and we each sank our hooks into a section and sang out: One-two-*three!* and heaved it over the side back into the sea. The flenzers had got down to the mother whale's backbone now, and her meat was splashing with the chops of the flenzing knives, and you sunk your pothook into a hunk of meat and maybe it was still attached to the rest of her or to a bone, and the flenzer had to come and chop away the connection. I went to the winch and the driver paid out cable to me and I led the cable round a capstan and over to the whale and Jakkals hooked the cable on to a section of rib-casing. The ribs were fifteen feet long. Then he signalled the driver to pull in on the winch and the winch rattled and gushed steam and the cable took the strain and the ribs began to bend and everybody stood well back. And then with a great wrench the section came away from the backbone and Jakkals hacked it clean off and the cable pulled it clear. Then I took a cable from a derrick winch above and I lashed it to the section of rib-casing and the winch driver raised it a little way off the deck and then Jakkals began hacking the flesh clean off the ribs. The other winches were tearing the rest of the ribs off the bloody backbone and the flenzers were working on the backbone with the big portable electric saws, and the other chunks of rib and backbone were lashed to derrick cables and the flenzers were hacking at the dangling bones. The ship was rolling a little, and the great bones were swinging through the air with the roll and the flenzers were swiping and the blood was flying and the winches were rattling. There was the mighty deafening clang of the giant slipway pliers dropping on to the tail of the next whale and the big amidships winch was dragging it up the slipway on to the skinning deck. The sun was down behind the icebergs and the sea was red and mauve and sparkling black and the icebergs were on fire and the sky was twisting and glowing, the yellow floodlights came on to the deck and the winches were rattling and the bonesaws were roaring and over the loudspeakers they were playing Oh What A Beautiful Morning.

Chapter Twenty

I showered and put on clean clothes and my new shirt, then I had one pint of beer in the Pig. I ate supper in the Big Mess, then I went to my cabin and poured myself a stiff brandy and smoked a cigarette. I was very excited. Then I brushed my teeth and walked aft through the factory up to Miss Victoria Rhodes' cabin. She had changed out of her uniform into a skirt and sweater and she looked tired.

'Hullo,' she said and she sounded strained. Her dark eyes seemed very big. 'Do you want to go for another walk like last night?'

'If you like,' I said. I did not want to go for a walk.

'Poor boy,' she said. 'You've been walking on deck all day, you don't want to go out again. I saw you working today.'

'Did you?'

'You worked very hard, much harder than anyone else, you're a good boy.'

'You were proud of me?'

'Oh yes! Very proud. Are you very tired?'

'A little,' I said. I was very tired indeed, for I was not used to lugging tons of meat around for twelve hours.

'You look very healthy though. Sit down and I'll get you something nice to drink.'

I went up to her and kissed her gently. She submitted but she was taut and then she turned away.

'Let me get you a drink, what would you like, brandy or coffee?'

'You've got brandy?'

'Only for my very important guests.'

She went to her locker and brought out a bottle half full and a tumbler. 'I can get ice if you want.'

'I have enough ice all day. Don't put any water in it.'

She smiled as she gave me the tumbler, then she sat down on the bunk with her hands between her knees to watch me drink it. She looked at the tumbler and then she looked at me and smiled brightly but she was nervous.

'Would you like to hear my record-player?' she said brightly. 'I've got a small record-player.'

'Come here, Vicky,' I said.

She was staring through me. She didn't do anything. I put down the tumbler and I went over to her. She was staring at my midriff now. I put my hand down under her chin and lifted her face. I bent down and kissed her on the cheek. I was trembling again.

'Vicky?'

'Yes?'

'It's all right, you don't have to make love to me.'

She just sat rigid with her face against mine.

'You don't have to do anything,' I said.

She still sat rigid. I stood up straight. She looked across the room.

'But you want to so much,' she said.

'Yes,' I said.

'I sort of led you to believe you could,' she said.

'That's all right,' I said. 'If you don't want to.'

I sat down beside her heavily. She just looked ahead.

'I suppose almost every man on this ship wants to,' she said. 'All men.'

'I guess so,' I said. I suppose I sounded nice and reasonable but I did not feel it.

'You're a nice man,' she said.

She turned and looked at me and then she kissed me on the cheek. I didn't say anything. I did not feel very nice.

'You're a good boy,' she said. 'You've been very good to behave like this after I promised to make love to you.'

I felt like saying 'Thanks.'

'You don't have to do anything you don't want to do,' I said.

'Oh I do want to!' she said earnestly. 'Oh *I do!*'

I looked at her. She looked away. She turned and looked back at me frankly.

'You see,' she said. 'That was all nonsense, that you loved me. You don't love me and I don't love you, how can we yet?'

'But I do love you,' I said.

She laughed and stroked my head.

'You're nice,' she said. 'Does it feel as if you mean it, darling?'

'Yes,' I said. 'It bloody well does!'

I put my arm around her and I kissed her hard and then I tipped her over backwards on to the bunk and I kissed her again. She lay rigid in my arms.

'I'm only kissing you,' I said, 'but you needn't if you don't want to.'

'Oh I want to kiss you,' she said.

I kissed her again and I was trembling to be kissing a woman, my arm around her was trembling, her lips and the smell and the feel and the taste and the feel of her under my chest, soft and woman.

'Oh darling,' I said.

'Darling,' she said. 'Darling darling darling.'

'I love you,' I said.

'Oh, I love you,' she said. 'I love you love you love you, tell me again you love me.'

'I love you.'

'Oh I really do love you too, darling. Say I love Victoria Rhodes.'

'I love Victoria Rhodes.'

'Yes, like that, I love you.'

And the feel of her legs in my hand, the thighs, woman-flesh, the feel of her between my fingers, her skin, so soft and smooth and woman and mountable and penetrable and glorious and soft and good and everywhere, the unutterable joy and want and revel and bliss of softness and smoothness and guts and kisses of love and loins and woman so you cry out and sob for joy and again and again and never never stop please God.

Chapter Twenty-One

When I woke up I was still in love with Victoria Rhodes. It was a shock to wake up in her cabin. We were very close together in her narrow bunk. It was very good to wake up to the clean sweet woman cabin. I woke up feeling good and happy. She was already awake, lying there.

'Good morning, darling,' she said. 'It's almost time for you to leave for the office.'

I smiled at the deckhead, I felt marvellous. 'Where's my breakfast, then?'

'Our cook Elsie is making you a lovely breakfast, darling. I said you wanted four eggs so you can make lots of love.'

I smiled.

'It feels like morning,' I said, 'not like sundown.'

'It should be morning,' she said. 'Today should have been last night, lovers are meant to love in the night.'

'Yes.'

'Tonight is our first day as lovers. Isn't it good? Tomorrow when we make love again the sun will be our moon. Was I good for you, darling?'

'You were beautiful,' I said. 'You were beautiful.'

'Did I do it right?'

'Oh, you did it so very right.'

'Did I make you happy?'

'You made me very happy,' I said.

'What did I feel like?'

'You,' I said. 'The best feeling in the whole world, there could not be a better feeling.'

She leaned up on her elbow and looked down at me.

'What did you feel inside me?'

I laughed.

'You're a funny girl.'

'I'm not funny darling, I'm just in love! Are you in love too, darling? It doesn't matter very much if you're not.'

'You're funny,' I said. 'Yes, of course.'

'It doesn't matter if you don't love me,' she said earnestly, 'it really doesn't, just so long as I can love you. I'll try not to be a bore. Do you love me a little?'

'I love you lots,' I said. 'And you're happy, you don't regret the jam you've got yourself into?'

'What jam?' I kissed her on the mouth and nose.

'You know,' she said. 'Men do get nervous about a girl in love. Especially in a place like this where there's no escape.'

It was all very wise but it did not matter a damn.

'I don't want to escape, Vicky.'

She kissed me very lovingly.

'Tell me what it felt like inside? So I can try to do better next time.'

I laughed. 'You felt warm and deep and blissful and you couldn't have done it better.'

'Did I really?' she said happily.

'Yes,' I said.

'Aren't all girls the same?'

'No,' I said. 'All girls aren't the same. You're the best.'

She lay back, then she snuggled into me. She was very happy. I thought she was a little crazy but I didn't mind at all, it felt fine. It felt like I was in love with her and it didn't matter what she was.

She said, 'Were you very cross that I wasn't a virgin?'

'No,' I said.

She got up on to her elbow again and looked down at me earnestly.

'It was only one man, darling,' she said earnestly. 'It was really and truly only one man. Do you believe that?'

'Yes,' I said. I did believe her.

'Only one,' she said defensively.

'Are you all right now?' I asked. I did not feel jealous.

'Yes, darling,' she said brightly, and she kissed me. 'Quite all right thank you!'

I smiled at the thank you. 'How long ago?'

'Oh quite a long time ago,' she said. 'But last night – last night I got over him.'

Then we were grinning at each other and then I felt her lusciousness again, her woman-flesh afresh and it was a huge joyous appetite again, and she rolled over on to her side, and then on to her back and she took me on to her and she opened her lovely legs to me.

Afterwards she lay stroking me and she said, 'Are you all right?'

I nodded.

'Poor darling,' she said, 'having to go to work. Just you look after yourself, see?'

'Okay,' I said into her shoulder.

'And you must have breakfast. Four eggs, eggs are very good for you, lots of protein.'

'Okay,' I said. I was feeling very beautifully exhausted.

'Poor boy,' she said. 'You must be exhausted, four times in ten hours, don't work too hard tonight, darling.'

'Okay,' I said. 'Tell the foreman.'

'I *will*,' she said. 'I'll say "Don't you dare work my James McQuade too hard, he's had a bad night!" Right?'

'Right,' I said. 'You tell him.'

'And now you must get off me, darling. Would you like some coffee and a cigarette?'

'Yes.'

'Come on then.'

I lay on my back in the bunk while she filled her little kettle. She looked at herself once in the mirror and said 'God, I look a mess.' She was naked and I was surfeited but not in the mind, and she was very very beautiful and gay and happy and loving making the coffee, long full legs and lovely breasts and her lovely woman face and her long black hair all over the place, and I saw that she did have the dim winter lines of her bikini, where her bikini had begun and ended.

Chapter Twenty-Two

That week I slept in her cabin every night. I did not love her, but it was very good. She was very happy and she looked after me and made me take vitamin pills because she said we did not get enough fresh vegetables and fruit. In the officers' Mess on the bridge the food was better, she said, and she brought back fruit for me.

'You needn't come to see me every night, darling, if you don't want to,' she said, 'you mustn't feel that I'm tying you down, if you want to go and drink with the boys in the Pig you must.'

'I want to come to you, Vicky,' I said. 'I've had enough of the boys, even in Cape Town.'

She hugged me.

'Oh yes,' she said. 'I love you all right.'

She set her alarm clock for five-thirty and I went back to my cabin and rumpled my blankets to make it look to my cabinmates as if I slept there. I don't suppose it did much good, and sometimes there were men queuing at the surgery corridor when I was leaving. My cabinmates said nothing, I hardly saw them: they were all three Coloureds and they seemed pleasant enough although the one called Pieter was surly. On the third night I was walking out down the surgery alleyway and there were no men queuing and Old Ferguson came out.

'Come here, James!'

I went back to her. She looked around, then took me down the alleyway to her cabin. She glared at me.

'James, I know you're sleeping with that girl!'

'Yes, Fergie?' I said.

'And don't say it's none of my damn business, because I'm in charge of this deck and you've no right to be here except on business.'

'Yes, Fergie?' I said.

'And don't say Yes Fergie in that tired voice! I could stop you, you know!'

'I know, Fergie.' She glared at me.

'James, are you in love with her?'

'Yes,' I lied.

She snorted. 'I'm not so sure of that! I know you boys. James,' she wagged her finger at me, 'don't you break that girl's heart.'

'All right, Fergie.'

'She's head over heels in love, I can tell! And I can tell you're making love to her, she's radiant. James!' she wagged her finger at me, 'Just you treat her right! She's not one of your whores.'

'I know that, Fergie.'

She wagged her finger at me again.

'And don't you get her into trouble!'

I nodded. She glared at me.

'Well, James? What are you doing about it? You didn't exactly come prepared on this whaling trip, did you, you're not that much of an optimist!'

I grinned at her. 'No, I didn't. It's nice of you to worry, Fergie. But don't worry, I've been around.'

'I'll bet you've been around!' Old Fergie glared. 'And don't think you can trust this rhythm method, young man! I've known plenty of young girls been beat on the rhythm method!'

'Rhythm Roulette?'

'Exactly!' Old Fergie glared. 'James? Now, I hate to be an old granny! But I've got a stock of those Board of Trade things we issue to the men in port. You'd better take some.' She was blushing suddenly.

'Old Fergie,' I said. I put my hand on her shoulder.

She was blushing and she shrugged my hand off her shoulder curtly.

'Don't you dear Old Fergie me! James? Take them, don't get yourselves into trouble, lad, she's such a nice girl.'

'Fergie, I won't use them.'

'Why not?' she snapped.

'I'm a Catholic, Fergie.'

'Catholic, my eye! You're an atheist, I've heard you!'

'I was brought up a Catholic, Fergie.'

'They didn't make a very good job of it!' Old Fergie snapped. 'Listen, James. Be a good boy. Even if just for the dangerous times. She's such a nice lass.'

'All right, Fergie. Thanks.'

'There's a good lad!'

She disappeared out the cabin and came back with a cardboard carton. Written on the outside was: One Gross. She was blushing again. She thrust them at me.

'And just you use them young man!'

I smiled at her.

'And James?' she caught my arm.

'Yes Fergie?'

She blushed again and her eyes were burning again and her chin trembled once:

'I'm so ... pleased for you two! I hope ...' she broke off and shook her head. 'Nothing! You're such nice kids ...'

'Thanks Fergie.' I put my arm around her big shoulders and gave her a kiss on her forehead. She loved it, all overcome, then she shook me off.

'Now off with you!'

'Good night, Fergie.'

'Good night, James dear.'

I walked up the alleyway smiling. As I got to the end Old Fergie's big voice boomed out, 'And just you use them, young man!'

I looked back and there was Old Fergie glaring, hands on her big hips. I waved to her.

On Old Year's Night we started drinking early on deck. The whaling was still booming. Most of the boys had hipjacks of brandy or whisky and Elsie ordered his messboys to bring the men pints from the Pig if they paid for it. They propped their beer mugs on a rail or on a winch, bedded in the blood, and took swigs between labour. The fleet only shot twelve whales on Old Year's Day because, rumour had it, The Kid was drunk. Rumour had it he had been threatening all day to harpoon the Mate, who was now in his cabin. Rumour had it that The Kid had advised the Mate, his Captain, that he, The Kid, was presently undecided whether or not to harpoon him only because he was worried about further spoiling the Company's already crappy product by chucking a load of crap like the Mate into the factory pots. He weighed against that, the rumour had it, the undoubted service he would be doing the Company by ridding it of the Mate, whom he insisted on calling Auntie. Rumour had it that The Kid was sitting down in the engine room of the Fourteen with the first engineer drinking Scotch and refusing to answer Auntie on the grounds that he could not hear him above the noise of the engines, which were only idling anyway because there is no point chasing whales without a gunner. Rumour had it that The Kid was saying he was going to knock my block off as well as harpoon the Mate. I pretended it was a joke. Rumours are rife on ships. I had a hipjack of brandy on the deck, and it made the work a lot less unpleasant. The boys were singing as they hacked and dragged the meat and blood and bone. When the midnight hooter blew there was cheering all over the ship and in the Pig the dayshift were singing Auld Lang Syne. I cheered a little and said, 'Hoo-bloody-ray, we're going home this year,' like I did every season but I did not mind the whaling nearly so much this New Year because of Victoria. Most of the boys shook each other's hands. I shook hands with a few. Jakkals looked at me. The blood was running off his face like sweat and he was drunk.

He said, 'Happy New Year, hey, Van, you *ou* bastard.'

He was not smiling and he offered his hand, full of blood. I thought he was waiting for me to call him an old bastard back, or ask him to wipe his hand. I shook his slimey hand.

'Happy New Year, Jakkals,' I said, and he grunted and turned away. I decided I was going to be very careful of Jakkals.

After the meal I lay down in the bloody alleyway outside the Mess in my oilskins to rest a little. It was the only way to rest and the blood does not matter any more in the oilskins.

That New Year's dawn there was a long range of icebergs to the east, two miles away, and the sky was on fire and the many faces of the ice caught the rising sun and for a long time the ship was bathed in moving spectrums, moving across the ship and the whales and the faces of men in many colours. It seemed the best Antarctic dawn I had ever seen and I wanted to shout out *Oh look at that!* And I thought *It's going to be a good year.* Oh yes it's going to be a good year! I sang as I worked in the dawn. We would almost finish the whales in tow by the end of our nightshift. Many of the men were drunk. Jakkals was so drunk the foreman sent him below to sleep it off, he was a menace swinging his flenzing knife. Jakkals lowered his knife and turned slowly on the foreman.

'I'll only fokkin' go if it doesn't come off my fokkin' wages.' His face was puffed and bloody and his eyes were bloodshot.

'Go below, Jakkals,' the foreman said. He was afraid of Jakkals.

'Does it come off my wages or fokkin' not?'

'We'll see about that,' the foreman said.

'You're fokkin' right we'll fokkin 'see about that,' Jakkals said. 'We'll see about it right fokkin' now!'

'You're drunk,' the foreman said. 'Go below, there's a good chap.' If it had been anybody else the foreman would have grabbed him by the back of his neck and thrown him down below.

'You're fokkin' right. I'm fokkin' drunk enough to stick this fokkin' knife right through your fokkin' guts!' Jakkals said.

The foreman took a step back. We in our gang had all stopped to watch.

'I'll forget you said that, Jakkals,' the foreman said, 'if you go below quietly.'

'And if I fokkin' don't?'

It was a very good question. The foreman hesitated.

'I'll report you to the bridge,' he said.

Jakkals wagged his finger. 'And if you report me to the fokkin' bridge you'll be very fokkin' sorry. Now does it come off my fokkin' wages or not, hey?'

The foreman blinked.

'Okay, Jakkals,' he said trying to sound brusque, 'seeing it's New Year an' all it won't come off your wages, jus' go'n sleep it orf, mate.'

Jakkals slung down his flenzing knife.

'It's a fokkin' good thing you fokkin' think like that, pallie.' He started plodding away through the blood. We were all watching him, his hull shoulders stooped, very broad in his bloody oilskins. He plodded ten paces and then he turned and shook his fist at the foreman.

'An' it's a fokkin' good thing for you too it's New fokkin' Year, pallie,' he shouted.

We all laughed except the foreman. Then the foreman laughed sheepishly, pretending it was nothing.

'Orl right lads!' he shouted. 'Where d'ya think ya are, on your daddy's fookin' yacht?' He came over to me, pretending he was just looking around. He was shaking, and it wasn't anger.

'Cheeky bastards. Jesus, no wonder you bastards don't like 'em.'

'Never mind, Fore,' I said. 'You put him in his place didn't you?'

'Yeah,' the foreman said, pretending to be looking down the pothole. He was still shaking. 'Cheeky bastards need keeping in their place 'an all.'

At six o'clock we were knocked off. There was only one whale left for the dayshift to work. I hung up my dripping oilskins in the changing room and then had a hot salt water shower. When I had finished it was six-thirty. I walked up the alleyways to Benjamin's cabin and knocked and opened the door. Only Geradus van Wijk was there, getting dressed.

'Evening,' I said. 'I'm looking for Benjamin.'

'Well he's not fuckin' here!' Geradus van Wijk said.

I looked at him, surprised, then I stepped into the cabin and shut the door.

'Why do you talk like that?' I said.

He was a little unnerved now. He carried on dressing.

'How else am I supposed to speak to you, hey? A man who's always hanging around with fuckin' Coloureds?'

'I beg your pardon, mate?' I said.

'You heard me, hey! You're a fucking *kaffir-boet!*'

I leaned back against the door.

'We're not at home now, mate,' I said. 'Anything else?'

'You fuckin' right we not at home,' Geradus van Wijk said. 'That's no reason to treat 'em like friends, fuckin' equals or something!'

'Is that right?'

'That's right!' Geradus van Wijk said. 'Why didn't you stand up for me on Christmas Eve, hey, about the Big Mess? We supposed to stick together. You're a fuckin' traitor to your race!'

'Anything else?' I said. I moved from the door.

'Yeah! An' now you're fuckin' a Coloured woman, a bleddy Tottie—'

'Jesus,' I said and I hit him. He wasn't expecting it and I hit him hard on the jaw so he crashed back against the bulkhead. I jumped after him and I hit him hard in the guts. He doubled up clutching his guts and I caught his neck and slung him down on to the bench.

'Get one thing straight, mate!' I shouted. 'She's not a Coloured! And get another thing straight! You're not at home and you're fuck-all on this ship!'

Jesus, I hated him. I hit him once more with the flat of my hand across his face. Then I walked to the door.

As I opened it, he shouted, 'You *kaffir-boet!* I'll see about you when we get home!'

I gave him the V sign and slammed the door behind me. I walked down the alleyway. I was furious, shaking. I had not hit anybody in two years; the last man I'd hit was The Kid, over the seals. The knuckles on my left hand were sore, I rubbed them. Jesus! Jesus Christ! I climbed up the companionway and walked along to the Pig. A number of dayshifters were hanging around the alleyway in their oilskins waiting to go on. The Pig was full of nightshifters and a lot of dayshifters too who did not seem to be about to take the New Year's Day shift very seriously. I was still shaking as I got myself a pint and took a long drink. I looked around the smoky beery Pig. Jesus, that bastard van Wijk! Most of the boys looked as if they had been up all night drinking. Jakkals was there in the corner holding forth, he had not gone below to sleep it off, I could have told the foreman that. Beulah and the other queers were there tarted up like sore fingers. Spike and Buzz were on the piano and the double bass. I saw Benjamin. He was sitting at a table of guffawing men, looking as if he wanted to topple off the chair asleep, but scowling away manfully. He had a half pint of beer in front of him. A man leaned out and made as if to prop Benjamin's eyes open with two matchsticks and Benjamin knocked his hands away with a fierce little scowl and nearly fell off the chair. They all laughed except Benjamin. I caught his eye and signalled him over to the hatch and he got up and nearly fell with a roll of the ship.

'Hullo, Benjamin,' I said. '*Gelukkige Nuwe Jaar!*'

I had stopped shaking.

'Hullo, Master James,' he scowled slowly, 'compliments of the season hey man.'

'Would you like a beer, ou?'

Benjamin scowled at my chest and nodded his head bravely.

'Half a pint here, Mac,' I called to the barman. As he handed it over I whispered 'How many has the lad had?'

'Maybe two pints all night,' he said.

'Cheers Benjamin!' I said. 'You been up all night boozing have you?'

'*Ja!*' Benjamin nodded vigorously at my chest. He did not take a drink of his beer.

'Aren't you a little tired?' I said.

Benjamin took a moment to register then shook his head at my chest vigorously. '*Ag nee wat!*' he said hoarsely.

'Well,' I said. 'You *have* had a good night. But it's only once a year isn't it?'

Benjamin registered this and then shook his head vigorously.

'Anytime's okay, hey!' he croaked.

'You stay up all night often?' I said, playing it along. Benjamin nodded vigorously and spilt some of his beer.

'Alla time,' he whispered. Then, 'Jesus Christ and bloody hell,' he said. 'I'm pissed hey!'

He gave a big stagger. He just looked dog-tired to me.

'Jesus Christ,' Benjamin croaked loudly in case I had not heard, 'I'm pissed mate!'

He staggered again and scowled as he thought.

'I'm fucking pissed like a ...' he trailed off. 'Like a *newt!*' he croaked suddenly.

'Like a newt!' I nodded.

'I wouldn' know,' Benjamin gave another stagger manfully, 'my ... my ... *cockfromabaconslicerl*' he croaked triumphantly at my chest.

'That's dangerous, Benjamin,' I said. 'What about work, you supposed to start work in fifteen minutes.'

Benjamin scowled-staggered-waved.

'Fuggwork!' he scowled-staggered-waved.

I decided he was finished anyway on sleep alone. I decided I might as well teach him something.

'Well Benjamin!' I said. 'Cheers! Drink it down down down *jong!*'

He knew that one too. He threw back his small curly head and the beer ran down his chin and chest and down his throat and then out his mouth and nose and then he dropped the mug. I grabbed him and I yanked him out of the Pig. I ran him down the alleyway to the open deck and I stuck his head out. As I got him out, up it all came in a rush. I held his forehead and said, 'Throw it up Benjie.'

Elsie came crashing down the alleyway and grabbed his waist and I squeezed Benjamin's forehead and up and out it came in a beery puke into the blood. Up at the door of the Pig some men were cheering Benjamin.

'Okay Bennie?' I said and Benjamin gave one dreadful shudder and then a gutsful dribbling cough and then he was still.

'He's asleep,' I said.

'That's the stuff,' Elsie said. His head hung down peacefully.

'Who've you got to do his work?'

'Mister van Wijk,' Elsie beamed.

'He's our man,' I said.

I ducked down and folded Benjamin over my shoulder and I carried him below and dumped him in his bunk. I took off his shoes and belt and I covered him with his sheet. He was very fast asleep.

It was nearly seven o'clock. I went aft through the factory and up to the hospital deck and padded along in my socks to Victoria's cabin and let myself in. A minute later she came in from duty.

'Darling!' she cried. 'Happy New Year!'

She threw her arms around me.

'And you, my love.'

'It's going to be a wonderful year for us I know. We're going to do great things this year!'

'Are we?'

'Oh yes we are, I know! Would you like a drink, darling, we must break the rule of a lifetime and have a drink this New Year.'

'Of course.'

'I nearly came to see you at midnight, to wish you a happy New Year, I was so in love with you, the Captain gave us champagne at midnight and I wanted to pinch some for you.'

'And did you?'

'Oh I tried so hard, but I couldn't get my dirty little paws on a bottle so I had to drink yours for you. I'll buy you lots of champagne in Cape Town darling! We'll have a lovely champagne holiday in Cape Town, won't we?'

'You're damn right.'

'I was so in love with you at the Captain's party, I wanted to make love to you there and then.'

'Come here,' I grinned.

'Do you want to make love to me now?' she asked.

I laughed.

'Yes but I'll wait—'

'You needn't wait darling, anytime you want just say the word and *zip!* off they'll come!'

'Come here Hotpants!' She came and put her arms around me and squeezed me hard.

'Damn right! But I'm only a hotpants for *you,* darling! I shouldn't joke about it should I?'

'I don't mind you joking about it,' I said.

'But a nice girl doesn't joke about it. Maybe I'm not a nice girl, do you think I'm a nice girl?'

'I think you're delicious.'

'Am I the most delicious girl you've ever slept with, darling? You needn't say you love me, just tell me if I'm the most delicious, I love you enough for both of us.'

'But I do love you,' I said before I realised it.

She toppled back on to the bunk and pulled me down on top of her and burst out laughing and hugged me and we were both laughing. Her cheeks were red and her big dark eyes were flashing merry and her wide mouth was sparkling and her hair was all over the place. She was very beautiful and she just lay underneath me smiling wide and sparkling at me and then her smile turned soft and began to go away and then it went right away and she said softly, 'Oh … I'm so happy.'

'And I,' I said, and I meant it.

'I'm so happy I came on this awful ship and met you. Old Fergie's sweet,' Victoria said, 'she's always saying the nicest things to me, about you.'

'Is she?' I was gratified. 'Old Fergie gave us a present today,' I said.

'*Did* she! What?'

'One hundred and forty-four French letters,' I said.

She looked at me, then she threw back her head and laughed. 'Oh James! Did she really!'

She was pealing with laughter.

'She thinks I might catch you with a baby!'

Victoria thought it was very funny.

'No,' I said, 'I think Old Fergie would regard that as satisfactory. She's worried about you.'

'Oh darling!' she laughed. 'Isn't that a scream! Is that a week's supply or what?'

'I thought you might mind,' I said.

'Of course I don't mind!' She stopped laughing and wiped her eyes. 'But darling?'

'Yes?'

'Do you mind using them? Aren't they awful for you, takes away a lot of the feeling?'

'Yes,' I said. It shocked me when she spoke like that, so knowledgeably.

'Do I shock you?' she asked.

'Sometimes,' I said.

'Poor darling! I'll try to be nice. Nice and sweet and virginal and innocent. That's me!' She blushed. 'I don't like them either. I don't mind if you want to use them though.'

'I don't like them,' I said.

'I just want to say you needn't worry about me having a baby. I'm a nurse and I know when it's pretty safe. I won't try to catch you with a baby, darling.'

I smiled at her.

'You're marvellous,' she said. 'And I really won't try to catch you with a baby.'

Later we went for'ard to the Pig to join in the New Year drinking. Most of the boys were pretty drunk and they gave a big howl and whistle and beat their beermugs when Victoria walked in. Victoria blushed furiously and laughed. Charlie pulled us over and shouted for beer, and the piano and the homemade double bass and the singing and the shouting and the smoke and the ship rolling. Beulah and Elsie and a lot of lads came over. Jock had passed out, and the rumour was that The Kid had passed out in the engine room of the Fourteen with the Chief Engineer. The lads laughed and sang and made a great fuss of Victoria, they were all in love with Victoria, and she was gay and laughing and saying funny things and I was laughing at her and very proud of her. The messboys were running beers out to the dayshifters on deck. Now and again a foreman came in to look for his dayshifters, but he didn't have much joy. We had a good time. I remember thinking it was the best New Year I had ever spent, and I still think it is. Afterwards, very late, we went back to her cabin, everybody knew where we were going and we didn't care.

Chapter Twenty-Three

That January was very good, a good beginning to a year. We laughed a great deal, even at things that were not really very funny, but they seemed funny to her and she laughed and played the fool, and then I was laughing. Then she was dead earnest and anxious about something and I thought she was funny then also, so I laughed. I did not mind the blood and the fat and the stink so much because I knew that when the shift ended there was Victoria, not the futility of the Mess and the Pig and the same old bullshit, the waiting and counting the days, the long grinding endurance test of your intelligence. It was not such an endurance test on the catchers, because at least there you are a seaman, working with the sea and using your knowledge of the ship, but on the factory deck you are an abattoir hand. We worked hard that January, the bloody whaling was booming. The Kid was excelling himself. The bonus to the crew of the Fourteen was going to be a third higher than to any other catcher. The story was that The Kid was being very funny with his new Captain, whom he called Matey; The Kid was still giving the orders anyway while saluting the Captain in a most exaggerated fashion every time he saw him, which delighted the crew who were still taking orders from The Kid anyway. The Mate was walking round in a constant bulbous pink-eyed rosebud-mouthed fury and every time he tried to pull his rank on him The Kid pouted and went all petulant and said if he wanted to be like that he jolly-well wouldn't shoot whales so *there!* which kept the Mate very jittery because he was a Company Man who used to be in the Post Office and should have stayed there. He would have made a good Post

Mistress. In early January The Kid came aboard in the derrick basket being swung aboard from the Fourteen and singing *Ein zwei drei vier* from "The Student Prince" as he came through the air with his arms outflung to us and the deck labourers cheered him, he was very popular because of all the whales he shot and because of all the funny stories about him. The basket landed and he vaulted out and fell on his hands and knees in the blood and everybody guffawed and he stood up and hollered, '*McQuade! Where's that awful man McQuade?*'

I was leaning on my pothook grinning at him.

'*Jesus Christ James my ship is awful, sell the pig and buy me out!*'

I grinned at him.

He shouted across the deck at me, '*You got no idea the awful men we got running the ship now, will you please sell the pig and buy me out?*' standing there beaming at me and dripping blood. Then he plodded and slipped over to my foreman and whispered to him and the foreman almost salaamed because on whaling ships good gunners are gods, and more so when they're the Chairman's son. Then The Kid plodded up for'ard towards the Pig and the foreman came over to me.

'Captain Child wants you in the Pig,' the foreman said, 'but don't make it obvious to the lads.'

I went below to the heads and I turned the salt water hose over my oilskins then I went up to the Pig. The Kid was propping up the bar. He had a pint waiting for me.

'Jesus Christ, James,' he waved, 'this is awful.'

'What is?'

'All this blood on thy fair hands and me without anybody to talk to on the Fourteen and that goddam pisswilly postmistress of a Mate chucking his freckled fat about the joint.'

The Kid was pretty drunk.

'Jesus Christ James,' The Kid said, 'I miss you, you miserable sanctimonious old sumbitch! Can you get me a job as potman?'

'It might be a bit late now,' I grinned.

'Do you think if I just went straight up to that pisswilly miserable shithouse of a pink-eyed sonofabitch Mate and just smote him one on his adenoidal nose for no rhyme or reason I might get demoted to potman too?' The Kid said.

'That wouldn't be fair on the lads,' I said. 'We need you on the harpoon.'

'You know what the lads have said they're going to do for me?' The Kid brightened.

'What?'

'They say if I keep this whale-shooting up they're going to lay on a party for me in Cape Town, lots of whores and we're going to squirt them with champagne and all run around bare-arsed screwing them! Won't that be nice?'

'That sounds fine,' I said.

'I'll see that you're invited,' The Kid said. 'I don't forget my friends. But James,' he said, 'that ship is awful now. What can I do to get you promoted again?'

He looked at me, then he grinned.

'But you don't want to be promoted, from what I hear you ole sumbitch,' he said.

'What do you mean?' I said.

'You and Vicky,' he said.

'What have you heard?'

'That you're down aft in her cabin every night,' he sighed.

I nodded. 'Uh-huh?'

The Kid nodded. 'I thought she was interested in you,' he wavered. 'She often asked questions about you and there was I with the clap and unable to get her mind off you!'

We both laughed.

'You lucky undeserving bastard!' The Kid said. 'Give her my love.'

'Sure,' I said. 'You must come and have a drink with us any time.'

The Kid nodded with a mouthful of beer. 'A drink with *us*!' he said regretfully. 'You know, I really liked that girl? I could see myself married to her.'

'Yes?'

The Kid gave a shrug.

'But *Jesus Christ, James*, my ship is awful!'

I did not mind the blood on my fair hands so much, I even began to take an interest in the oil tally because we were going to take a good holiday when we got back. We were going to load up the old V8 and have a carry-cold bag full of beer and champagne and a crate of champagne in the boot and drive away into the sunrise.

'And we'll just drive. Just think of that, driving! Mile after mile of open land. Free. Space. And as we drive we'll eat barbecue chicken and drink champagne.'

'And sing!'

'Sure we'll sing. Sing without worrying about other people hearing us. And at night we'll stay in the best damn hotels and lie in big soft double beds, and sleep as late as we like.'

'Without you having to get up and creep back to your cabin!' she cried. 'Won't that be lovely. Instead we'll make love when we wake up in the morning.'

'Afternoon is the best time.'

'Oh, afternoons are very, very good too, darling, I'm not turning my nose up at afternoons, no sir! But mornings are best 'cos I'm all soft and dreamy.'

'Oh very well then,' I said.

'And we'll have bubble-baths!'

'Okay,' I said.

'Every day we're going to have a bubble-bath. I'm going to get the fluffiest sexiest bubbles in the business. And we're going to jump in together and I'm going to soap you.'

'That sounds grand.'

'Oh it will be. And then after the bubble-bath ...'

'Yes?'

She considered.

'Well, we can make love on the double bed, or we can just make each other happy and then go down to dinner and make love afterwards at bedtime.'

'I see.'

'I mustn't exhaust you.'

'No,' I said.

Most days we walked for a while on the lifeboat deck in the cold sunshine. She was always happy. 'I wish I could *run* with you darling! Run and jump and tumble on the hot sand.'

'We'll do that at the Wild Coast,' I said.

'And run into the surf. And drive amongst the rocks looking for oysters! You know what oysters are good for, darling?'

'Maybe you're a sex maniac,' I said.

'Oh no, I'm just in love, darling, I want to make love the whole time. Sometimes in the surgery while I'm working I'm making love to you the whole time, you know that? And we'll go for long walks and sunbathe on hot rocks. But I'd better not sunbathe too much without my bikini,' she said.

'Why not? First time you've suggested wearing anything.'

'My bottom,' she grinned. 'I must keep my pale bottom to show those damn fool bus conductors when they try to make me sit upstairs!'

'They'll enjoy that.'

We had a good time.

And rolling through the Tzitzikama forests where the mountain brooks are ice cold running over hot rocks and the water is clear and the colour of Coca-Cola, and cooking the chops over the woodfire and the smell of woodsmoke and the forest and the warm rich earth again, the clean bloodless air again, and the beer and the wine getting good and cold in the Coca-Cola stream. And sleeping under the old rafters and thatch of the bungalows of the Tzizikama Forest, lying in the deep feather beds with the crick-cricking of the forest insects in the night and jungle night noises outside the windows. And through the green rolling hills of the Transkei, green open land as far as you can see, the land of the Red Blanket Xhosas, galloping horsemen and women smoking long pipes, and seeing cattle and sheep and goats again. Then out of the land of the people of the red blankets and down into the land of the people of the blue blankets, back down towards the sea along the top of the valley of the Umzimvubu, down to the Wild Coast. Where the sun shines hot and clean on green hills rolling down to the sea, and the sea is blue and white and there is no other person to see you and the gullies are deep and strong and full of big fish. And we'll walk and swim and play naked in the sun on the rocks and the beaches, and at night sleep deep under the thatch of the cottage. That's what we were going to do.

That January I stayed mostly in Victoria's cabin. I got Benjamin to do my laundry. He did it as if his seafaring career depended on it. I hardly ever went to the Pig: most nights I took a couple of pints of beer to Victoria's cabin. Victoria took the despair out of whaling.

Coming cold and bloody off the bloody deck with the knowledge of Victoria's warm clean woman cabin and the sweet clean Victoria smell of her powders and her face-cream and her lipstick and her hairbrush and her nail polishes on her little bunkside table and her hair clips and her hair ribbons and her orange sticks. Victoria curled up on the bunk sitting on her feet as only a woman can, warm and comfortable and talking and laughing, talking about everything, very serious and then very funny. She made me laugh. And the knowledge of her long strong smooth legs tucked under her, and her belly and the warm sweet bulge of her breasts and her wide mouth smiling, and full and red, and her big eyes sparkling, and deep and dark, Victoria taking off her clothes for me, looking dark and smouldering at me. Young and tall and strong and smooth and soft, and her legs were smooth and full and slender and her thighs touched each other, the smooth dark olive secret line where her legs touched, where it is such bliss to touch. And standing close and slippery together under her shower and her golden olive flesh wet and glistening and soft against me loving me. And she went naked to her bunk and lay down for me in the yellow bunk light, her breasts lying big and perfect on her, and her soft flat belly, she looked up at me and stretched up her arms joyfully and she opened her long soft legs.

Chapter Twenty-Four

That January the sun shone bright and blinded white off the ice and even the nightshift wore sunglasses on deck in the sundown and sunrise and we got very brown under the flying blood, the whaling was good and we worked hard. Mostly we seemed to be sailing west round the pole, following the sun and very close to the white Antarctic mainland. There were almost always the long solid line of ice cliffs to starboard, and the big bays and fjords stretching white and jagged up into the horizon. The cliffs and the fjords changed every season, the cliffs fell away with great cracks like thunder and the spray flew high in the air above the masthead, slow motion, and then there was a giant seethe and then a new iceberg came erupting up out of the blue frothing sea. The sun took a long time in setting in its vermilion flashings and sparkle and patchworks of spectrums. Victoria got very excited every time we saw a glacier breaking and from the cutting deck we saw her dash out on to the lifeboat deck with her box camera, but she was always too late and the men laughed at her. She tried very hard to paint the sunsets and got very frustrated. That January we worked very hard, against time, and afterwards the men ate their food and maybe drank a few pints in the Pig and then went to their bunks and slept. I woke up early and left Victoria and went back to my cabin while my cabinmates were still asleep, and I was the first at breakfast, and at lunchtime most of us slept in the alleyways in our oilskins, and men did not talk much, and they were irritable. There were some fights in January in the Big Mess and the Pig, some of the English amongst themselves and some of the Coloureds amongst themselves. There was some fighting talk between some Coloureds and some English, but there were no fights because the Englishmen pulled out of it or the English pulled him out of it. But I only heard of these things, because I was in Victoria's cabin when they happened. What I did see in the Big Mess was Geradus van Wijk working and the Coloureds were giving him a very hard time indeed.

The Big Mess was a pretty godawful place. Four Messboys feeding one hundred and fifty men, for Chrissake, and the ship rolling and the blood running off their oilskins and elbowed on the tables and fingerprinted all over the place, and the deck slippery with blood. The Big Mess was pretty godawful for Geradus Jakobus van Wijk. Apart from the blood, blood everywhere, and the sweat, worse than all that, much much worse: Geradus Jakobus van Wijk did not consider it a natural order of things that he should be waiting on Coloureds. *Got nee!* Not only was it downright unnatural, it was outrageous.

'Listen,' he had first said to Elsie, then to chef, then to the First Mate, 'What the hell's happening on this ship? First you make me share a cabin with a Coloured, then I've got to wait on them. It's not right, man.'

The Coloureds in the Big Mess thought it was all right. In January it was very bad indeed for Geradus Jakobus van Wijk in the Big Mess, for in January everybody was very sick of the whaling.

'Here comes the Government,' they said in the Big Mess in January, and, 'Thank you, *Baas,* sorry to trouble you, *Baas,*' and, 'Will the *Baas* please bring some more fucking potatoes before the *Baas* gets a fucking good hiding, *Baas,*' and, 'It's a bladdy shame the *Baas* is working for us Coloureds, Christ haven't they got any sense, can't they see the *Baas* is *white!*' and, 'Come here you fucking Dutchman!'

'*Voetsak you bladdy kaffir!*' Geradus van Wijk hissed.

'Jesus Christ!' Jakkals said and he lumbered up to him and stood there, and the men sat and watched.

'*Hoe se jy?*'

'*Voetsak,*' Geradus hissed, 'you bladdy Hottentot—'

Jakkals hit him in the guts and then slapped his face hard twice and he went down. There was a shout from the men and they scrambled up. Geradus lay there holding his guts.

'*Vat hom kerels!*' Jakkals shouted.

And they grabbed him and yanked him to his feet and hit him. He kicked and lashed out and they hit him and wrenched him. And lifted him right off the deck all kicking and shouting and trying to bite. And carried him kicking and fighting out the Mess room and down the alleyway out on to the bloody deck. And hurled him through the air on to the deck so he landed with a splash. And grabbed his legs and dragged him up and down shouting and kicking, and his face and nostrils and hair were clogged with red blood and fat.

That is how it was getting in January when the whaling was good. And then suddenly there were no whales again, and it was February.

Part Five

Chapter Twenty-Five

In February it was bad. There were no whales. In February began the time of waiting, waiting for whales, waiting for the tanker, just waiting and hanging around. And in men's loins the lust and in their breasts and arms and knuckles and teeth the tingle of fight. That February the weather turned also and the sky was grey and blown and the sea was greying, and sometimes the snow swirled and gushed in the wind so you did not walk on deck.

That evening in February McQuade lay in Victoria's bunk, his hands behind his head, smoking and watching her get dressed for duty. It was good lying stretched out, the whole bunk to himself, and he did not care at all about there being no whales. When you wake up is a good time to be with your woman. She made him coffee and fetched the daily newsheet from the surgery for him to read and she went to work. He lay reading the newsheet and drinking the coffee and smoking another cigarette until it was nearly breakfast time. Then he got up and showered in Victoria's little bathroom, then he tiptoed out of the hospital deck and went for'ard.

The alleyways were clean, no blood, and there was no vibration in the bulkheads from the factory. He walked along to his cabin and opened the door. He could smell the sweat and smoke as he walked in. The overhead light was burning and his three cabinmates were sitting at the table with a fourth whom he did not know. They were drinking beer.

'Good morning,' McQuade said. He walked to his bunk.

'*More*,' Januarie said. The others said nothing.

The laundry Benjamin had done was lying neatly on his bunk.

'Is it morning?' Piet said. 'I thought it was evening.'

'Morning for the nightshift,' McQuade said shortly.

'Nightshift?' Piet echoed. 'Who's working nightshift these days except the hospital, hey man?'

Oh so! McQuade thought. He picked up his laundry and slung it in his locker.

'I suppose it *is* morning,' Piet said, 'if you're in the hospital crew, isn't it, hey man?'

McQuade hesitated in front of the locker. Then he decided to let it go.

'Is the laundry okay, hey?' Piet said.

'Yes thanks.'

'You quite satisfied with the service on this ship, hey man?'

McQuade stopped. He looked at Piet. Piet looked at him. Januarie and the other man looked and then looked away.

McQuade said slowly, 'I pay that kid one pound a month to do my laundry.'

McQuade glared at him, then Piet looked away. McQuade walked back to his bunk.

'Where us *ous* come from,' Piet said defiantly, 'we do our own bladdy laundry, hey.'

McQuade did not look around.

'Good for you,' he said. 'You save money.'

There was a silence. McQuade picked up a book and turned back towards the cabin door.

'Money?' Piet said defiantly. 'Why pay for it when you got your own servant-girl, hey?'

McQuade stopped. He turned to the table and looked hard at Pieter. They all looked at him and then the other two looked away again. McQuade walked up to the table and leaned on it. He held his finger at Piet.

'Now listen chum,' he said quietly, 'I don't care a stuff what you think. I don't even care a stuff what you say when I'm not here. But if you talk like that once more in my presence I'll fuck you up, do you understand that?'

Piet opened his mouth.

'I warned you,' McQuade said quietly, leaning on the table.

Piet closed his mouth, he glared at McQuade.

McQuade straightened up. 'Right, gentlemen. Now we'll all mind our own business.'

He turned and walked to the door. His hands were shaking. He closed the door behind him firmly and walked up the alleyway. He was still shaking. He had thought there was going to be a fight in there. Maybe he had handled it wrong, maybe he should have ignored it or laughed it off or maybe sat down and talked it out nicely. But fuggem – cheeky bastard. Maybe that would shut him up. He walked up the companionway into the galley alleyway. Elsie was coming on duty.

'Come and talk, Elsie.'

'It's all right for some,' Elsie said. 'You bastards don't work when there's no whales but you still like to eat don't you?'

'Come and talk.'

Elsie sat down fatly opposite at the Mess table. The Mess was half empty.

'Lazy bastards,' Elsie said. 'All sleeping in 'cos there's no fish on deck. They needn't think they're getting a late breakfast out of me, I'm queer but I'm not crazy.'

'Have some coffee or something.'

'What's the matter with you?' Elsie said.

'Have some coffee and be sociable, can't you?'

'My-my!' Elsie said. 'We did get out of the wrong side of the bunk this morning. Get out the wrong side and smack your head on the bulkhead?'

'Yeah,' McQuade said.

'Or did she kick you out?'

'Okay Elsie,' McQuade said.

'Dear, dear!' Elsie said. He turned his fat waist and shouted at Geradus van Wijk, 'Messboy! Bring me some coffee please!'

Geradus came scowling with a pot of coffee. He poured it into a mug.

'Good morning!' Elsie said dangerously.

'Morning,' Geradus said and he walked away.

Elsie looked at McQuade, his fat blue jowls perspiring.

'Japie!' he said.

McQuade had helped himself to porridge, he started eating.

'Well?' Elsie said. 'We haven't seen much of you this past month.'

McQuade grunted.

'That's what those bastards in my cabin are thinking,' he said.

'Oh?' Elsie said.

'One of them tried to have a go at me this morning. They obviously don't like me seeing Victoria.'

'Seeing her!' Elsie said. 'Shacked up with her you mean.'

'Okay, Elsie.'

'It's no good saying "Okay Elsie" in that tone of voice as if it's none of my business. That's what you wanted to talk about isn't it? It's everybody's business.'

'Meaning?' McQuade said.

'Meaning everybody knows about it!' Elsie said irritably. 'Have you been under the fond impression that you've been keeping it a dark and sticky secret? Creeping back to your cabin just before everybody wakes up? Well you haven't.'

McQuade blew on his spoonful of porridge self-consciously.

'You used to be one of the boys in the Pig. Now? Have you given up drinking suddenly this season? Every night people see you going aft, every morning you're seen creeping forward.'

'Okay,' McQuade said. 'So what?'

'So *what?*' Elsie said. 'Listen James, I don't care if you're up there on the bridge screwing the Captain every night, except I rather fancy him myself. But Victoria? The eyes of the ship are on her – unfortunately.'

'What they see in her you do not know,' McQuade said. 'Carry on.'

'You're asking for trouble. There's bound to be trouble over a woman like that, men are animals you know that. The Company was *mad* to bring her, my eyes stood out like hat-pegs when I saw her. They'll have nothing but trouble, I said – look at you and Jock.'

'It's not that kind of trouble really,' McQuade said. 'This is politics.'

'What sort of politics?'

'South Africa.'

'Oh, I know that Jock was in trouble before you, I'm surprised you haven't had trouble before now.'

'Have you heard anything?'

'Only from Lodewijk.'

'What did he say?'

'Only that some of the Coloureds think she's Coloured too and you better be careful,' Elsie said.

'She's not, you know.'

'I don't know or care what she is. I don't understand what you Japies got your bowels in an uproar about. I'm just telling you you'd better be careful, those Coloureds'll cut your throat for tuppence.'

'What the hell am I supposed to do, stop seeing her because of those bastards?'

'It's the only way,' Elsie said.

'For Chrissake.'

'For Chrissake nothing!' Elsie said. 'Everybody else gets by. I'm in the same boat, nobody wants to screw me any more either because Elsie's getting old and fat, I'll have to wait until I get back to Cape Town same as most other people, except Beulah and Kitty, the lucky bitches. And *pay* somebody I suppose. Or are you in love with her?'

'I won't be pushed around by a bunch of Coloureds.'

'I'll tell you something else: the Bridge knows about it, Beulah told me.'

'*I* couldn't care a stuff about the Bridge,' McQuade said.

'Well, let me tell you the Bridge is watching you two like a hawk. They're turning a blind eye, they think if it wasn't you it would be somebody else.'

'Thanks,' McQuade said.

'Don't mention it, and they think you're a pretty reasonable type for the privilege. But if there's one sign of trouble over her,' Elsie wagged his finger, 'they'll put a stop to it. They'll transfer you to a catcher. And it *won't* be the Fourteen.'

'Umm,' McQuade said.

'In fact, don't stretch your luck, they might do it anyway, Beulah says – it would suit the Bridge's purpose: she probably won't shack up with anybody else while you're on the catcher, and everything will be harmonious.'

McQuade looked at Elsie.

'That's got you worried, hasn't it?'

'Well,' McQuade said. 'Well, well.'

He pushed his empty porridge plate aside and felt for his cigarettes.

'What about the eggs?' Elsie said.

'No thanks.' He lit a cigarette and looked at Elsie.

'So play it cool,' Elsie said, 'don't stretch your luck.'

McQuade puffed on his cigarette.

'Sleep a bit more in my cabin, you mean?' he said. 'Be seen more?'

'Be seen more, yes,' Elsie said. 'Go to the Pig, sleep in your own cabin. Sneak off and go and do what you want to do with her for a couple of hours if you must, but sleep in your own cabin. You've been stretching your luck.'

McQuade pulled on his cigarette.

'And don't get into any arguments over her,' Elsie said. 'Don't play the errant knight if the boys shoot their mouths off about her. One fight,' Elsie said, 'and you're *out.*'

Elsie grinned at him.

'You don't want that, do you darling?'

McQuade snorted softly.

'Don't stretch your luck,' Elsie said. 'Like you been doing.'

Chapter Twenty-Six

He and Big Charlie and Beulah were sitting in the corner of the Pig and later Izzy came in and sat down at the next table but he refused to talk to them today because they were sinners. Izzy had just woken up. The Pig was less than half full, because it was dawn and most of the nightshift had gone back to sleeping in the night, getting up for meals and then going back to their bunks. The galley refused to give any nightshifter any food during the day or any dayshifter any food during the night and if you slept through your meal you had to scrounge something off a messboy, talk very nicely to a messboy, or go without. Most of the messboys got as bad-tempered as the galley crew. Unless you were well in with a messboy, the only way to get a meal out of shift was to buy it with a pint of beer or a packet of cigarettes. Benjamin gave meals away for nothing, all you had to do was talk nicely to Benjamin. He gave them away with a scowl but he liked it very much when they spoke nicely to him. Even so Benjamin had credit for over a hundred pints of beer and every day Benjamin sat doggedly in the Pig. It made him nearly retch each swallow, and he held the beer in his mouth a long time before suddenly swallowing. He dearly wished that he did not have to drink the beer. He would like to have offered every man in the bar a beer to get rid of his credit, but he was too shy. When he had drunk three-quarters of a pint of beer he pretended to leave the Pig to go to the heads, and he did not come back. Usually he did go to the heads and vomited up the beer.

Tonight the Pig was quiet and surly. Jakkals came in. Behind him was the Coloured Piet and three other men McQuade did not know.

McQuade looked at Jakkals across the Pig and he could see he was drunk. Jakkals stopped near the door and looked around. McQuade knew Jakkals was looking for him, and he could feel his heart going faster. McQuade picked up his beer mug and took a long sip and he watched Jakkals' eyes over the rim of the mug. Jakkals saw him and stared at him a moment and then he started walking towards him. He walked with his arms hanging free, stuck out a little from his sides and his eyes looking steadily and his short cropped hair stuck up. The other followed him. McQuade lit a cigarette as he watched him come. Jakkals stopped opposite him. Everybody in the Pig was watching.

'I've been looking for you Van, pallie,' Jakkals said.

McQuade had his hands flat on the table. He looked up at Jakkals. 'Yes, Jakkals?'

'I wanna talk to you, man,' Jakkals said.

'You can talk to me outside,' McQuade said slowly.

'No I can't,' Jakkals said. 'What I got to say everybody can hear.'

'Is that right?' McQuade said. He still had his hands flat. 'Well you can talk to me outside or not at all.' He jerked his head at the other Coloureds, 'Without your pals.'

'You got a lot to say for yourself, haven't you Van?' Jakkals said, 'you seem to think you God Almighty on this ship – *Master* James.'

'Now lads!' Big Charlie said. 'Knock it off!'

McQuade held his hand up to Big Charlie without looking at him. 'I know my way around,' he said up to Jakkals. 'And I mind my own business.'

'Is the nurse your business?' Jakkals said.

McQuade snorted and nodded his head.

'Yes, Jakkals. The nurse is entirely my business.'

The men in the Pig were all watching. Jakkals looked at McQuade.

'You think you God Almighty, don' you *Master* James? Well I tell you something hey,' he held his finger out and the hard smirk went, 'The nurse is *none* of your bleddy business!'

McQuade stood up. He was shaking again.

'If you insist,' he said softly, 'on talking about this matter, we will do so on deck – alone!'

Jakkals' lips curled and he wagged his head haughtily.

'If you *insist* on talking about this matter,' he mimicked, then his face changed again. 'You're not in Cape Town now pallie! The nurse is none of your business Master James, she's a bleddy Coloured like me and if we peoples aren't good enough for youse at home you not getting *nothing* from us here!'

It was not as bad as McQuade expected. He had stood white and shaking ready to do something. He was relieved. He glared at Jakkals. If that was all Jakkals was going to say it was all right, he could let it go. It was almost reasonable.

'Anything else?' McQuade glared at him. He was quivering. He knew it was the wrong thing to say but he had to offer it.

'*Ja.*' Jakkals glared at him. 'Lay off her or else!'

McQuade stood there. Tense, half fists at his side, he looked full of fight. But inside he was relieved. He was prepared to let it go. If that was all the bastard was going to say it was all right. Let the bastard fuck off now and it was almost fair enough, they had both said their two bits worth. He stood staring at Jakkals, waiting for something.

Jakkals said, 'If you can't screw Coloureds at home you not to do it here.'

'Fuggoff,' McQuade hissed.

Jakkals swiped at him with his big flat hand across the face. McQuade's head jerked and there was a shocked instant's silence, then he bounded round the table at Jakkals.

'Jesus Christ!'

He had his arm pulled back in a fist, Jakkals stepped back crouched, waiting. There was a shout and Big Charlie and Beulah grabbed McQuade.

'*For Chrissake James!*' Big Charlie said.

Nobody was holding Jakkals. The men had scattered back in a big horseshoe, waiting.

'Get away you!' Beulah stamped his foot at Jakkals.

'For Chrissake, James!' Big Charlie shook him. 'You know better than that!' He turned red in the face to Jakkals. 'Get out of here or I'll call the Bridge down.'

McQuade relaxed and then he shook off Beulah and Big Charlie. He was white and shaking. Jakkals straightened up. He was grinning.

'Anytime, Van. Anytime,' he grinned.

'Fuck off you!' Beulah said.

'You better watch it too, pallie,' Jakkals grinned at Beulah.

'Shuttup Beulah,' Big Charlie snapped. He turned to Jakkals. 'Now scram or I'll call the bridge.'

'The fokkin' Bridge can go'n get fokked,' Jakkals said. He stood up straight and he dusted his hands elaborately. Then he shook his finger at McQuade.

'I warned you Van,' he grinned. He looked round at the big horseshoe of men. 'An' the same goes for the lot of you white bastards. Fair's fair. An' Coloured's Coloured!'

He looked around at them and then he shook his finger at McQuade.

'I warned you Van, hey? Non-Europeans Only. *Slegs Vir Nie-Blankes.* That's the way you want it at home, that's the way it's gonna be here!'

McQuade opened his mouth.

'Shuttup James,' Big Charlie shouted.

Jakkals nodded and grinned.

'That's right Van,' Jakkals smiled slowly. 'Jus 'you shuttup or else, hey? An' the same goes for the res' of you white bastards.'

He looked around and then he turned and walked through them towards the door. They made way for him and the five Coloureds followed him. Big Charlie pulled McQuade down on the bench.

'Quiet now, James. You played it fine.'

'Cheeky bastard!' Beulah fumed.

Jakkals got to the door and stopped and turned and looked back at McQuade and then shook his finger at him, 'I'll fok you up in the Cape, Van.'

McQuade lifted up his beer to his lips, watching him.

'Jesus,' Charlie said. 'Nice bastard, isn't he?'

'Isn't he a beauty?' McQuade took a pull on his beer and his mug was shaking. 'Take it easy, James,' Big Charlie said. 'You played it fine.'

'Well!' Beulah said. 'Well!'

Izzy spoke from the next table. He had not moved.

'The difference,' he said, 'is eschatological. Even in the Bible it says in heaven there is a great chasm between the blacks and the whites.'

'Oh shuttup, you,' Beulah said. 'Phew! That was close. Though I can't say you didn't have it coming to you, Professor.'

'Okay, Beulah,' Big Charlie said.

'I'm telling him for his own good,' Beulah snapped at Big Charlie. 'You better play it down Professor – even the Bridge is watching you two.'

The next day Old Ferguson heard about it. She said, 'Now stay away for a while James! Completely away. Let it blow over. Until the work picks up again or until the tanker arrives. If the Bridge hears about it we'll all be in trouble. They'll put you back on the catchers, James. Don't come near the hospital unless you're sick.'

Chapter Twenty-Seven

They squatted on their haunches in a queue along the surgery alleyway. The Kid had shot a few whales the past week, but few other gunners had. There was very little work but today there was blood again. The surgery alleyway was about the only part of the ship that never stank and slipped with blood. They waited in their socks. McQuade had a blind boil the size of a golf ball in his armpit. He did not want to take it along to the surgery, for he knew very well what would happen to him in there, but now the boil was so bad he could not lift his arm.

'He's a real bastard,' the Coloured man said. 'The doctor.'

McQuade nodded.

'Rough, hey? You get a splinter, he doesn't dig it out with a needle. He cuts it out with a razor blade, zip, like that.'

McQuade nodded.

'Dressings?' the Coloured man said cheerfully. 'He just rips them off, scabs and all.'

A shout came from the surgery.

'You see?' the Coloured man said.

McQuade's arm was so sore he didn't even want to lift it to roll a cigarette. It was all this no green vegetables. Many of the men started getting boils about February, it was the same every season.

'*Ou* Jakkals,' the Coloured man said cheerfully, 'he slugged the doctor. He was cutting out a splinter and *ou* Jakkals he got so mad he slugged him one.'

The man came out of the surgery. Old Fergie followed him.

'Next?' Old Fergie said.

She glowered at McQuade.

'And? What's wrong with you?' Old Ferguson demanded.

'I've got a boil in my armpit, Fergie,' McQuade said.

'And don't call me Fergie! Have you been taking your Vitamins C and D?'

'Yes,' McQuade said.

'Humpf!' Old Ferguson said, regarding this as a barefaced lie. '*When* you remember. Let's have a look at it!'

All of Old Ferguson's sentences ended in exclamation marks.

McQuade took his shirt off carefully so as not to move his shoulder too much. Old Ferguson watched him impatiently.

'What you going to do with the time you save, Fergie?' he said.

'Hurry up, young man!'

The shirt was off. He raised his elbow to shoulder height very gingerly. It was very painful.

'Let's see it.' Old Ferguson grabbed his elbow and shoved it above his head.

'For Chrissake Fergie!'

'Don't blaspheme, James!'

Old Ferguson peered at the red swollen armpit. 'Nasty,' she said. It was as big as half a golfball. She got her fingers round the boil and squeezed it experimentally.

'Christ!'

'Don't blaspheme, James. Hmmm, we'll have to open that.'

She led him like Madame Defarge into the doctor's room. He stood up from his desk.

'Boil, doctor,' she said.

The doctor looked at the armpit. '*Himmel*,' he said.

He prodded round the sides of the boil.

'Ow!' McQuade said.

'Sh-sh-sh-sh,' the Herr doktor said. 'Aren't you a soldier?'

'No,' McQuade said.

'Neffer been a soldier?' the Herr doktor said. 'Every yonk man should a soldier be.'

'I did my National Service,' McQuade said.

'You liked it, *ja*?' the doctor said. He was still prodding the boil.

'No,' McQuade said.

'*Ja,*' the Herr doktor said. 'We will have to an incision make. Shave the armpit,' he said to Old Ferguson.

'Lie down there, James,' Old Ferguson said.

McQuade lay down on the table unhappily. Old Ferguson came with a cut-throat razor and some soapy cotton wool in a kidney bowl. The doctor had gone next door. McQuade forced his elbow back above his head before Old Ferguson could shove it up. 'Why've we got to have the Gestapo on an English ship?' he complained.

'Sh, James,' Old Ferguson said. 'He's very efficient.'

'The Gestapo were all very efficient.'

'Sh, James!'

Old Ferguson dabbed the wet cotton wool on to the swollen armpit.

'This'll be a bit tender,' she said.

'You're telling me?' He clenched his teeth and jerked with each jab. 'Look Fergie – let me go below and shave it myself.'

'Come *on* James. Whoever does it, it is going to be tender.'

'*Tender,* she says.'

Old Ferguson pinched up some hair and pulled it up against the skin. 'Now, I'm trying not to pull, this is the quickest way.'

'Please,' McQuade gritted. 'Let me go and do it myself.'

'Come *on,* James!'

She slashed the base of the hair away with the cut-throat. Then she pinched up some more and she pulled it hard and the skin pulled up on the boil like tents.

'Je-*zuz!*' McQuade shouted.

'My, you *do* make a lot of noise.'

She threw the tufts of hair into the kidney bowl. She took another pinch. 'This way the blade only touches the hair not the skin,' she said. She cut and threw the tufts aside.

'That's enough,' McQuade said.

'That's the worst,' Old Ferguson said. 'Now keep still. I'm going to scrape it once.'

'Oh Jesus.'

'Don't blaspheme, James.'

'Oh Christ,' McQuade said, 'here comes the Gestapo.'

'What you say?' the Herr doktor said coming up to the table.

'Nothing,' Old Ferguson said, 'he's been a very good boy.'

The doctor winked at McQuade.

'Let's see it now,' he said. He gave it another press on the sides.

'Lock both your hands behind your head, so,' the doctor demonstrated. *'Gut!* Give me a scalpel,' he said to Old Ferguson.

Old Ferguson went to the steriliser. She came back with a wicked silver scalpel and stood over McQuade.

'Aren't you going to give me an injection?' McQuade said.

'Sh-sh-sh-sh,' the Herr doktor said, 'aren't you a soldier? This won't hurt much.'

'An injection will hurt as much as the incision, James,' Old Ferguson said.

'Just a little cut,' the doctor said. 'Strap his feet, Matron.'

Old Ferguson went to the foot of the table and buckled the leather strap over McQuade's ankles.

'This augurs beautifully,' McQuade said.

'Sh-sh-sh,' the doctor said. 'Hold his head.'

Old Ferguson went and stood behind McQuade's head and locked her palms over his forehead and pressed down firmly. She rubbed his forehead thrice with her little finger to comfort him.

'Got him tight?'

'Yes, doctor,' she said.

The doctor leant down and examined the boil closely. 'Hmmmmmmm,' he said.

'Oh sweet suffering Jesus,' McQuade said. 'Get on with it.'

Old Fergie rubbed her little finger on his forehead again.

'I'm looking for the best place,' the doctor said into McQuade's armpit, 'though so big is it I cannot miss.'

'Sweet suffering Jesus.'

'Sh-sh,' the Herr Doktor said. 'What would Sister Rhodes say? Got him tight?'

'Yes,' McQuade said.

The doctor jabbed the scalpel into the hump of red flesh.

'*Aaaaarh!*' McQuade screamed and bucked and Old Ferguson held him. The knife dug into the big red swell and the pain streaked through his chest and shoulder. The doctor squeezed the boil and a lot of muck came out. McQuade shouted again.

'Once more,' the doctor said. 'It's a double one.'

Jab went the scalpel again and McQuade bucked and cried out again.

'*Gut*,' the doctor said. He slapped a piece of lint on to the wound. Old Ferguson let him go and undid the straps.

'*Gut*,' the Herr doktor said. 'But for a soldier you make much noise.'

Old Ferguson shot McQuade a look to shut him up.

'*Gut*,' the doctor said. 'The next.'

Chapter Twenty-Eight

The snow was clean on the poop deck outside the hospital. There had been only three whales in five days but the poop and the fo'c'sle were still the only pieces of deck where the snow was white, not pink. The factory was rolling a little in the mid-morning sun, going God knows where. He no longer knew or cared. About seven days ago they were due south of Fiji, yesterday Big Charlie had told him they were due south of Perth. Sometimes, these days, the sun only set for a few hours, other times it was dark half the time. That depended on whether they were going east or west round the pole, following the sun or steaming away from it. All McQuade cared about was that it was February. Soon the tanker would come. Then only two months to go. The sea was blue black. There was one whale in tow behind the factory, bloated striped belly upmost and its six foot penis awash. The dayshift were working another whale on deck. Only three whales in five days. The whaling was finished. Man had shot them all to hell.

McQuade walked round the starboard side, going for'ard. He wanted to stay up on the poop, be alone. Most of all he wanted to be in that soft sweet-smelling cabin, but if he couldn't he wanted to be where it was clean and fresh and alone. Christ, that sickening bloody bullshit in the fo'c'sle. Three hundred men with nothing to do because there were no whales. The fights were coming every night now. The Mess room friendlies, the wrestling and the barefist sparrings that began because of talk, of demonstrations, just because men wanted to fight with somebody, the friendlies that turned into the not so friendlies. Men like to fight. It satisfied something, the being a man. And the fights that didn't start as friendlies, the ones that started with a word, or for just anything at all. The men were getting pretty sick of each other, and the sea and the ice. And the no women, not even any letters. It was the same every season. But this season it was worse, because of the no whales.

There was a very big iceberg to starboard. McQuade stopped and looked at her. She was only a mile away. She must have been a couple of miles long, lying there like a chunk of land with her long flat top with some jagged mountains of ice on top, and her sharp pearly cliffs two hundred feet high dropping perpendicular into the blue black sea. The sea was pale blue where the cliffs met the water, for under the water was a seabed of ice. Eight times as much ice under the water as the two miles of two hundred foot iceberg McQuade could see. There were bays and beaches on that iceberg, bays big enough for the ship to anchor in, and there was a big blue glittering grotto disappearing into blackness inside the iceberg. The iceberg was just like land. It was nice to see her there, something solid like land. After three months it was nice to see that. There was ice floe to port and maybe thirty icebergs. The sky was bright blue and hard and the sun shone white and clean off the icebergs so it hurt your eyes. Then McQuade came to the for'ard end of the poop deck and there below him was the stinking rattling vermilion carnage of the cutting deck. The dayshift working the first whale.

He climbed down to the factory deck and went to the galley hatch and got a mug of coffee.

McQuade walked into the Big Mess with his coffee. There were thirty or forty men sitting at the long tables drinking coffee and some of them beer, talking. The Mess deck had been scrubbed an hour before but now it was trampled thick with blood again. Big Charlie and Jock and Beulah and Izzy and Buzzy were sitting at one table and McQuade walked over to them and sat down.

'Today the tanker left Cape Town,' Big Charlie said brightly.

'Did it?' McQuade said.

Big Charlie nodded delightedly.

'She'll be here in a week, ten days. Letters, Jimmy!'

He nudged McQuade's arm delightedly as if it were a joke.

'God,' McQuade said, 'the tanker!' Only ten days away. Another ship, strange faces, from the world way up there, news, bringing fuel and taking away the whale oil. It really made you feel the season was nearly over when the tanker arrived with the fuel.

'Course,' Big Charlie said, 'it won't mean so much to you this season what with your own lassie aboard – but to *us.*'

'Sure,' McQuade said.

'There'll be some new photographs of the wife and the bairn,' Big Charlie said happily. 'I miss the wife, James,' Big Charlie said. 'You got no idea how much I miss her.'

'Sure I have,' McQuade said.

'Like you grafted on to her,' Big Charlie said. 'Like your flesh changes. So when you go away … man it's a shock Jimmy.'

'Sure,' McQuade said.

Big Charlie shook his head.

'It's hell every season,' he said.

Old Charlie, good honest Old Big Charlie. Him and his photographs. Women, sex, everybody thinking about it the whole time now. Everybody looking at the photographs of their women. And they asked you if you had a wife or a girl, and they asked to see the photograph, there is something about looking at the photographs of another man's woman after a while down at the Ice. And you showed them your photograph of your woman and they looked at her and then they went to fetch their photographs of their women to show you. It wasn't only the sex. It was the sight of woman you were craving, the presence of woman, the way they are, that is why you looked at the photographs. There was the other thing too, the brute gut sex, but that was a bit different from the photographs.

McQuade finished his coffee half listening to the talk. Then he went below to his cabin. He kicked off his bloody boots outside the door and stepped carefully inside. Januarie was sitting on the bench looking at the nudes in an old *Playboy*. Januarie was responsible for the glossy nudes pinned all around the bulkhead. McQuade had never bought a *Playboy* nor pasted up a nude in his life, even at the Antarctic, because the sight of all that perfect woman-flesh leering all over the joint made the whaling worse. McQuade did not notice the stink of blood and whale fat any more, but every time he went into the cabin he noticed the stink of socks and old body sweat. That was the worst of sharing with a Coloured, he thought. They sweat more. Don't shower enough. Maybe I stink too, he thought charitably. He got undressed. He slung a towel round his waist, put on rubber sandals and walked down the alleyway to the heads.

The heads had been scrubbed by the dayshift a few hours earlier but there was blood and fat on the deck round the urinals and round the lavatory bowls. He went into one of the showerbooths. The drain was clogged and he cleared it with his toe, a lump of hair. The salt water was not very hot. A dayshift potman came in dripping blood, shining yellow red on his oilskins, and went into the lavatory booth next to the shower and made a lot of noise and stink. McQuade thought of the smell getting into his wounded armpit.

'Jesus,' he said. He showered very quickly.

Januarie was in his bunk now, still reading the old *Playboy*. His thick socks were lying in a heap on the deck next to McQuade's bunk. Januarie only showered once a week or so. Where Januarie came from in District Six they did not have many baths. McQuade kicked the socks into a corner.

'Listen,' McQuade said, 'it's a rule of this cabin you don't leave smelly clothes lying around.'

'Do they smell?'

'I've told you before they smell. Now get up and shove 'em in your locker!'

Januarie got off his bunk sheepishly and obeyed. He didn't say sorry.

'And Janny?' McQuade said,

'Ja?'

How do you say it?

'It's time you showered again. There's a good chap.'

Januarie frowned.

'You mean I stink also, hey?'

'We all stink.'

Januarie wasn't taken in.

'You Whites ...' He hesitated. Then he decided to finish it. 'You always think you can boss us Coloured *ous* aroun.''

'Balls!' McQuade said. 'There's no apartheid on this ship. I'm telling you to go and shower because you need to go and shower. Some of those Pommies need to shower too.'

'Why don' you tell them to shower too?' Januarie demanded.

'Because they don't sleep in this cabin! Now go'n shower!'

'And if I won't?'

That was a good quesdon.

'Janny,' McQuade said quiedy. 'Will you please please please for Chrissake go'n shower?'

Januarie opened his mouth.

'I'll scream,' McQuade said.

Januarie was taken aback. 'You'll what?'

'I said,' McQuade warned, 'that if you argue and start bitching about politics and showering I'll go stark raving nuts!'

Jannie grabbed a towel and went out and slammed the door.

McQuade got into his bunk naked and lit a cigarette and lay there trying to read his paperback. Five minutes later Januarie came back to the cabin, trying to look clean. He hadn't had time to shower, but McQuade decided to let it go. He tried to read his book but he could not because he was thinking of Victoria Rhodes. Klaas came in and went to bed. They must have been going through pack ice or a big ice floe because the old ship slowed right down and there were loud bangs and knocks of ice against the hull. He lay there thinking of her so much he could almost feel her wide mouth pressing on his, and her breasts and her hips and the curve of her legs. And lying in the hot sun on his face half asleep and she came wet and cool and naked from the sea and put her arms around his shoulders and put her mouth over his ear and wriggled her tongue to make him burn for her, and then kissed him long and cool and tasting of salt water on his mouth, adoringly because she gave him such bliss. The white fat fumes from the factory deck came rolling up the accommodation alleyway, thick and billowing like steam, and it rolled into the cabin through the door on the hook, and slowly billowed up the whole cabin. And stinking of fatty gravy. McQuade turned on his side, so his back was to the fumes. Januarie's bunk above his began to creak rhythmically and then there were some slippery noises, and then Januarie began to breathe louder, and then very hard, and the creaks became louder. And then he sort of groaned softly, and then he was still. Januarie was thinking of his *Playboy* pictures again. Poor bastard, McQuade thought, an ugly bastard like Januarie.

Chapter Twenty-Nine

The next night McQuade went to the hospital to let Victoria dress his surgical wound. Ferguson had told her all about it.

'Good evening, Mr McQuade!' she said trying to keep a straight face. 'And what exactly appears to be the trouble, sir?'

'It's about this tingling in my loins, Sister.'

'Dear, dear,' Victoria said, her finger on her chin. 'How does it manifest itself exactly, Mr McQuade?'

'A pronounced swelling Sister. Very bothersome.'

'Dear, dear,' Sister Victoria Rhodes said with a straight face with her lovely finger still on her lovely chin. 'In the loins, you say, Mr McQuade?'

'It also bothers my head.'

'Yes, it would do, Mr McQuade. Tut-tut! And how long has this distressing state of affairs been going on?'

'Nearly two weeks, Sister, baby – two goddam weeks!'

'My-my! What can we do about *that*?'

'Just lie down on the operating table, Sister.'

'Oh darling,' Victoria hugged him. 'How lovely to see you! Isn't it awful, two awful weeks? Nobody can see us darling – how many men waiting in the alleyway?'

'I was the only one.'

'Oh darling, isn't it fun? I do wish you were really just a little sick so I could nurse you all the time in the sick bay, wouldn't that be nice?'

'Could you make love to me in the sick bay?'

'Oh, I would at nights when I'm on duty alone—'

'That would be first class. As your patient can I make love to you now?'

'Oh darling, perhaps we better not.'

'Just a quickie?'

'I don't want a quickie. I want a long long long one, all night. Soon we can, surely darling, we've been very good for two weeks.' She looked over her shoulder. 'I could do something for you that wouldn't be so dangerous, if it would make you feel happy and a little better.'

'Do you think you could?'

She looked over her shoulder quickly.

'Yes I could darling if you really want. It'll make you happy won't it? It's very unprofessional, against Florence Nightingale or something, but it is therapeutic' She laughed, then looked at him seriously.

McQuade grinned and kissed her. 'You're marvellous.'

'I will darling, if you like. I don't think you'll take very long, will you?'

'I'll wait,' he said. He kissed her and she stood in his arms with her head back a little and her eyes closed and her lips pouted a little waiting to be kissed some more, he kissed her again and she could feel him hard and wanting her against her belly and she rubbed herself against him, and then they broke the kiss. She took another big happy sigh. 'Isn't it good?'

She smoothed her uniform and said softly aloud to herself, 'I'm so happy.' Then she said with a smile, 'Business?'

'Okay.'

'Take off your shirt, darling.'

McQuade took off his leather windbreaker, then his sweater, then his shirt. She watched him.

'Shouldn't you wear vests?'

'I never wear vests.'

'All right darling. Can you lift your arm?' He lifted his arm and she eased off the dressing. McQuade winced.

'It looks fine. It must have been very sore.'

'It was.'

'Fergie told me you were very brave, I knew you would be.'

'Oh sure,' McQuade said.

She cleaned it gently. She was bright again now, not dreamy any more. 'I feel very important playing the nurse to you,' she said. 'I want to show you what a good nursing sister I am.'

'You *are* good.'

'Oh I'm very clever. Is that comfortable?'

'That's fine.'

'There you are then, darling. Come back tomorrow. *Night.*'

'Okay, Sister.'

She gave him a kiss on the mouth. 'Must you go?'

'No,' McQuade said.

She tiptoed to the doorway and looked into the alleyway and then came back beaming.

'Nobody. The whole hospital to ourselves! Sit down. I got you two bottles of brandy.'

'Did you!'

'I don't want you to be miserable, you're so cheerful when you have a nice drink of brandy.'

'Thanks, darling. I'll pay you for them.'

'You can pay me in kind, darling. If you want a drink now you can, though I'd rather you didn't just in case somebody comes.'

'I can wait.'

'I'll get your bottles of brandy,' she said. She walked out of the surgery.

She came back with the two bottles and gave them to him. He put them in his windbreaker and sat down. 'Are you okay?'

'I'm fine,' McQuade said.

She sat down opposite him and chewed her thumbnail once.

'What's the matter?' he said.

She looked at him with big steady eyes.

'Please don't be cross. This doesn't matter to you, it won't upset your life, you have not got to do anything, honest darling.'

'What?' McQuade said.

She took a big breath.

'I think I'm having a baby.'

McQuade stared at her. She looked at him apprehensively.

'Isn't that funny – a baby?' she said worriedly.

'A baby,' McQuade whispered.

'Yes. Just a little one. You don't have to marry me, honest. But isn't that good?'

'Good God!' McQuade said.

'Isn't that something, darling? You haven't got to marry me or anything but don't you think it's rather good?'

She looked at him earnestly. 'I'm really very very pleased with myself! I wanted your baby, you see, because I love you so much, you mustn't feel responsible. I don't even want any money I'm so happy.'

She was smiling earnestly at him.

'I would much rather have your baby than go without,' she said earnestly, 'so you see I'm really very lucky. You mustn't be cross, darling.'

'Ah, Vicky,' McQuade said.

'Are you cross, darling?'

'No, I'm not cross.'

You sure, darling?'

McQuade snorted softly.

'Quite sure, Vicky. That's okay. That's okay by me.'

He kissed her. He had never felt such a feeling. She broke off and laughed at him.

'Isn't it something!' she cried, 'a baby! Isn't that something!'

She gave a few little crying jumps for joy in his arms.

Chapter Thirty

McQuade walked back over the strawberry ice cream deck. There had been no whales that day. It was dark and cold, hard and biting. The ship was still, there was a catcher alongside bunkering and out there catchers' lights were twinkling small and dull in the night, waiting to come alongside, and there was nothing but ice and sea out there beyond. And up there in that warm clean white surgery his happy woman. He walked across the deck and then up the companionway on to the fo'c'sle head. It was frozen hard and dark up there. He walked up to the bows and then turned round and walked back again, and then up again. He walked up and down the fo'c'sle head thinking and examining the feeling, and then he turned and climbed back down the companionway back on to the cutting deck, then up the alleyway to the Pig. He went to the hatch and got two glasses and then he went and sat with Big Charlie.

'Have a drink, Big Charlie,' he said.

'What you looking so pleased with yourself about, James?'

'Nothing, Big Charlie.'

'You're very pleased with yourself about something.' Big Charlie said.

'*McQuade!*' a voice shouted. '*McQuade, this ship is awful!*'

The Kid was standing in the doorway, arms outstretched.

'*McQuade, hide me from that awful man!*' The Kid shouted. Everybody was watching The Kid, grinning, the darling of the fleet. He came hurrying across to Big Charlie's table.

'Hullo Kid.'

'Brandy!' The Kid shouted. 'McQuade give me some of your lousy brandy, if there's one thing worse than a Scotsman it's a detribalised Scotsman!'

'Sit down, Kid.'

'Is it true that round Aberdeen on Sundays you bastards still paint yourselves in woad and go round begging for meat? McQuade, my ship is awful.'

'So you've said.'

'Charlie,' The Kid said, 'do you love me dearly?'

'We love you dearly, Captain Child,' Big Charlie said.

'That's *right!*' The Kid said. '*Captain* Child, Big Bosun Charlie said. Respect, that's what we need in this vale of tears. Big Charlie will you please please please tell that awful shithead Mate to respect me?'

'Sure, Kid,' Charlie said.

'James, solace was never found in a bottle. James, it was a sad day when we sank the speedboat, mate. Any moment from now that gumboil is going to send his minions to flush me out before I have my solace found. James ... how is that glorious girl, Victoria?'

'She's fine, Kid.'

'Tell her ...' The Kid stuck out his arm and closed his eyes. 'Tell her I say ...' He opened his eyes. 'What does an English gentleman say? Tell her I say, "Tis better to have loved and lost than never to have loved at all."'

'Okay, Kid, I'll tell her.'

'Tell her I'm taking it like a man. Like an English gennelman should. Tell her I say she's got no taste whatsoever, that's her only trouble.

'Oh Christ!' The Kid said. 'Behold the minions.'

The deckhand from the Fourteen came up to him.

'Mister Child,' he grinned, 'the Mate wants you aboard, we're about to sail.'

The Kid listened, glaring at his brandy.

'I like that,' he said. '"The Mate." Yes I like that. Tell him you can't find me.'

'He knows you're in here, sir,' the sailor grinned.

'Sailor?' The Kid said, 'do you love me dearly?'

'Yes sir,' the sailor grinned.

'Then tell him I say I'm not here.'

'Yes sir,' the sailor grinned. He turned and walked out of the Pig, shaking his head.

'McQuade,' The Kid said. 'Succour me.'

'Let's go to Big Charlie's mess,' McQuade grinned.

'There will you succour me from the slings and arrows of outrageous fortune?' The Kid said.

They got up and walked out to the Sailors' Mess. McQuade looked through the porthole on to the deck.

'Here come the Slings and Arrows, Kid,' he said, 'seething with righteous indignation.'

'Oh Christ,' The Kid said. He clambered over the table to the broom locker and went inside. McQuade and Big Charlie were laughing. The Mate stomped up the alleyway to the Pig and then he stomped back down the alleyway to the Sailors' Mess. He stood puffing indignantly in the doorway.

'McQuade! I know Mr Child is with you!'

'He was here a minute ago,' McQuade said.

'Where is he?' the Mate demanded.

'I think he's brushing himself up,' McQuade said. Big Charlie laughed, then stopped.

The door of the broom locker burst open and The Kid fell out. The brooms cluttered on to the deck around him. McQuade and Big Charlie were laughing.

'Mister Child!' the Mate said pinkly.

'You spoke?' The Kid said. He dusted his hands.

'Were you trying to hide in there?'

The Kid looked at McQuade. 'Isn't he sharp? Boy, he's sharp like a marble. Yessir! No sir, I wasn't hiding, I was taking cover from the slings and arrows of outrageous fortune sir.'

He sat down and reached for McQuade's brandy.

'Mister Child!' the Mate burst out. 'You will return to the ship *immediately*!'

'I like that,' The Kid said to McQuade, 'the Royal Navy imperative. Yes, I like that, improves the tone donchathink? Goes with the shiny taps.'

The Mate swallowed furiously.

'Mister Child,' he said slowly, 'we are finished bunkering and we're about to sail.'

'Where to?' The Kid said, interested.

'To look for whales, Mister Child,' the Mate explained, 'you may have forgotten—'

'Where're the whales?' The Kid looked up at him, very interested.

The Mate took a big pink breath.

'Tell you what,' The Kid said very reasonably. You go find the whales and then come tell me, and I'll come and shoot them for you, I promise.'

McQuade whispered, 'Save his face for Chrissake.'

'Mister Mate, sir,' The Kid said. 'Will you have some of McQuade's brandy, Mister Mate?'

'Mister Child—'

'Request permission, Mister Mate sir,' The Kid said, 'to stay aboard till daylight sir. An unhappy gunner is a bad gunner sir!'

The Mate swallowed hard.

'Make a gunner feel loved, Mister Mate sir,' The Kid said, 'and you have a warm happy lovely gunner.'

The Mate opened his rosebud mouth.

'If you go away and fetch me at dawn, Mister Mate sir,' The Kid said, 'I'll be a nice smily submissive beautiful gunner; McQuade will see I don't get drunk sir.'

'*McQuade?*' the Mate said.

'Very responsible gennelman Mister McQuade is sir, comes from a long line of responsible gennelmen.'

The Mate was relieved to save face. It was nice for him to have The Kid requesting permission for anything.

'Bosun!' the Mate said fatly, greatly saving face, 'do you undertake to get Mr Child over at daylight?'

'Yessir,' Big Charlie said.

'Will you see he doesn't get drunk?'

'He is drunk, sir,' Big Charlie said.

'That he doesn't get drunk and incapable!' the Mate said fatly.

'Try sir.' Big Charlie said.

'Very well then,' the Mate said, very relieved. 'Carry on, men!'

The Mate marched away.

'Now, I ask you,' The Kid said, 'with tears in my eyes: as a tit, isn't he a collector's item?'

That is how it was in February and how The Party started. 'How them guys getting on?' men asked from time to time. Everybody knew which guys. The place changed from time to time. The guys were as follows: McQuade, Jock, Beulah, Big Charlie, fat Elsie, The Kid and Izzy Isaacson. Nobody was sure how Izzy Isaacson got in, because everybody was sick of Izzy Isaacson. The Kid could not stay at the party for as long as he wished because the Mate, who was now his Captain, would send seamen aboard to find him and flush him out. Having found him and having tried unsuccessfully to flush him out, the seamen would report back to the Mate and the Mate himself came.

'Mister Child!' the Mate said, 'we have finished bunkering and are about to sail!'

'Where to?' The Kid said, very interested.

'To look for *whales,* Mr Child – whales!' the Mate said. 'You may have forgotten ...'

'I tell you what,' The Kid said very reasonably, 'you find the whales and then you come and tell me—'

'You promised!' the Mate cried.

'But there ain't no bloody whales awhaleable,' The Kid wailed, 'and I'm having a whale of a time ...'

Very lousy puns but that's how you get with the whaling.

The course of The Party went like this: in the Pig until closing time, then to Big Charlie's cabin to finish McQuade's brandy, then to Jock's cabin to drink his moonshine, then to Elsie's cabin to drink his gin and Van der Hum, by which time it was tomorrow and the Pig was open again, then to the lifeboat deck to serenade Victoria Rhodes and borrow another bottle of brandy off her, to Jock's cabin to drink his moonshine that was still brewing, to the heads to give Izzy Isaacson a shower to stop him singing hymns, to the fo'c'sle head to sober Charlie up sufficiently to go on the bridge, to the galley to help Elsie cook, to the Fourteen to put soap powder in the Mate's mashed potatoes, to the amidships yardarm to rescue Izzy Isaacson.

'*Izzy, come down for Godsake,*' McQuade shouted up into the swirling snow night.

'There is no God,' The Kid sang.

'*Onward Christian So-ho-oh-holdiers ...*' Izzy sang from seventy feet up in the sky.

'*Marching as to-ooh war ...*' On the *war* a snowball hit McQuade in his upturned face. Izzy was astride the yardarm like a horse, peering down with deep interest as to his accuracy.

'*With the cross of Je-sus ...*'

'*Izzy!*' McQuade bellowed. '*Come down you sonofabitch before the Captain sees you!*'

'*Go-oh-ing on be-fore,*' Izzy sang.

McQuade dodged another snowball.

'*Izzy! Come down at once before you fall down.*'

Izzy shouted, 'There's angels up here, can hear their wings beating.'

'Ain't no such things as angels,' Jock said. 'He must be drunk.'

'Izzy!' McQuade shouted. 'Throw that bottle into the sea.'

'*Throw it into the sea,*' Jock shouted, '*and I'll climb up there and belt you one.*'

'God!' McQuade said. He started striding across the deck towards the mast ladder.

'Ain't no such person as God,' The Kid said.

McQuade started climbing up the mast ladder. He climbed five feet and fell. He persevered, getting the hang of it, got up fifty feet and slipped. He was holding on with only one hand and his legs kicked wildly trying to find the rungs.

'Careful, Professor, sweetheart,' Beulah called.

McQuade found the rungs. He clung there gabbling prayers to the God he didn't believe in. The snow beat in his face and his hands were sore and stiff, snow on his eyelashes so he could not see. He clambered on. Sixty feet, seventy. The yardarm Izzy was singing 'Closer my Lord to Thee.'

'Izzy,' McQuade croaked. 'Please come down.'

'Hi there,' Izzy said. 'Got any peanuts?'

'Izzy—'

'No peanuts?'

'No, I haven't got any goddam peanuts! Now—'

'Don't blaspheme. Olives then?'

'For Chrissake Izzy—'

'Don't blaspheme,' Izzy said.

'Come down, Izzy,' McQuade tried again, 'it's nice and warm in the cabin.'

'I like it up here,' Izzy said. 'Handy for the angels.'

'You can't stay up at the yardarm all night.'

'I like this yardarm,' Izzy said.

'It's a lovely yardarm,' McQuade said. 'But you can't stay up here all night.'

'I love this yardarm,' Izzy said, stroking the yardarm. 'I can't recall ever seeing a nicer yardarm.'

'It's the nicest yardarm in the business,' McQuade agreed, 'but you must come down. It'll still be here tomorrow.'

'It's a beautiful yardarm,' Izzy said stroking the yardarm. 'It's a magnificent yardarm,' he said cocking his head on one side and looking at the yardarm and stroking it.

'It's a splendid yardarm,' McQuade said. 'It's a shining example to all yardarms as to how a yardarm should be. But leave it alone now,' McQuade patted the yardarm affectionately, 'and come down.'

'I love this yardarm,' Izzy said. 'I'm going to spend the rest of my days sitting on this yardarm and loving it.'

'Izzy—'

'I *love* this yardarm,' Izzy declared. 'Do you love this yardarm?'

'I'm crazy about this yardarm,' McQuade said. 'Now—'

'It's the first time I've ever been in love with a yardarm,' Izzy confided. 'If you love yardarms ...'

Izzy broke off to think about yardarms.

'Izzy—'

'Well,' Izzy admitted, 'I've only just fallen in love with this yardarm. But I can't think of any snags in loving a yardarm. Not off hand.'

'I can,' McQuade said. 'Yardarms are ninety feet up in the sky. Now Izzy—'

Izzy felt inside his windbreaker and produced the bottle of moonshine. Both his legs swung free. McQuade started to scream 'Give me that bottle' and he strangled it in his throat down to, '*Give me* a drink Izzy, pal.'

'Sure,' Izzy said.

McQuade took it carefully clutching very tight on to the ladder.

'Now Izzy,' he said, 'come down.'

He was trembling.

'Gimme a drink,' Izzy said.

McQuade shook his head cunningly. 'No Izzy. Not till we're at the bottom of this mast.'

Izzy shook his head emphatically. 'Nope.'

'*For Chrissake Izzy, I'm getting tired of this!*'

'Don't stay,' Izzy said. 'Don't let me keep you.'

He felt inside his windbreaker again and produced another bottle. He took a slug of it.

'Oh God.'

Izzy swung his legs happily.

'Izzy,' McQuade pleaded, 'why did you run away from us up here?'

'Because,' Izzy pouted, 'you wouldn't let me sing hymns.'

'Izzy,' McQuade pleaded through the swirling snow seventy feet above the deck, 'if you come down I promise you can sing all the hymns you want.'

Izzy considered.

'And you?'

'I'll sing too, Izzy.'

'And Jock?'

'Jock too,' McQuade promised. 'The sonofabitch will sing all right.'

'The Kid and Beulah?' Izzy said eagerly.

'I promise you,' McQuade said, 'every bastard'll sing hymns and love it. Or else!'

'Promise?'

'Oh I promise you. Those sonsabitches.'

Izzy considered.

'I won't sing down below,' he pouted, 'unless we sing now.'

'For Chrissake Izzy—'

'Fair's fair,' Izzy pouted. 'You want to sing below, so, first we sing up here.'

'Oh Christ.'

'Gorn,' Izzy said. 'Sing!'

'What do you want me to sing?'

'Onward Christian Soldiers,' Izzy bounced up and down on the yardarm eagerly. '*Gorn* – sing!'

McQuade uncorked the bottle and took a swallow clutching on to everything very hard.

'Yippee!' Izzy bounced up and down. 'We gonna sing! Gorn – sing!'

'Okay, okay! Onward Christian Soldiers?'

'Onward Christian Soldiers. Gorn!'

'On-ward Christian Soldiers ...' McQuade began miserably.

'*Marching as to-oo war!*' Izzy bellowed happily. 'C'mon!'

'*With the Cross of Je-sus ...*' McQuade sang.

'*Go-ho-ing on be-fore!*' Izzy sang.

'*Go-ho-ing on be-fore!*' sang McQuade.

'Good!' Izzy said. 'Very good. Altogether now! A-one! A-two! A-three!'

'Onward Christian So-oh-holdiers,' McQuade sang with Izzy, seventy feet up from the deck in a snowstorm.

A figure came clambering up the mast ladder out of the snowstorm. Another snowy figure appeared below his.

'Sing!' McQuade shouted.

'Sing?' The Kid said.

'Sing!' McQuade shouted. 'You gotta sing or he won't come down.'

'Sing?' Jock said.

'*Sing you bastards!*' McQuade shouted. 'For God's sake sing! It's "Onward Chrisdan Soldiers!"'

'*Brothers we are trea-hea-hea-ding ...*' Izzy sang.

'All *together* now ...' McQuade shouted.

Chapter Thirty-One

The blood and the fat again everywhere, in the alleyways, in the cabins, in the heads, in the Mess rooms, fingerprinted and trampled, and out there on the deck a slough of blood and bone and fat, and the raw meat twelve feet high, and the blood gushing and gurgling and splattering and cascading, puddles and waterfalls and streams of blood into the fat congealing in the cold. And the loud rending noise of the winches ripping off the hide, and the gushing steam rattle of the winches and the shouts of the foreman and flenzers and winchmen and the swipes of the flenzing knives. And the limbs swinging from the derricks again, yards of bone and flesh and hide sweeping through the air dripping blood and the flenzers swiping at them with their five foot knives, and shouts and sometimes curses and sometimes laughing and singing, and the fumes rising up into the icy air out of the vat holes and the floodlights glaring yellow on the clamour and the flesh and the gore and the bloody men weaving and plodding and swiping and dragging. And the black night and sea outside and the dim cliffs of icebergs floating by.

Three days later they saw the tanker. The sun was still up flashing red off the icebergs. There was the tanker, on the horizon. God, oh God she was beautiful to see. She was keeping abreast, waiting for the morning to come alongside. They kept turning to stare at her that night, sitting low and black silhouetted out there on the horizon, a strange messenger from way out there up north where there was land and lights and people who lived on land. And their women. You had somehow forgotten what your woman was like, what it was like to be with your woman, it was sometimes like a thing that happened to you once long ago, and the tanker was like that. Then at midnight the sun went down and she disappeared behind the bergs. They did not work the last three whales. They lashed them in a row along the starboard side of the factory to act as fenders.

It was dawn when the tanker came alongside. They watched her all the way. She was clean and new and blue and beautiful. The factory cut her engines and she came up alongside, thirty yards away, and Big Charlie and his boys threw out the heaving lines and her winches dragged the mooring ropes over the water. Then the two ships heaved themselves alongside each other until only the row of whales separated them, the new blue tanker from way out there and the old dirty stinking factory with her rails of bloody nightshifters hanging over, staring down at her. She was quiet. The portholes of the bridge accommodation were dark and sleepy still. That was where the women would be, if there were any women. They stared at the portholes, hoping for the sight of women. There was no movement. The mailbag was sent over and taken up to the factory bridge for sorting. Then the two ships went quiet, waiting for the sun.

'Here we are just waiting to catch a look at it,' Jock said, 'and up there those lucky bastards sleeping on it.'

There were no more whales for the dayshift to work. Usually nowadays in the Big Mess they did not talk much but today they were excited because of the tanker. Outside it was cold and grey, the dayshift were hanging around, watching the tanker and waiting for the mail. The nightshift were still eadng when suddenly there was a shout and a big murmur from the deck and everybody in the Mess looked up and then somebody shouted 'There's a woman on deck!' and all hell broke loose.

The man sitting next to McQuade jabbed his fork into his lip and had to get it stitched later but it did not stop him at the time. Only McQuade and a dozen other men did not move. There was a big scrambling in the Mess, and a clatter. They surged for the door and pushed and shoved down the alleyway. Elsie was in the alleyway with a big basin of boiled potatoes and he was shoved backwards down the alleyway with his bluebeard cheeks bouncing and his potatoes were trampled to death.

'Men!' Elsie screamed. 'Animals!'

They surged out on to the deck, the men in front shoved by the men behind. There were over three hundred men on the deck straining to look. Then they saw her.

The woman was coming through the air in a basket, swung over by a derrick. There was an officer in the basket with her. The whalermen stared up at her coming through the air, three hundred faces gaping and waiting to see her properly to begin to lust after her, not a sound but the winch working the derrick, and the woman knew it about the men, she did not look down at them. She stood straight, very blonde and haughty and Swedish and groomed, she looked at the view as she was swung through the air.

The basket came down on the factory deck. Two Factory Mates saluted her, very English. She smiled brightly at the Mates. She was a little too strong looking, but that was good. She was not beautiful, she was even coarse, apart from her groomed hair, and her blonde face was hard, but she got them right here in the guts. They would have bludgeoned each other to death with their bare knuckles for her. The Mate helped her out of the basket. She lifted her knee on to the rim, then she swung her leg over and the toes of her high leather snowboots just touched the deck and her skirt was shoved up between her legs by the rim, then she lifted her other leg over and she showed a long white flash of her thigh. And it got them right here and a murmur went up from the deck.

Then they began to walk affably across the deck towards the Bridge companionway, and the big dense crowd of faces parted for them, staring. She was as tall as the Mate in her high leather boots up over her strong calves and her hips swung inside her thick skirt, and as she climbed they could see up her legs into the secret shadows of her skirt again and a murmur broke out from the deck again.

McQuade finished his supper listening to the talk about the woman, and smoked a cigarette. Then he got up and walked out on to the deck. It was grey and trying to snow. There were about a hundred men on the deck, waiting and looking at the tanker. The mail would not be sorted until half-past nine o'clock, the loudspeakers had said. He walked down the long cutting deck towards the slipway. Nobody spoke to him but he imagined the Coloureds watching him. He walked to the port hatch, next to the Smithy's shop, and through. There was some singing coming from up the alleyway. He came to the hospital companionway, and it was a small shock to him again to see how clean and nice it was. At the top he took off his boots. Then he walked up the surgery alleyway in his socks.

'James!'

'Jesus. You'd hear a cat on a carpet, Fergie.'

'Don't blaspheme. Where you going?'

'I am going,' McQuade said, 'to catch a bus.'

He had his hands on his hips.

'Very funny!' Old Fergie said. 'I suppose it's my fault, I should have nipped this in the bud when it began. Come here, James. You can't jaw in the alleyway!'

McQuade took a big breath and followed her into her cabin. She closed the door and looked at him.

'Well!' she said, 'I've heard what you've done to that girl.'

'Have you now, Fergie?' He was cross with Victoria for telling Fergie.

'Don't you get uppish with me young man, I feel responsible.'

McQuade took a breath.

'Fergie, I am free, white and twenty-one. It is my indaba, not yours.'

'I feel responsible.' Old Fergie turned away suddenly and she was crying.

'Fergie?' McQuade said.

'I feel responsible,' Old Ferguson sobbed. 'I encouraged you!'

She was shaking with her hands over her eyes.

'Fergie. You couldn't have stopped it. You could only have made it more difficult.'

'She's such a nice lass,' Old Fergie sobbed, 'and now she's in this dreadful trouble.'

McQuade took another breath.

'How did you find out?' He was cross with Victoria.

'Find *out?*' Old Fergie flicked his hand off her big shoulder irritably. 'I heard her vomiting, that's how! Every morning, morning sickness. Then she's radiant and bubbling with love.'

'Fergie,' McQuade said, 'everything is going to be all right.'

Fergie sniffed and then glared at him. 'You didn't use those things I gave you, did you?'

'Fergie you've been very kind, now don't you worry.'

'Don't worry?' Old Fergie said. 'With a layabout like you! Are you going to marry her?'

McQuade took a breath.

'Yes, Fergie.' He was feeling a bit sick of Old Fergie, he was feeling a bit sick of everybody.

Old Fergie glared then opened her mouth to say something, then she pursed it shut. Then she said, 'A young man who's never done an honest day's work in his *life!* Your drinking and your whores, oh, I've heard all about you! What do you know about the responsibilities of a wife and a baby?'

She said it grudgingly, she was going to say something much worse. McQuade waited, he had decided to ride it.

'What do you know about love?' Old Fergie said bitterly. 'All men are beasts, you've been cooped up on a ship for three four months without any woman except her, how can you say you love her? Would you marry her if she wasn't having a baby? When you get back to your Cape Town whores and your hormones are back to normal and your irresponsible judgement restored you'll regret this – and then you'll make her miserable!'

McQuade had to smile.

'It's no joke, young man!' Old Fergie glared. 'I've been on ships too long not to know what beasts men are! I don't want to see that girl unhappy, James!'

'Fergie,' McQuade smiled at her, 'I'm not a kid.'

'Oh James,' Old Ferguson's eyes went watery again, 'you mustn't marry her if you're only going to make her miserable, you're such a wild boy and she's so good.'

'Fergie ...'

'Look James,' Old Fergie took a sniff. 'Look: I'll adopt the child.'

McQuade smiled. 'Old Fergie.'

'I'm not so old, James! Look, I'd rather adopt the child than see the two of you make a mess of your lives. In fact, I'd like to adopt a child ...'

Old Fergie looked as if she might burst into tears again, then she stopped it.

'Fergie,' McQuade said firmly, 'you are very kind. But everything is going to be fine.'

She looked at him closely for a moment.

'Oh I hope so, James!'

'Sure it is. Now I better go, Fergie.'

'Oh James, I do hope so!' Old Ferguson said.

'Thanks Fergie. Now I better go.'

'All right, James, lad, I know you don't want to talk to a tearful old fool about it. You're a good boy, James. Good luck, good luck!'

'Thank you, Fergie.'

She opened the door and beamed at him tearfully.

'Go on then, James. And you know you can rely on me.' She was getting tearful again.

He walked back up the alleyway, relieved that was over. He knocked once on Victoria's door and walked in. He heard the sound of the shower behind the closed cubicle door. 'Victoria?'

The shower sound stopped instantly and she flung the door open.

'Darling!' she cried.

She was naked and wet, her long hair piled on top of her head. She dashed into the cabin and flung her arms around him.

'Darling, how wonderful you've come back, where've you *been*?'

She kissed him hard, warm wide saltwater lips and then leaned back in his arms, wet and curvaceous and bits of hair wet round her neck, and her breasts soft and perfect and her belly was pressed against him.

'Are you pleased you came back?' she beamed.

'Especially pleased I came back while you were showering.'

'Say I've come back to Victoria at tremendous risk.'

'I've come back to Victoria at tremendous risk.'

'Because I want to not because I had to.'

'Because I love you,' he said. She kissed him hard and long.

Chapter Thirty-Two

Benjamin Marais had never received a letter from anyone in his life, and he did not expect the tanker to bring him one. He was excited about the tanker because everybody else was excited about the tanker, and he pretended that he was expecting many letters from his girl friends, Sheila Pressure and others. The news that the tanker was coming, however, also served to remind him that the season was more than half finished and he still had not caught the thief. The thief had even got tired of stealing, he accused himself. He looked at the tanker morbidly.

Then a thought process occurred that so impressed him that he could hardly refrain from telling it at once to everybody in sight to show them that he was not jus' a bleddy little fool hey man. It went like this: if the skellum has stop stealing hey man you got to make him *want* to start stealing again hey man.

After considerable time the process continued: What you got to do is a trick hey man. What you got to do is trick the skellum to come to your cabin an' you hide in the cabin hey man an' then you *catch* him!

And after further time, with a burst of excitement: You got to tell everybody over the loudspeakers you lost the keys of your locker hey man and all your things is in there hey man! An' jus' now already the skellum comes along an' there you are and you *catch* him hey man!

Benjamin wanted to jump up and down.

And the time for announcing the loss of his keys, he concluded triumphantly, would be shortly before a filmshow, when the thief would consider it safe to strike.

Got hey man! It jus' a question of using your *kop*.

When it was nearly time for the mail to be handed out on the cutting deck, McQuade got off her bunk and started getting dressed. She lay on her side watching him. Then he kissed her and left.

There were still only about a hundred men gathered on the deck, waiting. There was still a quarter of an hour to wait. He felt very happy. He walked up the alleyway and into the Pig. It was full of men and beer and smoke and waiting. There was Big Charlie, leaning hunched against the hatch, rosy cheeks. He was happy by himself, thinking and waiting happily. McQuade did not really want to talk to Big Charlie, he wanted to talk about nothing. But Big Charlie's eyebrows went up and he smiled widely at him.

'Well, me old Charlie?'

'Well Jimmy, melad!'

'You're looking pleased with yourself, Charlie?'

'Ogh Jimmy,' Big Charlie beamed 'it's the letters that're coming be pleasing me.'

'You're a lucky man, me ole Charlie to be so happy about letters from your wee wifey.'

'Ogh Jimmy,' Big Charlie wagged his head happily. He dropped his voice conspiratorially. 'You've got a fine lass there too, Jimmy. And a lovely pair of shanks on her if you don't mind me saying.'

'I rather think so myself, Charlie.'

'I tell you,' Big Charlie lowered his voice, 'I tell you something. Jimmy: you get married, lad. Don't you leave it as long as I did. You don't know what you missing, lad.'

'Is that right, Charlie?'

Big Charlie burst into smothered laughter.

At half-past nine they were feeling pretty good when somebody shouted 'The Purser's on deck!' and there was a scramble for the door. McQuade was not expecting a letter from anybody more exciting than Sophie Marais, his housekeeper, and he waited at the hatch with his beer until the crush had subsided. Big Charlie slammed down his mug and said, 'This is it Jimmy!' and joined the crush.

There were nearly four hundred men on deck. The Purser with the big cardboard box was standing on a winch. He held up a bundle of letters.

'*Aardman.*' He pronounced it Artman. 'Akkerman – Aswegan – Anderson – Bancroft – Bull – Bosman – Burgher.'

The Dutch names belonged to the Cape Coloureds. McQuade saw Big Charlie. He still had a long time to wait before the Purser got to the Macs, but Big Charlie was watching the Purser intently in case he had got it wrong. He saw Benjamin Marais. Benjamin was shoved to the very back of the crowd and he could not see over the men to the Purser and every few moments he was jumping up and down to have a look. Then he stood, hands deep in his pockets and his chest stuck out and scowling at the shoulder blades of the man in front of him. He caught McQuade's eye and his scowl went and he gave a coy smile and hunched up his shoulders, then he went and stood where McQuade could not see him. Jock came up.

'Let's get a beer,' Jock said. 'It's a while yet before the Ms.'

There were only four men in the Pig, and the bartender. McQuade and Jock got a pint of beer each and Jock signed for them.

'Jesus,' Jock took a sip of his beer, 'wasn't that Swedish bird something?'

'Wassa matter hey Van?' Jakkals shouted, 'didn' any of your white whores write to you?'

Jakkals was sitting with three Coloureds against the far bulkhead. He had his legs crossed, smoking a cigarette. He looked very strong and relaxed and leering. The Coloureds were all watching. McQuade glanced at them, then he turned his back slowly and lifted his beer.

'Jesus,' Jock said. 'Lovely bastard isn't he?'

'Hey Van!' Jakkals shouted. 'I said whassa matter didn' you get any letters from your nice white whores?'

McQuade looked at Jock and Jock shook his head.

'Hey Van!' Jakkals shouted, 'you deaf or something hey, maybe you better go an have a shower like you ordered Januarie an' wash your ears!'

McQuade took a long pull on his beer.

'Take it easy,' Jock said softly, 'maybe we should get out of here.'

McQuade shook his head. 'Fuckem,' he said.

'I'm not scared of a fight,' Jock said softly, 'but I don't want to fight with no Coloured bastards if I can help it.'

'Hey Van!' Jakkals shouted, 'maybe we better give you a shower like you tol' Januarie and then you can hear nice.'

'Jesus,' McQuade said quietly. 'Who's your nice friend?'

'*My* friend,' Jock said. 'I thought he was *your* friend.'

'Hey Van!' Jakkals shouted, 'it's a bladdy shame you gotta share with bladdy Coloureds wot need a shower hey?'

'You're so right,' McQuade said under his breath, and Jock smiled.

'You see that?' Jakkals said loudly to the Coloureds, 'Van said something very funny 'cos his friend smiles so nice! What did you say to your friend Van?'

'All right,' McQuade said to Jock, 'let's get right out of here.'

'Hey Van ...' Jakkals shouted.

'Give us two more beers here please,' McQuade said to the man at the hatch.

'You boys better get out of here,' the bartender said. He drew the beers and McQuade signed for them.

'Whassa matter Van, you going or something hey?' Jakkals shouted.

'After you,' McQuade said to Jock, with his cigarette in his mouth.

'Hey Van you scared of a little talk or something hey?' Jakkals shouted at him. The other Coloureds were laughing. McQuade stepped through the door.

'You're dead right I'm scared or something,' McQuade said aloud in the alleyway.

'Jesus,' Jock said. 'Aren't they lovely people?'

'It's only because of Victoria,' McQuade said.

They walked down the alleyway and went into the Big Mess. It was empty except for Geradus van Wijk standing at the side. McQuade and Jock went into the farthest corner and sat down.

'I'm not so sure it's only Victoria,' Jock said. 'These bastards are gunning for anybody white, Victoria's just the excuse.'

'Let's talk about something else,' McQuade said. He was a little bit shaken.

'Talk about something else?' Jock said. He was a little shaken too. 'Listen, those bastards are gunning for you.'

'I'm doing everything I can to keep out of it, aren't I?' McQuade said.

'Except you're still ... seeing Victoria,' Jock said.

'Of course I'm still seeing Victoria, but only on the quiet. And that's my business.'

'Sure,' Jock said. 'I hope Jakkals and his pals are your business too, and not mine.'

'Let's talk about the Swedish woman,' McQuade said.

Jock took a long pull on his beer and then puffed his cigarette. They both took drinks of their beer.

'Well?' McQuade said. 'What's the story?'

Jock took a breath. 'Boy, I must be off my stroke. The story is she's married to the gent who came over with her, he's the Mate. And she screws.'

'Who told you?'

'The Swedish deckies. She's been screwing a few of them.'

'And hubby?'

'Hubby also screws her when he can. He's on watches, see.' McQuade smiled.

'She's a good screw apparently,' Jock said. 'Loves it. She's probably being screwed upstairs now by them all,' he said bitterly.

'And?' McQuade grinned at him.

'I got my plans haven't I?' Jock said shortly. 'And listen here!' he held his finger up at McQuade. 'Hands orf! You got your own. And pinched her from me you sonofabitch.'

McQuade grinned at him.

'Oh now Van's smiling too hey!' Jakkals shouted, 'so his nice friend is also a funny man like Van hey!'

Jakkals was standing at the door of the Big Mess now. He was holding a pint of beer and leaning relaxed against the frame and the three Coloureds were behind him in the doorway grinning. One was Piet.

'Oh Christ,' Jock said.

'Does your nice funny friend have a shower every day like you other people Van?' Jakkals said, 'or does he also stink like us Coloured *ous* you gotta share a cabin with?'

McQuade gave Jock a look.

'Issa bleddy shame you gotta share with us stinking Coloured *ous,*' Jakkals said. 'Christ, can't the Captain see you white?'

'Here we go,' McQuade said softly to Jock.

'But lucky for you you got lots of nice white funny friends who make you smile hey?' Jakkals said from the doorway.

Jock turned on him, 'I'll show you how fukkin' funny I can be, mate!'

'Shuddup, Jock!' McQuade said.

Jakkal's leer widened.

'Hey Van your funny friend says he can be very fokkin' funny, hey! That's nice, I like funny *ous*. Especially when they white, hey?'

'You shut up Jock,' McQuade said quietly.

'I wonder how fokkin' funny he'll be when I fok him up in the Cape, Van?' Jakkals said.

Jock muttered, 'A lot fukkin' funnier than you think, mate.'

Jakkals and his boys slouched into the Mess smiling. They sat down at the next table.

'Hey Van,' Jakkals said, 'is okay to work with Coloured *ous* an' make your money hey, but to share with Coloured *ous* wot need a shower is a bladdy shame hey man.'

McQuade took a drink of beer.

'An' is okay there by Oak Bay, you got Coloured *ous* running your fokkin' fishing boat hey, *that's* okay, but to share a cabin with them is too bladdy much hey?' Jakkals said.

'Jesus,' McQuade muttered, 'I'm getting bloody tired of this.'

Geradus van Wijk came walking slowly over. He stood against a stanchion and listened.

'But is okay to share a cabin with a Coloured *girl*, hey Van? Do you make her shower every day to make her white hey?'

McQuade looked at Jakkals.

'Is all in the colour of the skin hey, Van, you can't make her white by making her shower, man,' Jakkals smiled at him.

McQuade waited for him to say one more thing. He looked at Jakkals. Geradus van Wijk walked from the stanchion behind Jakkals and stood against the bulkhead to the side of Jakkals. Geradus van Wijk was watching McQuade.

Jakkals smiled at McQuade.

'I see you got your nice Dutchman friend come to your side Van,' Jakkals smiled. 'You whites gotta stick together hey man.'

'You fuckin' right we stick together,' Geradus van Wijk glared at Jakkals.

'You keep out of this!' McQuade snapped at van Wijk without looking at him. He said to Jakkals slowly, 'I am getting very tired of this. I am doing my best to avoid the fight you obviously want, but I am getting very tired of this. Now will you fuck off and leave me alone?'

Jakkals listened with rapt attention. All the Coloureds listened with rapt attention. When he finished Jakkals nodded his head up and down, up and down and smiled.

'Van's getting tired of us Coloured *ous*,' he reported to the Coloureds. 'He says will we please fuck off an' give him no more cheek. Van's a white man you see an' us Coloured *ous* mustn't talk to him like that hey man, is not right man.'

Then he looked at Geradus van Wijk in great surprise.

'But Van! – what's *Baas* van Wijk doing taking your side hey, doesn' he know it's illegal to fuck Coloured girls?'

McQuade put down his beer and stood up. He did not look at Jakkals. Then he started walking to the end of the table, and it looked as if he was walking to the door of the Big Mess. When he got to the end of the long table he walked round it into the aisle and stopped opposite Jakkals across the table, and as soon as he stopped he lashed out and hit Jakkals across the table. McQuade had been in too many seaman fights to have any qualms about hitting a man who is sitting down. The only purpose of a fight is to beat the man. He smashed him as hard as he could in the face across the table and Jakkals was knocked backwards off the bench.

Then everybody scrambled. McQuade vaulted over the table and as Jakkals scrambled halfway up McQuade hit him again in the face. There was blood all over Jakkals' face. He was knocked backwards on to the next table and McQuade jumped after him, and as he went for him the Coloured man Piet hit him. Piet hit him on the side of the head from the side and there was a dazzling blackness and then he was crashing sideways on to the table and then the Coloured man hit him again. Then McQuade was lifting his leg and he got the boot in the Coloured man's guts and he kicked out as hard as he could and he felt the man disappear and he scrambled up and then Jakkals hit him. McQuade took it on the side of the head and then he hit Jakkals again. And then suddenly there was a new body in the fight and it was Geradus van Wijk.

'You fokkin' Hottentots!' he was shouting and he hit Jakkals right down and then Piet was coming to him and he ducked and his knee came up and he tried to knee him in the crotch but he missed but he got the Coloured in the thigh, then he was after him and he kicked him in the chest. The other Coloureds were scattered around, they didn't know what to do and Geradus ran at the nearest one with a shout and hit him. Then McQuade was back up on his feet looking round wildly then he jumped at Geradus shouting, *'Pull him off Jock,'* and Jakkals was scrambling up and McQuade jumped and hit him and Jakkals went down cold. The other Coloureds were scattered. Jock let go of Geradus and the three of them stood there panting, the Coloureds were scattered and Jakkals and Piet were down. Altogether it had taken maybe twenty-five seconds.

'You fokkin' Hottentots,' Geradus panted – his face was red and he was crouched and ready, *'Come on you fokkin' Hottentots.'*

'Shuttup!' McQuade shouted. His face was red and his knuckles were bleeding. *'Get out of here!'* he shouted at the Coloureds, *'and take these bastards with you!'*

The Coloureds looked at him and did not move.

'I said,' McQuade shouted, *'fuck off and take these bastards with you!'*

Two of the Coloureds turned away uncertainly. The third one glared, '*Ek fok jou op in die Kaap!*'

'You can fuck off,' McQuade hissed, 'before I fok you op right here at the Antarctic!'

He was red and panting.

The Coloured stepped back. The two other Coloureds stood at the door already. They did not know what to do. Jakkals began to pick himself up off the floor.

'All right,' McQuade said. He walked over to Jakkals and he stood over him.

'Now get out of here Jakkals,' he panted, 'or I'll hit you as you get up.'

Jakkals got up slowly. His face was bloody and he felt pretty bad. He leant against the table.

'Three against one hey?' he said.

'That's right,' McQuade panted. He was ready to hit him. 'That's the only way to treat a bastard like you.'

'*Ek fok jou op in die Kaap,* Van,' Jakkals said.

'Get out of here,' McQuade panted, 'before I fok you op right here!'

Jakkals looked at him. His face was very bad with the blood. He knew McQuade would not hit him again unless he attacked him and he smiled, bloody mouthed.

'You bastards going to be very fokkin sorry,' he said.

Geradus van Wijk shouted, 'You'll be very fokkin sorry in a minute pallie if you don't fok off with your fokkin pals!'

'Shuttup!' McQuade said. He still looked at Jakkals. Jakkals edged to the bench and sat down and smiled at McQuade.

'All right,' McQuade said. He turned and walked to the door of the Big Mess. Jock and Geradus van Wijk started to follow him.

When McQuade was nearly at the door Jakkals shouted, 'You bastards going to be very fokkin sorry hey!'

'Ye-sus,' Geradus van Wijk said to McQuade and Jock. McQuade led the way down the alleyway and into the Sailors' Mess.

'Sit,' he said. 'I'll get some beer.'

He walked up the alleyway to the Pig. It was still empty.

'Three,' he said.

Chapter Thirty-Three

The Sailors' Mess had two long tables. The two portholes overlooked the cutting deck. McQuade came back with the beers. He put them down, his hands were still shaking.

'Jesus,' he said.

'"Jesus" is right,' Jock said. 'You know what happens now?'

'Listen hey!' Geradus demanded, 'why didn' we all fuck 'em up hey, like *that*?'

McQuade was lighting a cigarette. His hands were shaking.

'Listen,' he exhaled, 'you keep out of this! You rendered sterling service in there but it's none of your business, you only make it worse.'

'Could it be worse?' Jock said. 'Jesus – you know what's going to happen now with those bastards?'

'You keep out of it,' McQuade said to van Wijk.

'Except he's already in it up to his testicles,' Jock said.

'Listen!' Geradus van Wijk said to McQuade, 'we whites stick together hey!'

McQuade took a big trembling breath. 'Listen. You may not understand this, but you're what is euphemistically called an embarrassing ally.'

Geradus van Wijk stared at him. 'Embarrassing?'

'That's right. That means I'm grateful to you for pulling those bastards off me in there, but you're more trouble than you're worth because you're a goddam troublemaker.'

'*Troublemaker*?' Geradus van Wijk said incredulously. 'But those bastards were gonna make mincemeat of you!'

'It's no good,' Jock said.

'*Got!*' Geradus van Wijk said indignantly, 'here I am, once you fokkin' hit me down because of something an' as soon as you're in trouble I come an' help you, and now … ?'

'I know,' McQuade sighed. 'And I've said I'm grateful—'

'It's no good,' Jock said, staring at his beer. 'You're both in it up to your balls – and me, unfortunately.'

'An' you the one wot's caused alla trouble,' Geradus van Wijk said indignantly, 'you the one who's got the Coloured girlfriend not *me, ou!*'

McQuade rested his forehead on his hand and shook his head and said softly, 'Oh Jesus.'

Jock was grinning tiredly.

'Well, isn't it?' Geradus van Wijk demanded plaintively. 'It's cos of *her* you hit me that time, isn't it? *You* the fokkin troublemaker, pallie.'

McQuade shook his head in his palm.

'Well, isn' it?' Geradus van Wijk demanded reasonably. He drew himself up.

'Okay,' he said reasonably, 'maybe I don' blame you so much, she *is a* good-looking girl, you get some okay-looking Coloured girls I admit an' all cats are grey in the dark I admit.'

'Jesus,' McQuade said quietly holding his head.

'Hey?' Jock tapped Geradus on the shoulder, 'you better keep quiet.'

'But I *mean,*' Geradus van Wijk pleaded, anxious to be reasonable, 'I don' really blame him too much, I don' *blame* him 'cos I know wot it's like down here by the Ice an', I mean, Chris', a man's a man hey …'

Geradus looked at both of them anxiously.

'Yeah,' Jock said, watching McQuade. McQuade lifted his head and took a big drink of beer.

'Well for Chrissake!' Geradus van Wijk said injuredly. He looked at both of them.

'Drink your beer,' McQuade said tiredly.

'Well, for Chrissake hey!' Geradus van Wijk said.

They sat, dishevelled. Geradus glared at them and then glared at his beer. Three sailors came in with their letters and sat down at the next table. Jock tried not to smile then shook his head and smiled.

'What the hell you so happy about?' McQuade said.

'Jesus,' Jock grinned. 'Who're your nice friends?'

'Hasn't it been a dandy season?' McQuade said.

'Only two more months,' Jock said. 'If we survive!' he spluttered.

McQuade said nothing.

'And it couldn't happen to nicer guys,' Jock grinned. 'In it up to our balls.'

'What I mean is—' Geradus began.

'Okay,' Jock said. 'What's your name again?'

'Gert,' Geradus van Wijk said.

'Okay Gert,' Jock said, 'forget it, you did a good job, lad.'

'I say we should fuckem all up ...' Geradus van Wijk began.

Two more deckies came in. They were happy.

'How's the mail going?' McQuade stood up and looked out the porthole. The crowd had thinned right down.

'Aren't you going to see if there's anything for you?' Jock said.

'It'll find me,' McQuade said.

'Only two more months,' Jock said. 'Okay, maybe two'n a half. Then'—he punched his fist in his palm three times—'we'll screw 'em all in Cape Town, Professor. Right?'

'Yeah,' McQuade said looking out the porthole, 'that's right.'

Geradus van Wijk was glaring sullenly at his beer.

Through the porthole McQuade saw Big Charlie running along the deck. He was running from aft for'ard, as hard as he could. He looked very big, running. He ran through the men on the cutting deck. McQuade sat down.

'Charlie's running,' he said.

Then they heard him running up the Pig alleyway. They heard him clutter as he stopped at the Pig door. Then they heard him running down the alleyway again, then along the alleyway to the Sailors' Mess, and then Big Charlie burst into the doorway of the Sailors' Mess and hung on the frame, ready to run on. At first it looked as if he were happy. Everybody looked at him in surprise.

Then you saw he was not happy, he was angry. He saw Jock sitting there and he let go of the doorframe slowly while he looked at Jock, and Jock was staring shocked at him and Big Charlie whispered redly, 'My woman ...'

Jock stared at him.

'My woman ...' Big Charlie whispered and he lowered himself in the doorway watching Jock and he thrust his hand into his pocket and he pulled out an envelope and slung it at Jock. The envelope was torn open.

'My woman!' Big Charlie screamed and he charged at Jock.

He charged with his hands outstretched and clawed and his teeth clenched and bared and his face red and wild and his veins stood out.

'My woman!' he screamed and it was a roar of hate and spit, he was going to tear the bastard's guts and gullet out and stamp the bastard into the ground and kick his chest and head in and stamp him into the deck. Jock and everyone scrambled and there was a shout and a scatter and the bench went over and McQuade fell backwards on to the deck.

Big Charlie crashed into McQuade and Jock was scrambling up and jumping on to the table. McQuade was scrambling up and shouting 'For Chrissake Charlie! What's all this!' and Big Charlie heaved himself off the bulkhead with a roar and dived at Jock on the table.

'For Chrissake Charlie,' McQuade shouted and Charlie had Jock by the ankles, Jock jumped and crashed over the edge but Big Charlie still had his ankles on the table and he bit him. He opened his big crazy mouth wide and gave a roar and he sank his teeth into Jock's ankle.

'For Chrissake Charlie!' McQuade shouted and he got him by the collar to pull him off, Jock kicked and Big Charlie shook his big head and roared in his throat as he bit harder. Jock shouted, hanging head down over the edge of the table and he got his free leg in Charlie's face and he stamped hard. Big Charlie's roaring stopped with a thud and his teeth let go and he skidded back from the table with blood in his mouth.

The men were scattered around the Mess room. There were more in the doorway now, watching. Big Charlie was on his hands and knees, blood on his face. Jock scrambled back to his feet, he was white and wild-eyed. Big Charlie got up off his hands and knees and stood hunched and bloody faced and wild, panting under his big eyebrows at Jock. His eyes were red and his face was red and his hair was wild, blood on his mouth. The first rush was over.

'Now listen Charlie,' Jock said.

'My woman—'

He said it hoarsely and spit and blood ran down his chin. He moved forward slowly, hunched up round the table. Jock moved back, white. He looked behind him quickly, then he spread his feet and bunched his fists and he crouched down a little lower and waited. He knew it was no good to run. No matter how far and how long he ran Big Charlie would get him, so he waited and crouched a little with his fists bunched. Charlie stopped four paces from him with his head down a little, wild, and his fists at his hips and his shoulders heaving. Jock crouched down a little lower and they stood there looking at each other, Jock white and shaken and Charlie red and wild. And everybody knew it was no good trying to stop them.

It seemed a long time they stood facing each other like that, staring at each other in the eyes, there seemed to be no way the one could hit the other by surprise.

Then Big Charlie whispered, '*My woman!*' and his brain reeled red-black at the saying of it and he charged again. He charged for Jock's throat with his left hand, then he swiped with his right and then went in at the guts with his left and he crashed his head on to Jock's nose. There was a shout and a grunt and the thud and Jock's face was bloody. He swung his arm way back and swiped it up into Charlie's guts, and Big Charlie took it and swung at him. Charlie was fighting wildly. And then, suddenly, it was almost over. Charlie crashed his head on to Jock's nose again and you could hear the sharp bone gristle thump of it, then in came his fist at Jock's solar plexus. Jock grunted and staggered, blood all over his face, as he teetered there Charlie's fist crashed on the back of his neck. He crumbled down on to his knees and he was kneeling there bloody and groggy but still trying to regain himself. Charlie lunged at him again, he grabbed Jock by his hair and gave a big grunt and he swung him across the Mess room by his hair. Jock fell across the Mess room into the corner, and there was a handful of hair in Charlie's hand and Jock's scalp torn white and red.

Jock reeled propped into the corner with his smashed face hanging down and a handful of hair gone, and Charlie was after him again like a bull. He grabbed him by the hair again and yanked his head back so his chin was pointing upwards, and he swung his fist way back behind his knee. Way back behind his knee he swung, then he gave a big guttural scream and he swung at Jock's chin.

Jock sprawled on the deck out cold and bloody. Twenty men stood there, watching. Nobody said anything. Big Charlie stood crouched and heaving and red and wild-eyed over the body and nobody said anything.

The fight was over. There was nothing to do but wait for Charlie to come away. So nobody said anything as Big Charlie turned and walked towards the mess room sink. It looked as if Big Charlie was going to wash his hands in the sink and leave it to the men to clear up the mess. Big Charlie's face was still red and mad as he picked up the big bread knife. Then he turned with the big knife and walked back to where Jock was lying, and the men realised. McQuade and some others shouted. McQuade jumped after Big Charlie. Big Charlie spun round fiercely and held the big bread knife out at McQuade's belly and McQuade stopped.

'For Chrissake Charlie!' McQuade shouted, but Big Charlie just looked at him with those mad eyes, then he began to walk backwards down to where Jock was lying, and he still glared at McQuade.

'For Chrissake Charlie!' McQuade shouted again and he jumped after him, but Big Charlie stopped fiercely and jabbed the big knife out at McQuade's guts again and McQuade stopped, looking at the knife one foot from his guts. Then to make sure he got the message Big Charlie swiped at the air in front of McQuade's belly with the knife and there was a whistling sound of it.

'*Don't be a goddam fool!*' McQuade shouted, but Big Charlie walked quickly backwards glaring at McQuade the whole time with the knife held out at him. McQuade looked around for something to throw at Big Charlie.

'Get a chair!' he shouted and somebody turned and ran for a chair, or a stick or a broom.

'*Charlie!*' he shouted, but Big Charlie was still glaring at him as he leaned down over Jock and ripped Jock's fly buttons open. McQuade took a lunge at Big Charlie but Big Charlie swiped at the air in front of McQuade's belly again. Big Charlie was still holding the big knife out at McQuade's belly as he shoved his other hand down into Jock's crotch and pulled his testicles out. Then quickly he lowered the knife and jabbed it into the scrotum and sliced it right open.

Then he dropped the knife. He didn't care any more. McQuade jumped at him and kicked the knife away but Big Charlie did not care any more. He held the bloody mess in his hand and made a mad guttural roar fiercely at it and then he crunched them up and then he flung them on the deck and stamped on them. Over the loudspeakers Louis Armstrong was singing The Blues.

Chapter Thirty-Four

When midday came that was all over. First they locked Big Charlie in the padded cell while the doctor and the two nurses looked after Jock. Jock was going to be all right except he was never going to be the same old Jock. That was that, that's your lot mate. You had it coming to you. Okay, maybe not as drastic, as terrible as that but some day someone was going to have a go at him. He was lucky it wasn't a shotgun blowing his brains and his girlfriend's all over the wall. Some said it was all the girl's fault, the bitch, Big Charlie's wife, the little bitch. Maybe that was true. Of course that was true, but it's a first class shithouse bastard who has a go at his own blood brother's wife, a first class shithouse. And Old Big Charlie at that, a nicer gent. Your own brother. Fuckin' lucky he didn't slit his guts right open from his balls to his chin, that's what I'd've done. But Jesus – what a thing! It was all over the ship.

When the doctor and the Mate and Old Ferguson went into the padded cell to see Big Charlie he was sitting in the corner crying. They asked him what he was crying about and he said for his wife. He made no noise, only the tears. When they said they wanted to examine him he just stood up and stripped off his shirt and vest and his big hairy greying chest was quivering and the tears were running down his face. He did not look at them while they examined him, he just looked over their heads with the tears running down his face, sick fury in his guts. Then the doctor gave him a sedative and then the Mate told him he was to be confined to his cabin and they were sending him home on the tanker next week.

He lay on his bunk in his cabin with his sick fury in his guts and then the sedative took effect and he slept. It was the middle of the afternoon. When he woke up it was dark and the ship was going through some pack ice. It did not feel any different when he woke up, the rage and the outrage in his guts. He wanted to jump up off the bunk and crash out of the cabin and rush and smash and roar his outrage and leap off the ship on to the ice and run and run over the ice and roar his outrage.

That day McQuade did not sleep in his own cabin because he knew the Coloureds would be coming for him. He got permission from the day bosun to sleep aft in Jock's empty bunk. He knew the sailors in Jock's cabin. They knew the story about the fight with Jakkal's gang. Everybody knew the story, it was all over the ship, as well as Charlie's fight. One of the deckies did not want McQuade in the cabin.

'Listen mate, you fight your own fookin battles, we don' wanna get fooked up in Cape Town, mate.'

'I'm not asking you to fight any battles!' McQuade snapped. 'I'm trying to avoid getting my face slashed in my sleep.'

'Go'n report it to the fookin Bridge then!' the deckie said.

'It'll blow over,' McQuade said. '*You* go'n report it to the Bridge.'

'This is a British cabin, mate!' the deckie said.

'I thought it was a British ship,' McQuade said.

'But we don' wanna get fooked up in Cape Town,' he said, '*we* never made no trouble with fookin Coloureds.'

'Who had an Empire upon which the sun never set?' McQuade said.

But he did not think it would blow over. Before he went to sleep McQuade went for'ard to Elsie's cabin. Beulah was in there, talking about it all. Elsie lay in his bunk with his black curly hair sticking out the top of his frilly pink negligee and McQuade and Beulah sat on the deck against the bulkhead and they talked it out, Charlie and Jock and Jakkals' gang. Elsie was very worried.

'I think you better report it to the Bridge,' Elsie said.

'It'll blow over,' McQuade said.

'And if it doesn't?' Elsie said, 'you've only got one face, you know.'

'These plastic surgeons are marvellous,' Beulah said. 'But it costs yer.'

'It's nothing to laugh about!' Elsie said.

'I assure you I am not laughing about it,' McQuade said. 'I was laughing at Beulah.'

'Two hundred nicker,' Beulah said, encouraged, 'and Bob's your auntie.'

'If they come back and it's bad then I'll report it to the Bridge,' McQuade said.

'Of course they'll come back and of course it'll be bad!' Elsie said irritably.

'If he reports now they'll put him back on the catchers,' Beulah said, 'poor darling.'

'Exactly,' McQuade said.

'And if he doesn't they'll have to put him in the hospital!' Elsie said.

'They may forget about it,' McQuade said, 'after Charlie's fight.'

'Forget about it?' Elsie said. 'You know these bastards. And after that Japie messboy was on your side? You know how they love him.'

'We all love him dearly,' Beulah said. 'He's a dear boy.'

When he left Elsie's cabin he met Benjamin coming out of the heads.

'Hullo, *Boet*,' McQuade said.

'Hullo, Master James,' Benjamin said.

'Did you get a letter, *Boet*?'

'*Ja*,' Benjamin said, looking at McQuade's chest.

'From your Ma?' McQuade said.

'*Ja*,' Benjamin admitted to McQuade's chest.

'Is everything all right at home?'

'*Ja*,' Benjamin said. He looked around anxiously.

'Hey Master James,' he blurted, 'the *ous* come to *donner* you, hey!'

'Which *ous*?' McQuade said.

'Jakkals an' 'em,' Benjamin whispered. He looked around anxiously.

'How d'you know they come to *donner* me?' McQuade said. *Donner* is Afrikaans slang for 'beat.'

273

Benjamin looked as if he did not want to be seen talking to McQuade, he wanted to hurry away. McQuade led him into the heads, up to the urinal.

'All right,' McQuade said in Afrikaans, 'it looks as if we met here by accident. How do you know they want to *donner* me?'

Benjamin's eyes were big and he was breathing nervously through his mouth. 'They come to look for you in my cabin, hey,' he whispered.

'Why your cabin?'

'They said because I do your washing, hey, so maybe I know where you are 'cos you not asleep in your cabin.' Benjamin was shaking now.

'What else?'

'They said they gonna *donner* me if I do your washing, I musn' do no more your washing hey, that's what they said,' Benjamin whispered. He looked over his shoulder. 'An' they said they gonna *donner ou* Gert, hey, you an' *ou* Gert both.'

'Yes?' McQuade said.

'An' then jus' after they go away *ou* Gert comes back to the cabin hey, an' that *ou* Jackkals come back hey an' he tries to *donner ou* Gert but *ou* Gert pulls out a knife, hey.'

'Oh Jesus,' McQuade said. 'And what happened?'

'So he pushes *ou* Jakkals out the cabin an' locks the door, hey,' Benjamin whispered.

'How long ago was this?'

'Jus' now already,' Benjamin whispered. 'One hour ago.'

'Oh Jesus,' McQuade said.

Benjamin was trembling.

'Okay, *Boet*, thanks,' McQuade said. 'You go back to work.' He put his hand on Benjamin's shoulder. 'Don't worry *jong*, nobody's going to hurt you.'

Benjamin looked over his shoulder.

'Go on,' McQuade said.

Benjamin hurried out of the heads.

McQuade walked up the alleyway to Geradus van Wijk's cabin. The door was locked. He knocked loudly.

'*Wie's daar?*' came Geradus van Wijk's voice.

'*Dis ek,* McQuade.'

The door opened after a moment. Geradus van Wijk was in his pyjamas. 'Lock the bladdy door hey!' he said, 'jus' now a'ready they were here.'

McQuade locked the door and then sat down on the bench. There was a penknife open on van Wijk's pillow.

'Put that away,' McQuade said.

'*Jere!*' van Wijk said indignantly, 'jus' now a'ready the bastard was here!'

'They won't break the door down,' McQuade said. 'Put it away!'

Geradus van Wijk scowled at him.

'Yesus,' he said indignantly. He slung the knife on to the table. McQuade picked it up and closed it.

'Did you have to use a knife?' he glared at van Wijk. 'Benjamin told me.'

'That little bastard,' Geradus van Wijk said, 'I dunno why you so pally with them!'

'I haven't come to discuss your views on that!' McQuade said. 'Did you have to use a knife?'

'*Got!*' Geradus van Wijk said. 'I like the way you make out you some kind of schoolmaster or something – you the cause of the bladdy trouble, pal.'

'I haven't come to discuss that either,' McQuade snapped. 'The unfortunate fact is we're both in it together. You've only yourself to blame for being mixed up in it! Now shuttup and listen to me! *Don't start pulling knives!*'

Geradus looked at him incredulously. '*Got!*' he said. 'That bastard comes in here to *donner* me—'

'Was he armed?' McQuade snapped.

Geradus looked at him incredulously.

'Was he *armed* the *ou* says!' he looked at the deckhead. 'Listen pal, you know these bastards, they don' have to be armed to kick you in the balls and kick your head in, hey, what am I supposed to do, fight like a gennelman?'

McQuade knew it was a good question.

'That's your trouble with these bastards,' Geradus van Wijk raised his voice, 'you treat 'em like gennelmen or your friends or something, *ou*, you forget a Coloured is a bladdy Coloured!'

'*Shuttup!*' McQuade snapped. '*You don't pull a knife unless he pulls a knife – and that's only if you can't run like hell! Do you understand that?* We're in enough trouble without making this a knife fight!'

Geradus glared at him.

'Listen, pallie, there's only one way to treat a bladdy Hottentot and that's in his own language, that's your trouble, you think—'

McQuade stood up. He glowered at van Wijk.

'I'm not interested in what you think, van Wijk,' he said softly, 'I can talk till I'm blue in the face and you won't understand so I'm not going to try. *Shuttup!* But maybe this much you will understand: so far it's just a fight. There've been plenty of fights in the history of this company. If you keep your big trap shut and your goddam opinions to yourself it may stay that way. If you don't keep out it'll turn into a race riot! That's exactly what the bastards are hoping for! *Keep out of it!*'

McQuade strode to the door. Geradus was staring at him. McQuade stopped and glared at Geradus.

'And if you need me I'm sleeping aft in Jock's cabin tonight.'

He unlocked the door and flung it open. He stepped through and slammed it. Then he opened it again. Geradus was already at the door to re-lock it.

'And keep your big trap shut! *And don't use any fucking knives!*'

He slammed the door and he heard the lock turn behind him. Jock's cabin was also locked and he had to knock loudly and say who he was before they let him in.

When he woke up it was dark and the ship was going slowly through ice floe. The tanker was no longer alongside, she had emptied some fuel tanks into the factory and now she had gone away to clean out those tanks for the whale oil. The sailors had already gone to breakfast. McQuade got dressed quickly and then walked forward over the long snowed cutting deck in the dark, to the Big Mess. As he walked into the Big Mess nearly everybody stopped talking and watched him. Everybody knew about it, they were all waiting. As he passed him Geradus van Wijk whispered, 'I'm on your side, pallie.'

As McQuade sat down the loudspeakers spoke. They said tonight there would be a film show.

Down in his cabin Benjamin sat rigid when he heard the announcement.

'Oo *Got!*' he said. It took him some moments to remember what he had to do.

Chapter Thirty-Five

At half-past eight pm they were crowding into the Big Mess to see the movie show, smoke and excitement and beer smell in the air. McQuade leaned against the bulkhead near the door. His mouth was dry from smoking. The screen was at the far end, so most of the men had their backs to him. He looked at them, row by row, but he could not recognise Jakkals or Piet or any of the others. Old Ferguson and Victoria and the officers would come in after the striptease shorts. The Big Mess got more full, there were nearly three hundred men crowding in and finding places, squatting and crowding. After a long time the man came down from the Bridge with the boxes of films and began to step and climb over the men and a big cheer went up. It seemed a long time before he had the celluloid rigged through the machine. Then he called for the lights to be switched out and there was another cheer and then the flickering words came on the screen – *Climax Films Present,* and after that had shown a long time, the words – *I'm A Big Girl Now* and there was another cheer in the Big Mess. Then suddenly there was a blonde girl lying in a black negligee on a leopardskin couch and she had a black brassiere and very brief black pants and very white big breasts bulging out and she was pouting at the camera and she began to recite sulkily.

My boyfriend and I
Have come to the parting of the ways
'Cos he still treats me like he did
In our baby days ...

... and she began to rub her fanny.

Down below in his cabin Benjamin Marais was lying squeezed under the bottom bunk, behind all the shoes he had dragged under as camouflage. He had taken the bulb out of the overhead light so the thief would not be able to use it and the cabin door stood ostentatiously ajar on the hook and the full light from the alleyway shone in on his locker that was wide open. Benjamin Marais was trembling and he dearly wished he was up above in the Big Mess watching the film show where it was nice and safe.

Down aft in his cabin Big Charlie was hot. He stood at the porthole watching the black sea, the bulkhead and the porthole were very cold but he did not feel it. The lights from the ship shone dull out on to the black sea sliding slowly past, and on to the ice floe. The ice floe was thick and chunky, big and small pieces, some pieces stood four feet above the water and sometimes a pearly facet would catch the light and beam it on into the night and you saw a fleeting face of ice out there beyond, then it was gone. Big Charlie watched the pack ice and he was quivering.

Then he felt the engines slow right down, and then there was the grind and then the jerk and crunch of the bows against the pack ice. Then she ground forward again and then she stopped, then inched forward again and the ship went on like that. All the time Big Charlie was standing at the porthole and watching the ice floe and listening and feeling the cracks and grinds of the pack ice and he was wound up tight. When the ship was half length into it he could see the pack ice from his aft porthole, edging alongside down the ship, the lights shone white upon it, and his eyes opened wider. The lights moved slowly over the ice and it glowed and reflected and out there beyond the glow the ice stretched into the black. Big Charlie stood pressed against the porthole staring and his chest was heaving hard now and the tears were running down his face. He stood like that pressed against the porthole staring and crying and now the pack ice was hard alongside glowing white and hard and clanking against the ship. Big Charlie opened his mouth and lifted his head back a little and the tears were just running silently down his lined sweating face, then he took a huge breath and sobbed out loud and he turned and ran at the door.

He flung open his door and ran down the alleyway, sucking his breath through his mouth sobbing and the tears running down his face. He clattered up the companionway and ran to the hatch. He flung it open and the cold wind hit him but Big Charlie did not feel it. He flung out on to the lifeboat deck and skidded in the snow and fell. He scrambled up sobbing and ran at the rail and looked over. There below was the pack ice. The tears were running down his face, he was gasping and Big Charlie gave one loud sob and he slung his leg over the rail and he climbed up. He did not give a backward glance and he jumped out hard.

He landed with a crunch on the ice and fell forward on to his hands and knees. The ice cut deep into his hands and his right ankle buckled over and sprained but Big Charlie did not feel it. Big Charlie scrambled up and ran. His body was jarred sick from the jump. He ran and sucked in the ice air and he gave one long animal scream of hate. He ran and ran and fell and scrambled up again and ran on beating the air with his arms and his face was wild and his hair was flying and the tears were running down his face. He ran and scrambled and ran over the black ice as hard and long as he could and then he was finished and his ankle was lame and he fell down hard on the ice and lay there, finished. He was shuddering as he gasped lying sprawled there, then he twisted his contorted face and he looked back at the ship. It seemed a long way away now, the big black ship with the lights twinkling and the white glow of the ice near it, breaking its way through slowly. And Big Charlie did not want to run after the ship, all he felt was the hate, and he picked up his head and he crashed his forehead down on to the ice and gave a roar. He lifted his head and crashed it on to the ice again and again. His face was covered with blood then and the ice was bloody and then he collapsed and just lay there clutching the ice and crying.

Chapter Thirty-Six

When the striptease finished Geradus van Wijk ducked out of the Big Mess and went below to the lavatory while the main film was being threaded into the projector. He did not expect to meet any of Jakkals' gang but he moved quickly and kept his eyes well peeled. It was all quiet and deserted below decks. When he had finished in the lavatory he went quickly to his cabin to get more cigarettes.

He was angry when he saw the cabin door ajar on the hook, he always insisted that each man leave it locked, but he did not suspect an ambush. It was not until he flicked the light switch and nothing happened that he sensed danger. He stood crouched inside the cabin with the dull alleyway light shining in.

Benjamin Marais was lying curled up behind the bottom bunk and he had heard the man coming and he was so afraid that he could not think at all. He had forgotten all about catching the thief and how nice it would be afterwards. When Geradus van Wijk stepped into the cabin Benjamin had his eyes screwed up tight and his hands over his face and he was shaking all over. His breathing was roaring in his ears and then he opened his eyes and his horrified eyes saw a dreadful fiend crouched in the cabin and Benjamin scrambled in horror. He gave a gargled scream and scrambled out from under the bunk and threw himself towards the door in flight making his gargling noise. As he scrambled across the cabin in the dark Geradus van Wijk hit him. Geradus swung as hard as he could and Benjamin Marais ran straight smack bang into it and he was knocked cold across the cabin and his face was smashed and his four front teeth were knocked right out.

Then Geradus jumped on him and beat his head up and down on the deck a few times. Then Geradus went to the bunk light and put it on and then he stared and gasped and said aloud, '*Oo Got, sorry man Benjamin hey ...*'

Victoria Rhodes was going to go to the Big Mess to watch the main film and Old Ferguson was going to hold the fort for her for the hour. Victoria knew when the striptease would finish because the Chief Steward had told her at breakfast how long they would take. It did not matter if Victoria was a little late because there were seats reserved for officers and the films were very poor indeed. But all the same you always went to the movies because they were movies, except Old Ferguson.

Victoria Rhodes left her cabin. She was still wearing her white uniform. She intended going for'ard through the factory deck because it would be too cold crossing the cutting deck and she did not want to dress warmer because it would be hot in the Big Mess. She was humming as she walked down the companionway on to the lower accommodation deck, then she started walking down the alleyway towards the factory companionway. At the end of the alleyway there was a storeroom for brooms and buckets and rope and other gear. Victoria Rhodes was happy and she looked very beautiful. She was still humming when the man stepped out of the storeroom behind her and flung one hand hard over her mouth and his other hand tight over her breasts. Victoria Rhodes screamed but she screamed into the hard hand over her mouth and there was nobody to hear her. They dragged her backwards into the storelocker.

She could not see the men who seized her because it was black in the storeroom, but she knew they were Coloureds from the few words she heard as she fought and screamed. She screamed and screamed and bit and kicked and scratched and fought in the blackness but they had her from all sides with a hand hard over her mouth and they stripped off her clothes as she tried to fight. Then they threw her on her back on the deck. She shouted and screamed and bucked on the deck but her shouts and screams were smothered by the hard hands that squeezed her mouth tight. Two held her flailing arms and one held her kicking legs open as she bucked and fought. Then the first man got on top of her and she screamed and bucked and twisted under the hard hand across her face, her cheeks were wet with tears of horror in the grunting fighting sweating blackness. After the third man she stopped struggling because she was exhausted. She fainted several times. She was raped seven times.

Then they left her lying on the deck in the black room.

Geradus van Wijk found her when he was escorting Benjamin to the hospital. She was clothed again and she was slowly climbing the companionway back up to the hospital deck. She was crying and her face was red and bruised and her eyes were wild and her hair awry. Geradus knew what had happened to her when he saw her but she refused to tell him. She refused to be taken to the surgery to see Old Ferguson, she insisted she get to her cabin. The tears were running down her dazed face, making no sound. Geradus van Wijk took her to her cabin and she slammed the door behind her and threw herself on her bunk. Geradus ran to the Big Mess to call McQuade. McQuade burst into her cabin and Geradus waited outside. He heard her ruffled hysterical crying.

'Unclean! Get away from me I'm unclean – unclean!' and her crying again. Old Ferguson was coming up the alleyway to see what the commotion was about. McQuade stormed out of the cabin.

'See to her Fergie,' he snapped. He strode furiously down the alleyway, his eyes wild and his fists bunched, van Wijk after him.

'Was it Jakkals an' them?'

McQuade snapped, 'She doesn't know but I'm not giving the bastards the benefit of the doubt by Jesus Christ.'

Chapter Thirty-Seven

They were waiting for McQuade up for'ard on the cutting deck. The film show was just finishing. It had stopped snowing now and there was one floodlight shining amidships. McQuade saw them standing there as he stormed out on to the cutting deck from aft. He stopped when he saw them in the distance and then they all turned to face him in a line. Van Wijk stopped beside McQuade.

'I'm with you hey,' van Wijk whispered.

McQuade stared at them down the long snowy cutting deck and he was panting with rage and hate. They waited in a line.

'I'm with you,' Geradus van Wijk said.

'Okay,' McQuade panted. 'Okay, you bastards.'

McQuade bunched his fists.

'*Okay you bastards!*' he roared. Then started across the snowed cutting deck towards them.

'All right you bastards,' he whispered.

Geradus van Wijk was striding beside him.

When he got amidships into the floodlight he could see them better. They spread out a little in their line. Then they started walking slowly in a line towards McQuade and Geradus van Wijk.

'Okay you bastards,' McQuade whispered.

'I'm with you,' Geradus van Wijk said, 'all the fokkin' way.'

Some whalermen were coming out from the film show and on to the cutting deck now. Then more whalermen came out to see what was happening, then more. Then there was a surge of whalermen out on to the deck. Then there were two hundred whalermen for'ard on the cutting deck watching.

McQuade walked slowly across the cutting deck and Geradus van Wijk kept abreast of him. The line of Coloured men came on and then on a signal they were all grinning.

'Jesus,' McQuade whispered. 'Jesus.'

McQuade's hands were trembling, but it was with hate and rage, not nerves. His teeth were clenched, walking stooped forward a little and his hands were open a little away from his sides as he swung his arms slowly, and he watched only Jakkals. Jakkals was smiling at him. The whalermen were following behind the line of Coloured men. When the line was fifteen paces from McQuade, Jakkals said something and they stopped. McQuade came on three more paces and then he halted, panting. They faced each other in the dull floodlight on the deck. McQuade could see their knives on their belts.

'What's the matter, Van?' Jakkals smiled at him.

'Jesus,' McQuade said softly and his chest was heaving, 'you're going to jail, you bastard.'

'I dunno what you talking about Van,' Jakkals smiled. He appealed to his line of men. 'Anyone can see we jus' having a nice little walk an' here comes Van and Mister van Wijk to make trouble hey. Don't think because you white you can shove us Coloureds aroun' down here Van,' Jakkals said smiling.

'Jesus,' McQuade gritted, he was trembling, 'I'm going to put you in jail for a long fucking time.'

'I think maybe you the one in jail Van,' Jakkals smiled at him. The floodlight shone yellow on his fat brown smiling face. 'Ask your frien' Mister van Wijk about that one, I think maybe it's you an' Miss Rhodes in jail, pallie, after I finish talking with the police.'

'Jesus Christ,' McQuade whispered. Then he spread his legs and bunched his fists and his eyes went wild.

'*Jesus Christ!*' he shouted, '*come on out and fight you bastard!*'

He wanted to charge them but he dare not because of the knives. Jakkals grinned at him.

'Come and fetch me, Van,' he grinned.

McQuade's teeth were bared.

'Come out of that line and fight!' he roared and the veins stood out on his neck. Jakkals held out his hand and beckoned with his fingers.

'Come on, Van, come on,' he beckoned. There was silence on the deck.

'Come on *Baas* Jimmy,' Jakkals beckoned, grinning, 'an' I'll teach you to fuck aroun' with Coloureds, pallie.'

A man shouted from the crowd, 'Not six against one, mate!'

Geradus van Wijk shouted, 'Six against two, hey! That's all right, two of us is worth ten fuckin' Coloureds!'

Fat Elsie came through the crowd. He stood at the side with his hands on his hips and shouted at Jakkals, 'Come out and fight one at a time!'

Jakkals grinned at McQuade, 'Tell your queer *rooinek* frien' I'll fuck him up in the Cape, maybe he hasn't heard.'

'I'll show you what a queer can do an' all,' Fat Elsie shouted. He lumbered across and stood beside McQuade. McQuade did not take his wild eyes off Jakkals, but he thrust his arm out across Elsie's chest.

'Three's plenty for six Coloureds!' Geradus van Wijk shouted.

McQuade took a step forward, then another, then another, and he did not take his wild eyes off Jakkals. He stopped, standing ready ten paces in front of the line of Coloureds. They were all crouched a little now, waiting.

'Me an' all Professor!' Beulah shouted.

McQuade did not blink or take his eyes off Jakkals. Everybody was watching McQuade.

He said with teeth clenched, 'Now come out. Before this turns into a riot.'

Piet shouted:

'A riot's okay by us, ou!' He tapped his belt where his knife was. 'A riot's okay with us!'

McQuade did not look at him, he looked at Jakkals. Jakkals was crouched down now.

'Come on *Baas* Jimmy,' Jakkals said. 'Come on, *Baas.*'

'Jus' say the word hey!' Geradus shouted to McQuade, 'knives or no fukkin' knives!'

'*Kom, Baas!*' Piet shouted at McQuade. He tapped his knife with his elbow.

McQuade stared at the line of Coloureds waiting for him to come on. He knew very well what would happen if he came on. He hesitated, crouched panting there a long moment ten paces in front of the line of Coloureds. Then he unclenched his hands and he dropped them to his side. He stood up straight and he relaxed his shoulders. He had to force his shoulders and arms to relax. Everyone stared at him.

'Very well, Jakkals,' he said, 'you win.'

Jakkals stared at him. There was a murmur.

'All right Jakkals,' McQuade said shaking, 'I can't fight six of you.'

They stared. He took a big breath and started walking straight at the line of Coloureds to walk through them. They straightened and stared at him. When he was one pace from Jakkals McQuade hit him with all his might.

He hit Jakkals in the guts then he twisted and roared and he hit Piet in the guts. A roar went up from the whalermen. He threw all his weight into both swings.

'*You bastards!*' he roared. He was fighting mad and did not care about the knives any more.

'*You fucking bastards!*' he roared and he was already on to Januarie. Januarie scattered back shocked swinging wide at McQuade and McQuade was so fighting mad he was wide open but he crashed through his swings and he hit him with all his might in his guts also and Januarie reeled right across the deck before he sprawled. McQuade did not hear the shouting, he only knew his eyebrow was bleeding. He bellowed a roar of hate and turned to run back and hit somebody and there was Piet coming at him and then there was Geradus. Geradus swung at Piet and he was down again.

'*Any more?*' Geradus shouted. '*Any fuckin' more?*'

McQuade looked wildly for the other Coloureds and there was Beulah swinging wild as Jakkals hit him. Jakkals was swinging from way behind his back and Beulah had his head down and the blood was splashed over his face and he was crouching backwards as Jakkals hit him. McQuade roared and ran at Jakkals and he dropped his shoulder and hit Jakkals at full run with all his hate with his shoulder and he felt the great jar and then they were both reeling across the deck. Then Beulah was staggering after Jakkals and the blood was splashed down his face and neck and chest from his nose and mouth and Geradus was screaming '*Okay*' and running after Beulah and McQuade scrambled up blindly.

'Leave him!' McQuade bellowed, '*the bastard's mine!*'

He grabbed Geradus and swung him aside.

'*Leave him Beulah!*' he bellowed. Jakkals was on his side on the deck. Geradus was looking around for more, Beulah was reeling, blood streaming. The blood was running down McQuade's face, blood in his eyes. Jakkals was clutching his side where the shoulder had hit him.

'*Come on!*' McQuade roared at him and his brain reeled black with rage and he bounded at Jakkals and kicked him with all his hate.

'*Get up you sonofabitch!*'

He kicked him savagely again.

'*Get up unless you want the next one in the head!*'

Jakkals rolled over and in a flash he had his knife and lunged at McQuade's legs with it. McQuade jumped back with a shout. He did not hear the roar of the whalermen. Jakkals was scrambling up. He crouched there with the knife. McQuade was heaving wild-eyed, he began to skip in a circle round Jakkals while he unzipped his leather windbreaker with a shout. He yanked off his leather windbreaker and seized it by the cuffs of the sleeves as he danced round Jakkals crouched there with the knife, turning with McQuade. McQuade whirled the leather windbreaker round his head like a lassoo as he danced around Jakkals and his eyes were mad and teeth were bared and the big leather lumberjacket made a loud beating sound in the air.

'*Fucking brown bastard!*' McQuade was screaming.

He whirled the windbreaker as hard as he could and Jakkals was turning, turning with him.

'*Faster you sonofabitch*,' McQuade shouted, '*faster!*'

He was five feet from Jakkals and the windbreaker was whipping in front of Jakkals' face, the big circle of men was spinning round and round about them.

'*Come on*,' McQuade roared. Jakkals swiped at the windbreaker with the knife. McQuade lashed the air outside Jakkals' reach with the windbreaker. Jakkals lunged at the heavy leather windbreaker and McQuade whirled in and lashed him with it. He lashed him across the head and face with all his might then he let go and he charged in with a scream. The world was reeling about him, all he knew was the dark lashing shape flailing under the windbreaker and the sharp swirl of sweat and the knife flashing. He lashed with all his might and hate and he lunged with his shoulder and he swiped with his other fist and then again. Something hit him on the side of the head and he did not feel the knife get him in the forearm. He felt the hair rasp his face and the sweat again and he swiped into the chest with all his weight and he smashed up his knee with all his hate and he hit and hit and swiped and hit again and he felt the man stagger. He swung his arm way back behind and he could not see for blood in his eyes and he shouted as he swiped wildly. Then he was reeling bleeding dizzy and looking wildly for the man through the blood in his eyes, clutching for breath and reeling, then he saw him. He was on his hands and knees shaking his head and McQuade shook his head fiercely to shake the blood out of his sight and he gave a roar of hate and he only knew the bastard was down, he ran at him with all his weight. He swiped him at full tilt on the head with his fist and the man sprawled and he reeled after him. He leapt on him with a roar of hate and he seized him by the hair and yanked his head up high and he drew his fist far back with a shout and he smashed him again. Then he sprawled on top of him and he grabbed the man's hair in both his hands and he crashed and smashed his head up and down and up and down on the deck and he was crying, '*You bastard – you fucking Coloured Hottentot bastard—*'

Then they pulled him off.

The next day McQuade approved when the Mate ordered that Victoria Rhodes be sent home on the tanker when it left in five days' time. The Mate was not told of the rape of Victoria Rhodes but he knew she was the cause of all the trouble. He was sending her home, he said, for her own safety, and McQuade approved. The Mate transferred Jakkals and eight other Coloureds to nine different catchers. He placed the afterdecks out of bounds to McQuade until the tanker sailed; he was forbidden to see Miss Rhodes. Every night for the next five nights McQuade slept in Miss Rhodes' cabin with her.

Chapter Thirty-Eight

The night before the tanker left Victoria was transferred over on to it. There had been eight whales that day and The Kid had shot four of them, but the dayshift had worked them. They had to keep the last three whales to lash alongside the factory for fenders so there were none for the nightshift to work and the deck was hosed down. The tanker had pumped over the last of the fuel oil and now she was taking on the last of the whale oil. She would stay alongside all that night and leave at dawn.

At eight o'clock that night they transferred Victoria Rhodes over. Two sailors carried her suitcases and Old Ferguson and the Mate walked with her to see her off. There was a big crowd of whalermen on deck to watch. They started clapping when she came out, for she was very popular.

A man chanted 'We want Vicky! We want Vicky!' and then they all took up the chant, 'We want Vicky!'

Victoria blushed and waved embarrassedly. The big basket was waiting for her, suspended from the derrick. The Mate helped her over the rim of the basket and when she showed some of her leg the whalermen shouted 'Ooooooooh!' and then kept on chanting. The whalermen started singing For She's a Jolly Good Fe-Hell-Ow and then the steam winch rattled and pulled the big basket up and Victoria Rhodes went up, up, and away and over, and there were the Swedish deckhands and the Swedish Mate on the tanker below to receive her.

When both ships were quiet again McQuade went down below to the factory deck and between the boilers to the "French" windows. The factory was going full blast, processing the new whales' meat and you would not have been able to hear a man speak unless he shouted. There outside the French windows was the deck of the tanker and eight feet below were whales. McQuade had fixed it up with the Swedish Bosun's Mate. McQuade pulled his snowcap down low over his forehead and put on his sunglasses for all the good they would do him. Then he climbed out of the window and lowered himself down on to the whale. It was dark down there between the two ships. The whales were bumping up and down ponderously and the black sea was smacking and sucking. He clambered over the whale and over on to the low tanker deck. He was back in the light now and if anybody on the factory was looking it was too bad.

The Swedish Bosun's Mate led him for'ard to the companionway up into the accommodation. He took off his spiked boots and walked in socks. The tanker was new and everything was very clean and bright and he knew again why he was a sailor instead of an icthiologist.

The Bosun's Mate took him to a door and grinned and said 'There in.'

He knocked and the door opened and there was the Swedish woman and behind her was Victoria. The Swedish woman smiled, she looked very nice.

'How do you do,' she said with her Swedish accent, 'I will leave you now.'

Victoria came up and put her arms round him and kissed him excitedly.

'She says you can stay as long as you like! She's the Captain's *wife!* She says she can handle the old Captain, isn't she a nice woman?'

'The Swedes are very broadminded.'

'I've met the old Captain and everybody and they're all very charming,' she said. 'It's very good.'

'They kicked the poor old radio officer out for me,' she said.

'He'll probably expect to come back at nights,' McQuade said, 'the Swedes are very broadminded.'

'Oh no!' she said. 'I belong to you, darling. Oh I *wish* you were coming!'

'It'll only be two months,' he said. 'Maybe only six weeks.'

She sat beside him on the bunk. Now she looked miserable.

'Darling,' she said, 'I feel such a failure, being sent home and everything.'

McQuade took a deep breath.

'It's not your fault Vicky,' he said. 'Now don't think about it.'

It made him furious to think about it.

She shuddered. 'I'm sorry. I won't talk about it.'

'You aren't unclean,' he said hotly. 'Now for Christ's sake! You were a great success. Everybody's sorry, you heard them on deck.'

She looked at her hands. 'All right, darling.'

He said nothing. She looked around the cabin miserably.

'I'm sad to leave my good little cabin. It's all empty now. Didn't we have a fine time in it?' She was trying to change the subject.

'We had a grand time,' he said.

'And the surgery and Old Fergie and the boys and all. I did like it so, everything except the killing, that's terrible.'

'Yes.'

'But wasn't it fun in our own cabin?'

'It was grand,' he said.

'It was our first home, wasn't it?' she said. 'I'll always remember it as our first house. And where we started the baby.'

'We'll make another house soon in sunny South Africa.'

'Oh I'm dying to have this baby! Aren't I *lucky?*' she beamed at him. 'Do you mind about my baby very much darling?'

'No,' he said, 'not any more.'

'Did you mind much at first?'

'A little,' he said. 'I've never had a baby before.'

'Nor have I, darling. Don't you think you've left a few babies somewhere in the world, darling?'

'Maybe one,' he said.

'Where, darling?'

'Italy.'

'*Italy?*' she said.

She stared at him.

'Oh I don't *mind!* The world must be a better place each time a McQuade draws a breath. I'd love to see your Italian baby. Do you think we will one day?'

'I shouldn't think so. She may even have had an abortion. She was very rich.'

'Oh, I'd *hate* her if she aborted your baby! You never told me about her.'

'There's quite a lot of things I haven't told you yet.'

'Have you *many* other children darling?' she said, fascinated.

'I don't think so,' he said. 'I suppose I would have heard.'

'Did you love her?' she said jealously.

'No,' he said. 'But she was very nice.'

'Why didn't you marry her if she was rich? Then you wouldn't have to be a fisherman and come whaling. No!' she said, 'then I wouldn't have met you. And that would have been *terrible!*'

She kissed his cheek, dismissing the Italian girl. 'Have a drink, darling!'

'All right,' he said, 'even if it is only breakfast time.'

She went to her new locker and pulled out the brandy bottle and two glasses.

'It's early for you,' he said.

'I've been awake all night,' she said. 'It's not every day I leave my love.'

She poured the brandies. 'Here's to us.'

They both took a sip. The brandy went down well.

'Be careful crossing back to the factory,' she said.

'How have I managed at sea,' he said, 'for ten years on and off without you?'

'God only knows,' she said.

'Tell me more,' she said brightly. 'I love to hear you talk. And you get so cheerful after a few brandies. Tomorrow I won't hear you for two months.'

'*Then* we'll talk,' he said.

'Boy,' she grinned. 'I'm going to be on the quay to meet you and I'll have a magnum of champagne waiting in the taxi!'

'I'll be imagining it for the next two months.'

'Except that you won't have much chance to talk,' she said, 'because I'll be smothering you with kisses.'

'And I'll be too busy tearing your clothes off.'

'You better wait till we get to the hotel darling! Or are we going to your house?'

'The best damn hotel.'

'And a bubble-bath! Oh, we'll have a proper bubble-bath and I can slip and slide all over you while I smother you with kisses! Isn't it going to be fine?'

There was a knock on the door and Victoria said, 'Come in,' and the Captain's wife looked in.

'The Captain says will you join us for dinner, but I said to him you would like it better here alone,' she smiled.

'Oh thank you!' Victoria clasped her hands. 'Would you like a drink?' Victoria said.

'No-no-no,' the Captain's wife smiled, she waved her finger. 'I will send the steward.'

Straight away there was another knock. Then a steward came in with a trolley. He carried in a collapsible table and set it up. McQuade tried to help him. Then he spread a white tablecloth and laid the table. Then he asked them if they would like soup. No thank you, they said, no soup. Then he put out plates and carried in a salver of roast chicken. They sat side by side on the bunk while he dished it out.

'Red or vite vine?' the steward smiled.

'*Wine*,' Victoria said with big sparkling eyes. She could not believe all this.

'The Captain always like vine,' the steward said.

Victoria looked at McQuade happily.

'Red,' he said, 'please.'

The steward went to the door and produced a bottle of red wine.

'Thank you!' Victoria smiled dazzlingly at him, 'very much.'

'*Bon appetit*,' the steward smiled and withdrew.

'Well,' McQuade said. 'Who are your friends?'

They ate the dinner and got very merry on the wine. When they finished the wine they carried on with the brandy. It was excellent chicken. On the whalers they only got chicken once a season, at Christmas time, it was a great treat. When they finished the dinner the steward came back with ice cream and frozen strawberries.

'Those bloody Limies should see how the Swedes run their ships,' McQuade said. 'But that's the English. Bangers and mash and a stiff upper lip, lads.'

'They *need* a stiff upper lip,' Victoria said. 'Poor bastards.'

'That wine's done you the world of good,' he said. 'Never let an Englishman near you. He'll open the nearest window and give you pneumonia. Look at that Kid.'

'The Kid's a good bastard,' Victoria said happily.

'The Kid's a champion bastard,' McQuade said.

'Wasn't that a good dinner? Haven't we had a good time together?'

'I didn't realise you had such a hearty appetite, I've never seen you eat.'

'There's a lot of things we don't know about each other. And already we're having a baby, that's a good start. I've got a very good appetite, I'm a strong healthy girl, I'm farmer's wife material. Or a fisherman's wife.'

'Yes, your strength would be wasted on an icthiologist,' he said.

'An ichthiologist's wife would be grand. It's not that I'm choosy, I'm just a snob. But you needn't change if you don't want to.'

'Thanks,' he said.

'You're the boss, darling,' she said. 'I'll always do whatever you say. Oh, it's a grand life we're going to have! And our holiday to the Wild Coast?'

'Absolutely. Champagne all the way and the best damn hotels.'

'Do you think I'll have trouble getting into the hotels, darling?' she said.

'Of course not, Vic. Don't talk like that.'

'I'm really not a Coloured girl, darling, I don't think so, anyway, despite what everybody says.'

'Of course you're not. Don't talk about it!'

'I'm sorry, darling. But you see why I'm so sensitive? It's happened *again,* five thousand miles from the nearest damn bus conductor and cinema cashier.'

'This happened because you're a good-looking woman on a ship with a load of sex-starved men!' he said angrily. Thinking about it was making him furious again. 'It was nothing to do with your damn complexion!'

She stared at the deck. So did he. She dared not contradict him.

'All right darling,' she said, 'I'll be a happy girl now.'

'You'll make a fine wife, Victoria,' he said. 'Shall I get undressed now, darling?'

He looked at her. He felt very good and fullsome with the brandy and his woman. She stood up and she watched his eyes the whole time and when she was naked and he looked at her he thought of those bastards between her olive legs, and he got sick with fury again inside. She saw it in his face and she quickly kissed him and pressed him over on to the bunk and said into his mouth, 'Don't think about it, just think about me and how happy we are,' and she started unbuttoning his shirt.

After a long time she went to sleep in his arms and he lay there, looking at her lying sprawled out and her long black hair all over the pillow. Her breasts were cream coloured and you could see the line where her bikini had been. She was very beautiful lying there deep asleep full of good dinner and wine and love. He wondered if it would feel any different after she had gone, or when he got back and saw other women again, but he could not feel how it felt when you see other women. He wondered how he would feel when she was big with the baby or if she did turn out to have some Coloured blood in her and he decided that it would not matter provided nobody else knew and gave them a hard time, but he could not feel it. After a long time he went to sleep.

When he woke the sky was beginning to grey through the porthole. She was already awake and she had pulled a blanket over them.

She said, 'I was watching you.'

'Did you sleep well, darling?'

'I had a lovely sleep,' she said. 'I think two people draw strength from each other when they sleep together.'

They got dressed. There was a range of icebergs to port and one of the catchers was already waiting to act as a tug.

'It's beautiful,' she said. 'I've got so used to portholes and masts and winches and icebergs and now I'll never see them again.'

There were some sailors on the fo'c'sle.

'Shall I try and get us some tea? They'll call us when you must go,' she said.

'No,' he said. 'Let's say goodbye now.'

'All right darling,' she said.

'Goodbye Victoria,' he said.

'Goodbye darling.'

'Remember to write.'

'I can't write to you, can I?'

'It was a joke,' he said. 'Look after yourself and young Victoria.'

'Don't worry, I'm making you a grand baby, darling. I'll be on the quay to meet you no matter what time of day or night.'

'Good! Goodbye, darling.'

'Goodbye, my love. Take care.'

He walked through the door. As she was closing it, she said, 'I'll wave to you when we go, look for me.'

'All right,' he said.

He went back to the factory over the whales. It was very cold outside after the central heating and Victoria's warm bunk. The ship was quiet but there was a wind coming up from the west carrying snow and the sea was beginning to chop.

At sunrise when the tanker left the wind was swirling snow hard. There were few whalermen on deck to watch her sail, only the sailors to untie her. The two catchers sent out stern lines and hooked up to the tanker, one to her bows and the other to her stern. Then the lines were thrown off from the tanker to the factory, and the tugs took the strain and she began to draw aside. He looked for Victoria but he could not see her. Then the tanker swung around and he could see her porthole, and there she was waving. He waved. She jerked her thumb over her shoulder and then held her collar as if she was cold and he realised she meant for him to get in out of the snow. Then the tanker was swung right around and he could not see her porthole any more. Then she cast off the two catchers and she gave three whoop-whoop-whoooops on her funnel and the factory and the catchers answered *whoop whoop whoooop* and she rang up full ahead, heading due north.

Part Six

Chapter Thirty-Nine

Now in March it was autumn and on deck your feet ached even though you wore three pairs of thick wool socks, and you could not feel your toes. In March, very soon it is the winter when the whole sea will freeze over. Your face is frozen always and your fingers ache inside your gloves if they are not first class gloves, and if you take them off out there on deck to roll a cigarette the gloves are stiff when you pull them back on, and they feel as if they are cutting your fingers and your fingers are aching down at the bone. In March the days are getting much shorter, it is not the falling snow any more, it is the snow that blows over the spreading ice and you can hear it. The snow hits you in the face and you have to keep your eyes screwed up, and your wet breath freezes icy on your moustache, and your chin is numb and the snow encrusts white on your eyelashes and beard. In March there were whales again but you did not care about the money any more and you thought: the fucking whaling. And you wanted to scream out: The *fucking FUCKING FUCKING WHALING*. March is the month of waiting, waiting for the long beginning of the end, an end to the blood and the fat and the sea and the ice and the bulkheads about you and the deckheads above you and your goddam bunk, an end to the blood in the showers and urinals and round the lavatory seats and the blood on the tables and on the plates and knives and forks, the blood and the stink of blood and the slip and the slime of blood and the sight and the sounds of blood, waiting for the end of the stink of the whale oil fumes rolling up the alleyways and seeping into your sheets, an end to the whole goddam godawful godrotten ship and its godrotten crew, the same goddam godawful godrotten faces doing the same godawful godrotten things every goddam godawful day and the same oaths and eating the same way the same time in the same seat the same godawful godrotten food. March is the month of fights every day, and loving every swipe and shout and curse and bloodcrunch. Waiting, waiting for Stopvangst, the glorious order from Oslo. *There will be no more hunting of any species of whales except sperm whales after noon tomorrow* – Stopvangst, the international order that makes whalermen shout and laugh and kick the blubber and throw blood and fat and snow at each other, when all other whaling fleets turn around and go home. Except the All England Whaling Company, mate, and the Russians and the Japanese. We poor bastards stay down at the Ice another month till the bitter end, till the sea begins to freeze, hunting the goddam sperm. Come, Stopvangst you bastard, for Chrissake come. But no, not yet, not in March. In the good old days when whales were plentiful it used to be in March, but not any more. The movies, nearly very other day the movies in March, Berlin Boogie Woogie and Caribbean Nights and Oo La-La, three hundred whalermen who had not been with a woman for four months lusting and shouting and whistling, *Berlin Boogie Woogie* and the bar girl with the hundred Mark note in her suspender jumping up to the hot hot music and her tits and hips and shoulders and thighs vibrating so her breasts vibrated out of the top of her blouse and shaking her arse arse arse under the short black satin at you and her thighs with the hundred Mark note jumping around right there fifteen feet in front of you large as life at the Antarctic, by Christ so it got you right here in the guts and the loins so you didn't know what to do.

And outside the Mess room there's only steel and blood and fat and stink and men and guts and bone and cold cold snow and sea and ice ice ice, and you've been here forever and you've got for ever to stay here, and the girl and her smooth flesh loins belong of long long ago.

And oh my Vicky, my Victoria Rhodes.

Chapter Forty

In March Jock came often down to the Pig and stayed all day drinking although he was not supposed to drink too much yet. He was over the shame of it now, the shame of no longer being a man and the men looking at him like that, now it was some kind of bad joke amongst the men. Jock did not think it was a joke but he was no longer ashamed.

'I can't sleep, Professor.' He was shaky.

'Why didn't you go back on the tanker?' I said.

'Because I want to adjust,' Jock said. 'Before I see the outside world so it doesn't drive me mad. But I can't sleep at nights.'

'So drink,' I said.

'Sure. Why not? What does it matter if I drink myself to death? There's no point in being healthy, is there? But I wish I could sleep.'

It's difficult to know what to say to a man who's had that.

'It won't be so bad,' I said. 'You'll feel different and therefore it won't be so bad.'

'It's up here, Professor,' he tapped his head. 'It's up here, mate. You remember what it's like, mate. When you see a woman you remember and you still want it, mate. But you can't have it, mate. Oh Jesus.'

His face was drawn from thinking about it and the bad sleep and his eyes were red. That was also from the drinking.

'It's still up here, mate,' Jock said. 'You spend your whole life thinking about it, you're conditioned by it, you're not going to stop your mind thinking about it, are you? Not you and me anyway, mate, who like it so much. It's our whole reason for living, mate, crumpet is, isn't it? Who d'you always say was the bloke who said that?'

'Freud,' I said.

'That's the bloke. He wasn't talking bullshit, Professor. He wasn't talking bullshit, that bloke,' Jock said. 'When you see a woman's legs'—Jock half closed his eyes—'when you see her legs when she walks past, and her arse and her tits an' all – Oh Jesus … Oh you still want it all right. I didn't deserve that, mate,' Jock said.

'No, you didn't,' I said.

'Not that, mate. Death, maybe, but not that. You go to the pictures,' Jock said, 'and what's it all about? Crumpet. How this guy's getting it or he's not getting it because some other guy's getting it. Everybody's trying to get it, that's what the pictures are all about. Books, it's the same with books. How this guy's trying to get his end away with the bird. Advertisements, everything, Maidenform bras or raincoats or sportscars, it's all about crumpet and how the raincoat or the sportscars are going to get you more crumpet,' Jock said. 'And guys like you an' me who think about it more than anybody else? – how'm I goin' to stop thinkin' about it?' Jock said.

I did not think it would be as bad as that but I did not want to contradict him. A man in that position needs to be right, because everything else is wrong now.

'I didn't deserve that, mate. She threw herself at me. Always shaking her arse at me, she was. Stupid bitch, writing to me down here. Poor ole Charlie. At least we kept it in the family.'

It sounded funny although he did not mean it like that. I had to cough to keep a straight face.

'Maybe I deserved to get my throat cut,' Jock said. 'But not that. What's the point in working to earn money? What's the point in nice clothes? *Crumpet,* right? Take away crumpet and you might as well be … I dunno what.'

'You've still got your painting,' I said.

'And what did I ever paint? Crumpet! I once went to the pictures about a guy who painted birds an' all the crumpet he got that way, that's why I took it up. It worked, an' all. I wish I could sleep,' Jock said.

'It's all up here,' Jock said.

Jock would not go to the movies they were showing every other night in the Big Mess. It became a very bad joke for everybody, except Jock.

In March the whaling fell off again.

The Kid found me lying in my cabin. There had been some whales on deck but we had finished them by midnight and The Kid's boots were bloody. 'Take your boots off,' I said, 'if you want to come in this cabin.'

'I've brought us a bottle of whisky,' The Kid said, 'and all you tell me is take my boots off.'

'Go and take your goddam boots off.'

I got up off the bunk and got some glasses.

'And tomorrow and tomorrow and tomorrow,' I said, 'creeps on this petty pace.'

'Shakespeare,' The Kid said brightly.

'*Very* good,' I said. 'Cheers.'

'What's the matter with you?'

'Tomorrow and tomorrow and tomorrow,' I said.

'What're you bitching about?' The Kid said. 'Who's had it made all season, who's been in the sack every night with—?'

'Okay, Kid.'

'Are you in love with her?' The Kid said. 'To the best of my knowledge.'

'What's it like? I been in love so many times I think I may be unreliable on the subject.'

'Unreliable, the man says. You've got a second pair of testicles where your heart should be.'

'I like that! Are you going to marry her?'

'Yes,' I said.

'How does it feel for a gentlemanly bastard like you to be committed? I know how I've felt, I've been committed up to my nostrils umpteen times, fathers with shotguns and all, but I'm not a gentleman.'

'And how did you feel?'

'Terrified,' The Kid said cheerfully. 'Are you terrified?'

'No,' I said.

'Babies and nappies and hire-purchase and in-laws?' The Kid said hopefully.

'Sometimes a little. But I don't think about it.'

'You better think about it pretty damn quick. Christ,' The Kid said. 'You're a goner, mate.'

'Sure,' I said.

'Are you getting married as soon as you get back?' The Kid said. 'Boy, will we get blind! We'll be staying in Cape Town a week.'

'I don't know. Maybe.'

'Have some more Scotch. Just the thing for your liver. You're a goner,' The Kid said. 'I'm glad I didn't get mixed up with the South Africans.'

'How are things on the Fourteen?'

'Auntie starts crying whenever he sees me these days. I've promised to use my influence to get him his job in the Post Office back.'

'Will you get your command back next season?'

'Who's the best gunner in the fleet?' The Kid said happily. 'The Chairman understands. The Chairman's very bright, like his son.'

'You're a spoilt bastard,' I said.

'I'm also the best gunner in the fleet,' The Kid said happily. 'How're things here?'

'They're all English in this cabin now,' I said, 'thank God. Except they don't shower as often as they might either. You'd think they had to put fourpence in the gasmeter each time.'

'Only dirty people need to wash,' The Kid said. 'We English are a very clean race.'

'Poor bastards, living on that miserable island. No wonder they colonised the earth.'

'Old James. I miss you on the Fourteen, you know that? Never mind,' The Kid said, 'next season I'll insist you sail with me again.'

'There's not going to be a next season for me, I've had a gutsful,' I said.

'I've heard that every season,' The Kid said.

'No, I've really had a gutsful.'

'That's Victoria speaking,' The Kid said.

'No, it's not. I'm just sick of spending half my life like this.'

The Kid grinned at me. He was very charming.

'You'll be back, domesticity or no domesticity, you've been a bum too long to resist it,' The Kid said.

'I'm sick of everything,' I said. 'The no sex. The killing and the goddam stupefaction. The whaling's finished, anyway. We've butchered them all.'

'Stupefaction,' The Kid smiled. 'That's good, very good. What does stupefaction mean?'

'You won't understand,' I said. 'One's got to have brains to experience stupefaction.'

'Let's have another Scotch,' The Kid said, 'and get stupefied.'

This is how it was those days.

Sitting around in the Pig, the big Big Mess, the Sailors' Mess, Elsie's Catering Mess, drinking; coffee, tea, beer, moonshine, talking, arguing, just sitting and saying nothing, reading, quarrelling, just sitting, sometimes working, waiting, waiting for something to happen, waiting for the whales, waiting for March to go by, waiting, waiting for the next meal, which is something to do. And out there, just hard blue black sea, bitter salt ice cold, and the white ice, thick and chunky and drifting, and the icebergs, huge and solid and like land, drifting, drifting north, just ice ice ice and sea sea sea, all the way on all sides, all the way to the horizon and on forever. And behind the ship the slow blue black wake for half a mile, aimless, slow, coming from God knows where and heading for God knows where, heading nowhere really, waiting for the catchers to find sperm whales. But they found few whales because Man had destroyed them all. But we need have no concern, Izzy Isaacson advised, because within the next forty years the Batde of Armageddon was scheduled to take place.

'And all the Angels of the Lord will fly into mighty combat against all the Angels of the Devil. And all the people of the world will be destroyed, except fifteen hundred, who will live for eternity like in the Garden of Eden.'

'No clothes?' The Kid asked, interested.

Izzy considered. He hadn't thought of that one.

'No, I guess we'll wear clothes,' he said, 'except maybe the children.'

'Can queers get in?' Elsie demanded. 'Can queers go?'

Izzy had no doubt about that one. 'No. No queers.'

'Of course not, Elsie,' The Kid said. 'They couldn't have you touching up all the little bare-arsed boys. Not in the Garden of Eden, the Garden of Eden is a respectable joint.'

'God made me,' Elsie pouted, 'so why can't I get into the Garden of Eden?'

'Only fifteen hundred get in anyway, Elsie,' The Kid consoled him. 'The Garden only holds fifteen hundred.'

'You guys better be careful talking like that,' Beulah said.

'I thought you didn't believe in God?' I said.

'Yeah,' Beulah said, 'I don't. But God gets pretty sore with guys making jokes about Him.'

'Damn right,' Izzy said.

'But why am I a queer?' Elsie demanded. 'Not that I *mind* being queer, but why is God going to *punish* me for making me a queer?'

'Izzy, why is Elsie a queer?' The Kid said.

'Predestination,' Izzy said stiffly.

'There you are, Elsie,' The Kid said. 'Predestination, see? Your grandpa did something wrong, see, which God predestined also, and then God got so sore with your grandpa for doing it that He took it out on you by making you queer. It all figures, Elsie.'

'But I *like* being a queer,' Elsie said, 'I don't *want* to be any other way.'

'Izzy,' The Kid said, 'Elsie says but she *likes* being a queer.'

'That's the devil talking,' Izzy said. 'God's going to punish Elsie for that.'

'Elsie,' The Kid said, 'it's a rough life. The bad thing which God predestined your grandpa to do must have been awful bad, because not only is God punishing you by making you queer, denying you admission to the Garden but he's going to make it real hot for you because He also decided to make you a happy queer. God just can't stand that.'

'This is disgraceful,' Izzy said. 'I'm going to pray for you all.'

'Pray for more whales, Izzy,' Elsie said.

Sometimes I could see her face. Right clear in front of me when I wasn't trying to picture her. Sometimes when I was ploughing through the blood, leaning forward dragging the big hunks of bleeding meat through the fat and blood to the big steaming pothole, suddenly I would see her face, her big brown eyes crinkled, and I could hear her happy laugh. Sometimes the foreman gave me the job of driving the winch, dragging big chunks of meat and skeleton and hoisting big bones aloft on the derrick so the flenzers could hack the meat off, I liked that job because I could dream a bit while I pulled the levers mechanically and the others did the hard work, and I glimpsed and heard her often then, but the foreman didn't give me that job often because I dreamed too much, and finally the foreman never gave me the job again, on account of I dropped a five foot chunk of whale fin on him when I was dreaming, which endeared me to everybody except the foreman.

And lying in my bunk and staring at the deckhead – *I should have loved her more*. I should have kissed her more, I should have looked more at her mouth and felt it with my fingers, her cheeks and her nose and her chin and the line of her neck. And her long thick straight black hair, I should have stroked it more and looked at the sheen of it and felt the warmth of it and the thick silkiness of it, and looked much more into her eyes and remember every fleck and flicker of them. I should have kissed her more, felt her more on my lips, the feel and the smell and the taste of her. I should have stroked her more and examined her more, to commit her to memory, I should have lain more long and quiet beside her and looked at her, each line and curve and dimple of her, I should have caressed her more, her thighs I should have stroked and caressed and rejoiced in them more so my hands forever remember the feel and the softness and the smoothness and the line of them more, the sweet line of her back and her strong smooth thighs so my hands more remember her softness and clefts and curves, oh I should have loved her and kissed her and tasted her and smelt her and seen her more, so I could feel and taste her still.

And oh when this fleet comes sailing in and there is Table Mountain and the loudspeakers are blaring When Johnny Comes Marching Home and we've been laughing and drinking since midday watching that horizon and now the crowds packed on the quays all shouting and waving and cheering in the floodlights and you cannot hear yourself on deck for the shouting, you'll be down there somewhere waving and laughing with the taxi waiting and the champagne and we'll shove laughing and hugging through that crowd and jump into our taxi and we'll crack that bottle of champagne laughing and kissing in the back seat and we'll go to that best damn hotel and eat the best damn dinner with the best damn wine and then we'll go laughing upstairs to our big bedroom with its thick soft carpets and its deep soft clean white bed. *Oh for Chrissake Stopvangst when will you come* ... And then at last in March the Stopvangst came from Oslo, and there was a bitter cheer. Because we still had to stay and hunt the sperm.

Chapter Forty-One

And then at last one bitter cold and bloody April night it came with a crackle over the loudspeakers.

'This is the Captain speaking. There will be no more hunting of any species of whales.'

Stophunt! Stophunt oh Stophunt hurrah you lovely bastard! Stophunt hurrah yahoo goddammit you beautiful bastard! Like a goddam golden incredible trumpet blast you darling bastard Stophunt! We're going home my darling bastards yahoo! And cheers and shouts and yelping laughing all over the ship and stamping and thumping in the goddam blood. They dropped their knives and pothooks with a shout and threw their snowcaps in the air and stamped and danced in the blood under the snowing floodlights and kicked the blubber and one man tried to do a somersault and ricked his back and it was terribly funny. Stophunt for Chrissake you lovely bastards, we're going *home!* We fell upon the last gaping whale and hacked and tore it apart and rammed the flesh down the vats with a *ha! you bastard,* we slung the stinking entrails into the sea and we were singing. We turned around.

Now, this is how it is when the whalers turn around: there is much drinking and nobody cares a stuff. There is work also, the tearing the blood-rotten planks off the deck and heaving them over the side into the sea, and the scrubbing of everything, caustic soda sloshed and slapped and scoured down into rotten cracks and crevices, a hundred men with buckets and brooms not caring a stuff. And after the scrubbing there is the painting, strong paint slapped everywhere with gay abandon, a hundred men with paintbrushes not caring a stuff; and all the time the drinking beer sixpence a pint in the Pig and the Pig is open twenty hours a day, beer at smoke-ohs and beer for lunch and beer for tea and fuck the foreman beer on the job and fuck the scrubbing and the fucking painting too *fuckemall I says*. It is very good. Fuck the whaling fuck the Mate fuckemall *we're going home boys!* And in the Pig at night the drinking and the singing and the dancing and the laughing and the bullshit. There are only ten days to go. And all the time the excitement in your guts when you think about it, about the land and the lights and the brass band singing over the loudspeakers and the thronging and shouting and waving and the tugs and the crowds on the quay, and her. The snow dropped off the tawny ship now, and there were much fewer icebergs, and the sea is lighter and the air warmer and all the time the scattered fleet ploughing north with the snow and the ice dropping off, and everybody happy all the time. No icebergs today boys, not one godrotten iceberg in sight today boys, just look at that sea and feel that air, boys! Pray the Roaring Forties aren't aroaring boys. Altogether now – *pray* you sonsabitches!

It seemed to take a long time all the same, in spite of all the drinking and the laughing and the bullshit. The English are the wittiest race even if they don't bath enough. The English may be pains in the arses but you cannot beat them as a race. The English cannot help being funny, even the toffy bastards. The English are funny when times are bad, they're a bloody scream when it's going well. They were very funny indeed homeward bound, it was the same every season, but it took a long time all the same. We were all back on day work, except the sailors. In the mornings we were given a Job and Finish by our foremen. A Job and Finish means that when you've finished the job you are finished for the rest of the day. You had had a few already by the time you'd finished the job and then you went to the Pig. The Pig was always full. The piano and the double bass was always going and there was always singing. The SPEBSQA boys did a great deal of woodshedding. At mealtimes there was a lot of breadthrowing and laughing and singing, except at breakfast when everybody was hungover. In the afternoons I slept off the beer. Then I went and sat in a towel in the steam room to sweat the rest of the beer out. I wanted to be fit when I got back to Cape Town. It was not intended as a steam room but that's how it was because one of the big steam pipes leaked and it did a good job. Then I went back to the Pig and undid all the good steaming out I had done. The Pig was always jumping. There was an ugly rumour that we were running out of beer but it was only a joke and everybody was very relieved. Then it settled down to just solid drinking. That was when it seemed a long time. Then we hit the Roaring Forties and they were flat that time and we celebrated that and we steamed across them in a day and then it really felt we were coming home and it started getting wild again. Only four days to go boys, only four effing days! Four days, three days, two days, Jesus, and the delicious laughing feeling in your guts. Then the loudspeakers said, 'At approximately twelve hundred hours tomorrow we will sight the Cape of Good Hope,' and it got its wildest in the Pig.

And that night the naked splashing and the shouting and the singing in the showers and the squirting water and throwing soap and towels and sponges, soap everywhere, scrubbing the stink of whale fat out of your hair and ears and pores for the Cape Town girls and out of the clothes that would never be unstunk. And in the Pig that night the roar of drinking and laughing and singing.

And all the time that delicious laughing nervous incredulous joy in your guts.

Chapter Forty-Two

Now, at first on the horizon there is just a spot which you cannot be sure is not just another ship, and we stood on the bows in the sunshine wind watching it. It was chill sunshine and there was a big swell running, the beginning of the great Cape Rollers, and the factory was pitching and rolling and now and again we got a little wet up there on the bows. The spray did not matter much but you had to be careful not to let it go in your beer. The message got around and a lot of men came running up from the Pig on to the fo'c'sle to see the line. When there was a big swell they cried 'Woah!' and took the strain and ducked for the spray and put their hands over the tops of their beermugs. There was a lot of laughing and wisecracks. The fleet of catchers was spread about us, riding very high and low in the swells and the spray was smacking over the bridges. The Fourteen was about a mile ahead of all of us. I could imagine The Kid on the bridge with his bottle of Scotch baiting the Mate and stamping his foot and saying *faster you bitch*. I was very fond of The Kid, I had done five seasons with the bastard and I had only had to hit him once, over the seals. He had made me a lot of money. I went below to the Pig and got another pint and I tried to drink it there but after a while I went back up on to the bows. The line was a little thicker. Then somebody shouted my name from up on the bridge and there was the Fourth Mate holding a piece of paper and I climbed up. It was a wireless message from the Fourteen which read:

mcquade land a-effing-hoy you ole bastard shall I give auntie a kick
for you leave any messages at the company offices so long you old
sonofabitch luv kid captain repeat effing captain.

From the bridge you could see it better, the line was a row of humps
now, it was the Apostles all right. Jesus, they looked good. You could
see the sun on them and the shadows between, but you could not
see the green yet, they were mauve. By God they looked good, the
first land in five bloody months, you felt you wanted to shout. Land
ahoy you bastards, land goddam land! I clattered down from the
bridge to the Pig and got another pint.

There were some English singing,

'*Even though I'm a Londoner, Cape Town will fookin do …*'

… and some of the Coloureds were singing,

'*Bokkie*
Jy moet nou huistoe gaan
Want die trane die rol
Oor jou Bokkie …'

… and I could feel my own *trane*, my own tears, and I was very glad
I was a South African. I went over to the group of Coloureds and we
sang *Nkosi Sikelele Afrika* which means *Lord look after Africa* which is
the Bantu national anthem and you've got to harmonise it. Then the
English sang *The White Cliffs of Dover*, so we sang *Uit Die Blou Van*
Onse Hemel which is the South African national anthem. We all felt
very good. Down at the end of the Pig there was nearly a fight
between a Coloured and two Limies but we shut them up.

The Coloured said, '*Ek fok julle op in die Kaap vanaand, outjies!*' and
he walked out. The two English looked worried about that.

The Coloured next to me said, 'The fokkin English, give me a
fokkin Dutchman every time, at least you know where you are with
a fokkin Dutchman.'

I didn't know what the quarrel was about and I didn't care.

The Coloured said, 'What about the Notting Hill Gate riots, *ou?* The English think we all fokkin kaffirs or something.'

'Forget it,' I said. The singing had taken up again. I could not resist going up on deck to see if the Apostles were closer any. They were well above the horizon now but they were still hours away before you would see the green. Christ, the green! I went below to look for Elsie. He was sitting in his cabin with Beulah.

'Hello darling,' Beulah said.

'Have a pink gin, Professor,' Elsie said.

'No,' I said. 'I want to be more or less sober when we get in.'

'Have a gin darling,' Beulah said. 'You've never got in sober all the years I've known you.'

'All right,' I said. Elsie got a glass.

'Are you going to come back next season darling?' Beulah said.

'No,' I said.

'You say that every season,' Elsie said.

'I hear there was a fight in the Pig,' Beulah said.

'Nearly,' I said. 'It was broken up.'

'Them Coloureds,' Elsie said.

Beulah was sitting with his legs crossed smoking with his long cigarette holder. He smiled his lovely smile.

'You coming back, Beulah?' I said.

'No, darling. I'm absolutely sick sick sick of the fucking whaling.'

'She'll be back an' all,' Elsie said. He was sitting bulging on the bunk in his chequered chef's pants and tee shirt.

'I won't,' Beulah said serenely. 'I'm like the Professor, I'm going to get married an' settle down.'

'Who're you going to marry?' I said.

'I was only joking darling. But I'm going to have the knife.'

'You serious about this?' I said.

'Absolutely darling, if I can,' Beulah said serenely. 'I'm going to go into it very thoroughly.'

'It won't be the same,' Elsie warned him, 'it won't feel the same.'

'They can do wonderful things nowadays, Elsie dear,' Beulah said calmly.

'But it won't *feel* the same,' Elsie said. 'You better stay a regular homo.'

'You won't be able to go into the men's showers any more, Beulah,' I said.

'There'll be compensations,' Beulah said.

'I don't like it,' Elsie said, 'it's unnatural.'

We all laughed at that.

'I'll get my nose re-done at the same time,' Beulah said.

Elsie said, 'So, tonight you'll be with your girl, James.'

'Yes,' I said. It felt very good.

'Be careful,' Beulah said, 'remember what happened to my Pete. That sonofabitch.'

'Beulah's only trying to be funny, James dear,' Elsie said soothingly. 'You shouldn't say things like that,' Elsie said to Beulah.

Beulah looked surprised.

'*I* wasn't being funny. I thought that's what the bejeezuz big fight was about with that Jakkals sonofabitch!'

Elsie glared. 'Now stop it, Beulah!'

Beulah looked all hurt. 'My, we are touchy.' He glared at Elsie, 'Don't get your knickers in a knot, you fat old whore. I was just trying to be *help*ful! Tut!'

'You a fine one to talk about whores!' Elsie said.

'Ladies, ladies,' I grinned. 'It's all right.'

'I just didn't want to see the Professor in *jail*,' Beulah said to Elsie, 'like that sonofabitch Pete!'

Elsie turned up his palms and rolled his eyes.

'All right girls, knock it orf.' I was laughing.

We had another gin, then we said goodbye. You never say goodbye to all the people you meant to say goodbye to on a ship. I said I would come and see Elsie next season when the fleet was back in port.

'You'll be sailing an' all,' Elsie said.

I wished Beulah luck with his surgery.

'As long as I have better luck than I did with my nose,' Beulah said.

I went along to my cabin. I wanted to go back up to the Pig and get another pint but I knew I must not drink, I better try to sleep. I wanted to be fresh tonight. My things were packed, on the bunk. Just seeing them there all packed made me excited again. The big twinge in your stomach. All the alleyways were strewn with rubbish the South Africans had thrown out in their packing. The ship had an air of gay abandon. God, the coming home is marvellous. It is the best part of being a sailor. You marvelled that it was actually happening at last, you've thought about it so much. And oh my Victoria! I knew I would not sleep. I turned and walked up the alleyway to Benjamin's cabin. He was sitting with his hands between his knees. On one side was a big old suitcase and on the other was a big bundle of a blanket with things inside, all ready to go.

'*En toe, Boet?*' I said.

'Hullo man Master James.' I sat down on the bench. He smiled and wriggled. It was a very toothless smile. Then he scowled at the deck. I thought: his ma's not going to be pleased about his teeth.

'Are you pleased we're getting home, *Boet?*' I said.

Benjamin scowled.

'It's okay man Master James,' he said.

'Your ma's going to be pleased to see you,' I said.

Benjamin scowled. He didn't want his ma going soppy over him.

'Is she coming to the docks to meet you?' I said.

Benjamin looked horrified. 'Of course not man!'

'Well,' I said, 'where're you going to sleep tonight if she doesn't come and fetch you?'

Benjamin frowned.

'I'm sure she's coming to fetch you to spend the night in her room at my place,' I said. 'But you may miss her or maybe she hasn't found out we're coming in tonight. If you miss her, take a taxi out to my place.'

Benjamin looked at me with big eyes. I gave him the key to the back door, off the ring. He looked at me with big eyes.

'If your ma isn't home, you better stop at the police station and tell Sergeant van Tonder Mr McQuade says you're to wait in my kitchen. Otherwise they may think you're a burglar.'

Benjamin clutched the key. 'Thenks hey Master James man.'

'Tell your ma I'll be home for dinner tomorrow night, ask her to roast me a duck, will you remember that?' Benjamin nodded vigorously.

'Tell her I'll be bringing somebody to dinner, Benjamin. I'll be bringing Miss Rhodes,' I said.

Benjamin's eyes opened wide and I thought he was blushing. I stood up.

'One thing Master James, hey,' he said.

'Yes?'

Benjamin looked very embarrassed. He hung his head and twisted.

'Don' tell my ma how I lost my teeth, hey,' he said.

'Okay, Benjamin,' I said.

As I turned to the door it opened and Geradus van Wijk came in.

'Hullo Jimmy, *ou,*' he said, *'fere, Got,* you seen the *ou vaderland* hey?'

Benjamin walked round him and out.

'Yes,' I said.

'Jere, but it's going to be nice to get back where they got a bit of bladdy sense hey?'

I shook my head, I couldn't help smiling.

'Well, cheerio, Gert,' I said. 'See you on the Christmas tree.'

'Anytime, *ou,*' Geradus van Wijk said. 'No hard feelings hey?'

'No,' I said.

'I'm sorry about the little bastard's teeth hey,' he said. 'I reely didn' know it was him.'

'It can't be helped,' I said. 'As long as you've apologised to him.'

'Of course, yes, I apologised, man,' Geradus van Wijk said. 'He's not such a bad little bastard reely, I quite like him reely.'

'He worships you,' I said, 'like a brother.'

Geradus van Wijk thought that was very witty, he laughed.

'Jere, but I'm happy to be getting off this fokkin ship, *ou.* I tell you, it's not so much the Coloureds, we understand each other, it's these English bastards I really can't stand – no offence, hey, I mean you're a South African.'

I shook my head and smiled, I couldn't help it.

'So long, Gert,' I said.

'No offence, hey? But don't these English bastards get on your tits hey? You never know where you are with a *rooinek.*'

'Something terrible,' I said.

'No, but don't they give you the shits, hey? Always so bladdy superior, even there in South Africa.'

'Absolutely,' I said. 'I must go.'

'Okay, so long, hey. *Hou vas!*'

'*Totsiens,*' I said.

I walked back to my cabin. I thought: you better go and say goodbye to Old Fergie and Jock. But I could not face Old Fergie lecturing me on how I must stop being a layabout and start being an ichthiologist now that I had responsibilities. I would make a point of seeing them before the fleet sailed next week. I wanted to try to sleep. I moved my things off my bunk and lay down and closed my eyes. I could hear the singing in the Pig, far away. I lay there trying not to think about how good it was, how bloody marvellous it was, *Christ.* After a long time I went to sleep.

When I woke up it was half-past five. There was loud singing in a cabin down the alleyway. I slung a towel around my waist and went down to the heads. It was cold but I didn't care: it was good Cape cold. I had a cold salt water shower and I kept my head under it to knock all the sleep and thickness out of me. Then I dried myself until my skin felt red. I looked at my face in the mirror. I wanted to shave, feel the clean skin, but I decided to leave it. Then I decided to shave. I fetched my razor and gave myself a good shave. My face was pale where my beard had been. It was never a very good beard anyway. I gave my teeth a good brush. I went back to the cabin and I poured some brandy in the palm of my hand and slapped it on my face. It burned and felt good. I felt good and clean and rested. I poured the last of the brandy into a glass and took a good swallow. I got dressed in clean clothes and put on my sports slacks and sports coat and my veldskoens for the first time in five months. They felt very loose and comfortable but very formal. I tied my snowboots and my gumboots and my spiked deck boots to the haversack. God, it felt good. I swallowed off the brandy and savoured the burn, then

I walked out the cabin, to the Pig. I was grinning. It was a bloody good life. Only the sailors know what it feels like.

I got a pint in the Pig, the Pig was roaring, then I took it up on to the fo'c'sle. The sun was low and the old ship was rolling in the big Cape Rollers. As I climbed up on to the fo'c'sle the twelve Apostles hit me big and mauve and green and gold in the sundown. God, they looked incredible. They had swung right away to starboard and now we were heading past Llandudno and could see the Lion's Head and behind it the Table Mountain. And the houses by Christ! There it all was! And the fleet scattered all about and pitching and rolling in the big swells and the spray flying. By Christ. And you could make out the road leading round to Hout Baai and you could just make out a car driving along the road, and far ahead the houses. Houses with home things in them. There were about fifty men. They were laughing and joking and singing and drinking. Most of them were Coloureds. The wind flapped their trousers. They were all very happy.

The Apostles swung right astern to starboard whilst I stood there and then the great giant flat topped Table Mountain was swinging round in all her glory, in the sunset, and the mat of lights coming on below, the glorious harbour lights of Cape Town.

'Oo Got,' a Coloured said, 'there lies trouble,' and we all laughed.

And up there amongst those lights the women, wives and sweethearts and whores and just women with tits and arses and thighs and crotches that could be grabbed and splayed and mounted and shot up and manhandled, women fat or thin white or brown cool or sweaty clean or smelly it doesn't matter a damn because they're women.

And somewhere up there amongst those lights is my Victoria, tall and slender and clean and sweet-smelling of Victoria and she is sick with excitement also and I wanted to shout and laugh I loved her so much.

Chapter Forty-Three

At eight o'clock the tugs had us inside the harbour, swinging us round. The catchers were all around. The loudspeakers were playing When the Saints Come Marching In and four hundred whalermen were on the floodlit cutting deck singing and shouting and waving. There were hundreds of people on the quay in the lamplights, a mass of waving shouting faces. And the women, white women and brown women, fat ones and slim ones, the wives and sweethearts and the whores from the Fisherman's and the Fog Horn and the Tavern. You still could not recognise people. The tugs swung us right round and then they pushed us broadside and now the loudspeakers were playing Daar Kom Die Alabama and then the heaving lines were thrown out fore and aft, snaking through the yellow night air, then out went the shore lines and as they were dropped over the bollards a roar went up from us and the loudspeakers burst into Tipperary. We were only twenty yards from the quay now and the crowd were waving like mad and the whalermen were singing and shouting. You could make out faces now but there were hundreds of them. And the din, and everybody surging. I was standing on the starboard rail winch.

'Victoria!' I shouted into the din, 'Victoria!' but there were so many faces. We were almost alongside now and already the amidship derricks were slung out over to hoist up the gangway. Now the whalermen were surging down the deck to where the gangway would be and the crowd was surging along the quay to the same place. Many of the whalermen had seen their women but now they lost them again. The shouting and the surging and the loudspeakers blaring Tipperary. I still could not see Victoria but I kept shouting. I stayed on my winch.

'Victoria!' I shouted. The crowd was a big mob round the gangway. The gangway came up from the quay and a dozen hands grabbed it, before it was lashed down the whalermen were jumping down it and the crowd was surging up. Then everybody was swarming on the gangway. And the loudspeakers still blaring, now it was When Johnny Comes Marching Home. Some whalermen got halfway down the gangway and then climbed over the handrail and jumped down on to the quay. There was the roaring of greeting and kissing and hugging and laughing faces in the yellow light. And the loudspeakers singing. There were people from the quay running on to the deck now, running and hugging and milling and surging, everybody mixed up and milling now under the yellow lights and the blaring loudspeakers, whalermen on the quay and women on the deck.

I pushed through the crowd to the top of the gangway. I climbed the rail at the top of the gangway and hung on to a cable. I was very excited. I did not want to go down the gangway in case she was trying to come up. I shouted her name. There were many women with black hair in the big crowd and it was difficult in the patchy yellow lights. And the noise. There were cars coming up along the quay now, taxis and private cars in a line. I kept on the rail, looking and shouting her name.

After a time the surging and the milling slowed down. Everybody who wanted to be up was up and the men who wanted to be down were down. A few were still going up and down the gangway. Everybody seemed to have found everybody they wanted. The cars were driving off down the quay, most of the English had already clattered down and zoomed off to the Navigators and the Fog Horn and the Tavern and the Night and Day with a whoop and a holler. The whores were already aboard. A few more cars came, all taxis, but there was nobody in them, they had come to look for whalermen to take to the bars. After a while even the loudspeakers stopped. There were no other men waiting around on deck now, everybody had found everybody and now there were only groups going down the gangway to the taxis laughing and talking. I went down and walked a little way along the quay and I forgot to think of the concrete under my feet and say to myself *Christ – Land,* like I did every year. Of course there was nobody waiting in the shadows along the quay and I walked back and I waited at the bottom of the gangway. Then I climbed up and waited at the top where I had a better view. The crowd had almost all gone now. I hung around the top and the bottom of the gangway a long time, figuring she had got held up by something. I was very disappointed and impatient but I knew it was some mistake, and we had only been in an hour. Then when there were no more people coming and going anywhere I went down to my cabin to get my gear.

It seemed very quiet and clean down below without the vibration of the engines and the blood. There was nobody about, then I heard some laughter, men and women's. It sounded like a good time. I flung open my door and grabbed my case and haversack and started down the alleyway. I felt good now I was moving again. A door up the alleyway opened and there was the laughter again and half a naked woman stepped half through and a hand grabbed her back and she squealed as if she was trying to run away. As I passed somebody shouted 'Hey Jimmy!' I stopped and looked in and grinned.

'You doing all right, Spike?'

It was the Spike who played the double bass in the Pig.

'Hava drink Jimmy,' Spike shouted. The girl was hiding behind him giggling, pretending to be shy about me seeing her. Spike was stripped to the waist and he had a brandy bottle. Buzzy was lying on top of the other broad in the bunk. Buzzy had his pants rolled down over his arse and they didn't care about me.

Buzzy said 'Is that good, honey?' and she jerked her hips and said 'Uh-Uh ...' and then took a slug out of a bottle over Buzzy's shoulder. They were both white broads. Spike's whore was still crouching behind him giggling.

'Yirra, close the door man,' she giggled. They were having a good time.

'Cheerio Spike,' I said, and shook hands. 'Say cheerio to Buzzy for me.'

'Hava drink for Chrissake!' Spike shouted happily.

'See you, Spike.' I picked up my bags and walked on up the alleyway. Spike and Buzzy were having a good time. The deck was quite empty now. When I got to the quay I looked up and down then I started walking towards the lights of town. I was happy again. A taxi came round the warehouse and I flagged it. I slung my bags in and I gave the driver the address of Victoria's flat in Oranjezicht.

'How does it feel to be back, hey man?' the driver said.

'Bloody marvellous,' I said.

They did not bother about us at the Customs gate. I sat in the back and let it all wash over me, the joy of riding to her flat in a taxi, coming back from the Antarctic. I wished I had a drink, I wanted something big. When we got into Adderley Street there were girls walking and by Christ it looked good, girls and lights and cars and a soft seat under my bum going to Victoria's flat. I was very impatient at the traffic lights. Oranjezicht is not a very classy area of Cape Town, but parts of it are all right. It is old. Oranjezicht means View of the Oranges. The taxi took me up the long street and then up a side street and then stopped outside an old block of flats. It had been built in the Victorian days. The street was narrow and there were cars parked on the pavement. I was very excited. I climbed the stairs and walked down the back access verandah and there was her number on the door. There was a light burning in the frosted kitchen window. I put down my bags and I was grinning as I knocked loudly. A woman came to the door. It was not Victoria.

'Doesn't Miss Rhodes live here?' I stared.

'No, I think before I came. I've been here a month already.'

I stared at her.

'Do you know where she went?'

'No,' the woman said.

My heart was beating hard.

'Didn't she leave any forwarding address?'

'No,' the woman said.

'A message?' I said.

'No.'

I looked at her. I was astounded.

'Can I use your telephone if I pay for it?'

'All right,' the lady said.

I went inside to the telephone. The telephone shook in my hand. First I telephoned my house at Oak Bay. After a time Sophie answered. I cut her short and asked if there were any letters or messages for me. No, Master James. She knew nothing of Miss Rhodes. Then I telephoned the local office of the All England Whaling Company. It rang a long time and there was no reply. Then I looked for her mother's name in the telephone directory. The pages rattled as I turned them. I did not know her mother's address and there was no Rhodes who lived anywhere near Woodstock. I didn't know what to do. I didn't know what to think.

'Thank you very much,' I said to the woman. My eyes felt burny, I could not believe it.

'Are you a sailor?' the woman said.

'Yes,' I said.

'Agh, shame,' she said. She looked very kind.

'Thanks anyway,' I said.

'No,' she said, 'I don't want your money. Never mind, maybe you'll find her in the morning.'

'Maybe,' I said. 'Good night.'

'Good night,' she said. 'Cheer up.'

I walked down the stairs to the street. I did not know what to think. I was bewildered. I did not know what to do – there was nothing more I could do until the morning when the Whaling Company's offices opened for the pay-off. I walked down the street the way I had come in the taxi. I could not believe it. When I got to the corner I started walking down the hill. When I got to the bottom of the hill a taxi came along and I flagged it. I got in and I wondered where to go.

'Take me to a hotel,' I said. 'Take me to the Phoenix.'

The Phoenix is an old hotel. A lot of sailors and whores went there to drink in the bar-lounges. It also had a Non-European Bar and an Indian Bar. I got a room. The Coloured taxi driver carried my case upstairs ahead of me and I carried the haversack. You could hear the noise from the big bar lounge. The stairs were made of wood painted grey, with linoleum. When we were walking up the stairs a woman started walking down. She was chewing gum and she wasn't pretty but she was stuff all right. The Coloured taxi driver passed her and then he stopped and winked at me and nodded his head at her. He knew I had come off the whalers. The girl was looking at my sea boots and she was slowing right down.

'Hullo, man,' she said.

'Hullo,' I said. She was stuff all right.

'How about a drink hey man?' she said. She was smiling. I had stopped. I could have done with her all right.

'Later,' I said, I started on up the stairs. 'I'll meet you in the bar lounge.'

'When, hey?'

'Two minutes,' I said.

'Okay,' she smiled.

I followed the taxi driver down the narrow linoleum passage. The walls were painted grey and there were fire buckets with cigarette stubs in them. We came to my room. It had an old fashioned brass handle that the management had got sick of cleaning and had painted it over and the paint had worn away and he had got tired of painting it too. It was a narrow room. I put on the light. There was a brass-railed bed and a cupboard and a marble topped washstand with an enamel basin and enamel jug of water. Outside was Adderley Street and across the street a blue neon sign flashing Players Please. It was very depressing but I did not care. I was going to get drunk.

'Do you like the girl hey?' the Coloured taxi driver said.

'I'm crazy about her,' I said. 'What do I owe you?'

'Why didn't you bring her straight to the room man, some other bugger's got her now.'

'It's nice of you to worry. How much?'

'Ten bob,' he said.

I didn't argue, seeing he'd carried the bag and worried about the girl.

'Tell the manager to send a bar waiter please,' I said.

'Why you look so sad hey man, you must give it hell your first night back,' the Coloured taxi driver said.

'You're a good bloke,' I said. 'Good night.'

'Good night sir,' he said, 'and give it *hell* man!'

I sat down on the bed and looked at my bags on the floor. I didn't know what to do. I looked round the room. Some room. Some first night. Some Victoria. I knew then it was finished, it had all gone wrong. The bar waiter knocked. I ordered two cold Castle beers. Then I added a double brandy. I did not want to go out yet, before I felt a bit drunk. I lay down on the bed and looked at the Players Please sign, waiting for the drinks. I wasn't thinking yet, I was only feeling. The waiter came back and I got up and paid him. Then I picked up the brandy and took a big swallow. I heard Victoria saying *You're always so cheerful after some brandy, darling,* and my eyes were burning. Christ, it all seemed ages ago but yet it could have been yesterday. There was a knock on the door and for a wild moment I thought it might be Victoria and I flung open the door. It was the girl from the stairs.

'You said two minutes, hey,' she said.

'I'm terribly sorry,' I said.

'Can I come in hey?' she said.

'Of course.'

She came in and looked round the room. I closed the door.

'I see you already drinking, hey,' she said.

'Yes. Will you have one of the beers?'

'I drink brandy, man,' she said. I took a big breath.

'Okay,' I said. 'We'll go out and drink brandy. And get blind drunk, you and me.'

She giggled. She came up to me and kissed me. She felt good and cheap and sharp with perfume.

'You stink man,' she said, 'of the whalers. It's the same every season.'

'Do I?'

She flicked her fingers on my sportscoat. 'You'll have to get rid of this,' she said. 'Chuck it out. It's the same every season, man.'

'Okay, I will,' I said. She smiled.

'You're a *lekker ou*,' she said. 'You stink, but I don' care, hey.'

She put her arms around my neck and I was kissing her again and she fluttered her tongue inside my mouth. What the hell, I thought – *what the fucking hell – why shouldn't I?* But in the back of the lust and confusion I thought: if I find her this will spoil it all.

And I broke the kiss and I said, 'I want brandy too.'

As we walked down the passage I thought: that's the only virtuous thing you've done for a hell of a long time, McQuade.

Chapter Forty-Four

In the morning it was raining. It was cold and wet, the beginning of the season of the Cape of Storms. It was Sunday.

I walked in the rain from the hotel to the company's offices in Port Road, there near the docks. The company rents two rooms in an old building which also houses a few gentlemen in the import-export business, the passages are unpolished wood and there are always crates of stuff being unpacked. There is also a stevedore agency and there are always Coloureds and natives hanging around to see the stevedore agent, and usually they sit on the import-export crates while they wait. There was already quite a queue of Cape Coloured whalermen outside the company's door, queuing for their pay-off. They were very cheerful.

I walked to the top of the queue and one of the Coloureds shouted, 'Back of the queue, hey Van!'

'I'm not coming for my cheque,' I said.

I went into the office. There was a counter. Two clerks were standing at the counter and one was calling the whalerman's name off a register and the other found the cheque in a box, then they asked the whalerman to sign for it. I called to a typist and told her I wanted to see the Company Secretary. I had never seen this girl before and she was trying to be very efficient in her English way. What did I wish to see the Company Secretary about? It was, I said, very personal. Could I not write a letter? No, I could not write a letter. The Secretary was very busy, was it about employment? No, I said, it bloody well was *not* about employment, I had been employed for five stinking seasons by her outfit and I was going to see the Secretary or else. Who should she say was calling? Captain McQuade, I said. Yes sir, she said.

The Company Secretary was not amused about having Captain McQuade shown in. He was also an Englishman and the English are great ones for their appointments and ivory towers. If in doubt, chuck 'em out. There's the story of the man who had been trying unsuccessfully to get an appointment with the boss of an English firm for so long that he finally had a gift wrapped parcel delivered. Inside the parcel was a caged carrier pigeon with a note:

> *I can't get past your secretary, please put a note of the time you will see me in the pigeon's ring and release it out the window.*

I have sailed for many English shipping companies and the shore administrative staff are all the same. The deck officers are different, they're usually gentlemen. The Secretary of the All England Whaling Company's Cape Town branch office, two lousy rooms in Port Road, did not approve of whalemen. In particular, he did not approve of me, never had. Never would. My South African accent had a lot to do with it. And he knew about the van Niekerk part of my name, of course, which was very off. Not on, my dear fellow. What the devil did I want, and what did I mean getting in here by masquerading as a captain, didn't I know the fleet was in and he was frightfully busy? Yes, I said, I did know the fleet was in on account I had come in on it. I wanted, I said, to know the address of Miss Victoria Rhodes, the Sister of the company's clinic. And what, he wanted to know, as if he knew all about myself and Miss Rhodes and thoroughly disapproved, did I want to know that for? That, I said, was my business. Then I could wait until tomorrow and enquire at the company's clinic when it opened. No, I said, that was where he was quite wrong, I would *not* wait until tomorrow. He considered that an impertinence but for the sake of getting rid of me he would look up her file. He looked up her file: he told me the address of her next of kin and snapped the file closed. And now would I kindly leave? Yes, I would kindly leave. And it *may* interest me to know that Miss Rhodes was *no* longer employed by the All England Whaling Company.

'*What?*' I said. My heart was knocking hard again.

'You heard me, now will you please leave!' the Company Secretary said.

'When did she quit?' I said.

'Two months ago. Now will you leave?'

I was too astonished to dislike him. He waved the back of his hand at me towards the door. I just looked at him, then I turned and walked out of the offices of the All England Whaling Company and out of the old building into Port Road and the rain. I did not have a raincoat but I did not care. I started walking hard down Port Road towards town, looking for a taxi.

Then I took a taxi up over Constantia Nek and down into Hout Baai and through to Oak Bay to fetch my car. It was beautiful going over the wooded Nek and the cottages of the Coloured folk amongst the oak trees looked cosy. It rained all the way.

Maybe once upon a time there was a pinetree in Pine Street, Woodstock, but there are no trees now. The semidetached houses in Pine Street were depressing and old, but they were all right, I have seen many like them in England and very many worse. I stopped the old Ford about halfway down Pine Street. I was very excited again. I walked through the rain to Victoria's gate and across the narrow red cement stoep and knocked loudly. My heart was beating wildly as I heard the footsteps coming. The door opened and a middle-aged woman was looking at me.

'Mrs Rhodes?' I said.

'Yes?' she said.

She looked very like Victoria, her hair pulled back in a bun.

'Is Victoria here?'

She looked at me. I was smiling but she did not smile.

'Who are you?' Mrs Rhodes said. She had a strong South African accent.

'I am James McQuade. I was at the Antarctic with Victoria.'

I could tell she knew my name by the look in her eyes. I was not overconfident of being very popular as the man who had made Victoria pregnant.

'Victoria doesn't live here any more,' Mrs Rhodes said.

I stared at her.

'Well, where does she live?'

Mrs Rhodes' lips were pursed thin. She looked at my eyes the whole time.

'Where does she live?' I repeated. She waited a second.

'Come in,' she said.

She led the way down the short passage. On the left was a door to the main bedroom and on the right I knew would be the sitting room. At the bottom of the passage was the back door and on the left would be the kitchen and on the right another bedroom. Outside the back door would be the lavatory and bathroom. I followed her into the sitting room. Everything was old and neat and shiny, it was very seldom sat in. She did not ask me to sit down. She turned and faced me.

She said, 'She doesn't want to see you.'

I stared at her.

'I insist on seeing her,' I said, 'Mrs Rhodes.'

She stared straight back at me. I could not believe her, I was incredulous.

'Why do you insist on seeing her?' Mrs Rhodes stared.

I was beginning to get angry now.

'*Why*? Mrs Rhodes, it happens that I love your daughter and I was under the impression that she loved me.'

'She doesn't want to see you, Mr McQuade. She told me to tell you that if you came.'

'For Christ's sake, Mrs Rhodes, if you don't tell me where she is I'll find her somehow!'

'Do you know she's pregnant?' Mrs Rhodes said bitterly.

'Of course I know she's pregnant, Mrs Rhodes, I happen to be the man.'

'Then I'll tell you where she lives,' Mrs Rhodes said bitterly. 'Despite what she said.'

She was crying.

Chapter Forty-Five

In District Six there is a street called Second Avenue but there are no trees. The constables patrol the beat in pairs, in District Six. There are many skolly boys and many robbings and stabbings and gangfights. District Six is an unlovely place in the summer when it's hot, in the winter it is mean and dank and ugly.

Halfway down Second Avenue is a church. There is a wall around the church-yard with broken bottles planted in the top, and on both sides are old double-storeyed buildings with some shops underneath and on top are dwellings. It was still raining. There was an old Coloured walking down the street with his cap on the back of his head swinging along in a hurry with his old sports coat flapping and he had a demijohn of vaaljapje wrapped in newspaper under his arm. I could hear them singing in the church, it did not sound like many voices. The church-yard was narrow and muddy and there were green weeds standing wet in the rain. I walked round the side of the church to the house of the Coloured parson at the back. The house was built right up to the back of the church-yard wall. There was no stoep in front of the house. I knocked on the door and a small Coloured boy answered.

'*Is Mejevrou Rhodes tuis?*' I said. Is Miss Rhodes at home?

The boy had short frizzy hair and his nose was running but he was neatly dressed.

'*Ja, Meneer.*'

'Take me to her please,' I said. I did not want her to come to the door. My heart was beating hard again. The boy turned and ran down the short passage excitedly to the back door. He hung on the handle.

'Open the door, *jong*,' I said.

Outside was the open back yard. It was cemented and on one side was the kitchen window and on the other was the lavatory. On the opposite side against the church-yard wall was another room with a window looking into the yard and the door was closed.

'All right,' I said to the boy, 'I'll go alone.'

I walked into the rain and I stopped at the door. The boy was still hanging on to the door staring at me. I jerked my head to chase him away, but he still hung on to the door. My heart was beating very hard now and I was happy again in spite of everything. I knocked. I heard her move, then it was quiet again. Then I opened the door.

She was sitting on the bed, staring at me. Her hands were wedged between her knees and her eyes were big and nervous and her face was bleak and her long hair hung straight down the sides of her face. She looked as if she had sat down suddenly. We looked at each other. My heart was pounding.

'Vicky?' I said.

'Hullo darling,' she said. She sat there looking at me like that.

I closed the door behind me. 'Oh *Christ*, Vicky!'

'What, darling?' Her eyes were brimming.

'Oh Christ, what have they done to you?'

She closed her eyes and two tears rolled and she nodded.

'What indeed.'

'Oh *Christ!*' I pulled her up and hugged her tight and kissed her and kissed her and clutched her and hugged her and I felt my throat would burst and she clutched me tight, Oh Vicky, what have they done, what have they done? I kissed her wet face and neck and mouth and chin and her eyes and salty tears, she hugged me and kissed me salty tears wet smooth face wet and long hair sticking tears and sobs and she was crying *Oh darling darling darling* my love my lover my darling. Then she broke apart and her tearful eyes were sparkling suddenly and she stood back and smoothed her dress over her body.

'Look,' she said, wet red happy eyes and her hair sticking to her cheeks. I could not see any difference but she expected me to.

'Very good,' I said. It was lovely to see her happy. 'Isn't that something?'

She was holding her dress smooth and looking up at me with sparkling wet eyes. 'You see I really am having a baby!'

'Certainly you are.' I tried to laugh.

'Maybe you can't see it so well now but you would with my clothes off darling,' she said. She was the same old Victoria now.

'I can see it now,' I said.

She was still holding her dress smooth over her belly so I could see and her eyes were still sparkling wet and I was trying to laugh with her and my eyes were burning, and then she froze like that and the laugh died out of her face as she looked at me, her hands rigid on her belly, then her lip curled over her teeth and the tip of her chin crinkled, then she dropped her head and cried 'Oh God Oh God Oh God—'

'Victoria.'

I was holding her tight again and there was the sweet smell of her hair.

'Oh God Oh God Oh God,' she cried. I held her tight.

'Victoria,' I said, 'Victoria ...'

Then she stiffened and turned out of my arms with a big sniff.

'The boy's at the window,' she said flatly.

I looked, the boy's head was disappearing. A second later it came peeping back. I went to the door and flung it open. The boy was running in the back door.

'Stay away!' I said. He hung on the back door again and stared at me.

'It's no good,' she sniffed. She was sitting on the bed again. 'Church will be over soon and they'll be back. You better go.'

'Don't be crazy, Vic.'

She looked red-eyed across the small room at the window.

'I'm not crazy darling, you aren't allowed here, if there's talk there'll be a policeman around in five minutes.'

She said it flatly and she stared at the window with wet eyes. 'Where did you park your car?'

'Out the front.'

'You see?' she said without looking at me then she blew her nose. 'Somebody's bound to have seen you come here and you'll be in trouble. Nobody comes here in a car.'

I was feeling dizzy and confused.

'For Chrissake!' I said, 'let's get out of here.'

She laughed once flatly, looking at the window.

'Don't be daft, that's worse, darling. If they see us driving off there'll be all kinds of talk and the police will hear about it in five minutes.'

I stared at her. She looked at me then she dropped her head again.

'Oh God,' she said, 'Oh God!'

'Victoria.' She held her face and her shoulders were shaking. I held her shoulders and squeezed her hard. 'Victoria listen, it doesn't matter, I'll find a way.'

I felt desperate.

She shook her head. 'Of course it matters darling.'

'I'll do something,' I said, desperately.

'Of course it matters!' she cried into her lap. 'Do you think I haven't thought it all out the last two months, thought every conceivable thing about it? Why do you think I wasn't there on the quay when the fleet came in, why d'you think I didn't even leave a message?'

She was looking up at me now with red wet angry eyes.

'Why darling?' she cried. 'Because there's *nothing* we can do! Because I'm a Coloured girl now and you're white, it's all nice and official now darling!'

'Victoria—'

'Because I'm not allowed to marry you or live with you or make love to you any more. I'm not even allowed to live with my mother because *she's* white. Because I'm not allowed to go to the same places as you any more or to the same parties or the same beaches or sit on the same benches in the park as you darling! *Because you're not allowed to be here in this room at this moment!*'

She was angry now while she cried. She pointed at the bed she was sitting on. 'Because I want to lie down on this bed right now and make love to you because I love you but it's a *crime* now and we'll both go to *jail!* Because while I'm sitting here I'm worried sick about where you parked your car, the whole time I'm listening for the policeman, that's *why why why* darling.'

She stopped. Her eyes were wide and angry and wet and she was panting.

'I know Vicky,' I said.

'You *know!*' she cried angrily. 'You *know?* Oh darling you *don't* know or you wouldn't be here. I told my mother not to tell you because *I* know, I've lived with it! You don't realise yet this has happened to us! To us us *us!* Not those poor wretches you read about in the papers – this is us!'

She tapped her breast angrily. She was almost shouting now.

'I know because I've lived with it, all my life I've lived with the terror of it, so *I* know!' She stared at me, then looked away. 'Oh I *knew* all right, darling. Deep down in here I knew, although I denied it, even to myself. I *knew* in here those damn bus conductors were right. I knew even though my mother denied it, even though we lived in a white street and I went to a white school and worked in a white hospital. I *knew* what the kids at school thought and what the neighbours thought and what the bloody halfwit bus conductors thought. I knew what you thought the first time you saw me, I could see it in your eyes. Don't shake your head darling, I *knew!* I knew what the Coloureds on the whalers thought, even you, though you persuaded yourself otherwise, so we've only ourselves to blame.'

'That's rubbish!'

She snorted softly. 'That's not rubbish darling, you suspected me at first, like half the South Africans who I meet, so we've only ourselves to blame.'

'I'm not blaming you or me!' I said angrily.

She snorted tiredly.

'Mom knew, of course,' she sniffed. 'She knew, poor thing. But you can't blame her, when she married my father it was legal, it didn't matter in those days. She was Poor White anyway. Half the

Cape's got some Coloured blood in them if you scratch back far enough.'

I wished I had a drink, for both of us.

'Mom knew,' she said dully to her lap. I sat down and held her tight. I was only half listening, I was trying desperately to think. 'She always denied it when I first started asking her. It didn't matter until a few years ago when the witchhunts started, but she denied it. We were white. *White!* We lived in a *white* railway house in a *white* street. That's why she encouraged me to leave home and get a place of my own in a decent area – so I'd be safe, away from the street where the neighbours whispered I was Coloured because my father was one-eighth Malayan.'

She looked at me beside her. Her eyes were red from crying.

'That's what he was. Although Mom denied it. Dad was white white *white!* She always said.' She looked ahead again. 'I don't remember him much. I've seen photographs of him, though Mom keeps them locked away. You can't tell from the photographs, he looks all right.' She looked back at me. 'He was quite handsome,' she said.

'I'm sure he was a fine man,' I said.

She looked at me red-eyed, then she smiled gently tearful. 'You don't have to say that, darling.'

'I wasn't being patronising.'

She smiled at me. 'You see what happens darling? I've got such a chip on my shoulder. All right. Anyway that's what he was, Malay. But only one-eighth,' she said pretending to be bright, 'as Mom so repeatedly emphasises now that it's all come out.'

I looked at her.

'Oh Christ. How did it all come out?'

She sighed. She said tiredly, 'God knows. Informers, that's all I know. Some nice neighbour wrote to the Board, I suppose "We can't have a Coloured girl living in *our* nice Pine Street!" Or one of your Coloured whalermen friends who had it in for you and me sent a letter with the tanker. I don't know how but that's how the Board usually gets to hear about borderline cases, through informers.'

'Jesus Christ,' I said.

She smirked bitterly. 'Jesus can't help, He was a borderline case too, darling. You can count Jesus out, darling. The next thing I know is I get a letter. Dear Madam, In accordance with Section so and so of the Population Registration Act of 1954, you are hereby required to appear before the Population Registration Officer at 9 am on such and such, bring your birth certificate and any witnesses with you, I have the honour to be, Madam, your obedient servant.'

She took a breath and I could feel it quiver.

'So. So I went along. I took Mom as my witness,' she said. 'Poor Mom, she was going to tell them a thing or two. It's just an ordinary Government office, with a counter. There were lots of people waiting and I was the whitest of them *all* – you'd have been very proud of me darling!'

I squeezed her shoulder.

'Go on Vic.'

She rubbed her forehead. 'You had to take your turn. Then when my turn comes, I go up to the counter and this officer gets out my file and says he's received information that my race is mixed and what further proof have I got? The whole time he's looking me over, he was quite an elderly man. Meanwhile I'm nearly fainting and dear old Mom blows her top. *Me!* she says, *I'm her proof, I'm her mother, I should know, take a look at me!* She kicks up such a fuss and you've seen her, she's dead white.'

She looked at me intently. I nodded.

'So,' Victoria said and her breath quivered, 'he refers the matter to his boss, in another office. So, in we go to the boss.'

She paused and rubbed her forehead.

'Go on Vicky,' I said.

'Well. The boss is very nice. He's also elderly. He tells us to sit down. He reads my file. Then he smiled at me and he can see how worked up I am and he says "Now relax, Madam."' She smirked again. 'Relax. Then he says did I want a lawyer? A *lawyer?* I've never met a lawyer in my life and I don't want to! No, I didn't want a lawyer, I said. Very well, did I have my birth certificate? No, I'd never seen my birth certificate, which is true. So he says was this good lady my mother? Mom's very upset now and she says yes. Well, he says, didn't *she* have my birth certificate? Mom lied, she said no she'd lost it years ago. Then he said well where was I born and where was my birth registered? And Mom told him, she could hardly say she didn't know. Well, he says, thank you, would we come back next week so they could get a copy of my birth certificate. And he tells Mom to bring along her marriage certificate. Then when we got home poor old Mom broke down in tears and told me she did have it, my birth certificate. She dug it out and there it was in black and white: Race of mother white, race of father *mixed!* Then she tells me about father being part Malay.'

She looked at me and her eyes were full of tears again. 'She was so ashamed.'

Her chin dimpled and she was going to cry and I held her tight.

'Don't cry, Vic.'

She started crying again, I hugged her shoulders.

She sobbed, 'Poor mother – to be so ashamed ...'

'Go on, darling,' I said.

'I'm sorry darling,' she sniffed. She sat up, eyes and nose red.

'Well,' she said, 'the next week he's got the birth certificate and Mom has to show him her marriage certificate. Well,' she took a breath, 'that was it. He said he's very sorry but the certificates accord with his information *and,* he says, with his own observation – and he says he's got his duty to do. "Victoria!" He called me Victoria. Not *madam* any more.' She looked at me. 'And Mom just about faints. And we're both crying. And he sends one of his minions to get a taxi for us and he says he's very sorry. But, he says, I can appeal against his decision.'

'And did you appeal?' I demanded.

She sniffed and nodded.

'Yes,' she said dully. 'We had the whole rigmarole over again at the Race Classification Appeal Board or whatever it's called. That finished a week ago, I was lucky I only had the suspense for six weeks, it usually takes months. I lost the appeal,' she said flatly.

'There's a further appeal to the ordinary Supreme Court,' I said angrily.

'Yes,' she said, 'I went to see a lawyer after that.'

'And are you appealing?'

She shook her head.

'No darling,' she said. 'What's the use?'

I stood up and punched my palm.

'You're bloody well appealing,' I said angrily.

She looked at me tearfully.

'What's the use darling?'

'What's the use?—of *course* you're bloody well appealing!'

She looked at me with red dull eyes, then they came more alive.

'But the baby,' she said firmly, *'he's* all right. He'll only be one thirty-second non-European so he's white, after one-sixteenth you're all right, thank God.'

I wasn't even thinking of the child, it didn't seem real yet. She rubbed her forehead feverishly.

'We're appealing,' I said.

'He'll have to live with my mother though,' she said earnestly, 'if he lives with me I'll have to have him classified as Coloured also the lawyer says.' She looked back at me earnestly as if she were saying that she had decided to send her son to boarding school because it would be good for him. Then her lip trembled and it curled over her teeth and she dropped her head and cried out loud.

'Victoria!' I said angrily, 'get up and pack your things!'

She stopped crying. She looked up at me with wet cheeks. I was very determined and sure and angry.

'What?'

'I said get up and pack. Go on!' I went to her cupboard and flung it open and grabbed two handfuls of dresses hanging there and flung them on the bed.

'Darling—'

'Go on and pack!' I slung more dresses on the bed. 'Where're your suitcases?'

She sat on the bed staring at me. 'Darling you can't take me anywhere.'

'I'm taking you home! Where're your bloody suitcases?'

'Darling we'll go to jail!'

'Pack, woman!'

I grabbed her suitcase off the top of the cupboard and slung it on the bed and flung more things into it. She was standing now staring at me.

'*Will you for Chrissake pack?*'

'James do you realise what you're doing?'

'Yes.' I slung more things in.

'But what can you do?' Her hands were clenched.

'I'll do something I promise you Victoria Rhodes. Now *pack!* Before somebody comes!'

She stared at me wide-eyed, her hands clasped at her belly and the tears shining on her cheeks, frightened. She looked very afraid standing there and I thought my heart would break. I went to her and held her tight and kissed her face.

'It'll be all right Vic,' I said, I was very determined. 'Nobody knows you out at Oak Bay. Now do as I say.'

I felt my heart would break for her standing there and what they had done to her and I wanted to shout a fierce *Christ you bastards,* and fight and trample any bastard underfoot who tried to stop us just let any bastard come ...

Chapter Forty-Six

Quickly we slung her things into the suitcases. She was tearful but she was not crying any more, she was working feverishly, obediently, she would do as she was told. She was a criminal now that she had begun to follow me, we were both criminals and we both knew it, it did not seem unbelievable that we were breaking the law, it was real all right. She was frightened but she would do it all the same, she was reckless now. She threw her clothes into her suitcases and I flung her other things into a cardboard box. She had to carry her coats.

'The rent,' she cried, 'I haven't paid the rent—'

'How much is it?'

'Five pounds a month, I owe a whole month.'

I pulled out my pocket and threw five ones on to the bed. 'Write a note, say your mother's very sick.'

She scribbled the note. I opened the door. The parson's son ran to the back door. I picked up the two suitcases.

'I'll put these in the car, wait here.'

I crossed the yard with the suitcases. The boy retreated backwards into the kitchen. I stopped and glared at him.

'Tell your father that Miss Rhodes had to leave suddenly because her mother is very sick. She has left one month's rent in the bedroom. Understand?' I spoke in Afrikaans.

The boy stared at me and said nothing. I turned and strode down the passage to the front door and out into the church-yard. They were singing something else now. I was very glad it was raining because not many people would be standing in the rain. The church-yard was drab and muddy. I strode through the gates into the wet street. The gutters were running with dirty water. I cursed that I had not parked my car away from the church, I had not thought of that. I unlocked the car and slung the cases on the back seat. There was an old man sitting on the verandah of the house opposite and up the street there was a man coming but there was nobody else watching. It was lucky it was raining. Then I looked behind me and there was the boy standing at the gate staring. I locked the car again and strode past him back through the gates. They had stopped singing in the church now. There was the sound of running and the boy overtook me and he ran into the house and slammed the front door.

I ran to the door, it was locked. I beat as loud as I dared.

'Open up!' I called as loud as I dared. I beat the door again. 'Open up!'

The boy shouted through the door, '*Wat maak jy hier?*'

'*Maak oop die deur!*' I shouted. 'Open the door.'

I beat with my hand.

'Victoria,' I shouted, 'Victoria – open the door.'

I heard Victoria running up the passage. '*Gee pad!*' I heard her say and the sound of the boy squealing then the door flung open. Victoria was looking wild-eyed and breathless. The boy was cowering in the passage. He ducked past us out the front door and ran round the side of the church.

'Hurry now!' I said.

We snatched the rest of her things from the room. I carried the box, she carried her bundle of coats and bedding. She was looking very afraid.

'All set?' I said.

She nodded and her hair was over her face and her face was white.

'When we get outside, just walk normally.' She nodded.

'If anybody challenges us, don't say anything, leave me to talk.' She nodded desperately. I tried to smile at her. I was very nervous myself.

'All right Vic,' I said.

I started walking down the passage and out of the house into the rain, Victoria followed with her bundle. They had not started singing again in the church. When we got to the corner of the church I said without looking round, 'Relax.' She didn't say anything. As I approached the gate I heard a rumble in the church of the congregation pushing the benches back and standing up. I walked quicker and I heard Victoria take a few running steps to catch up. I was panting now. I thought the congregation was coming out.

'Quick,' I said. As I walked through the gates I said, 'Please Christ, no cops.'

There were two policemen a hundred and fifty yards up the street. They were in their winter uniforms, walking slowly down the street towards us. They were wearing mackintoshes, walking slowly, chins a little tucked in against the rain. They were looking straight down the street towards me. They were both white policemen, though I don't suppose that makes any difference. I put the box down and I felt for the keys. Victoria was right behind me.

'There's two police,' she whispered desperately.

'I saw them.' I rattled the keys in the door. 'Open you bastard!' I hissed.

The door opened. The rain was coming down on my back. I turned to Victoria and grabbed her bundle. She was shaking and her hair was plastered to her pale face. I slung the bedding and coats into the back seat. Then I pushed the box in on top.

'Get in.'

She scrambled into the seat and sat hunched down, the rain running off her. I slammed the door and started round the car to the driver's side. Then I realised the keys were still in her door and I cursed and had to go back. The two policemen were a hundred yards away now. I heard the organ in the church starting up.

'Sing, for Chrissake, sing,' I whispered. I was shaking now. I tugged the keys out of the door and hurried round to the driver's side. The police were seventy yards away now. Victoria was sitting hunched down in the seat, she looked at me with a white face. It smelt damp in the car. I put the keys in and trod on the starter. The windshield was misty inside and wet outside. The two policemen were distorted. They were looking right at us. The old car started.

'Sit up straight,' I said. She sat up straight. I rammed the car into gear and let out the clutch. I was looking dead straight ahead but I was watching the policemen. They seemed to be looking right at us. We started down the street towards them and as we drew level they both had their heads turned looking at us. As I was level with them I put on the windscreen wipers. Then we were past them. Victoria was looking straight ahead.

I looked back through the rear view mirror but I could not see them because of the rain on my back window. At the corner I turned right. I did not know where that led to but I wanted to get out of that street.

'Light us a cigarette Vic,' I said. I was shaking.

'Where are we going?' she whispered.

'Home,' I said. 'Home, home, home.'

Then I laughed once, a burny laugh and she looked at me and then she laughed once and she said, 'Home! Isn't it exciting darling!'

Then she started to cry.

It rained all the way through District Six and through Woodstock back into Cape Town and up and up over Constantia Nek, cold, and the windscreen wipers were going slosh-slosh. We did not talk. I was driving hard and very carefully. There was not much traffic on account of the rain. When we got out of the urban area up into the Constantia Nek between Table Mountain and Devil's Peak we both felt better. She was cold and shaking and now I was feeling the cold too. I put out my hand and squeezed her knee and she looked at me.

I said, watching the road, 'We're having hot brandy and then roast duck and champagne,' and I smiled at her and then she smiled at me. She looked very strained.

'Are you frightened?' I said.

She was quiet a moment and then she said, 'Are you, darling?'

'Not any more,' I said. 'We're going home.'

She took a big breath.

'Nor am I then, darling, if you're not.' But I knew she was still frightened.

'Everything's going to be all right,' I said.

'We'll do something,' I said. 'Everything's going to be fine.'

I looked at her.

'Get that straight, Vic.'

She smiled again, tearfully. She nodded.

'Isn't it?' I said. I felt lightheaded now. I felt strong and happy. Christ, I wanted a hot brandy lemon. God, I was so happy to be with her. It didn't matter so long as I was with her.

'I love you, Vic,' I said. 'I love you.'

Her eyes were full of tears again but she was smiling.

'I love you too,' she said. 'Very much indeed.' I wanted to laugh. I loved her so much and I was glad of what I had done. The pines and the oaks were wet and dripping and there was a big white mist table cloth tumbling down over Table Mountain. I did not mind it, I like it when it is the Cape of Storms. I wanted to shout and laugh for my woman. The rain was slanting through the pines and the oaks down on the Coloured folk's cottages and they looked good and cosy and warm and the road over the Nek was beautiful in the rain, and my woman beside me.

'Look!' I said. 'This is where we're going to live, isn't it beautiful, this is home!'

And she was caught up in my happiness and she said, 'Oh yes, darling, oh yes it's beautiful!'

I really felt that I was coming home. And I was very proud of the fine old Dutch-gabled house amongst the oaks and the vines, it was a fine house to call your own and to bring your woman to and say *This is the home I am taking you to.* And when I come back from the fishing trawl she will be down there on the jetty to meet me when the boats come in, and we would jump into the old car and go back to our fine house on the slopes of the Nek amongst the oaks, is there a finer life for a man, his sea and his land and his woman? I was very lightheaded as we drove up the drive and there was the old house standing in the rain.

'Oh it's a grand house darling!' she said.

'This is where we're going to live,' I said.

'Hadn't we better park at the back darling?' she said.

'No,' I said.

The house was shuttered and locked, which meant Sophie was not in, she had probably taken Benjamin into town. I took Victoria down the old passage to the parlour. The cobbled floors were cold and the house was dull with the windows all closed. She was shivering. The fire was laid in the parlour, ready to be lit. The Dutch built their fireplaces big. I lit the fire and it crackled. Immediately the room was cheerful and it felt very good to be home.

'Home is the sailor,' I said, 'home from the sea.'

'Is it a lovely feeling darling?'

'It's grand because you're here.' I kissed her. 'Take off your wet coat, I'll get the things out of the car and make us some hot brandy toddies.'

'I'll make the toddies darling,' she said.

'All right, there should be brandy in the pantry.'

I went back out in the rain to the car and got out the two suitcases. I put them in my bedroom. Sophie had written in soap down the wardrobe mirror in big letters: Welcome Home! She had done that every season, and even when I was a boy coming home from boarding school for the holidays. When I went back outside to the car I saw Sergeant van Tonder's car driving along the road at the bottom of my land. I bent inside the car and said to myself *For Christ's sake don't come now, Van.* I got hold of her bundle of bedding and backed out of the car. Sergeant van Tonder's car was coming up the drive in the rain. When I got on to the stoep I waited with the bundle in my arms. Sergeant van Tonder hooted and he was grinning. He pulled up behind my car and rolled down his side window. There was a Coloured policeman beside him in the front seat. I was glad of that. I knew him as Klaasie.

'Hullo, Mac, you back, *jong!*' Van shouted.

'Hullo Van! Hullo Klaasie,' I said.

'Hullo, sir,' Klaasie shouted.

'I saw in the newspapers the fleet was in and I was just passing and saw your car. Welcome back, *jong!*' He was grinning all over his big old face.

'Thanks, Van. How's business?'

'No shortage of crime, *jong*,' Van grinned. 'Did you have a good season?'

His engine was still running.

'Bad, Van. All the whales are dying out. I won't ask you in, Van, I've got company.'

'Sure, *jong*,' Van grinned knowingly. He presumed it was a woman. 'Just saw your car, I'm going to the station anyway. Come down to the station soon for a dop and a skinder.'

'Okay Van,' I grinned. He revved the engine and put it into reverse. 'So long Van! So long, Klaasie!'

'So long, sir,' Klaasie shouted.

I stood on the stoep watching until he had swung round. He gave a short hoot and went down the drive. I went into the house with the bundle. I dumped the blankets in the corner of the bathroom. I could feel my heart pounding. I went back for the box. Victoria had the brandies ready. She was standing in front of the fire staring into it.

'Hullo darling,' she smiled.

'Hullo my love, how're you feeling?'

'Who was that at the front?'

'A friend of mine, he was passing.'

'Oh, I thought it might be your friend the police sergeant,' she said.

I kissed her face. 'Why did you think that?'

'I'm just nervous darling,' she said.

She smiled. I kissed her again.

'Drink your brandy,' I said.

'Oh darling,' she said, 'I'm so worried. Hadn't I better go back before it's too late?'

She looked at me with big worried eyes. I kissed her again and shook my head.

'No.'

'But we'll go to *jail* darling! And the disgrace!'

'Disgrace for who?' I said.

'For *you* darling! You'll be finished if this comes out—'

'Victoria,' I said, 'drink your brandy, you need it. We're going to appeal. I'm going to see a lawyer now.'

'When?' she said, surprised.

'Now. While you're having a very hot bath. Here's your brandy.'

I handed it to her off the mantelpiece and I held up mine.

'Here's to us,' I said. I was happy again.

She smiled wanly. Her eyes were still bloodshot and she looked cold.

'To us darling,' she said.

She drank it and shuddered.

'Golly, that's good.'

'Now go and soak in a long deep hot bath,' I said. 'I'll be back in half an hour, that's all.'

'What about the front door darling?' she said worriedly.

'Okay,' I said, 'I'll lock it.'

Chapter Forty-Seven

Driving through the rain from Oak Bay over to Hout Bay I was thinking how to put it to Fanie de Villiers. Fanie was short for Stephanus. Fanie de Villiers had been at university with me. He had worked harder than I, he was a very bright young attorney. He was a partner in one of the young go-getter firms, I had gone to him to set up my fishing company and occasionally to get him to placate my bank manager. Fanie had a very nice house on the Chapman's Peak road on the other side of Hout Bay. It was after twelve noon and he was having a beer before lunch.

'Mac!' he said. 'I saw in the papers the fleet was back!'

He looked very prosperous in his very nice house. He took me into the lounge grinning.

'Look who's here!' he grinned. His wife was sitting in front of the fire. She had been at university with us, she was a very pretty and pleasant girl. She was English. They had gone steady all through university and married as soon as he qualified. She stood up with a big smile.

'James!' she said, 'how lovely to see you. Did you have a good season?'

Fanie gave me a beer.

'Lousy, Marjorie,' I said. 'I'm getting too old.'

'It's really time you got married, James!'

Your university women friends always feel sorry for you if you haven't got married, as if you're unloved in this world.

'Can I have some advice, Fanie?' I said. Fanie raised his eyebrows.

'Shall I go?' Marj said.

'Sure, Mac – you go, lovey.'

Marj twiddled her fingers at me saucily. 'Nice to see you back, James. Get married this time home.'

'What's the trouble Mac?' Fanie said. 'What you done now?'

I took a pull on my beer.

'How clued-up are you on this Population Registration business, Fanie?' I said.

'Fairly,' Fanie said guardedly. 'I don't do much of that sort of thing.'

'A girl I know,' I said, 'is a borderline case. She's just been classified as Coloured. She's appealed once, she wants to appeal to the Supreme Court or whatever it is.'

Fanie looked at me soberly and nodded. He took a sip of his beer, he looked into my eyes. 'Go on,' he said.

'She's pregnant,' I said. 'The man's white and they want to get married.'

'Oh Jesus,' Fanie said. He walked to the settee and sat down. 'Is this you, Mac?'

'No,' I said.

'Mac,' he said, 'you can tell me if it's you, I'm your lawyer and whatever you tell me is secret and privileged information.'

'It's not me, Fanie,' I said. I lied because I wanted an unbiased opinion from him. If your lawyer is your friend he starts getting too avuncular. Fanie had been avuncular before over my affairs and it had made me nervous. I also did not want Fanie to think badly of me. Enough people were going to think badly of me soon enough without anticipating it.

'Mac,' Fanie said. 'Does she *look* white?'

'Yes. Her mother's white, her father was one-eighth Malay.'

'One-eighth hey?' Fanie said nodding. 'Pity it wasn't a sixteenth. But she passes as white?'

'Most times. Some people suspect, others don't, she's one of those. She's a nurse.'

'She's been living as a white woman, in a white community, *accepted* as white?' Fanie said.

'Yes,' I said. 'Poor lower middle class, railway family. Apparently there's been talk for some time in her neighbourhood that her father was part Malay, but nobody has done anything about it until this new thing started. Then somebody informed.'

'Oh Jesus,' Fanie sighed. 'Well,' he said, 'she's got a fifty-fifty chance on appeal, it sounds to me at first blush. The Supreme Court is very lenient with these borderline cases, they try their best to let them in, though the Government doesn't much like it.' He went on, 'The test nowadays is whether the appellant has been generally accepted as white by his community, kept the company of white friends and so forth. Has she?'

'Yes,' I said.

'And the man is unquestionably white?'

'Yes. He's been classified.'

'Has there been any prosecution under the Immorality Act?'

'No.'

Fanie took a breath.

'Mac,' he said, 'the trick is that she's got to show the Supreme Court that she *looks* white, that she *is* very nearly white, that she leads a *white* life, and is *accepted* as white. Then she'll get away with it. Anything that shows she is settled as a white person helps her.'

'What if she were to get married to him?' I said. 'I mean secretly.'

'She can't get married to him,' Fanie said flatly, 'because she's already classified as Coloured. If she gets married with false papers she commits an offence, Mac,' Fanie said pointedly, 'just like bigamy. Even if she had married him years ago, before she was even classified, the effect of her being subsequently classified as Coloured is to *dissolve* the marriage, although on appeal the fact that she *was* married to a white is a strong factor in her favour in proving she is *accepted* as white – because she had a white husband.'

Fanie looked at me. 'But I must warn you, Mac – she'll have to wait something like a year before her appeal is heard.'

I stared at him.

'A *year?*' I cried.

Fanie nodded. 'I'm afraid so, Mac. There's an enormous backlog of these appeals waiting to be heard.'

'A *year!*'

Fanie got up and walked to the fireplace then turned back to me.

'Oh for Chrissake,' I said.

'I'm sorry, Mac. And there's nothing can be done about that. I heard, I don't know how true, but I heard there are over thirty thousand appeal cases pending, mostly in the Cape.'

'A *year!*' I said. 'Oh Jesus.'

Fanie walked to the liquor cabinet and snapped the cap off another beer. He brought it to me.

'Mac? Are you in trouble?' he said. I poured the beer.

'No,' I said.

'You sure? You should tell me.'

'I'm sure, Fanie.' He didn't believe me.

'Mac? You know about the Immorality Act?' he said.

'Of course,' I said.

'Okay, Mac,' Fanie said. He still looked at me. 'Anything else?'

'That's all Fanie,' I said. 'Thanks.'

'Send her along to me if you like,' he said. 'I'll do what I can. Send her along next week.'

'Thanks, Fanie,' I said.

'I'm tied up in court the next few days. Send her along Thursday or Friday, tell her to make an appointment. But make it soon.'

'Thanks, Fanie.'

'It's a hell of a business isn't it?' Fanie said. I snorted.

'Drink your beer,' Fanie said. 'I'll tell Marj to come back.' Marjorie came back.

'Well!' she said brightly, 'business over? Now tell us about your love-life, James. Have you come back to half a dozen pining ladies?'

'Tell me,' Fanie said, 'why do thirty-year-old bachelors so fire the imagination of dull respectable matrons?'

'I'll dull respectable matronise you!' Marj said.

'They can't bear to see the lucky bastards happy,' Fanie said.

All the way home I was thinking about what Fanie had told me. A *year!*

Sophie had come back from the city and she heard me coming up the drive and she had the front door open as I was coming up the steps.

'Master James!' she beamed all over her fat old brown face with her grey hair. She gave me a bear hug.

'Hullo Sophie, *ou ding*,' I squeezed her broad fat shoulders harassedly. 'Is Miss Victoria all right?'

Sophie held me at arm's length and her smile was gone.

'Miss Victoria? Yes, she's bathing still, I got a *skrik* when I come home and find a stranger in the house, Master James!'

'Yes?' I tried to smile cheerfully at her.

Sophie looked over her shoulder then she closed the front door so we were alone on the stoep.

'Master James – who is she?' She spoke in English.

I smiled at her.

'She's my fiancée, Sophie. She was on the ship.'

Sophie stared at me.

'Your *fiancée*?' she whispered.

'Yes, Sophie.'

Sophie still stared at me.

'Benjamin tol' me about her, she's the nurse, he said you bringing her home to dinner,' she said.

'Yes, and she's staying, Sophie,' I said.

'You mean you going to *marry* her, Master James?' Sophie stared.

'Yes, Sophie.'

Sophie took a big breath, then looked over her shoulder again. Then she took my elbow and led me further down the verandah. She stopped squarely in front of me with her hands on her hips.

'Now you listen to me, Master James! Do you know what you doing in that *kop* of yours?'

'That's enough, Sophie,' I said.

'You listen to me Master James!' Sophie hissed. 'And jus' you remember I remember the day you was born! I remember the day your pa first started stepping out with your ma! Remember that!'

'Okay Sophie,' I said tiredly, 'say it.'

'If your ma was alive today she'd be saying the same as me Master James! I know every crazy thing you done enough to turn your poor ma in her grave so you listen to me for once!' Sophie glared.

'For once?' I said tiredly. 'Go on, Sophie.'

Sophie glared at me.

'Master James – I don't think that girl is white!' she hissed.

'Well she *is* Sophie,' I said angrily. I began to turn away, Sophie caught my arm.

'Master James – I admit she's nearly white but I don't want no trouble with the police, what would your ma say if she knew?'

'Sophie, the subject is closed.'

'Master James – have you seen her ID card?' Sophie pleaded.

'Yes,' I said, 'and it's got the magic letter *W!* Miss Victoria happens to be part Portuguese.'

Sophie's fat old brown face looked nonplussed, then very relieved. She looked sorry.

'Agh I'm sorry man Master James, sorry hey, I was only worried—'

'That's all right Sophie. We'll say no more.'

'I was only worried in case you messing roun' with Coloured girls and getting into trouble, Master James,' Sophie said. 'What would your ma say?'

'Of course, Sophie,' I said.

'She's a very nice girl reely Master James,' Sophie apologised.

'Sophie,' I said, 'you are not to say one word about this to anybody, anybody at all. You're not even to say Miss Victoria is staying here. *Verstaan?*'

'Understand, Master James,' Sophie said apologetically, 'of course yes.'

'All right Sophie,' I said. 'Now bring me a brandy, *ou ding.*'

We started back to the front door.

'Welcome home man Master James.' Sophie waddled behind me remorsefully.

'Thanks Sophie. How was the fishing, have you got the accounts?'

'*Ja,* I bring them now Master James. I think that coxswain is crooking you but it's not too bad.'

I knocked on the bathroom door.

'Vic?' I said.

'Come in darling,' Victoria said.

It rained all that afternoon. We had lunch in the parlour in front of the fire. We could hear the rain on the tin roof and it gurgled down the drainpipe outside the window. It was blowing now, in off the sea, you could hear it in the trees and in the chimney. It was good in front of the fire, the firelight flickering yellow and gold on her face and in her big eyes, on her long shiny hair. She looked very clean and tired, her face shiny from the soap and her lashes were thick and dark. She wore a long woollen nightdress and a long white towelling dressing gown tied in a knot at her waist. She was very worn out but her big eyes were dry and warm, and I loved her so much I kept wanting to stretch out and touch her. I said 'I love you, Vic,' I kept wanting to say it. I was very happy and also I felt very desperate. I had told her only part of what Fanie had said, that she could still appeal and that she stood a good chance on appeal but I did not tell her it would take a year. All the time I was thinking about what we had to do, and about what Fanie had said. If she lost the appeal. If the police came. If it came to the worst we would have to run away. I tried not to think about all these things, I tried just to give myself up to her and the fire and the brandy and the food but every time I looked at her I was thinking about it again. I did not want to spoil the homecoming any more. It was good now in front of the fire with the wind and rain outside. I was home again from the Ice at last with my woman in my own house and it was getting to be something like it was meant to be, and after a while the other thing seemed unreal and it felt that if we did not think about it nobody would ever know as long as we never thought about it. And when we were good and full and warm with food and the brandy and the wine I took her hand and led her out of the parlour and down the passage to the bedroom, with my arm around her waist and her arm around me. The bedroom was good and warm and dark and flickering in the fire Sophie had lit, and there was the big old bed with the covers turned back, and it was warm inside and blowing and raining and cold outside. It was the best and most right thing in the whole world and I undid the knot in the girdle of her towelling dressing gown as she kissed me. I looked at her naked there in the firelight, her long smooth lines and shadows and softness and I was so happy and proud of her and lustful and the aching sob after all the time, it was the best feeling I had ever had in my life.

Afterwards there was no sadness of afterlove, but it was all coming real again. I lay on my back and looked at the ceiling thinking and she lay holding me. Her eyes were wide and starry in the firelight, not dreaming.

She said, 'What are we going to do, James?'

I lay looking at the ceiling.

'I'll do something,' I said but I did not know what yet.

She said nothing for a while and then she said, 'How can I stay here?'

'You're going to stay here.'

'These appeals take time. In that time they'll find out about me staying here. And if I lose the appeal?'

'We won't lose the appeal,' I said.

'I've lost one already, darling,' she said.

I was thinking hard.

'If I lose I'll have to go back. If they catch us we'll go to jail, then I'll have to go back.'

'No, you won't,' I said. 'You won't go back.'

She said nothing.

'We'll leave, Victoria,' I said.

She shook her head against my chest. 'We can't leave.'

'Why not?'

She lay there listless. 'Because. Because of everything. This is your home.'

'And yours.'

'Home for me is where you are, darling. But it's not the same for you. This is your home.'

'You're my home,' I said.

'It's not the same for you, darling,' she said.

I lay there and I was slowly making the decision I had been making all afternoon since I spoke to Fanie. It was very clear suddenly. And once it was clear it was all right. I sat up and then I swung off the bed.

'Get up, Vic. Would you like to get married the day after tomorrow?'

'*What?*' she said.

'I said, Get up, we're getting married day after tomorrow.'

She stared at me.

'How?' she stared.

'In Bechuanaland. Over the border in the British bloody Protectorate of Bechuanaland. It'll take us two days hard driving to get there. Then we'll come back *married*. South Africa recognises Bechuanaland marriages and divorces. What can South Africa do about *that*, when two South African subjects are *legally* married *outside* South Africa?' I was excited.

She stared up at me.

'They can hardly prosecute husband and wife under the Immorality Act can they? They'll make a laughing stock of themselves. They may dissolve the marriage but they'll *have* to allow your appeal!'

It was all very clear now. She looked at me and then she sat up. Her hair loose down over her lovely breasts. I wanted to laugh at her.

'Darling? Hadn't you better ask Fanie about it?'

'No,' I said. It was all very clear. 'Fanie will get his bowels in an uproar and start shouting about social ostracism. How can we go wrong, unless we're caught before the border? If you are *already* married to a white husband it is a factor in your favour when you appeal, Fanie said. We cannot aggravate our position by getting married outside South Africa. *that's* not a crime. And how can they prosecute us under the Immorality Act if we're married? It's the complete answer, woman! Get dressed!'

She still sat up in bed. She was looking frightened again. 'I haven't got a passport.'

'Well, I have. We'll cross the border at night and you'll hide in the car. Now get dressed, Vic.'

She sat there. 'Darling, I'm scared.'

I was getting dressed. 'Of course you're scared. You'll be a damn sight more scared living here unmarried to me. Do you want to marry me?'

'Oh *yes* darling!' she said.

'Then get dressed.'

Chapter Forty-Eight

It was dark when we got out of Cape Town on to the Cape Flats, the rain was slanting across the road through the headlights and the car leaked a little and it was cold but our feet were warm on the floor boards against the old engine. After a while, when we got out of town and we stopped looking out for police, it was good in the car with the rain beating and the wipers going slosh-slosh and the dashboard lights shining into the cab, and our feet warm. At first she sat rigid while we made the long drive through town, looking out for policemen, then when we got on to the Flats she relaxed.

'Relax darling,' I said. 'You must be happy, it's not every day a girl drives to her wedding.'

She smiled at me, 'I am very happy really, darling.'

I said, 'Get me some brandy please,' and she got one of the two bottles out of the picnic basket that Sophie had packed for us. 'Have a swallow first, Vic,' I said and she took a big swallow out of the neck and shuddered. 'Have another one,' I said, and she took another swallow and shuddered again and then she passed me the bottle.

'Now you darling.'

It burned down to my stomach and I felt good. It was good solid brandy. It seemed to spread out into my arms and shoulders.

'That's much better,' she said.

'Sure it is,' I said. We drove through the drab Flats in the cold night rain and then the sandy scrub gave way to pines and dark soil again and gum trees, then the road began to wind slowly up into Hottentots Holland Mountains and the old V8 began to boil.

'Is it all right for her to boil like that, darling?' she said.

'She always boils,' I said. 'These old cars go best when they're boiling,' but I knew it was not good for her to boil all the way, as she would at this speed. The speedometer was marked up to one hundred, but she could only do sixty, flat out. With a following wind. I knew I should not be pushing her flat out. We climbed the long winding road up into the mountain, you could still see the glow of the lights of Cape Town faraway through the rain. The wind was blowing hard on the top and you could feel it beat the car. Then we entered the du Toit's tunnel with a whoosh and the rain and the wind and the faraway lights of Cape Town were cut off and it felt better.

'Better?'

'Yes, darling,' she said.

'We won't meet any police now,' I said. Then we came out of the long tunnel into the rain again, going down into the valley and I switched off the engine and freewheeled to cool her down.

Driving. When we were over the du Toit's Kloof it felt better, we had got away and at first it felt better and we settled down to the long hard drive through the night and tomorrow and tomorrow night before we came to the border. Then when we felt quiet and there was only the noise of the car and the rain, and our staring through the windscreen into the wet night, then we started thinking again, the seriousness of what we were doing, and the fear came back and I could see it in her face, staring through the windscreen. I told her to pass the brandy again and I made her take a big mouthful, to try to stop her thinking and to make her sleep. Then we ate the food Sophie had packed for us and we opened a bottle of the red wine and ate and drank while we drove, and for a while it became as if we were on a great adventure and we felt strong and a little heady from the brandy and the wine and the driving over the Kloof and now we were on the open road, almost free, and we talked. Then the talking and the brandy stopped and there was just the driving again. We drove up the valley and then the long climb out up into the Karoo plateau, the vast hard flat scrub country, and we left the storm clouds of the Cape behind. The night sky was clear and there was a moon and it was cold. The car stopped boiling. The moon shone pale silver on the vast flat land and the broad black tar national road was a dead straight ribbon going on to the horizon and the short scrub began at the edge of the road and extended on forever. There were very few cars on the road and you could see them from a long way.

At Five Sisters I stopped for petrol and oil and water. It was nearly midnight and the Shell station was about the only light burning in the village. Next to the garage was the Dutch Reformed Church with its high steeple stretching up into the moonlight. Across the road was a cafe with a sign *Vyf Susters' Kafee,* in darkness. Next to it was a butcher shop owned by Mr Hendrik Muller, but the paint on the wall had peeled off in places and it read *Hen Mul Fam Butch.* At the edge of the tar road there was a gravel verge and then a concrete gutter and then a dirt sidewalk. I hooted outside the Shell station and nothing happened. Then I got out of the car. It was bitter cold outside. I walked over to the glass office. It was good to stretch my legs and back. The native pump attendant in his green overalls was asleep on the floor inside the office. I knocked on the window and he woke up and looked at me sleepily. He came out.

'Sorry, sir,' he said in Afrikaans.

'Fill her up please,' I said in English, 'and check everything.'

'Yes sir,' he said in English.

'Cold hey?' I said.

'Very cold, sah,' he said. 'Super or regular, sah?'

'Regular,' I said. 'That old car doesn't know the difference.'

He was rubbing his hands and his breath steamed. He was a fat young man. He went to the pump and unlocked it.

'Is the toilet open?' I said.

'Gents sah, but not the Ladies.' He felt in his pocket and gave me a Yale key. I went to Victoria's window.

'Want to go to the lav?' I said. 'You better.'

'Yes,' she said. She threw off the blanket and climbed out. She was wearing slacks and a sweater and she hugged herself.

'Golly it's cold,' she said. I gave her the key and she went off round the side, still hugging herself. I went to the Gents. On the door it said Gents Europeans Only Slegs vir Blankes. It was messy inside. I decided to go round the back of the garage. When I got back he was checking the oil. He showed me the dip stick.

'Okay,' I said. He started checking the tyres. Victoria came back.

'Was it clean?' I said.

'Not very,' she said, 'but I'm a big strong girl.'

She climbed back into the car and huddled up under the blanket again.

'Brrr,' she said. A figure came out of the night walking slowly into the lights of the Shell station. It was a native policeman, patrolling in his khaki greatcoat and khaki helmet and he was carrying his knobstick. He had the three stripes of a sergeant on his sleeve. He looked at us but I was not afraid of him.

'*Goeie avend*, Sergeant,' I said.

He smiled in his black face and saluted as he strolled by.

'*Goeie avend, Meneer*,' he said. '*Koud, ne?*'

'Very cold,' I said. 'You should go back to the station, there are no criminals in Five Sisters.'

'We have a peaceful place,' the Sergeant said. 'Where is the *Baas* going?'

'To Johannesburg,' I said.

'Ah! You must be careful there,' the Sergeant said. 'There are many *tsotsis* in Johannesburg.'

'That is true,' I said.

'That is true, sir,' the Sergeant said. 'Here we have a peaceful town.'

'Good night, Sergeant.'

'Good night, sir, good journey,' the black sergeant said.

I paid the petrol pump attendant and I tipped him a shilling. He put the back of his hand to his forehead and then shot his hand up sideways.

'"*Nkos!*"' he beamed. 'Please call again for Shell Service with a Smile, sah!'

He was still saluting as I drove off. Victoria was smiling. 'Wasn't he sweet?'

We drove up the tarred road through Five Sisters. The roads leading off down to the houses were gravel. We passed the police station with its blue light. Then we were back on the road through the Karoo and there was only the sound of the engine.

'Try to sleep Vic,' I said.

'What about you?' she said.

'I'm all right.'

'I'll stay awake to keep you company,' she said.

'I wish we had coffee,' I said.

At about two o'clock I felt her head against me and she was fast asleep and I settled down to driving. After she had gone to sleep the brandy and the strain caught up with me. I wished I had coffee, but every town was fast asleep. My eyes began to play tricks and the road looked as if we were travelling uphill. Victoria was fast asleep. I rubbed my eyes and screwed them up but I only cleared them for a moment. At half-past three I blinked and for a moment I was asleep and when I woke with a jerk I was heading off the road at fifty miles an hour and I swung the wheel back. That's it, I thought. I pulled right off to the edge of the scrub and switched the engine and the lights off. The engine kept turning over for a few seconds, it was so hot. Suddenly it was very quiet. In an instant I was asleep.

When I woke up it was just beginning to get light over the Karoo and I was freezing cold. Somebody was tapping on the window. When I came to I saw it was a Provincial Traffic Patrol policeman. His patrol car was parked on the road. I sat up and rolled down the window. My heart was pounding.

'Good morning,' I said.

'Good morning, sir,' the traffic patrolman said, 'are you all right?'

'Yes, thank you,' I said. 'We were trying to drive through the night but couldn't make it.'

'No, I was just passing and saw your car and wondered if you were all right hey,' he said.

He was smiling. He was a young blond man. I was praying Victoria would not wake up. He could only see her long mass of hair.

'Sorry to wake you,' he said.

'Thanks for stopping,' I said.

'*Jere*, but aren't you cold hey?'

'Frozen,' I said. There was frost on the ground and the inside of the windows were misted. Victoria suddenly sat up, blinking. She looked straight into the face of the traffic patrolman and her eyes widened.

'Good morning, madam,' the patrolman smiled and he touched his cap, '*Jere*, but you must have had a cold night.'

'The patrol officer was passing and stopped to see if we were all right,' I said.

'Oh thank you,' Victoria smiled nervously at him.

'Well thank you,' I said. 'How far to the next town where we can get some coffee?'

'Thirty miles, sir,' the patrolman said, 'but you won't find nothing open, it's only half-past five.' He looked eagerly at Victoria. 'Would you like some coffee madam? I always carry a few thermos flasks.'

'Oh no, we couldn't take your coffee,' I said quickly.

'Oh we couldn't,' Victoria said.

'No, no trouble, sir,' the patrolman said. 'I just fill it up the next place, but you won't get no coffee till seven-thirty earliest.' Before we could stop him he turned and walked to his car.

'Christ,' I said to Victoria.

She looked at me, frightened.

'Stay inside the car,' I said. 'Just flap your eyes at him whenever he looks in, he likes you.'

The patrolman was coming back with the thermos, I got out of the car so he would have to stand to talk to me. I stretched.

'Man, a man gets bladdy lonely in this job hey,' he said. He was enjoying himself.

'You must do,' I said.

'I hope you like it with milk and sugar madam?' he leaned down and smiled in at Victoria.

'Yes, lovely, thank you so much,' she smiled.

'Agh, it's nothing,' the patrolman said.

He had three plastic mugs, he passed Victoria's to her through the window. Thank you, we both said. I was very tense but he clearly did not see anything wrong with Victoria. He took a noisy sip, he was enjoying himself.

'How long were you driving hey sir?' he said sociably.

'We left Cape Town at six last night,' I said. 'We hoped to drive right through to Jo'burg.'

'What's the hurry hey?'

'My fiancée's mother is very sick,' I said.

'Oh I'm sorry to hear that, man,' he said. 'I'm a Jo'burg *ou* myself, whereabouts your mother live, hey, madam?' He leaned down to look in at Victoria. He was determined not to have her left out of his chat.

'In Rosebank,' I said. I did not know Johannesburg but I knew there was a suburb called Rosebank.

'Oh very nice,' the patrolman said. 'I live, I mean my mother lives in Hillbrow. But now mostly I go down to the Cape for my holidays.'

'Oh yes?' Victoria said.

'Did you go to school in Jo'burg then, madam?' the patrolman said.

'No,' Victoria smiled at him. She looked lovely. 'My mother moved to Jo'burg only recently, I was brought up in the Cape.'

'Agh, the Cape's lovely, hey?' the patrolman said.

'Oh, isn't it?' Victoria said. 'I wouldn't want to live anywhere else.'

'No man, the Cape's lovely. But Jo'burg is gayer, hey?'

'Oh Jo'burg is very gay,' Victoria smiled, 'though I don't know it very well.' She had never been to Johannesburg.

'Pretoria,' the patrolman said, 'now you can keep Pretoria, man. But Jo'burg's also nice.'

'Too many damn civil servants in Pretoria,' Victoria said gayly, 'and not much nightlife.'

I thought she was doing very well but I wished she'd let me do the talking.

'No, you can keep Pretoria,' the Patrolman agreed. 'Would you phone my mother in Jo'burg, madam?' he leant in.

'Certainly,' Victoria said.

'Just tell her you met Hendrik on the road and had a cup of coffee with him. She'll like that.'

'Of course we will,' I said. 'Give us her number.'

He wrote it down and passed the note to Victoria. He looked very pleased. 'She'll like that. And tell her I'm writing some time.'

'Yes, you write to your poor old mother you naughty boy,' Victoria said.

Hendrik laughed, he liked being teased. 'Will you have some more coffee?'

'No thank you so much,' I said, 'we really must be going.'

'It's a long way,' Victoria said, 'in this old car, thank you very much.'

Hendrik looked disappointed. 'I've got another flask,' he said.

'No really, thank you,' I said. 'You've been very kind.' I shook hands with him. 'Goodbye, officer.'

'Cheerio, sir,' Hendrik said. He leant in and shook hands with Victoria. 'Cheerio madam, and ring my mother, hey, just say Hendrik sends his love.'

He stood beaming next to his patrol car while I manoeuvred back on to the road. I gave a hoot and waved and Victoria waved energetically and Hendrik saluted. I drove off down the early morning road.

'My God, darling!' Victoria said. She wasn't smiling any more.

'You did very well,' I said. 'He fancied you.'

'My God I got a fright, my heart's still pounding.'

'His coffee was all right though, wasn't it?'

'Wasn't it good? He was really very sweet.'

'You and your Pretoria nightlife,' I said. 'You see – you don't look Coloured.'

'*Agh sistog Master James, ek is only one-sixteenth Malay hey!*' she said in a Cape Coloured accent, and we both laughed.

'The Malays have lovely skins,' I said.

'Provided you a bit colour blind like Master Hendrik, hey Master James?' she laughed. 'We shouldn't joke about it darling!' she said. 'Supposing he'd been suspicious it was a stolen car and asked for our ID cards!'

'Nobody would steal this heap.'

'She's doing beautifully,' she patted the dashboard.

At eight o'clock we stopped in a town to fill up with petrol and wash and use the toilets. There were two cafes and a hotel. A native youth was herding some sheep down the main road, he was whistling and all the sheep were following the leader. I was still very tired but Hendrik and the wash had woken me up. I parked outside the cafe.

'Come on,' I said. 'Nobody will know.'

'We better not, darling,' she said. 'Better you go in and order us some sandwiches to take away.'

'It's early and you look fine,' I said.

'Oh darling?' she said, 'just suppose somebody kicks up a fuss and they call the police?'

All right,' I said. I was beginning to feel tired again. I went into the cafe. A black waitress was behind the counter, she was the only person inside. It would have been all right. I ordered coffee and six fried eggs and bacon and chips, then I went back to the car to fetch Victoria.

'Come on. The place is empty and there's a table in a far corner. It will do you good.'

She got out of the car very reluctantly. It was a typical South African cafe with formica tables and chairs and on the walls there were advertisements of beautiful girls drinking Coca-Cola and some Schweppes and Hubbly Bubbly and Cadbury's advertisements. There was a formica milk bar and a big display window with old lace curtains and some potted ferns. There were racks of newspapers, *Die Volksblad* and *Die Burgher* and *Die Stem* and yesterday's edition of *The Cape Times* and *The Cape Argus,* and there were *Superman* and *Batman and Robin* comics. In our corner there was a juke box. I wondered how only the South Africans can make their cafes so deadly uniform. It is something we got from the Victorians. Victoria sat with her back to the rest of the cafe.

'Swinging joint,' I said.

'I don't believe I'm missing much darling.'

'Oh it's a swinging scene behind you,' I said. 'Cheer up.'

'I feel like a criminal,' she said. 'I am a criminal.'

'Hold your head up high, this time tomorrow we'll be safely married. Mrs *McQuade,* what more could a maiden ask for?'

'Absolutely nothing. You're awfully cheerful, darling.'

'Here comes the coffee,' I said.

The black waitress slapped the coffee pot down and walked off. The cups were thick.

'That's what I like,' I said. 'Class.'

The coffee cheered her up. Then the eggs came. It was all good and greasy and hot. It made me feel happy to see them. Victoria put one of her eggs on to my plate, so I had four.

'Good for your hormones, darling,' she said.

'Tonight,' I said, 'in the Francistown Hotel in a deep feather double bed with clean crisp sheets, after a hot deep bath and on a full gut and a couple of bottles of wine, you're going to rue that fourth greasy egg.'

'Oh I won't rue it darling! Oh isn't it going to be lovely! To be unafraid and all legal!'

'We're going to win the appeal, Vic,' I said. 'It's going to be every night from then on.'

'Do you think we'll still manage to go to the Wild Coast one day darling? Swimming and goggle-fishing and all?' Her eyes were happy now and I loved her so much I wanted to laugh. I rubbed her head behind her ear. I thought of the hot sand and the white beaches and the old homemade beds under the thatch, the beer and the wine and the deep fried fish and tired and healthy and brown from the sun. And I knew it must all be all right soon and I wanted to eat down the eggs quickly and get going for Bechuanaland.

'Where are you going, darling?' she said.

'To get the brandy,' I said, 'to lace the coffee. You don't get married every day.'

I poured a tot of brandy into each coffee cup. There was still nobody in the cafe except the native waitress. While we were finishing the coffee the European man came in and went behind the counter. He was the owner. Outside on the cold sunny pavement people were going to work. We got up and I went to the counter to pay. Victoria stood with her back to the counter pretending to look at the newspapers. The owner studied her as he handed me the change. I bought a slab of chocolate.

'That your Cape Town car outside?' he said in Afrikaans.

'Yes,' I said.

He nodded. 'Holiday?'

'Honeymoon,' I said pointedly. I said *wittebroodsdae* which means literally white-bread-days. I could not tell if he was being friendly or not. I took my change and walked out with Victoria beside me. She had gooseflesh on her arms.

'You see?' she said.

'He was just inquisitive,' I said, 'about a pretty girl.'

'He thought I was Coloured,' she said.

'Nonsense,' I said.

At the next town I went into a Woolworths and bought a big thermos flask so we would not have to go into cafes. In the mid-morning we were out of the Karoo and climbing into the bo-land where the Witwatersrand and the mighty Johannesburg lies. At lunchtime I went into a cafe and got coffee in the flask and some hamburgers. I bought some beer at a liquor store and I opened one for Victoria. I wanted her to go to sleep.

'What about one for you darling?' she said.

'No,' I said, 'it'll put me to sleep.'

I badly wanted a beer to make me feel good but I knew that after that it would make me sleepy. I was feeling very tired again.

'Let me drive, darling,' she said.

'No,' I said. 'All we're short of is for you to go through a red light.'

At noon we saw the first gold mine dump rising high and yellow out of the undulating green-brown plateau. Next to the dump was the shafthead with the big cage wheel turning. On the other side of the road was the miners' compound, neat rows of brick houses with a soccer field and a beerhall. There was a traffic sign: *Beware Miners Crossing.* They were changing a shift and I had to stop at the crossing. The natives coming off shift still wore their helmets and boots and carried their meal tins. They were big fine looking men. They were singing as they crossed the road. One stopped in front of the car and he clapped his hands at us and then put a tin whistle in his mouth and started giving sharp shrill blows on it and then he held out his hands and shuffled back across the road while he whistled and then

he lifted up his right knee as high as his shoulder and then stamped
his boot down on the ground with a shout. Then some others joined
him and they got into a line and shuffled in unison with him as he
shrilled his whistle and then suddenly they all lifted up their right
legs and stamped again. It was the beginning of a dance. The other
miners crossing the road were laughing and some of them were
doing it as they walked across. They were doing it for our benefit.
Then their dance got quicker and now they were stamping with
both legs and then slapping their gumboots with their hands. It was
very good. Some more cars were waiting now. Then the last of the
miners were crossing the road and the dancers broke up and they
loped across the road grinning and waving. Victoria was clapping.

'Oh wasn't that marvellous!' she said. 'What rhythm!'

'They're Zulus,' I said. 'They love to dance.'

The countryside became more lush and built up and there were
more mine dumps and compounds and mills. Sometimes there were
gumtrees planted alongside the road and there was plenty of traffic.
There were more signboards warning of cyclists and miners. There
were roads leading off to the other towns of the Witwatersrand, the
gold towns. All the way there were mine dumps now. The new
mining towns were mostly built back from the road and you had to
turn off to go to them. Sometimes there were miles of new brick
houses in lines, the new native townships built to replace the shanty
towns. Victoria did not go to sleep, she was watching the countryside.
We bypassed Johannesburg and we came out on the Pretoria road.
It was lined with trees and there were some gracious houses built
back from the road. There was a lot of traffic and there were signs
warning careful driving. There were a number of cars full of
natives. We passed two speedcops on the Pretoria road. We drove
through the outskirts of Pretoria and then over the long hill of
Wonderboom and then we were on the Great North Road that leads
up out of South Africa and across the Limpopo and then across the
Zambesi, and all the way up Africa to the Nile. It was afternoon,
Monday, and we were very tired.

'Four hundred miles to go,' I said.

Chapter Forty-Nine

The great plateau of the Transvaal was brown and the farms are far apart. There are few trees, except round the farm homesteads far back from the road. The Transvaal is almost entirely Afrikaans but the homesteads are not Dutch-gabled, like in the Cape. The Dutchmen had forgotten about the gracious gables by the time they had trekked up to the Transvaal. There were gaunt steel windmills pumping in the cold dry afternoon. Alongside the broad straight national road the farm fences were four-strand barbed wire. The natives we saw on the roadside wore old white man's clothing and they were runtish. They were not big and proud-looking like the Zulus and the Xhosas who go to work on the mines of the Witwatersrand. The Zulu nation had passed through the Transvaal on their way south and had decimated the native people before they reached Natal and met the white Voortrekkers going north. Then Mzilikazi had led his splinter tribe north again back through the Transvaal heading for Matabeleland across the Limpopo, and he had had another go at the Transvaal natives. Mzilikazi took their cattle and women and butchered their men. There had not been much left of them by the time the Dutch Voortrekkers had arrived, trekking away from the English occupation of the Cape. The Voortrekkers fought the Zulu Wars in Natal and when they had won the English came and occupied Natal also. So the Dutchmen trekked north again to the Transvaal and set up their Boer Republic, which means Farmers' Republic. Then the richest gold reefs in the world were discovered in the Boer Republic and so there was the Boer War. That was sixty years ago. The Voortrekkers had a gutsful of the English and of the natives. They are not fond of the English in the Transvaal. The Transvaalers are very hospitable to individuals but they don't like the Union Jack. When the Royal Family toured South Africa after the Second World War the Afrikaans newspapers in a back page advised their readers to keep off the streets as reliable sources had reported that some irksome foreigners were at large.

In the late afternoon we came into Potgietersrus. The shadows were getting long and it was colder again. Potgietersrus is a farmer's town in a farmer's land and it is where you turn off the Great North Road and go west through the bush to Bechuanaland. Victoria had not slept, she had kept awake to keep me company. We filled up with petrol and I bought a six-pack of cold beers. At the petrol station Victoria wanted to go to the lavatory.

'I can hang on till we're out of town, darling,' she said.

'Maybe you'd better,' I said.

In Potgietersrus the tiredness went and a new tension began. This was the last lap, then the border and the smuggling her across. It could all blow up in our faces at the border. She was quiet, sitting there in the front seat staring through the windscreen. I put my hand on her knee and she looked at me without smiling.

Then she said, 'James, are you sure you want to do it?'

I did not want to do it at all.

'Yes,' I said.

'We can turn back,' she said.

'No.' I put the car into gear and we turned off the Great North Road on to the dirt road to Bechuanaland. 'Are you very scared?' I said.

'Oh darling, I'm so scared. Are you?' She looked at me.

I looked straight into the late afternoon sun. I was scared all right.

'No,' I said. 'We'll sail through that border post easy. Open a beer for yourself,' I said.

'And for you?'

'Later,' I said.

'I'll wait, then,' she said.

The dirt road was wide. The grass was taller and greener in the Western Transvaal and the road did not wind much. It was flat and now the thorntree country was starting, the trees that grow all over Bechuanaland and the north-western Transvaal and across the Limpopo and up across the Zambesi, right up to the Congo. It is cattle country. We met no cars on the road. Sometimes we passed a native walking along the road and one raised his old hat to us as we went past. We met a herd of cattle being herded by two small native boys. One had a long whip of rienipe attached to a long slender pole and he cracked it over the backs of the cattle to get them on to the side of the road for us and he whistled and shouted at the beasts. They were Afrikaaner cattle, brown and big with very long horns. They moved off the road under the whip but we had to stop for one beast that turned and stared at us. The native boy lashed it across the face with the whip and it turned and lumbered off with the rest.

'Hey!' I shouted out the window. 'Don't beat the cattle like that!'

The boy stared at me then he said, 'They are my father's cattle,' as if that made it all right. The sun began to go down and it was very quiet. The sunset shone into our eyes and it made the trees gold and then red and then mauve. Then it went under and it was the quiet twilight of the African bush, the best time, and the night insects started crick-cricking. Then the moon came up over the dark thorn trees. It was a half moon and the sky was clear black and full of stars. We had not spoken for a long time.

'Open me a beer now, please,' I said.

When she handed it to me I said, 'Don't you want one?'

'No.'

We drove on. The beer made me feel stronger, like food. I had been smoking a lot. The headlights threw long shadows through the bush. I saw a pair of eyes flash and they were probably a leopard's because they were quite big and lower to the ground than a buck's would be. Her face was gaunt in the panel lights. She felt me looking at her and she turned.

'We'll get through easily, Vic,' I said. 'They very seldom search.'

When I estimated we were three miles from the border I stopped the car off the road. I took a towel from our case and I wet the corner from the water bottle and wiped my face clean, to look respectable for the immigration officers. I put on a clean shirt, then

I combed my hair. She watched me and when I had finished she stretched out her hand and stroked my face once.

'All right,' I said. 'On to the back seat.'

She got out of the car and climbed into the back seat and lay down curled up. I put the suitcase on edge at her head. At her feet I put the hold-all. Then I heaped the blanket on top of her. No part of her was showing. Then I slung my jacket on top of the blanket carelessly. I chucked the cushion on to the side. Then I took the six-pack of beer and placed it where her waist was. It was all very conspicuous but it looked like a heap of bedding of a man travelling alone.

'Can you breathe, Vic?'

'Yes,' she said, very muffled.

'Breathe very lightly,' I said, 'and don't move.'

The blanket nodded.

'All right darling,' I said.

I started the car. I opened the brandy bottle and took a big swallow. I was very nervous now. All right, I thought. I put the bottle on to the seat beside me and I started down the road.

The South African Immigration post was just a small white building with a flagpole. Beyond the building was the boom across the road and a native sentry in a khaki greatcoat was sitting. He had a brazier burning in a paraffin tin. There were lights burning in the building and there was a place to park cars at the side. I decided I would not park the car at the side, I stopped in front of the building, in the yellow lights from the window. I took a deep breath and then I climbed out of the car and slammed the door loud. I tried to look normal as I walked towards the building and I felt abnormal trying it. The tiredness had all gone. I blinked in the strong light inside. There was only one officer on duty. I decided to speak in Afrikaans.

'*Goeie avend*,' the Immigration Officer said resignedly. He got up and came to the counter.

'How many people?' he said in Afrikaans.

'One,' I said, 'myself.'

'Only you?' He was looking at me.

'Yes.' I was putting my passport down in front of him. He picked it up and at the same time he slid a form to me. I slid it across the counter towards me. I was glad I did not have to pick it up because it would have rattled in my hand. I put my hand in my jacket pocket for my pen and clenched it tight as I brought it out.

'*James van Niekerk McQuade,*' the Immigration Officer read aloud. 'That is an unusual name for an Englishman.' He sounded amused.

I had my head over the form. 'My mother was an Afrikaaner,' I said, 'and she didn't want me to forget it.'

He liked that.

'That's why you speak such good Afrikaans,' he said. I was very relieved. I was filling in the form, pressing hard with the ballpoint.

'We spoke both languages,' I said. 'But mostly Afrikaans,' I lied.

'Ah, so.'

I was filling in the form rapidly.

'How far to Palapye Road?' I said for something to say.

'Eighty miles,' he said. 'You look tired,' the officer said. He sounded friendly.

'I feel terrible, I drove through the night.'

'You staying in Francistown tonight?' he said.

'Yes.'

'Just a visit?'

'Personal business,' I said. 'I may have to go on to Mafeking,' I said to get his mind off Francistown. He probably knew everybody in Francistown. 'God, it's cold.'

'*Ja*,' he said. 'You drove through the night all the way from Cape Town?'

'*Ja*,' I said, 'and let me tell you those Voortrekkers deserved that monument.' He thought that was very funny.

'Is that a Ford you're driving?'

'*Ja*.'

'Those old Fords are good,' he said. He was looking through the window at it. 'I had one like that,' he said. 'Best car I ever had.'

'They're good.'

'They built cars in those days,' he said. 'What year?'

'Thirty-nine.'

'That's the one. Best car I ever had.'

I was nearly finished the form. He came round the counter and stood at the window looking at the old V8. 'Wonderful cars, man.'

I finished off the form. 'Finished,' I said loudly. I was still scribbling my signature.

He turned from the window. He took the form and looked at it, then he stamped it. Then he stamped the passport.

'Nothing to declare?' he said.

'No,' I said.

'No gold or diamonds?'

'No,' I said. 'Wish I had.'

'Okay,' he said. He stamped a slip of paper and wrote *one* on it.

'Thanks,' I said.

'All in a night's work, man.'

'*Totsiens*,' I said. I was grinning.

'*Totsiens, meneer*,' he said. 'Probably see you on the way back.'

'Good,' I grinned. I sincerely hoped he was on duty on my way back. '*Totsiens*.'

I walked out to the car. I had to stop myself from grinning. When I got to the car I looked back at the window. He was standing there. I got in and trod on the starter. I put on the headlights and up the road the native sentry stood up and walked to the boom and waited. I let out the clutch and she started forward.

Then the Immigration Officer shouted.

'Hey!' he shouted. 'Hey!'

Suddenly my heart was banging in my ears again. I pretended not to hear. The boom was halfway up. I revved hard and let the clutch right out and the car jumped and stalled. I looked back and Victoria had jerked forward on the seat.

'Cover yourself!' I hissed.

The Immigration Officer was trotting out to the car. He came up along the driver's side. He had his hand out.

'Hey, you forgot your pen, man.'

Christ. I stretched my hand out and took it.

'Thanks very much,' I said in English. 'So sorry.'

'That's okay, man. Now you've stalled it,' he said in English.

I trod on the starter. The engine turned over and over but she did not start. He peered in the window at the milometer.

'Nearly a hundred thousand, hey?' he said. '*Jere*, that's good hey? I bet you she's good for another hundred thousand.'

She had still not started.

'Now you flooded her,' he said. 'Take your foot off the accelerator.'

I tried her without the accelerator. She just ground over.

'You flooded her, man,' the officer said regretfully. 'Try again.'

We were speaking English all the time. My heart was pounding. I tried again with the headlights off. *Start you bitch*, I willed her.

'You'll wreck the universal joint,' he said, 'stalling her like that, man. Try again. Open the bonnet man,' he said, 'and let's have a look at your carburettor.'

'A push will do it,' I said. 'Give me a push.'

'Open the bonnet, man,' he said. He was walking round to the front. He opened the bonnet himself. '*Flitslig*, Tagwisa,' he shouted at the sentry. The sentry came running with his torch. He bent inside the bonnet with it. I got out of the car so he would goddam advise me at shoulder height. He was shining the torch over the engine caressingly.

'*Jere*, you should clean it up, man,' he said. 'Give it a scrub with a brush and petrol. Look at that crap, man.'

'I will,' I promised him. I was shaking.

'Look at that crap, man,' he said irritably. 'You could paint it also, you know, you can get special paint for engines.'

'Really?' I said.

He undipped the distributor cap expertly and shone the torch into it.

'Look at those points!' he said disgustedly. He yanked off the rotor arm and held it up. '*Jere*,' he said. He slapped it back on. 'No wonder,' he said. 'You need a new rotar arm and new points,' he said. 'They only cost a few bob man!' as if I had been holding out on him. He tugged at the sparkplug leads. He tapped the fanbelt. 'And you must tighten the fanbelt,' he said.

'I will,' I said. 'Can you give me a push?'

'*Ja*, man,' he said, reluctant to finish with the engine. He called to the native sentry, '*Kom stoot*, Tagwisa.'

Tagwisa, the sentry, raised the boom then he came running. I gave him the slip of paper and they walked round to the back of the vehicle. I got in and put her into second gear. The officer and the sentry were ready to push.

'Now start you old bitch,' I whispered.

'All right,' I shouted.

They started pushing and the car rolled forward.

'Top gear, hey!' the officer shouted.

'Shut up,' I whispered.

I let them shove me right through the gate out of South Africa into Bechuanaland, then I let out the clutch. She coughed and jerked and then she roared and jerked forward and we were off down the night road into Bechuanaland. I was grinning and shaking and I wanted to laugh. I looked in my rear view mirror. They were standing in the lights of the Immigration building, watching. I hooted three short blasts and they waved.

I wanted to laugh.

'All right, you can sit up now.'

She swept the blanket aside and sat up. 'Oh, darling!' she said.

'It's all over Vic,' I laughed. 'We're safe!'

'You were marvellous.' She sounded shaky.

'I am bloody marvellous,' I said gaily. 'Can you climb over?'

'I can jump a ten foot fence, darling!'

'Come on, then.'

She clambered over and knelt on the seat and hugged me. She was laughing and shaking.

'Your hero,' I laughed, 'wants a stiff shot of brandy.'

'So does the heroine! Oh darling weren't we brave!'

'Aren't we bloody marvellous? Where's the brandy?'

'Here you are kind knight. Oh darling, you were good!'

'I was shaking like a leaf.' I lifted the bottle and took three long swallows. I only tasted the third one and then my throat and chest and belly were burning gloriously. I felt good and very happy. I passed her the bottle. 'A long one,' I said. I laughed at her as she lifted the bottle and swallowed.

'Oh, I feel marvellous! Wasn't he funny about the engine!'

'He was a scream,' I said. 'Didn't you hear me sniggering all the time?'

'Oh darling, I'm so happy!'

'It doesn't matter what happens when we re-enter South Africa. If they do happen to catch us at the border, we'll be already married! That'll fox them! They can't refuse us entry to our own country. We'll be legally married!'

'Oh darling, aren't we clever?'

'We're marvellous. Pass the bottle.'

'Finish it darling, there's only one swallow left.'

'One swallow doesn't make a summer. We're having champagne in Francistown.'

We were happy all the way to Francistown. We parked right outside the old hotel with the red stoep verandah. The wide road was only tarred down the centre, the wide verges were dirt. There were some old general dealer stores opposite. It looked a lovely sleepy old town. Down at the end of the verandah was the bar with men in shorts drinking. A native porter in white uniform came and took our bags. He had to go and call the receptionist. She came out smiling. She was middle-aged and bosomy.

'A double room with a bath, please.'

'I'm afraid we have no rooms with bath attached, sir,' she said.

'Your best room,' I said.

'Double bed or twin, sir?' she asked.

'Double,' I said.

'I think so,' she beamed at us. 'Sign here please.'

I filled in the register.

'Tea or coffee in the morning, sir?' she beamed.

I didn't know what Victoria liked in the morning.

'One tea, one coffee,' I said with a grin. I didn't mind. 'And can you serve dinner in the room? And breakfast?'

'Certainly, sir, there's a shilling extra service charge. There's no *a la carte*, I'm afraid, only the menu.'

'That's fine,' I said. 'What champagne do you have?'

'Only South African, sir,' she beamed, she was very friendly, she liked us. 'Grand Mousseux.'

'Can you send two bottles along right now?' I said. 'Immediately.'

'Certainly, sir. Shadrech,' she said to the porter, 'call a wine steward.'

'Yes mam!' Shadrech beamed. He liked us too. We were infecting everybody.

'And can you have a bottle of champagne served with breakfast too? That's most important.'

'My!' she said, 'certainly. Are you celebrating something?'

'Something,' I grinned.

She flashed Victoria a conspiratorial smile. Victoria looked lovely, grinning there.

The porter carried our bags to the room. It was a fine old room at the side with a wooden floor and a great soft bed. It had French doors opening on to the verandah. I tipped the porter half a crown and he shot up his hand in salute and grinned white teeth all over his black face. 'Thank you sah!'

Victoria was bouncing up and down on the bed.

'Darling, feel this bed!'

Before the porter closed the door, the wine steward came with the two bottles of Grand Mousseux in an icebucket and two glasses. He wore a wide red sash over his shoulder. He was also grinning. I think everybody loved us, we were so happy. He opened one bottle while we watched him. The cork popped loud and shot across the room. I gave him half a crown also and he saluted.

'Nkosi!' he beamed.

I passed Victoria her glass. Then I kissed her happy smiling face.

'Here's to us that love us well!'

'And all the rest can go to hell!'

We were both laughing.

The next morning, clean and rested, after a big breakfast and champagne, under a cold blue sunny sky, on payment of five pounds for a Special Marriage Licence, the Assistant District Commissioner married us at the courthouse. We had more champagne after that and after lunch we slept in our room, and that night we drove back across the border.

Part Seven

Chapter Fifty

In summer it is the Fairest Cape of All, and they call it the Cape of Good Hope: winter is a bitch, and they call it the Cape of Storms. That late April the leaves were nearly all going from the oaks and the vines, and it was blowing. It was still raining on the Thursday night when we got back to Cape Town and the sea was grey and the rollers were big and the spray flew back off them all the way in, and when they hit the rocks they made a great crash and flew high. It had been too rough for the fishing boats to go out. It was raining hard with the wind when the police came for us.

They had been watching the house for two days and nights. I don't know who had put them wise to us, whether the parson she had boarded with, or Jakkals, or maybe even Geradus van Wijk. They had watched us come home in the dark and carry our bags in. They had waited while we bathed and ate. They had waited until we had gone to bed and every light in the house was switched off. Then they had come through the dark garden in the rain and the sergeant put a constable to guard the front door and a constable to guard each side of the house and he had taken one constable with him as a witness and first they had woken up Sophie and shown her their warrant and ordered her to unlock the back door. Victoria was already asleep. I heard the back door click and I thought it was only Sophie coming in for something. Then I heard the sound of male footsteps coming. I got out of bed and pulled on my dressing gown quickly. I knew from the first who it was. I could feel the anger coming up inside me. I did not care any more. I looked at Victoria and she was still asleep. I stepped into the dark passage and closed the door behind me. I could see a figure at the bottom of the passage. I snapped on the light.

'*What the devil do you mean by this?*'

I had expected to see Sergeant van Tonder. It was a sergeant I had never seen before, frowning in the light. By Christ, I hated him.

'*What the hell are you doing in my house,*' I shouted.

The constable came up beside him. Sophie was standing in the kitchen doorway. I walked towards them. I was full of fight.

'You get out of my house,' I shouted. The sergeant had the warrant in his hand.

'Sir, I have a warrant under the Immorality Act to enter and search your house—'

'*Get out!*' I shouted. The constable ran past me for the bedroom door. I lunged after him and the sergeant jumped at me. I swung at the sergeant with all my might and I got him on the chest and he went down. The constable had flung open the bedroom door and the light was on.

'*Get out of my house—*' I roared and I flung myself at the constable. Victoria was sitting up in her nightgown with the blankets bunched to her chin. The constable turned on me and I hit him flat out with my shoulder in the chest and I swiped into his stomach and he was hitting me on the back. I got him by the collar and slung him sideways and hit him again. Then the sergeant was on to me and I lashed back with my elbow and I got him also and then the constable was scrambling up and as I tried to hit him the sergeant got my arm.

'*Get out of here you sonsabitches,*' I shouted. Then the constable had my other arm and I was struggling wildly and shouting. Then Victoria was beating at them with her fists and her hair was flying and shouting, '*Leave him alone how dare you,*' and then two more policemen were running up the passage and one grabbed Victoria, I kicked out at him and got him in the thigh and he shouted. Sophie was screaming. Then they got my hands behind my back and I felt the handcuffs snap on and then they had Victoria handcuffed and she was still kicking and she was crying. The constable was bleeding from the nose. Everybody was panting. The sergeant picked up his cap, panting.

'I arrest you both ...' he panted, 'I now caution you ... you are not obliged to say anything ... but if you say anything it can be taken down ... and given in evidence ... do you understand that, hey?'

First they took us to the Oak Bay Police Station and booked us both under the Immorality Act and for assaulting police officers. I had told Victoria to say absolutely nothing until I had spoken to Fanie. They gave me permission to telephone him but there was no answer. It was only ten o'clock. They asked me if I wanted any other lawyer. I said no. When they asked Victoria her full names she glared at them and said, 'I refuse to say anything.'

'You've got to tell us your names,' the constable said.

'You warned us that we need not say anything!' I shouted, 'and she's telling you nothing.'

'Okay,' the policeman shrugged. 'We know it anyway.'

'We want bail,' I said.

'Only the magistrate can give you bail for this offence, man,' the sergeant said.

'I want to see Sergeant van Tonder,' I said.

'He's coming,' the sergeant said.

After they had booked us they put us in separate cells. I heard the sergeant instruct a constable to go and take photographs of the bedroom and wait for him there. The cells were at the back of the station. I could not see the females' cell. My cell had a steel door with a grill and there was a latrine bucket by the door. There was a pile of blankets folded neatly on the floor and the room smelt of disinfectant. There were some drawings on the whitewashed walls. There was an electric light burning high in the ceiling. After five minutes the door opened and Sergeant van Tonder stooped in.

'I'm sorry, Mac,' he said, 'I told them not to put you in the cells. Come, *jong.*'

I glared at him.

'What about Victoria?'

'She's in the females' cell,' Sergeant van Tonder said.

'Are you letting her out too?' I demanded.

'Where'll we put her?' he said.

'Wherever you put me!' I said.

Sergeant van Tonder shook his head.

'She'll have to stay in the cells, Mac.'

'Let her out for Chrissake!' I shouted.

'Listen, Mac,' Sergeant van Tonder said, 'you're not in any position to demand anything, *jong*. I'm letting you out meantime as a favour.'

'For Chrissake, Van ...'

He stared at me then he shook his head. 'Okay,' he said. He said to the Coloured constable behind him, 'Let the woman sit in the Charge Office. Come,' he said to me.

I followed him back and through the Charge Office. There were two Coloured Constables checking in from their beat. I knew them both, they looked at me. Sergeant van Tonder led me into his own office and waved me to a chair and closed the door. He sat down behind his desk. He looked at me and then he gave a big sigh and shook his head.

'For Chrissake, Mac. Why did you do it?'

'Can you give us bail?' I said.

'Only the magistrate can, you can apply in the morning when you go to court for remand. Why did you do it, *jong*?'

I just looked at him.

'For Chrissake, Mac,' Sergeant van Tonder said, 'you know the law, now look what a mess you're in. You've had it, *jong*.'

'Can you get me Fanie on the phone?' I said.

'I'll try,' he said. He picked up the telephone and dialled and listened. Then he shook his head and replaced the receiver. 'Not home.' He looked at me. 'I admit she's a pretty girl, *ou*. But Christ, Mac, you know better than that. Was it because you were crazy for a woman after the Ice, *jong*?'

'I'm not saying anything, Van,' I said angrily.

He smirked mirthlessly.

'For Chrissake, Mac, I'm not trying to trap you into a confession. Why d'you think I didn't lead the raid myself, hey? Because I didn't want to have to give evidence against you.'

I said nothing. I hated the bastard.

'I can understand it maybe in a youngster or in one of those English whalermen, but Christ *you,* Mac?'

I waited.

'Listen,' Van leaned forward on the desk and dropped his voice. 'Listen: you must say you didn't know she was a Coloured girl.'

I looked at him and waited.

'When the case comes up, say you didn't know. Because she looks so white. Say it was dark an' you never knew, Mac.'

He waited for me to agree.

'You hear me Mac? I'm trying to help you, *jong.*'

'I hear you, Van,' I said. I wondered now how much they knew.

'Say it, Mac,' Van urged. 'The magistrate'll believe you, *jong,* she's so white. Say you met her on the docks or somewhere when the fleet came in an' it was dark and so forth and you just thought she was a white whore from one of the bars. You never saw her in daylight, etcetera.'

He looked at me.

'Where did you meet her Mac?' he said.

'I'm saying nothing, Van,' I said. I thought: so he doesn't know about her being on the whalers. 'What put you on to us?' I said.

Van sat back.

'Information received,' he said flatly. 'I won't tell you any more. Except we checked up on her and we know she left her room in District Six on Sunday without telling anybody. Christ, Mac, you been with her since Sunday, that's bad.'

I said nothing.

'Listen, Mac,' Van leaned forward again. 'I'll tell you one thing: all we can actually prove is what we saw tonight. Don't say you were with her since Sunday for Chrissake, say you only saw her one night, in the dark.'

I waited.

'All right, Mac,' Van sat back. '*Jere,*' he said, 'a respectable *ou* like you!'

He was through with the advice.

'What happens now?' I said.

'When they come back from photographing the room they'll take you into town, to Caledon Street. You'll have to stay in the cells. In the morning they'll take you in front of the magistrate for remand,' Van said.

'What's that?'

'Adjourn the case for two weeks to get the file ready. They'll ask you whether you plead guilty or not guilty tomorrow before the magistrate. Plead not guilty, hey. Then the magistrate'll remand you for two weeks. Ask for bail, hey,' Van said.

He sat back and looked at me sadly.

'*Got, jong,*' he said, 'a well-brought-up chap like you.'

Chapter Fifty-One

It rained all that night. In the morning the wind was harder driving the rain in from the sea and I knew the swell was big out there.

In the morning they took me with the other prisoners in a black maria from the Caledon Street police station up to the magistrate's court. I had not yet seen Victoria since last night. They put us in a big holding cell below the court rooms. The policeman read from a list and made us sit on the benches in the order that we were to be called up. We were all Europeans. There was a lavatory at the end of the cell. The female cells were elsewhere in the building. One side of our cell was bars and the other side the bars was the Coloured male cell.

At ten o'clock I saw Victoria when they took me from the cells up to the court. She was walking down the corridor towards me beside a policewoman. She looked shocked and the hate welled up inside me. She was pale and her hair was uncombed and her big dark eyes were wide and under them the skin was dark and her lips were very pale and her dress was crumpled. She smiled faintly when she saw me and I started down the corridor towards her and the policeman grabbed my cuff. I shook my wrist free and he hurried after me.

'Hullo darling,' she said. 'Are you all right?'

'Yes, darling, I'm just very tired.' She said it dreamily and her eyes were a little glazed. The policeman was plucking my sleeve nervously.

'Come, now,' he said. He exchanged looks with the policewoman.

'Is Fanie here?' she said faintly.

'No, Vic. Just plead not guilty and let me do the talking.'

'Yes darling,' she said.

The policeman had steered me round, *'Kom nou,'* he said again.

The policewoman put her hand on the small of Victoria's back. They walked on either side of us towards the courtroom.

'Everything is going to be all right, Vic,' I said.

'Ssh!' the policeman said.

'I'm sure it is, darling,' she said.

We were at the door of the court, walking through. There was the magistrate sitting up on the bench. He was saying something and then a European man was walking out of the dock with a policeman beside him. He was scowling angrily. Then a policeman was standing up at the bar singing out our names. The people in the gallery were turning to look at us, expanse of faces turning. The magistrate looking at us. Walking side by side down the aisle of the court and there's the wooden dock with the door open, walking in and it closing behind us. Everybody looking at us, the two pressmen at the press table scribbling hard in their notebooks, the police prosecutor reading the charge and there was a new shuffle in the gallery of people craning when they heard it.

'Do you understand these charges?'

'Yes,' I said.

'Do you plead guilty or not guilty?'

'Not guilty,' I said loudly.

'Not guilty,' Victoria whispered.

I felt for her hand and it was trembling, she was trembling all over. The magistrate was writing and the two pressmen were scribbling and the police prosecutor was applying for a remand for two weeks.

'I want to apply for bail, your Worship,' I said loudly.

'Yes?' the magistrate murmured, he still had his head down writing. 'What do you say to that, Mister Prosecutor?'

'The Crown opposes bail, your Worship,' the policeman was saying, 'he's a violent man and he may abscond.'

'They broke into my house—' I shouted.

'We had a warrant!' the policeman said loudly.

'Quiet please, quiet,' the magistrate said.

'They forced their way into my bedroom,' I shouted, 'where my wife was lying—'

'Your *wife?*' the magistrate said. He looked up.

'My wife!' I shouted. 'She's my legal wife ...'

Wife wife wife was buzzing round the courtroom. The prosecutor was looking astonished. Victoria had her eyes closed.

'What do you know about this suggestion, Mister Prosecutor?' the magistrate said.

'They can't be married,' the prosecutor said hotly. 'We've got extracts from the Population Register,' he rattled a document up in his hand, 'and she's a Coloured so they can't be married ...'

The pressmen were scribbling frantically, one got up and hurried out of court.

'*We were married,*' I shouted. The magistrate held up his hand.

'That is something to be investigated at the trial not now,' he said. 'In the meantime I will grant you bail in the sum of one hundred pounds each in your own recognisance, you must surrender all travel documents to the Clerk of Court and report daily to the police. And for your own sakes I must give you the following serious warning.' He paused and looked sternly at us. 'Are you listening James McQuade and Victoria Rhodes?'

I nodded. Victoria was trembling beside me.

'Yes, your Honour,' she whispered.

'You are both on a very serious charge indeed,' the magistrate said flatly, 'the maximum penalty for which is three years' imprisonment with hard labour. Now, I have agreed to let you both out on bail pending your trial.' He wagged his finger. 'But do not imagine that because you are on bail you are at liberty to commit further offences of this nature during that period. I warn you both that any further acts of sexual intercourse between you while you are on bail will be additional offences for which you can also be further tried and further punished. Let me make that very clear, for your own sakes. Do not think that being on bail leaves your own positions or the legal position undecided: the law is clear and, in its wisdom, it takes a very serious view of these offences. As to your claim that you are married, that will be gone into at your trial, but I point out that the effect of our legislation is to dissolve any marriage between Europeans and non-Europeans. Now, I've warned you. For your own sakes you should have nothing further to do with each other. Go back to your own respective areas and have *nothing* further to do with each other except in the presence of your lawyer. Now, I've said all this for your own sakes, because you seem attached to each other and I don't want you to be under any misapprehension as to the legal position.' He looked at us.

'McQuade, do you understand that?' The pressmen were getting it down verbatim.

I nodded.

'Victoria, do you understand?' the magistrate said kindly.

Victoria had her eyes closed. 'Yes, your Honour,' she whispered.

'Very well, then,' the magistrate said. 'Your trial will take place in two weeks.'

The policeman was plucking at my sleeve to lead me out of the dock. Turning in the dock, the expanse of faces in the public benches all watching, the two pressmen leaving their tables hurriedly, following the policeman up the aisle and all the faces turned to us. The prosecutor was calling the next case. We got to the door of the court and the two newspaper reporters were on to us. I took Victoria's hand. She was walking dazedly, her hand limp and moist.

'Excuse me Mister McQuade can you tell me about your being married—' The policeman was still holding my sleeve, he tugged me forward, I shook my arm free.

'*Let go of me!*' and my voice sounded loud.

'I've got to take you to the Clerk of Court,' the policeman said plaintively.

'*Take your goddam hands off me—*'

'Excuse me Mister McQuade will you tell us how—'

'*Get out of my way!*' I said.

'Miss Rhodes, will you tell us—'

'*No, she will not, get out of the goddam way!*'

They followed us down the aisle still scribbling. *And despite the magistrate's warning the two accused left the courtroom hand in hand.* The policemen hustled us down the corridor with the pressmen following. Into the Clerk of Court's office and signing the bailbonds, the pressmen hanging on behind waiting for us. I threw down the pen and took her hand and turned and barged through them. They walked alongside us.

'Mister McQuade, is it true that you have just come back on the whalers—?'

'*Leave us alone for God's sake,*' I said.

'Miss Rhodes, is it true you were also on the whalers—?'

She was clinging to my hand running every few steps to keep up with me. We clattered down the stairs to the main entrance and there were the newspaper photographers and the pressman snapped his fingers. The photographers ran in front of us out into the rain.

'It's no use covering your face,' I said to Victoria, 'it looks worse.'

We clattered down the front steps into the rain, the photographers skipping in front of us.

'Mister McQuade—' The rain was teeming down, slanting with the wind. I pulled Victoria up the pavement looking for a taxi, the photographers trotted along and ahead. Her dress clung wet and long hair was sticking to her face and her eyes were wide.

'For Chrissake leave us alone!' I shouted. I was ready to take a swipe at the next one who came near. I shouted at a taxi. The taxi pulled over and I flung open the door and Victoria climbed in. The photographers were still with us. I slammed the door and sat back. The rain was running off us. She sat back in the seat with her eyes closed clinging on to my hand.

'Where to, sir?' the taxi driver said.

'Just drive, get away from here.'

I looked at Victoria. I squeezed her hand and she opened her eyes. Her hair stuck lank to her face.

'Hullo darling,' she said faintly. 'It's all over now.'

'It's all over, Vic, everything is going to be okay.'

'I know it is, darling,' she closed her eyes again and sat very limp, 'if you say so darling.'

'We're married,' I said. 'They will have to allow your appeal, that's the main thing.'

'Of course darling,' she said. 'I'm so terribly cold darling.'

I put my arm around her. 'You'll be warm and dry soon,' I said. 'And we'll have something hot to eat.'

'Yes, I'm hungry too darling,' she said. 'I'm very hungry.'

She sounded far away and dreamy.

The rain was beating on the taxi and the windscreen wipers were going flat out. The streets were distorted with the rain on the windows. There were very few people on the streets, scurrying under umbrellas.

'Where to now, sir?' the driver said.

'Just keep going,' I said. I was trying hard to think.

'Darling, I'm very cold,' she said, she was shivering now. I squeezed her shoulders. I was trying desperately to think where to go. It was all very confused. She was shivering and hungry and telling me and I could not think what to do, where to go. It felt desperate. The taxi turned out of Adderly Street past the Grand Parade on to the Peninsula road, driving slowly.

'Can you hold on Vicky?'

'Yes I can,' she said dreamily. 'Don't you worry about me darling.'

'We'll go somewhere now, we'll go home,' I said.

'We can't go home, darling,' she said dreamily. 'You heard what he said, the police will be watching for us, darling.'

I felt desperate.

'We've got to go there to fetch your things for Chrissake!' I said desperately.

'And then where will I go darling? I can't go to my mother's place either.' She still had her eyes closed.

'Oak Bay,' I said to the driver. He trod on the accelerator.

'Darling I can't stay at Oak Bay with you,' she said. 'You better take me back to District Six and I can fetch my things later.'

'You're *not* going back to District Six,' I said.

'Darling you heard the magistrate,' she said. 'If I stay with you we'll be back in jail tonight.'

'You're not going back to District Six!'

'I can't go to my mother,' she said, 'and I can't stay with you, so I must go back. I must get dry and lie down soon darling, I feel so sick.'

I hugged her close and I did not know what to do. I looked through the rear window to see if a police car was following us. I could not let her go back to District Six, back to that room. Marrying her would help her in her appeal, a strong factor in her favour Fanie had said, but it did not help us right now. The appeal would still be months away and there was still the legal uproar in between, the screaming uncertainty, the appeal was not important right now, what was important was the here and now, in this taxi with her asking to lie down and no place to go, where to go here and now. I did not care about the appeal, it was no comfort here and now.

'Please, darling, take me back to District Six,' she whispered, 'I must lie down.'

It made me desperate to hear her, impotent furious confusion and I saw her lying down shivering on that bed in that room at the parsonage, covering her with a blanket and asking the parson's wife to look after her, and then leaving her. And having to go back to Oak Bay alone and collect up her things and drive back with them to District Six, and carrying them through the back, back into her room and putting her cases and her cardboard box down on the floor and kissing her wet eyes goodbye and driving away leaving her again. I could feel a howl of fury in my throat, impotent rage and fight but you can't win, you can only lose there is absolutely nothing you can do every way is blocked and you run frantically to the next one and it is blocked also, and the next one and the next one, she was begging to lie down and be warm and there was no place I could give it to her, my woman and my wife, there was nothing and nowhere whichever way you turned, I could not even stop the taxi to take her to a place for some hot milk, there was nothing nothing nothing we could do. And I knew then there was just one thing I could do and it was the only thing and it was what mattered right now, I tapped the driver hard on the shoulder ...

'Go to the docks,' I said.

'Where, sir?'

'The docks.'

'Where're we going darling?' she said.

'You're going to England,' I said. 'On the whalers. Fergie and Elsie and The Kid will help you.'

She opened her eyes wide. '*Me*, darling? What about *you*?'

Her eyes were wide and frightened.

'I'll come to England later, Vic,' I snapped.

'I'm not going without you!' she cried incredulously.

'I can't go today for Chrissake Vic! I've got to wind up my affairs—'

'Oh no!' she cried, her big eyes were desperate. 'Oh no! No! No!'

I held her right. 'You've got to go Vic! I'll come soon I promise—'

'No!' she cried fiercely. 'No! No!'

I held her tight and squeezed her. 'Vic don't be a fool!'

She shook herself free and her eyes were red and hysterical. 'No! No! I won't! Not without you, I won't!'

I shook her. '*Vic listen to me—*'

She was hysterical and wrestling me and her fists were clenched. '*I won't go alone, I won't—*'

'*Vic you've got to go, I'll come I promise—*'

'I won't!'

'All right, darling,' I said, and I felt desperate I loved her so much. 'All right ...'

'I won't go alone!' she cried still, fighting, 'I won't go—'

I gave her a slap. She stopped suddenly, panting and shocked.

'All right, darling,' I said.

She stared at me wild-eyed.

'All right, darling. I'll come with you. Today,' I said.

She stared at me wild-eyed.

'I'll come,' I said. 'We'll go together.'

We were still driving for the docks. Sanity came back into her eyes.

'You can't go,' she said, 'and I'm not going alone without you.'

'I can go, Vic,' I said, I can and I will, now calm down darling.' She stared at me red-eyed.

'We haven't got passports darling,' she whispered.

'We don't need them on the whalers,' I said. 'Now calm down.'

I held her tight.

Chapter Fifty-Two

Down at the docks it was blowing harder than uptown, straight in from the sea. The swells were breaking, crashing against the breakwater and leaping high in the air. Inside the harbour the water swelled and the wind was blowing it into high chops and the swells were heaving and sucking at the ships and the mooring ropes and straining. And all the time the rain lashing in and across from the sea.

There was little moving down at the docks, most things were battened down for the storm coming. Men stood in the doorways of the warehouses and watched the rain. We had to stop to let a harbour goods train shunt across the road. The engine driver was not leaning out of his cab because of the rain. Far down the road through the warehouses you could see the sea leap up into the rain after it hit the breakwater. Victoria was still shivering but her eyes were wide and alert now, she was tense.

'Soon you'll be safe and warm and dry,' I said.

'Are you sure this isn't a crackpot idea, darling?' she said.

'What other idea is there?' I said. I could feel my hands trembling too. It all seemed unreal.

She squeezed my hand.

'I'll do whatever you say, darling,' she said.

'We'll be fine,' I said.

'We'll have a grand life together,' she whispered. She wasn't thinking of the grand life, she was saying it to comfort me.

'Are you afraid, Vic?' I said.

'I'm afraid they're going to catch us again. Or send us back from England.'

'They won't catch us,' I said. 'And they won't send us back from England.'

'Are we going to be icthiologists in England, darling?' she whispered. She was staring through the windscreen.

'We'll be first rate red hot icthiologists,' I said.

'It'll be lovely when we're on the ship again!' she said. 'Maybe they'll give us our old cabin back. We had a good time in that cabin didn't we, darling?' She was talking to give us courage.

'We had a grand time,' I said.

'The Captain will be mad with us when he finds out, darling,' she whispered. There was no need to whisper.

'He'll be mad all right but we won't give ourselves up till we're far away. Elsie will hide us.'

'Fergie too,' she said.

'We won't compromise Fergie,' I said. 'Elsie will do it.'

'The Kid would do it,' she whispered.

'The Kid would think it's a lovely idea but the Mate would blow his top.'

'You and The Kid could drink brandy all the way to England, darling.'

'I wish we had some now.'

'Beulah will get you some from the Bridge, darling.' She was sounding dreamy again. 'We're going to have a grand time.'

'You've had a bad week,' I said. 'You need a good rest, you'll have a good rest on the boat.'

The train passed. We were driving between the warehouses. A man in a khaki smock was standing in the big doorway of a warehouse looking out at the rain. There was nothing he could do about it. We drove a long way down and then turned right and through another avenue of warehouses. The rain was teeming down. Way ahead were the ships. Then we came to the last warehouse and you could feel the wind bite the car. There were all the ships in the Duncan Basin, and down at the end the Icehammer. There seemed to be nobody moving on her but she was getting steam up. The catchers were tied up to each other about her. She looked nice standing there. Her gangway was down.

'There she is,' I said. My heart was beating hard again.

'She looks super, darling,' she whispered.

I paid the cabby and we climbed out. The rain was lashing. I grabbed her hand and started running up the gangway. The deck was swept by the rain. From the deck you could see better the waves crashing on to the breakwater out there. She had to run every few paces to catch up with me. Her hair was stuck to her face again. We got into the galley alley and I wiped my face on my sleeve. Two galley boys were working but not Elsie. There were some men sitting in the Big Mess with some women. We hurried down the companionway on to the accommodation deck. I could smell it again, the whale oil. There was nobody about. We hurried up the alleyway to Elsie's cabin. I knocked and opened.

'Professor *darling!*' Elsie squealed, 'ooh – *Victoria!*'

'What time are you sailing Elsie?'

'Four o'clock, darling, weather permitting.'

'Listen Elsie—'

We sat Victoria on the bunk and Elsie looked the other way while she took off her clothes. We gave her Elsie's dressing gown and a blanket and a brandy. She was shivering and very cold. The whole time I was explaining it to Elsie. Elsie's rosebud mouth was open in astonishment.

'All you've got to do is hide us for twenty-four hours, Elsie,' I said.

'But of *course*, Professor darling!' Elsie said.

'When we give ourselves up to the Captain we won't tell who helped us.'

'Darling, it'll be too easy on this ship. But supposing we don't sail today because of the weather?'

'We'll worry about that when the time comes.'

'Has the poor child eaten anything?'

'Can you get her something hot Elsie?'

Elsie beamed at her. 'What would you like, luv? Some nice soup?'

'Soup would be excellent Elsie,' I said.

'I'll get her some proper clothes from Beulah, Beulah's more her size,' Elsie said busily. He was enjoying it now.

'Now listen, Vic,' I said. She looked up with a vague startled look. 'I'm leaving you here with Elsie and I'll be back—'

Her face went anxious. 'Where are you going, darling?'

'I'm going back to Oak Bay to get some things for us.'

She made a startled movement.

'There's enough time, we've got over two hours, we can't go with nothing.'

'Darling,' she cried, 'we can buy clothes and things.'

'We're going to need all the money we've got, Vic,' I said. 'Now listen to me.'

'You better make it snappy,' Elsie said.

'There's ample time,' I said. 'I've also got to leave instructions about my property and so forth, Vic,' I said. 'It's all very important. Now you stay here and don't worry.'

'Darling, suppose they *catch* you! 'she cried.

'They can't catch me for anything, Vic,' I said. 'We're on bail. If they see me they'll just think I'm collecting your things.'

'I'll go and get her some food,' Elsie said. He hurried out of the cabin. I sat down on the bunk beside her and put my arm tight around her.

'Oh darling,' she said anxiously.

'What?'

'I don't think you should go. But if you're going, for God's sake go quickly!'

I squeezed her shoulders.

'There's ample time darling, it's only half an hour each way and it'll take me only an hour to tie things up, now relax. Are you warm?'

'I'm warm, darling,' she said anxiously.

'Let me have a shot of brandy,' I said.

She stared at me as I poured it. I swallowed it in one go and poured another.

'Five minutes, Vic,' I said, 'and I'll be gone with the wind.' I sat down and she stared at me agitatedly. I took a swallow of the second brandy. The first had made me feel much stronger. The second was good. I looked at her and I felt I loved her so much I wanted to cry out.

'Everything's going to be fine darling,' I said.

'Darling, you must go now.'

I took a big breath to keep the tremble out of my voice.

'Now listen, Vic. Everything's going to be okay, I'll be back in plenty of time. But if, repeat if by any faint chance I should come unstuck and miss the boat—'

She jerked and stared at me. I held her tight.

'I'm *not* going to miss the boat, Vic,' I said, 'but if I do, *don't worry.*' She was staring at me. 'Because if I miss the boat I'll be in England long before you are, probably I'll jump on an aeroplane—'

'But you've had to surrender your *passport!*' she cried.

'I'll manage something,' I said soothingly. 'My father was British and I'm entitled to a goddam British passport, I'll swing something even if I have to go back to Bechuanaland. Or sail my own goddam boat to England.' I squeezed her hard. 'But it's all right because I'm *not* going to miss this boat, darling.'

She looked very worried and I could feel my eyes burn. 'Oh, darling?' she said.

'In a few hours we'll be as free as the air. I'll bring a few bottles of champagne from home, Vic.'

'Darling, you're not planning to let me sail to England without you and follow later are you, I couldn't bear that.'

'Of course not, Vic.'

'I'd run right off this ship right now if I thought that. Promise?'

'I promise, Vic.'

She looked at me. 'I wish I could have said goodbye to my mother,' she said tremulously.

'In England we'll make so much money we can pay her fare there for a holiday,' I said cheerfully.

'I wouldn't be any good to her here as a daughter would I?' she said.

'It wouldn't be any good at all,' I said.

'Darling?' she turned to me, 'I'm sorry I've been such a damn nuisance.'

I tried to laugh. 'You haven't been the nuisance Vic,' I said.

'Darling if you're going hadn't you better go now?' she said anxiously.

I nodded. I stood up.

'Right Vic,' I said. I held her hand and there was the ache in my throat again and I could have cried very easily. It felt terrible to be deceiving her like this. I thought: you mightn't be seeing her for six months or a year, if it doesn't go right, you must bank on it going wrong, you'll be lucky if you get away with it. Unless you're very lucky she'll have the baby before you see her again. And I wanted to hug her and feel her and love her close for the last time in a long time. She was looking up at me anxiously. I pulled her to her feet and hugged her close.

'What's the matter, James?' she said anxiously.

'Nothing,' I said. 'Everything's going to be fine.' I put my hand inside her gown and felt her beautiful breast and there was a sob in my throat and I was glad of everything I was doing.

'You must go now, darling,' she said.

'All right. Bye, Vic,' I said. 'I won't be long. Lock yourself in and don't let in anybody except Elsie.'

'Yes, darling,' she said anxiously.

'All right Vicky darling,' I said.

'Godspeed darling,' she said. She was looking calmer now and I wanted to shout I loved her so much. I kissed her once hard then I turned and walked out the cabin. I waited until I heard her lock the door, then I walked up the alleyway. I climbed the companionway to the galley. Elsie was standing at a stove making her soup.

'Good strong soup and three scrambled eggs will pick her up, James.'

'That's good of you, Elsie.'

'What else are friends for?' Elsie said. 'Though what you see in girls I do not know.'

I tried to smile. I was suddenly deathly tired.

'You better make it snappy,' Elsie said. 'You've only got a couple of hours.'

'Elsie,' I said, 'I'm not going with the ship.'

Elsie stopped stirring and stared at me.

'You're *what*, James?'

'I can't leave yet, Elsie. There's too much for me to do.'

Elsie was staring at me open-mouthed. 'But what about Vicky?'

'She'll be all right. It's imperative she gets out of the country, I can't risk her going to jail and living in a slum. I'll come to England as soon as I can.'

'But ...' Elsie looked around exasperated. 'Who's going to look after her in England?'

I closed my eyes, I was very tired.

'I'll see the British Embassy here and explain it all. The Kid will help that end and so will Fergie. I'll come as soon as I can. She's big enough to look after herself, anyway, just as long as she's allowed to stay in England.'

'Why can't you come now?' Elsie demanded.

I sighed. 'Elsie, I've got a house to sell. Debts to pay. I've got a goddam fishing company to wind up. I've got four thousand quid's worth of fishing trawler unpaid for yet and five thousand quid's worth of house and Christ knows how many hundred quid's worth of debts. I can't dump all my assets and liabilities on some stranger's lap, I could lose thousands.'

'But,' Elsie said, 'you'll go to jail, I thought that was the whole idea.'

'For her, Elsie,' I said wearily. 'She's got a baby inside her. And until the appeal she'd have to live in limbo in goddam District Six, it would kill us. It would kill me anyway just thinking about her. It's much better this way.'

Elsie looked at me very worriedly. He could see it now.

'But does she know about this?'

I shook my head. 'No, Elsie. If she knew she wouldn't stand for it. She's in a high emotional state and she'd kick and scream and try to fight her way off the ship and louse it all up.'

'So you're not going to your house?'

'No. I could never have made it anyway.'

Elsie gave a big sigh through his hairy nostrils.

'Oh, James, you do get yourself into messes.'

'I'm sorry to land you with it, Elsie. I'll go and warn Fergie presently.'

'*Fergie'll* kick and scream,' Elsie said. 'You better leave Fergie to me, I'll tell her.'

I nodded. 'Maybe. Got a drink Elsie?'

'In the pantry, darling,' Elsie said. 'Poor old James, wait here.'

I sat down at the big kitchen table. It was scrubbed white and the wood had chips out of it. When I sat the tiredness came over me down to my bones and I felt my wet clothes again and the tiredness was an ache. When I sat down I felt I had to hang on tight not to sob out loud. Elsie came back with a half-jack of brandy.

'I must write Victoria a letter, Elsie. Can you get me some paper and a pen?'

'Easy.'

'You're a good friend, Elsie.'

'Nonsense,' Elsie said, embarrassed.

I rubbed my head. 'God I'm so tired, Elsie. Listen, get Fergie to give her a sedative to knock her out after you've sailed.'

'That's an idea, James. What are you going to do now till we sail?' Elsie said.

I tried to pull myself tight together.

'I've got to write that letter. And I must go to the Fourteen and see The Kid and tell him what he's got to do.'

Elsie snorted. 'I wouldn't bank on getting much sense out of The Kid at this stage of the fight. Rumour is he's been having a whale of a time.'

'Old Kid.'

'Isn't he a beauty?' Elsie said.

'Elsie,' I said, 'can you get me that pen and paper now?'

I poured myself a big shot of Elsie's brandy and I sat down at the kitchen table to write to Victoria. I was very tired. I thought of her sitting down there in the cabin in Elsie's dressing gown exhausted and frightened sick about me not making it back in time and my eyes burned as I wrote.

'You've still got an hour, luv,' Elsie said as he came back.

'How is she?' I said.

'She's had her soup and eggs and she's fine. She's wound up tight as a clock but who wouldn't be? She's lying down now.'

I thought of her lying down there.

'She's being very brave,' Elsie said. 'You got yourself a good girl there, James.'

'Sure,' I said.

'What are you going to do now?' Elsie said.

'Here's the letter, Elsie. I'm going to go now.'

'I hope you're going to get tight tonight and then collapse in hoglike sleep.'

'I will,' I said.

'It'll feel better once we've sailed and it's all over,' Elsie said. 'Take the brandy.'

'Thanks Elsie. Oh well,' I put out my hand, 'goodbye Elsie and very many thanks.'

'Thanks nothing,' Elsie said. 'It's not costing me anything is it? Will you come and see me in England?'

'You bet, Elsie,' I said. 'We'll have a helluva party.'

'I'll take you down to our local,' Elsie said. 'We'll get Beulah and The Kid along too.'

It made me smile just to think of it. It also made me very sorry that I would never sail on this fleet again. And I did not want to leave my country for ever and go and live in England with the dear goddam English.

'James?'

'Ja?'

'How long are you going to be in prison?'

It didn't seem real any more but made my pulse trip hard. I was very tired. 'Six months, I guess. A year at the outside. That's what you read about people getting in the newspaper.'

'Aren't you scared?'

'I'm sick in the guts Elsie. But I may get away with it.'

'How?'

'Lie. Say I didn't know. There's also this trick about being married.'

Elsie looked at me with his head on one side. 'It's rotten luck, James.'

'It's not luck, Elsie. It's law. I must go now. Goodbye, Elsie.'

Outside the rain was slanting across the long bare black deck with the wind. You could not see Table Mountain through the rain. There were men coming up the gangway, heads tucked down and their raincoats flapping. They were happy drunk. There was a lot of noise of men and women on the ship now. I was going to run across the deck to the gangway but I took three strides and then I walked. I was too tired to run and it made my heart beat in my ears. The wind buffetted me as I walked and the rain swept me but I didn't care. It didn't matter. I was walking through the rain off the ship without telling her, without even saying goodbye to her and the sob ached hard in my throat but it wouldn't come out. It seemed a little mad and unreal walking through the storm off the ship and then it was screaming real. The cold and the rain began to pull me round and clear my head. I came down the gangway on to the quay. The catchers were scattered along the quay astern of the factory, tied up to each other. Most of them had their steam up, coming whispy out their funnels and swept away in the wind and rain. The rain had brought me right round and now I was cold and shivering and tired again. I came alongside the Fourteen and went aboard. The Kid was not in his cabin. I went up to the Bridge but there was nobody up there. There was singing in the Mess room. I looked in but The Kid was not there either. They called me but I pretended I didn't hear. As I got on to the deck a taxi pulled up and The Kid reeled out.

'*McQuade*,' he bellowed. 'Professor Goddam McQuade you detribalised Dutchman ...'

I waited for him to come over the gangplank. He was grinning all the way and when he got to the end and fell, I helped him up. He hung on my neck happily panting and plastered wet. 'James ... you should have been with me ...'

'Kid, I've got to talk seriously to you ...'

'James, when it comes to serious talk,' he hung beaming from my shoulder, 'I'm your only man ...'

On the way to his cabin he was trying to tell me something about how he had resolved to walk on water in some public fountain somewhere and it hadn't worked. 'And I had faith, James – I'm bitter because I had faith. And I rebuked the wind.'

When we got to his cabin I managed to shut him up and I told him about it. He scowled as he tried to concentrate. He was pretty drunk but he was all right. It took a great deal to knock The Kid out. When I finished he said 'Jesus' and he went to his showerbooth and put his head under it, then he came back a little more sober. He poured us both a drink.

'Tomorrow,' I said, 'when she gives herself up, will you speak to the Old Man?'

'James,' The Kid said, 'I will tell that goddam Old Man that Mrs James McQuade is my bloody guest on his stinking factory.' He thumped his breast. 'My guest!'

'Thanks, Kid,' I said.

'Listen, James,' The Kid said aggressively, 'Victoria is my goddam guest! Who shoots the most fucking whales in this tinpot fucking outfit? And shall I tell you something?'

'Yes?'

'Nobody knows it better than that half-arsed Old Man and my old man and the Board of Effing Directors. I'll have the whole goddam McQuade clan as guests if I goddam want!'

'Thanks, Kid. Now what can you do with the Immigration authorities in England, without her passport?'

'Listen, James,' The Kid said aggressively, 'my old man may be a miserable old shithouse but he knows more high-ups and bloodies on that dark island of England than Carter's got pills. He's known them,' he said, warming to his theme, 'since Pontius was a Pupil Pilot. And I,' The Kid said, 'will personally commit all my vast wealth as security that she does not become a charge upon the State, they'll let her in all right. Would you like that in writing, James?'

'No thanks, Kid.'

'That's my James-baby, smiling again! You're a good bastard James you know that?'

'Thanks, Kid,' I said, 'you're a good bastard too.'

'Certainly I'm a good bastard,' The Kid said. He was through with being sober now. 'Let us two good bastards drink to Victoria McQuade.' He held his glass high. 'May she live long and die beautiful! And here's another to you, you old sumbitch.'

'Thanks, Kid.'

I knew he would do everything he promised. He had woken me up, but now I was relieved and feeling the tiredness again, deep down to my bones. I knew I needed some hot food in my gut but I wasn't hungry. The Kid was talking and I had to pull myself back to hear him. There was a shout below deck: *'Stations! Stations! Stations for Blighty, lads!'*

'I must go, Kid,' I said, 'it's Stations.'

'Balls,' The Kid said. 'That's only the first call.'

I wanted to get out of the cabin or fall down in a heap and stay there.

'I must go, Kid,' I said.

There was a knock on the door.

'Come in!' The Kid bellowed.

A deckie put his head in. 'First call for stations, sir,' he said.

'Did the goddam Mate send you to tell me, Woods?' The Kid said.

'Yessir,' Woods said.

'Woods,' The Kid said, 'will you do something for me?'

'Yessir,' Woods grinned.

'Will you convey my compliments to the Mate, Woods?' The Kid said.

'Yes sir.'

'And tell him that as he thinks he's fuggin captain of this fuggin ship he's big enough and he's certainly fuggin ugly enough to get the fuggin thing under way without me. Will you do that for me, Woods?'

'Yessir,' Woods grinned.

'Thank you, Woods,' The Kid said. 'And Woods.'

'Yes sir?'

'Tell that goddam self-styled Captain Bligh that if he thinks I'm going out on deck in this weather he's crazy because I may catch my death of cold, Woods.'

'Yessir,' Woods grinned.

'Thank you, Woods,' The Kid said. 'Will you have a drink?'

'Thank you, sir,' Woods said.

'Give Professor McQuade another drink too, Woods.' I waved my hand and stood up.

'No, I'm going now, Kid,' I said.

'Give the goddam party-pooping professor another drink for Chrissake, Woods!'

I took my hand off the top of my glass and let Woods put one shot into it. We all tossed it back.

'Thank you, sir,' Woods said. 'Dismissed, sir?'

'If you like, Woods.'

Woods disappeared. The Kid reached for the bottle.

'No, Kid,' I said firmly, 'I want to go.'

I put out my hand and took his.

'So long, Kid,' I said.

He looked at me.

'Okay, James. So long, you old bastard.'

'And many thanks.' I was feeling emotional, but I guess it was the strain of everything.

'Nothing,' The Kid said. He was suddenly serious through the drink. 'I'll look after her, James.'

I nodded. I shook his hand again and then I turned and walked out of the cabin. I was feeling very bad now. There was loud singing below. As I stepped out on to the deck the wind and rain hit me in the face. I slammed the door shut and made for the gangway. The gangway was heaving slowly up and down. There was nobody on the quay opposite the Fourteen. I looked to the Icehammer through the rain and she was lying there big and black and white and heartbreaking and there were some sou'westered sailors on the bows crouching around against the wind and rain, getting ready to single up to fore and aft. There were warm lights twinkling on her bridge. The rain was coming in swirls with the wind and I could hear it splatter against my wet chest. There were some cabin lights on aft. By God, they looked good and warm and happy and laughing, sailing back to Blighty tonight, lads, there'd be a lot of beer-swigging and belly-laughing and happiness tonight by God in those warm lighted cabins and in the Pig by God. And down there in the cabin my woman sitting and waiting for me, counting the time now and her big dark eyes anxious and darting, hugging the blanket to her and jerking and listening with every clatter of feet on the companionway. She could hear the noise and she would know that everybody was back and she was almost ready to sail. And her eyes would be getting panicky now. And here I was standing on the quay. I was tricking her into going away illegally to a strange land with a baby in her belly. Without a passport without any clothes without even saying goodbye to her, without explaining it. And when she felt the ship moving without me she would be panic-stricken. I turned and walked down the quay.

There was a cafe at the end of the quay. When I had walked a hundred yards there was a big whooooop-whoooop from the factory and I jerked and looked back. But the gangway was still down and it was only a warning. I went into the cafe bringing in a gust of rain with me.

'My, you're very wet,' the European lady said.

'Can I have some very hot strong coffee please,' I said.

I sat down at a formica topped table. The chairs were formica too and the table rocked a little because one leg was shorter than the others. It was warmer in the cafe. There were the goddam Coca-Cola ads on the walls and some ads for Wall's ice cream. The rain beat on the big windows and I could only just make out the ship way down the quay. A Coloured waitress brought the coffee. There were no other customers in the cafe. I pulled out Elsie's brandy bottle and poured a strong shot into the coffee. My hand was trembling. I took a big sip. Then with the comfort of it I had a big ache in my throat.

'Are you off the whalers?' the European lady said from behind the counter.

'Yes,' I said. I did not look at her.

'You better hurry up,' she said.

'I live here,' I said. The ache was hard in my throat.

'Oh,' she said. 'Nice to be home?'

I nodded. 'Yes.'

'It must be lovely to come home after so long away,' she said. 'I've watched them come and go for six years now, they're so excited.'

'Have you got a hot meat pie?'

The waitress brought the pie on a plate. I took a bite and it was hard to swallow. I forced myself to eat the pie between sips of the hot spiked coffee. It made me feel better. When I was finishing the pie the funnel went Whoooop-Whoooooop faraway. I got up and went to the rainy window and peered through. I could make it all out clear enough. The for'ard tug was hooked up and the factory was singled up fore and aft. I could see the deckies on the fo'c'sle in their sou'westers. The gangway was still down and there were some people climbing down it. Most of the catchers had moved out. The Fourteen and the Twelve were already headed for the mouth. One of them blew Whoooop Whoooop Whooooop and then the other took up the blowing too. I could only hear distantly. It sounded reckless and gay and very sad. The other catchers were scattered about, heading round. There were no more people coming down the gangway now. A sailor came halfway down the gangway and lashed the derrick cable on to the gangway then he ran back up on to the deck. Then the gangway was lifted away and lowered down on to the quay. The people on the quay waved a little, but there were only a few of them. Then she blew, Whooop Whoop Whoooooooooop, and it got me right here.

I could see the aft tug too now. Their lines were taking up the slack. Then the man on the quay threw the for'ard shore line off the big quay bollard and I saw it splash in the sea. I could not make out the aft shore line. The lines of the tug were taut now, and then I saw that the bows had already swung a little way out from the quay. Then the factory gave a big Whoooooooop on her funnel and the tugs answered, and now they had her heaving slowly off from the quay.

I watched through the rain battered window and I lit a cigarette and I quivered as I inhaled it big and my eyes felt blurred. She was nearly halfway swung around now. I uncorked the brandy bottle and I took one swallow, and it was empty, then I opened the door and the wind and rain blew in and I stepped out into the rain. I started walking against the wind down the other arm of the quay to the mouth so I would be near when she went through.

Chapter Fifty-Three

I walked along the side of warehouses watching her being swung around by the tug and I had to screw up my eyes from the rain. I had plenty of time. Then I came to the end of the line of warehouses and the wind and rain were fiercer and there was the loud crashing of the sea on the breakwater. It was about a hundred and fifty yards from the last warehouse along the breakwater to the mouth. On the sea side of the breakwater it was a jumble of big concrete blocks. Now I could really hear the sea. The big swells were smashing with a great thud and then grey spray flew high and wide and the wind smashed it on and it swept with a clatter across the breakwater. The catchers were heading into the mouth now and now they were feeling the big swells. I thought dizzily: if the swells were any bigger she could not make it, she would have to wait. I kept close to the harbour side of the breakwater as I made my way along, watching the Icehammer. The spray hit me like pellets every time there was the crash of the wave on the breakwater. The big sea was grey and disappeared into the rain and there was no Table Mountain and you could not make out the warehouses clearly across the harbour. The Fourteen and most of the catchers had already gone through the mouth, riding high and plunging low as they hit the swells. The Icehammer was swung clear around as I got near to the head and then there was the churn from her screws and she cast off the tug. She gave her final blasts and the tugs answered Whoop Whoop Whoop, faintly against the wind, and then her propellers gave a big churn, and she was away.

I was at the mouth now. There was a big bollard and I leant my right knee against it to give me support against the wind. The swells came in a big running dune from out there through the rain at an angle, running with the wind and then they hit the breakwater with the crack of thunder and the hard spray flew and the rest of the swell surged big and sucking through the mouth with a deep treacherous trough, and then the swell that had hit the breakwater surged back with a mighty deep sucking roar and then the next swell came rushing in and hit the back suck of the last one and then crashed the breakwater and the spray leapt again. It was a bad sea but it was not too much for the Icehammer yet. I would not have taken my own boat through but I would have taken the Icehammer or one of the catchers, just. In a few hours, maybe in one hour it would be too much, even for the Icehammer. The mouth was plenty wide. Now I could only just see the last catcher out there, dim through the driving rain. The rain and wind beat me and each time the swell hit the breakwater the edge of the spray hit me and I was deadly cold again. Walking along the quay had done me good but now I was aching down to my bones again. I wished I had more brandy. I watched the Icehammer coming and it felt as if my heart would break. She was only seventy yards off now and she had hit the swelling in the harbour. The swell curved up her bows and then she went laboriously down into the trough. She did not yet have enough speed up to take them better. I could see the big churn of her screws behind. Her navigation lights and her bridge lights twinkled through the running rain. The rain was beating my back and I had my hands to my eyes like blinkers to keep the rain out of them. My hair hung matted over the top of my eyelids and I swept it back and then it fell back again. She was only fifty yards away now looming big through the grey and now she was hitting the bigger swells but she had more speed up now and she was still pitching but she was doing all right. I could see her bridge and porthole lights clearly now and I could see the Old Man and two Mates at the long glass of the bridge. There was a deckie on the fo'c'sle head and another in the crow's-nest, poor bastards. I had a big pain in my throat. I was not feeling the wind and the rain and the cold and the exhaustion any more, I was only feeling Victoria. She knew I was not on the ship now. I could see the scream in her big brown eyes and the terror in her face as she realised it. I prayed that Elsie was already with her telling her everything, that now she had my letter and she believed that what I had done was for the best as I could see it. I could no longer see it myself clearly, I only knew as the rain beat me and the ship came on that I had once long ago this morning deemed it best and now it was done, for better or worse, right or wrong I had done it now. It did not matter what happened to me any more, that was way ahead in the future tomorrow, what mattered now was what I had done to her in that cabin in that ship leaving our land behind her for ever. She could never come back, now. She could never come back now and after this was over nor could I. We could never come back now, it was over, dead, behind, finished, a memory. That was all right. All that mattered this moment was that big ship heading through the swells to the harbour mouth and my woman somewhere down there inside realising but not understanding yet because she was crazed. I did not feel the wind or the rain or the cold or the exhaustion or tomorrow, all I felt was my woman.

The ship was only twenty yards away now, and she was in the bad big swells and for all her speed and weight up she was riding them badly. I could see all of her clearly now, she was holding for the middle of the mouth. I thought: *For Christ's sake helmsman keep her steady.* She looked huge and blind coming on into the swirl. There was a crack like thunder behind me and then the spray hit me and the swell heaved into the harbour with a rumble all the way and her bows were way down in the trough in front and there was a thud above the wind and the spray and her bows came up and I thought I saw her lurch.

'Steady steady,' I shouted with the wind, '*steady and hard ahead for Chrissake ...*'

I was shouting to the helmsman. It all rested with the helmsman going through a gate like this, the Old Man knew where he wanted her but it was for the helmsman to hold her there. She came down with a lunge into the trough and the swell curved up her bows and then she steadied and I fancied I heard the telegraph ring. And her screws caught the swell as it heaved through underneath her and she surged and she was into the mouth. She was surging past me. She was screwing big and black and white before me through the mouth now and her portholes were twinkling. I could have tossed a stone and hit her. She looked good and big and impregnable like she had so many times from the deck of the Fourteen, and she was carrying my woman away. I had worried in the mouth only because she was carrying my woman and now I was cheering her inside as she went through safely. *Goodbye Goodbye* I was shouting inside. I could hear the wind and rain and crash again now and it was all right. I stood up straight on the mouth with my feet apart and I waved her through and, I remember, I was smiling into the wind.

She was three parts through now. The aft accommodation was coming up and surging down and you could hear the throb of the screws. I could see no person anywhere. I had stopped my waving now. I was looking almost into the wind and the rain was hitting into my face now and I had to screw up my eyes. Now the stern was level with me and now I could see up into the slipway. She was lunging into the next swell now and her bows went down and then the stern came up high with the crack of the swell on the breakwater and the screws came half out of the sea and roared thrashing in the air, and then the hard spray from the breakwater hit me. When I unscrewed my eyes I saw Victoria through the wind and rain.

She was running out on to the rainswept deck aft of the hospital where we had often walked. She was wearing jeans and Beulah's blue anorak and her long hair was blowing wet in the wind and she was lurching with the heave of the deck making for the rails. She was only twenty years away.

'Victoria!' I shouted into the wind '*Victoria!*'

I had both arms thrown up and my heart was hammering in my ears.

'Victoria!' I shouted and the wind smashed the words away. 'Victoria.'

Then she saw me. She lurched against the rails and clung there and the stern swooped down and she lurched and I saw her shouting to me but I could not hear.

'Victoria,' I hollered into the wind and rain, *'It's all right Victoria, it's all right.'*

She was clinging to the rails leaning over screaming to me and her hair was flying and her face was desperate. I heard 'James' once faraway. She was shouting and shouting and the rain was battering her and the wind smashed it away and the stern was swooping up now on the next swell.

'Victoria,' I bellowed, *'it's all right it's all right I'll come to England,'* and the wind smashed it to nothing. She had her hands to her mouth shouting to me, I could see her mouth moving and she was leaning over the rail and the stern was crashing down now.

'Get back Victoria,' I bellowed, *'Get back.'*

Then the swell hit the breakwater and the world was nothing but hammering spray.

When the spray was gone I saw her again. The stern was swooping up on the next swell. She was clambering up on the after rails, the wind blowing her hair in front of her.

'Victoria,' I screamed, *'Get back for Chrissake,'* and my scream smashed back into my mouth. *'Get back for Chrissake Victoria,'* I was screaming and I was wild with fear – *'Get back get back!'* – But she was clambering up higher on the rails. She had her right foot on the second uppermost rail and her head down. The stern was coming down now, thirty yards past the mouth now.

'Stop get back Victoria,' I roared into the wind, *'get back get back,'* and my heart was roaring in my ears. *'Get back for Chrissake you fool—'*

Then came the crash of the swell on the breakwater and I was flailing the spray with my arms. Then the stern was swinging up again through the rain.

Then she swung her left leg over the handrail and her anorak was flapping in the wind. I was roaring at her into the wind and the whole world was crazed. Then Elsie came running round the starboard side flapping his arms. And big Elsie threw up his hands and then threw his arms around Victoria and tore her off the rails and the stern swooped up and they sprawled, then Old Fergie came lumbering round the starboard rail and she ran at them.

'*Thank Christ!*' I was roaring into the wind. '*Thank Christ Elsie Thank Christ,*' and the rain was beating hard deafening in my face. '*Thank Christ*' I cried, '*Jesus Christ Thank Christ,*' and the wind and rain beat me with the massive crash of the sea on the breakwater and then I could not see. The rain beat into my eyes and when I could see Elsie and Fergie and Victoria were gone. Then there was a crack like a cannon and a big spray hit me harder than a man can stand and there was nothing in the world but the deafening crash of sea beating me and I was reeling and then I fell and the spray was beating down loud in my ears on the concrete, and the massive crack and shudder of the big sea, then the spray was gone and there was only the wind and rain and then I was crying. It seemed a long time I lay there on the concrete, the rain and the spray and the wind, and I did not care, I did not care about anything. Then I got up and I could not see the Icehammer or any other ship, and I started back along the breakwater. The rain and the wind and the sea spray got me all the way, and the crash and roar of them, and I didn't care.

Then I got to the end of the breakwater and started along the quay, and then I was a little bit in the lee of the warehouses. I did not know what time it was, only that it was very nearly dark.

Chapter Fifty-Four

I saw the lights of the cafe at the end of the warehouses. There were no other lights on the quay. When I was nearly at the cafe the stationary car headlights suddenly came on in the road and all I could see was the glare and the rain slanting bright silver in front of me. Then somebody shouted, 'Hey Mac!'

The glare and the beating silver rain blinded me and my eyes were screwed up and my heart was pounding hard, I was finished. The cab light went on.

'It's me, Mac – *kom hierso, jong.*'

'Fuck you, Van,' I shouted, 'if you want me you can come out and get wet.'

I just stood there, I was too finished to care about anything. The door opened and then van Tonder came hunched through the glaring rain and wind.

'Come into the car, Mac.' He had his hand on my elbow.

'Are you arresting me?' I did not have the strength but I would take a token swing at the bastard.

'Mac – come to the car, *jong!*'

He pulled my elbow gently. What the hell, I thought. I didn't care any more. I did not fucking care. I let him take me to the car and I got in and suddenly it was warm and the rain was crashing down on the roof. Van got in and slammed the door. I held my face in my hands and I was shuddering.

'What do you want?'

'Do you want a drink, Mac?' Van said.

'Yes.' I heard him open the dashboard and then he pushed the neck of the bottle into my hands. I didn't care what it was and I lifted it up and took four long swallows and I could not taste it and then suddenly it was raging in my guts and the fumes scorched my nostrils inside and my guts heaved. I got it down, and swallowed and then it was good in my guts. I was shivering. I looked and Van was holding a lighted cigarette out to me. I took it and my hand was shaking. I inhaled deep and then my breath quivered and I wanted to cry and I screwed my eyes up tight once.

'I want to see Fanie,' I said loudly and my voice shook. 'I refuse to say anything except in the presence of Fanie, in which case he will say it for me.'

The rain was hammering on the car. Van sat old and wet behind the wheel and he said to the windscreen, 'Fanie says he's waiting for us at his office now. An' the bladdy Press most probably, if I know the bladdy Press.'

I looked at him, shaking.

'What do you mean "Fanie says he's waiting now?"'

'I telephoned him,' Van said tiredly.

'How d'you know he's at his office now?' I demanded.

'I telephoned him, Mac,' Van said. 'Go use the cafe telephone an' check if you want.'

I stared at Van, shivering.

'You mean,' I said, 'you mean that you saw us?'

Van said to the windscreen and the rain beat down hard loud silver, 'I said I telephoned Fanie an' told him you would want to see him.'

There was a ringing in my ears. I took a big swallow of the brandy bottle and I wanted to sob.

'How did you know I was here?'

Van snorted softly, old and tired.

'I didn't know nothing. But it didn't take much intelligence.'

I did not know what to think, I was too finished. 'Why didn't you stop us if you saw it?'

Van said to the windscreen, 'I'm not saying I saw anything, Mac.'

I was shivering and my heart was knocking as if I had run a long way, and the ringing in my ears. I took the brandy bottle and took another swallow and then shuddered and I just wanted to lie back in a warm place and sleep. I shook my head.

'What happens now?' I said. It sounded faraway.

Van puffed hard once on his cigarette, the rain was beating down on the car.

'I must arrest you, Mac.' He put his left hand on my shoulder. 'James van Niekerk McQuade, I arrest you on suspicion of aiding and abetting the breach of bail and escape of Victoria Rhodes. I also re-arrest you on the original charge of contravening the Immorality Act. Understand?'

He looked at me, old blue Dutch eyes. 'Understand, Mac?' he said.

I didn't say anything.

'I now caution you, Mac. You are not obliged to say anything but anything you say may be taken down in writing and used as evidence in future. *Verstaan?*'

He was looking at me in the eyes the whole time.

I nodded.

'Okay,' Van said. He turned the ignition. 'I have to do that, Mac,' he said.

'Pass the brandy,' I said. I did not know what to think, I did not know and I did not care, all I wanted to do was to cry and sleep. I did not care. I took a big swallow of the brandy and it burnt down into my guts and then I wanted to retch and then it felt good. We were driving through the dark docks and the rain was hammering down and when we went round a row of warehouses the wind hit the car, and then the rain again. The black roads and railway lines shone wet black beating silver.

'What will I get?'

Van did not look at me. He looked old in the panel lights. He took a breath.

'Nine months, altogether,' he said. 'Maybe a year.'

The rain hammered the car.

It did not mean much, and then it meant a lifetime, and then I did not care about anything, I would care tomorrow when I had slept.

Then I thought of Victoria, in London and the cold of winter and the snow and the flat we would have and Victoria all warm and laughing with me and we would go for rides on buses and tubes and go to pubs and newsreels and plays and we'd buy a cheap car and when I came home there would be Victoria, Victoria lying on the ship with the baby in her belly, and Fergie and The Kid and Elsie would look after her in England and when she was ready she would go to a big grey stone hospital, and the rain sleeting down and her soft flat belly big and beautiful, and Fergie or The Kid or Elsie would send me a telegram, and it would be nearly time for me to come out of prison.

By John Gordon Davis

Leviathan

A compelling novel of adventure and intrigue, 'Leviathan' tells the unadulterated and at times terrible story of whaling, partially from the perspective and mind of a whale. The novel concentrates the senses in terms of willing conservation, whilst entertaining with a varied mixture of characters, some of whom would be classified as eco-terrorists. There are thrills, adventure, battles and heartaches in the story which is taut with human drama, and the author manages to convey the underlying message without preaching, or propaganda.

The Years of the Hungry Tiger

Set in the years of Mao and prior to the handover, 'The Years of the Hungry Tiger' is the story of McAdam, a Hong Kong policeman who is unhappily married. Then he meets Ying-ling, who is a schoolmistress, and he falls headlong for her. This, however, makes him a security risk as she teaches at a communist school, and to make matters worse her father lives on the mainland and so McAdam becomes immediately vulnerable to Chinese pressure. Ying-ling herself is a 'starry-eyed' Marxist with resulting conflicting loyalties. In a novel which contains more than a smattering of realism, the author thrills with a tale of political intrigue, espionage, riots, sex, and the underworld of the island, along with it surviving typhoons, economic crises, and everything a hostile regime can throw at it.

By John Gordon Davis

Taller Than Trees

For many years hunters had tried to kill Dhlulamiti, but he had survived. An elephant some thirteen and a half feet tall – his name translated to 'Taller than trees' – and weighing in at twelve tons he was a giant even amongst the largest species of mammal ever to have inhabited the earth. In his early days, he had roamed the savannah in Africa as a killer, attacking every man that came his way, but now wiser thoughts prevailed. Inevitably, one day Dhlulamiti met up with Jumbo McGuire, a hard hell-raising Irish hunter who was renowned for the number of 'kills' to his credit. As the predators circled with a hope of cashing in on what would seem to be the inevitable outcome and an easy meal, the final epic struggle between elephant and man began.

Hold My Hand I'm Dying

A stirring and compelling story, full of adventure, set against the background of the move to freedom in Africa. In the face of opposition, hatred, violence and death, the gentler human feelings of friendship and love are nonetheless maintained. Joseph Mahoney is the last Colonial Commissioner in the Kariba Gorge, faced with easing the transition to new rule. To complicate matters, his servant Samson has been accused of murder, and he is drifting apart from Suzie, whom he loves very deeply. Yet personal matters apart, he must deal with the simmering undercurrent of violence and revenge that might envelope the countryside at any moment.

Printed in Great Britain
by Amazon

54384384R00251